D1202052

PERSIE MERLIN AND LEVIATHAN'S GIFT

Harley Merlin 18

BELLA FORREST

ONE

Persie

There is nothing I would not do for those who are really my friends. I have no notion of loving people by halves, it is not in my nature. Jane Austen's poetic gem resonated with me. Which was why I was letting my friend, Genie Vertis, drag me into trouble once again. Although, she was doing it for me, so maybe we were both guilty.

I say "friend" but she was more of a sister, really. And siblings had a way of getting each other into a whole lot of trouble. At least, that's what I'd gathered from my mom and Uncle Finch's epic gab sessions. They were the stuff of SDC legend, and both could wax nostalgic for hours. As for me, I didn't have siblings to test the theory on. Only Genie. But she was all the sibling—and all the trouble—I'd ever need.

"I'm sweating bullets, here!" I hissed to Genie. She waltzed beside me, not a care in the world, having picked the smaller pile of books to "carry back to the library"—the shaky story we'd decided to go with. In comparison, I looked like a juggler with a severe hand cramp, trying to keep the tomes from toppling. I didn't want to drop them. For one, they'd clatter and make everyone stare. For two, I hated books getting damaged, which was why I always glared at page-folders and spine-benders. *Bookmark, anyone?*

Genie smirked. "I'd say you've got more of a glossy sheen. It suits you. Like I keep saying, you should come running with me. Cardio is good for the soul."

"Running is for psychopaths." I swerved to keep my tower of books steady. "Seriously, why aren't you nervous right now? I've never seen anyone so calm about sneaking into the Bestia—"

"Shh!" She put a finger to her lips. "First rule of sneak club, you don't talk about sneak club. Besides, I have a naturally innocent face." Her slate-gray eyes twinkled. Wherever there was mischief, my friend was never far behind. And neither was I, since I was never far from her. Wrong place, wrong time, all the time. Though she rarely got as much heat as me, even with an Atlantean dad. That was what happened when your parents were the Merlin-Crowleys—I *always* took the rap.

"Like one of those Russian hamsters that look super cute but won't hesitate to take a chunk out of your finger?" I peeked at her over my books, though my sardonic smile went to waste behind the leathery, musty blockade.

She stuck her head out to the side and puffed out her cheeks. "Hamster? I'm more like a duck."

"Everything rolls off your back?" I teased.

"Nope, though I like the way your mind works." She paused to shuffle her feet wildly, making me snort into the spine of *Rare Purge Beasts of the Northern Seas*. "Serene on the surface, paddling like heck underneath!"

With laughter in my belly, the nerves ebbed, and we slunk farther up the main hallway of the SDC toward the Isadora Merlin Library. It had been renamed after a great-aunt I'd never met, though I felt as though I knew her from the stories I'd heard. Tales told by firelight lingered in the mind, conjuring unforgettable memories that seemed as real as my own. That branch of my family name had been a double-edged sword throughout my almost eighteen years on this earth. On the one hand, I absorbed the old stories like a sponge, desperate to learn everything and anything about the characters whose lives had enriched my ancestry. On the other, you really couldn't look anywhere in this coven without seeing the Merlin name somewhere, an ever-evolving fanfare of triumph and magical success—and a sharp contrast to my own shortcomings.

It was a cosmic joke with me as the punchline: a Merlin with no magic.

"Incoming!" Genie shoved me into the shadow of one of the imposing bronze dragons, the ever-dutiful sentinels of the SDC, standing guard with watchful gemstone eyes. I hoped they wouldn't snitch on us.

"Who is it? I'm flying blind here." I nodded to the stack of books, the dust of them itching my nostrils. One sneeze, and the whole thing would tumble floorward. *You poor babies... I'm going to take good care of you until we put you all back in alpha-*

betical order. I tended to immerse myself in the vivid worlds of fiction and the escapism within their creamy pages, but non-fiction served its purpose. Yes, I might have associated non-fiction books with endless study sessions and weighted eyelids, and I might have cursed their names when the words wouldn't stay in my skull, but that didn't mean they deserved rough treatment. It wasn't their fault that I associated them with a bad time.

"The Levi-Catemaco clan." Genie ducked around a metal trunk of a dragon leg and peered into the corridor, putting on her best espionage performance. *Genie Bond, license to cause mischief.*

I wished I'd gotten a look. Marius Levi-Catemaco, the eldest of Raffe and Santana's four adopted kids at nineteen, had the sort of heaven-sent face that could've been torn out of *GQ.* Ruggedly Spanish, all dark and tan and good enough to nibble on, he set many hearts aflutter. And neither Genie nor I—otherwise sensible young women—were immune.

"It's like everything slows down when he walks," Genie whispered dreamily. "He must have a personal fan with him. Nobody's hair moves like that without outside help."

"I'm about to need some outside help myself," I huffed. The books were getting heavier by the moment.

She winked back at me, her Atlantean face tattoos shining slightly. "We can't go anywhere until the Osmonds have passed. Might as well enjoy the view." When she went outside, the tattoos were hidden by an embedded magic, but she preferred to go au naturel inside the safe confines of the SDC.

"How do you even know who the Osmonds are?" As far as I knew, Atlantean integration hadn't covered the history of popular music.

"Blame your uncle. He blasts that stuff from his car when he thinks no one's around." She grinned from ear to ear. "But I'm *always* around. You should enlighten him about new music, to save his dignity. And get him to update his technology, too. He still uses CDs."

I smiled, thinking of my favorite uncle. My only uncle, but still my favorite. "I think that'd be like trying to close the stable door after the horse has bolted." Fortunately, I hadn't developed my musical tastes from him, but I owed him for my love of literature. He'd given me a pile of classics at age eleven or twelve, and I'd never looked back, devouring every novel the library held and beyond, like a regular Matilda. Only, I couldn't move things with Telekinesis.

"Okay, the coast is clear. Tip some of those books onto mine." Genie shuffled up to me and let me tip the top tome onto her stack, in a precarious exchange. Not much of a relief, but enough to keep me going. With the load a bit more even, she stepped out of the dragon shadows, dusting off her ripped band tee. I doubted she'd ever heard a single song by Prince and the Revolution. She just wore it to annoy her dad, who'd have preferred to see her in the adapted traditional attire that most integrated Atlanteans wore.

"You know, it's funny that he's called *Marius*." She flashed me the look that let me know a punchline was coming.

I humored her, the constant comedy enabler. "Why's that?"

"Because I wish he would." She cackled, flipping her long silver braid over her shoulder. The white-gold feather barrette at the top of the braid glinted in the coven's warm, atmospheric lighting. Her Esprit.

I rolled my eyes. "How did I not see that one coming?"

"You had to have known. You know me too well." She gave me one of those looks that existed solely between life-long friends—an expression of love that encompassed almost eighteen years. She'd been alive way longer than that, given the formerly extended lives of Atlanteans, but I'd known her all my life, from day one. Before that, actually, as my mom liked to tell us. Genie had been there when my mom had found out about me, and our friendship had been sealed by the fates from that day forward. But her papers said she was nineteen, so that's what she went with.

We pressed on up the hallway, weaving in and out of dragon statues, and took a left, avoiding as many people as possible. Not easy in a packed coven, but Genie had surprising stealth and a good nose for suspicious glances. Everyone knew us here, and everyone knew our past endeav-ors: practical jokes and harmless tricks, mostly.

"Are you playing a game, or something?" A voice brought us to a sudden halt. A boyish face appeared shortly afterward, poking around the side of a reptilian limb. Kestrel Merlin—my cousin. My uncle swore he'd named him purely after a bird, like he himself had been. But I knew better. *A Kestrel for a Knave* was one of Uncle Finch's favorite books—mine, too—and he'd traumatized me with the film when I was prob-ably too young to see it. I still hadn't gotten over that ending.

"Kes! You scared the life out of us!" Genie sank against the wall with a dramatic sigh.

He looked slightly abashed. "I'm sorry. I didn't mean to. I just wanted to know what you were up to."

"Who says we're up to anything?" I blurted out. Rookie mistake. I sounded as guilty as I felt.

He swept auburn curls out of his blue eyes. "I meant, I was just curious about what you were doing. It looked like you were playing a game." He observed the dual stack of books that Genie and I had split between us. "Or doing some light reading?"

I tried to shift the weight of the books and almost upended the entire stack. "Sorry, Kes. We've got to get these back to the library before we get a fine."

"Oh, well, let me help you. I don't mind heading that way." He reached out for my books, but Genie wedged herself between us like a human barricade. He was a sweet kid, not a bad bone in his body. A relief for Uncle Finch and Auntie Ryann, considering the rotten eggs that had cropped up in the Shipton line, but we couldn't have any witnesses to what we were actually doing. Especially when I'd been forbidden from doing exactly what we were about to do.

"We appreciate the offer, but we wouldn't want to dent our strong, independent woman image." Genie cut in.

He stepped back and raised his hands in understanding. "Of course, my bad. I keep forgetting when it's appropriate to be chivalrous. Dad says I shouldn't bother, but then Mom smacks him and tells me to ignore him, so it's hard to know."

"I love chivalry, but we're working on our biceps." Genie

offered him one of her most dazzling smiles. The shine reflected in his eyes, and a flush reddened his cheeks, bringing out his freckles. She had that effect on most of the opposite sex, even kids like Kes, without intending to.

He chuckled awkwardly. "Well, you... uh... do that, then. I'll just... uh... be on my way." He gave a peculiar half-bow. "I hope you don't get fined."

"Same here. I could do without another lecture from my dad on how to be a responsible adult." Genie laughed like she was joking, but I heard the truth in her words. These days, she always seemed to be at odds with her dad. I supposed that was part of growing up, but I knew it bothered her. She loved her dad. She didn't want to fight with him, but she also felt like they were from different worlds. And she wasn't entirely wrong.

Kes waved before heading back down the hallway. He turned back once or twice, his expression bemused, but he didn't try and investigate further. Where our family was concerned, sometimes it was better not to.

We carried on, my arms about ready to give out. With the strain tingling through my veins, rendering my hands numb, I began to doubt our cover story. We could've gone with something easier to carry. Essays, perhaps? Or a few folders that needed to be returned? It was too late for that now.

"How are your arms?" Genie picked up on my ongoing struggles.

"Arms? What arms? I can't even feel them anymore."

"Then give me another book, and let's hurry." We made another wobbly exchange, and she pushed forward with renewed energy. I struggled to match her, lagging behind on the last stretch. But at least we were almost there.

After a few more minutes, we finally reached the library entrance—an elegant feat of architecture, with two pillars to either side, carved vines twisting up them to form a triangular archway. A frieze within the archway depicted stone intellectuals in elegant poses: reading books, strumming lyres, and scribbling on curved scrolls. And, at the triangle's apex, a large version of the Merlin pendant stood in pride of place, gemstones glittering. An homage to the woman who'd once worn it: Isadora Merlin.

"We need to be seen, right?" I checked in with my accomplice. We could've dumped the books on the side table by the entrance, but I wanted to make sure these books went back to their proper homes.

Genie nodded. "We should head in, make sure we get seen by Mrs. Tibbs, and slip out again *without* her seeing."

"Okay." I sounded more confident than I felt. I knew I'd have to rally strength from somewhere. This was only phase one—the ruse. Phase two had yet to be put into motion.

Genie led the way into the library—one of my favorite places in the whole coven. Wall-to-wall worlds, each one brimming with adventure, romance, characters waiting to be fallen in love with, and villains a person could love to hate. I adored the smell more than anything, the musty, inexplicable scent of escapism.

"Hi, Mrs. Tibbs." Genie wriggled a hand free to wave at the sourpuss who sat at the reception desk a short distance ahead. She didn't wave back. She never did. "Ah, ever the chatterbox."

I stifled a giggle. "You'll get us kicked out!"

"That'd mean her having to get out of her chair. I think we're good." Genie hustled toward the returns cart and toppled the books onto it with an overly loud thud. I winced, certain it would draw attention to us. I waited for the cry of, "Girls! What are you doing?" but it didn't come.

Hurrying in case it was only a delayed reaction, I performed an awkward squat so the books wouldn't get hurt. I set the whole pile down with as much care as possible before flexing my aching arms.

"That feels good."

Genie stepped forward to give my forearms a squeeze, massaging some life back into them. "You ready for phase two?"

"I hope so," I replied uncertainly.

"You've got this, Persie. You've been waiting to speak to that monster for years. And I'm not going anywhere. I'm with you, all the way." She smiled, and I felt a bit of courage stir inside me. Her pep talks never failed to make me feel braver.

I drew in a sigh. "Okay. Let's do this."

"That's my girl!" She dove in to give me a quick, necessary hug before dragging me into one of the stacks. "Now, I need you to hold very still. This is one of my grandpa's tricks. I've been practicing like crazy so it'd be perfect for today, but my skills are still a bit glitchy."

"Glitchy how?" It always made me nervous when she said things like that.

"Let's just say, fifty percent of the time I've phased in and out."

My heart pounded harder, like a runaway horse. "Phased in and out of what?"

"Visibility. Relax, I've got backup tricks, and if we get caught, I'll say it was all my idea." She held my shoulders. "Now, remember to stay still. We're going to have to be up close and personal until we reach the creature's box."

"He has a name, you know." A stiff chuckle puffed out of my nose.

Genie raised a finger. "Ah, but when you name something, you give it power. If you keep thinking of it as just a creature, you won't be so afraid."

"Huh. That actually makes a lot of sense."

She tapped the side of her head. "Not just a hat rack, my friend. Now, shush, I need to concentrate."

Neon-green Chaos sparked out of her body as she gripped me tight. It flowed from her chest to her arms, and into me, without so much as a twitch of her fingers, since she was a Sentient. The telltale sign of an Atlantean. I had no idea what sort of spell she was using, but her grandfather had been an infamous thief who'd never been caught. That called for a trick or two, and she'd certainly picked up a few family secrets.

Suddenly, the pain hit. A fierce heat that began at the point of contact and pulsed through the rest of me at lightning speed, as though someone had doused me in fire ants. Judging by the strained expression on her face, she felt it too.

"Is it supposed to... feel like this?" I gasped, my throat burning.

"I... think so," she gasped back. "A few minutes... of pain, to get... answers. That's got to be... worth it, right?"

It hurt too much to reply.

"I think we're good... to go. Stay... close," she instructed, after a few more agonizing seconds.

Remind me never to get on your bad side. Genie never failed to amaze me with her brilliance, but it could also be a little frightening at times. She literally had no fear whatsoever, and a whole box of tricks at her disposal, courtesy of her grandpa. A trait I envied and admired.

Pulling me with both hands, she headed for the library door. Mrs. Tibbs would be our alibi, if anyone asked where we were. She'd seen us come in, but she wouldn't see us go out. At least, that was the plan, providing nothing... glitched.

At the door, my entire body tensed up against the pain and the fear of discovery. I glanced back at Mrs. Tibbs, but her head stayed down, as she was evidently transfixed by something on her desk. If rumor was to be believed, she frequently enjoyed a bodice-ripper while wiling away the hours in the library. And the smirk on her face suggested she'd delved into the kind of book that would've had my beloved Austen turning in her grave.

Still holding on to each other, we bolted out the door after someone else entered. If we'd opened it ourselves, it would've sounded alarm bells. Not literally, of course, but Mrs. Tibbs had a renowned eagle eye. Our window of opportunity had opened. Sucking in a deep breath, I hurtled alongside my friend, grateful that the shield around us stopped anyone from seeing. My version of running wasn't graceful. Give me a set of pencils and a fresh page in a sketchbook, and I could toil away for hours without breaking a sweat. Give me a novel and I would demolish it, front to back, without pausing. But give me a sprint... and I looked like a frazzled crab trying to figure out how all its legs worked at once.

Fortunately, our destination lay a short distance down the hallway, but that didn't stop the nerves pounding in my chest, like a marching band had taken up residence between my ribs. I realized, with some disappointment, that I'd have made a terrible spy. I didn't have the calm for it. Even familiar faces proved unsettling. I spotted two men wandering up the corridor toward us and grabbed Genie, pulling her back into a recess, the two of us pressing as flat as possible, even though we were hopefully still invisible. *Dylan and Garrett!* Two guys who might as well have been uncles! The sight of them had almost given me a coronary.

"Don't... worry. They can't... see us," Genie wheezed through the pain. Both of us poked our heads out like meerkats, still connected. "If we wait a few... more seconds, they'll... be gone."

"I'm starting to think this... was a bad idea," I admitted. Genie tended to be the guts of our operations, while I provided the anxious hair-pulling. In fact, she'd been the one to suggest we do this. I'd spoken about a certain creature so many times, I'd finally broken the camel's back. She'd all but insisted we take matters into our own hands and actually act on my curiosities instead of just speculating.

"We're so close, Persie. Leviathan… is within shouting… distance."

At the sound of his name, a fresh wave of anxiety washed over me. "I think I'm going to… be sick. But that might… be the pain." It simply wouldn't let up. "Anyway, I thought… we weren't using… his name?"

"Argh… sorry, I forgot. This pain… is messing with my head." Genie chuckled and gave me a nudge in the ribs. "It's okay, I… promise. I know a thing or two about… sea beasts from my mom's old journals. There's nothing in there… that you can't handle. And Leviathan… is frozen in a box. He can't hurt… you. This is your shot at getting answers, Persie. Or do you want to carry on, never… knowing what the deal with him is? If that's the case, we can turn around."

Genie stared at me expectantly, the green-tinged force-field swimming around us.

She was right. I needed answers. But… *What if he says something I don't want to hear?* I didn't say it out loud.

See, when I was a kid, I'd wandered away from my parents while they were speaking to Tobe in the Bestiary. I remembered feeling a weird pull, magnetic and intense, toward a certain door, and I'd beelined to it. I managed to push the door open and take a few steps into a strange, huge hall with a large box at one end. If I closed my eyes, I could still see every detail, down to the elaborate patterns of frost on the panes of the box, like breath in winter. Anyway, my mom and dad had caught up to me before I could get any farther, and that was when they'd laid down the ban. From that day forward, I was forbidden from entering that hall, and Tobe had made sure to keep watch and see that the embargo prevailed.

What don't they want to tell me? I'd tried to pry answers out of them, but they refused to discuss it. Actually, no, that's not specifically true. They'd given me a tantalizing nugget that I couldn't forget. They'd said, "Leviathan is dangerous and presents an unknown threat to you." And that was all they'd say. So, here I was, edging closer to potential answers. Despite the potential for danger.

"Keep going or... give up. Your choice." Genie delivered an ultimatum. One I needed to hear. If I left now, I'd lose my nerve and have to stay silent on the subject forevermore. But if I steeled myself, then I wouldn't have to wonder anymore. I could know, one way or another, if Leviathan had answers for me. That was worth being brave for.

I flexed my hands a few times to dispel the nerves that had gotten bunched up in my fingers. "Let's keep... going."

She gave my shoulders a squeeze. "You're doing... the right thing." She peered around to make sure Garrett and Dylan were gone. "So, we should probably... hurry up before I... can't hold this anymore."

I've come too far to turn back now. I repeated the mantra, trying to stave off any more doubts that might send me back the way I'd come. After all, I didn't carry those books and endure this forcefield for nothing.

Genie pushed me forward on the home stretch. She stayed beside me with her hands on my arms, acting as my cheerleader, until we reached the Bestiary doors just up the corridor: two enormous black monstrosities with golden lion heads roaring out in place of handles. This time, we had no choice but to open the door ourselves. I only hoped Tobe's security system wouldn't pick up on the anomaly.

Opening it just enough, the two of us crept into the vast expanse of glass boxes and Purge beasts beyond. My eyes darted toward the formidable atrium at the center of the space, fueling the magical world one Purge beast at a time. It never failed to amaze me. All these beings, swirling inside their boxes, had come from magicals, hurled into existence when the time was right.

Another thing I'll never get to experience. I didn't mind that one so much. The creatures might have been wild and wonderful, morphing out of black mist into beasts that littered mythologies and legends the world over, but it sounded like a painful feat for all involved. And I doubted I could ever have lived up to my mom's benchmark of birthing a freaking Child of Chaos. Yeah, my mom was cooler than most. A gift and a curse.

"This is… it," Genie whispered excitedly. With my friend tucked behind me, we stalked toward the far door, where Leviathan's secrets awaited me. And, since Tobe hadn't come screeching between the boxes to catch us in the act, I guessed her trick was working, and we hadn't been spotted coming in.

Just keep going. Just keep going. Just keep going. My nerves were alight. I looked around for signs of Tobe, knowing he could appear at any moment and blast this attempt out of the water. But the avenues between the glass boxes stayed empty, and we continued walking. It was almost more than my nervous heart could bear.

A sharp clatter sounded to my left, and I clamped my hand over my mouth before a proper scream could unleash itself, echoing out into the Bestiary and ruining everything. A gargoyle slobbered on the glass pane beside me, bumping its ugly head against the box as though it wanted to make dinner out of me.

"Easy there, jitterbug. They can't hurt you. Those boxes are designed to keep them in," Genie reassured me, her voice more even. I guessed she'd gotten used to the burning sensation. "Anyway, it can't see you with the shield up."

"I feel like it... can! What if it cracks the glass?" I hissed, my eyes glued to the monstrous face only inches from my own.

She laughed softly. "It won't be a gargoyle that cracks one open, that's for sure."

"That's... not comforting." I curled my hands into fists and tried to pull myself together, as Genie continued her advance toward Leviathan's hall.

I tried to focus on the glass boxes instead of my imminent breakdown. Whorls of black smoke twirled inside, like ink dropped in a glass of water. When I painted, there was nothing more satisfying than that first dip of a paintbrush into the water... I loved it. Plumes of pastel, twirling in the liquid, creating beautiful shapes that invited the eye to interpret. I saw whole worlds in one cup of water. Worlds I could never emulate on paper. They belonged to the transient medium of that solitary glass—a temporary glimpse of beauty that wasn't made to last.

"Here we go!" Genie said excitedly, breaking me out of my reverie. At least I felt calmer. Or I had, until she'd spoken.

She pushed through the door into Leviathan's hall, keeping the shield up to avoid any watchful security. "I can't keep this going for very long," she explained. "You've got about five minutes until I have to admit defeat. This is killing me, and I don't imagine it's a walk in the park for you, either, but it was the only thing I could think of to fox Tobe's security system."

Five minutes... will that be long enough? At the far end of the cavernous hall, which echoed emptily, there stood a huge glass enclosure. It was just as I'd remembered it, down to the frost patterns that dusted the surface. Behind the frost, however, I saw something that hadn't been there before. Subtle movement, shadowed and furtive, making it seem as though the box were full of beings that drifted in and out of view. Or perhaps that was just my eyes playing tricks on me.

"I can't do this." I stopped abruptly, my heart beating out an entire carnival in my chest. The idea had been easier to deal with than the reality. Now, faced with what I wanted, I didn't know if I wanted it anymore. There was something... *off* about this room. The space thrummed with menace, cold and biting, sending up the hairs on the back of my neck. And that glass enclosure stood at the center of it all, the core of the danger.

Genie whirled around. "You're kidding, right? But he's right there!"

"I know, but..." I trailed off, my mind sparking in a thousand directions. I wanted to find out more about him, direct from the source. I wanted to understand this strange connection between us—the one that had driven me to this very door, twelve years ago. I wanted to understand why I wasn't allowed in here and what my parents weren't telling me. Leviathan had the answers. I just needed to keep going and get them.

Genie pressed on. "Look, I know you're freaking out. It's only natural. You're about to speak to an ancient monster about some weird bond between the two of you. *I'd* be having a bit of a freak-out as well, if I were in your shoes."

I sighed. "No, you wouldn't. You'd stride up to that box and... demand answers. You wouldn't hesitate."

"It's all about faking it until you make it, Persie. I act brave when I don't feel brave. I act confident when I'm not. I trick my mind into believing it." She smiled at me. "Your mom and dad don't have the answers you're after. Only *he* does. And the truth can set you free. But if you really don't want to do this, we can go back. I mean it. I'm not going to make you do anything you don't feel ready for. Just know that I'm going to support you through this if you do decide to go for it. It's totally up to you."

Why does this feel all wrong? I wondered if the dutiful daughter side of me was getting in the way. I rarely set a foot out of line, and when I did, I was always quick with an apology, ready to face the consequences. But this had something to do with who I was. Leviathan held the key to a door that had been locked all my life. A door I would never have known existed, had I not stumbled on this place when I was little. And that magnetic pull would only continue to grate on me if I turned back now. Besides, wasn't it better to ask forgiveness than permission?

"You're right." I made my choice.

Genie offered me an encouraging look. "I'm here, no matter what. I'm not going to let anything happen to you. I know this is what you need to do. But I've got you, okay?"

"Thank you." It didn't seem like enough, but it was all I had. I only wished I didn't have to rely on her to stop anything from happening to me. If I'd had magic of my own, I'd have been able to protect myself. Truthfully, I'd never felt the absence of Chaos more keenly than I did at that moment. Nobody really wanted to be the damsel of their own story. Still, if I had to have a white knight, I was glad it was her.

With the shield still up, we approached Leviathan's enclosure. Our footsteps ricocheted faintly between the vast walls, sounding small and insignificant. I fixed my eyes forward, not wanting to look away from the glass box. Fear, anticipation, dread, hope, and a million other emotions swarmed inside me like the mist I thought I'd seen inside this box, behind the frost and the ice.

"He's... coming." I gulped. A core of black throbbed in the center of his frozen block, and a sudden vibration cut right through the heart of me. It shot out from the middle of the box and didn't stop, a steady thud, like war drums approaching. And I didn't know if it was just my imagination, but I swore I heard the sound of ice cracking. I might not have been able to see the monster yet, but I could feel him. His presence shivered up my spine, prickling the hairs and making my hands shake violently.

Suddenly, a voice boomed through the yawning hall, and the forcefield vanished. The sound had startled Genie so hard that she'd let it go.

"Iphigenia Vertis and Persephone Merlin-Crowley!"

I whipped around, lightning fast, to find myself face-to-furry-chest with a very grumpy, very disapproving Tobe. I tilted my head up to look him in his feline eyes—a beautiful shade of layered gold and chartreuse and bronze, with flecks of brown and green and silver that made the color impossible to replicate. Believe me, I'd tried.

"We... uh... I just wanted to... uh..." I gave up. It was obvious what we'd been doing.

"You both know that this place is prohibited." Tobe strode ahead of us and waved a chunky paw across the front of the enclosure. A sheen of bronzed light shot up, concealing the box from view. He'd raised a barrier to prohibit sight and sound, and now I couldn't see or hear anything. I couldn't even feel the unnerving coldness that whispered of menace. In a split second, that barrier had blocked it all.

And we've just been caught breaking a major rule... for nothing. Genie and I exchanged a glance of dread. Tobe was level-headed, and though he might have been disappointed, he hadn't yelled or gotten angry with us. But it wasn't the Beast Master I was afraid of.

TWO

Harley

I stood out on my office balcony, mug of coffee in hand, and let the perfect San Diegan afternoon wash over me. Gulls wheeled overhead and the trees whispered their secrets, egged on by the balmy breeze that swept over the national park. I took a sip and nestled farther into my light sweatshirt. I didn't get peaceful moments to myself like this very often. Still, life as a whole was quieter than it used to be. Nearly twenty years had gone by since Atlantis rose, and no shiny new tyrants had reared their ugly heads since. Apparently, they'd gotten the message.

The world, magical and non-magical, is for no one's taking. I took a longer sip and winced as it scalded my tongue.

These days, I viewed the past and present as pre-Persie and post-Persie. I saw the passage of time in her growth and in the mirror every morning. Pesky new lines around my eyes, my skin a little less elastic, regardless of what pricey creams I piled on. But Wade still loved me, no matter how time changed me. And I loved him. Differently, I guessed, from those heady days when we were young, but oddly the same. We were just a bit softer, maybe.

"Eighteen..." I said the number aloud against the bronzed landscape. "How can she be turning eighteen already?" It seemed like the more years went by, the faster they came.

I vowed not to cry into my coffee. My emotions were all over the place, and seeing my baby grow up wasn't the only thing I had to worry about.

I closed my eyes and recalled the fateful day that Persie had come into the world. I had barely been able to enjoy my pregnancy due to fear, and I'd even had Melody delve into her Librarian back catalogue to surround me with as many protective hexes as possible, in the hopes it'd keep Leviathan away. But there had been no escaping him.

Exhausted from the birth, and sore in places no woman deserved to be, I'd drifted off to try and claw back some energy. I don't know how long I was out, but something woke me sharply. Like bursting out of a nightmare, sweaty and breathless. I blinked awake to find a swirling mass of water leering over the cot beside me. My nameless newborn's cot, with her inside it, pink and new and beautiful. Leviathan had come to seal the deal that I'd made with Echidna, Mother of Monsters. And, somehow, he'd managed to send out his mind and manipulate the water in the Infirmary from the safety of his Bestiary box to make it happen.

"You put in a sterling effort," he said.

"Go to hell," I replied, trying to will strength into my weakened form.

He ignored me. A faceless churning of water. If only he'd been voiceless, too. "I have come to name the child."

"I didn't think you were here to bring balloons."

He laughed. "So beautiful. So fresh." He reached forward with a tendril of water to touch her hand, and I lashed out with a jolt of Air to push his tendril away. A warning.

"Don't touch her!" I snarled. I felt an overwhelming instinct to protect my child from him, spurred on by rage and panic. He'd caught me at my most vulnerable, but I still had some fight left when it came to my baby. I'd always have some fight left for her.

"Temper, temper." But he retreated. "I do not want unpleasantness."

I flipped back the covers, making to get out of bed but hoping he wouldn't call my bluff. "Then go away!"

"Stay at your bed. Rest." He bobbed around to the far side of my little girl's cot. "She will need you to be strong."

"I'll show you how freaking strong I am." I swung my legs over the edge of the bed and prayed for Wade to come back from grabbing coffee. Undoubtedly, Leviathan had waited until I was alone.

"There is no need." Leviathan reached forward again. This time, his watery touch brushed her cheek, leaving a glistening streak. "She is Persephone. She has been named. And when she reaches maturity, I will bestow a second gift… Happy Birthday, my darling." A glowing green bead of light floated out of his watery form and sank into my baby's chest.

She didn't stir, as though nothing had happened. I tried to lunge for him, to stop it, but he'd already gone. Leaving a puddle on the floor where he'd been.

The deed had been done. My daughter had been named, and I'd had no say in it whatsoever. And if I went against him... well, it wasn't worth facing the consequences of breaking a deal like that. The only thing we'd been able to do was shorten her name to Persie, so we didn't have to be constantly reminded of the creature who'd tied her fate to his in some unknown way.

Some unknown way... That was the worst part. He hadn't left us any instructions or details. He'd swooped in, named her, told me about a gift, and left again. The gift concerned me the most, especially as Persie edged closer to eighteen. I'd tried to get more out of him several times, but his lips had been sealed. Which proceeded to worry me even more over the years. Deliberate silence represented a greater threat than frank honesty.

Feeling the familiar anxiety grow, I watched a plump brown bird flutter to its nest. Chicks chirped, open-mouthed, for juicy worms. If only human parenting were that simple. Keep them fed, keep them alive, then kick them out when they were ready to fly. I'd tried to be a normal mom, I really had. But with Leviathan's shadow over our lives, I'd turned into more of a helicopter parent than I cared to admit. Always hovering over Persie, trying to protect her from just about everything. I'd shot a fireball at a bumblebee once, and even pushed a nasty older kid who'd been bullying her into a pond with a sneaky push of Telekinesis. Not my proudest moment. Maybe it was partially the foster kid coming through, too. I'd never known safety or consistency as a kid. I might have gone overboard with Persie, to make up for what I'd only found with the Smiths, years too late to make much difference.

"Go easy on her, sis. Squeeze too tight and she'll try to wriggle free," Finch had advised, a long time ago. He'd been a bit more cavalier in his approach to parenting. The "let them eat mud and fall out of trees so they'll learn their lesson" kind of dad. Typical Finch. Then again, he had two of the politest, most levelheaded kids in the known universe: Diana and Kestrel. Kes couldn't do enough for people. Kind and sweet and earnest at thirteen years old, I occasionally doubted he belonged to Finch at all. Diana, on the other hand, had more of an edge to her. Six months younger than Persie, she was whip smart, like her mom, with the same dry humor as her dad. A potent mix of genes that made for one formidable young woman. They had Ryann to thank for that, for sure. She had this natural maternal instinct about her that I envied. It had never come intuitively to me. I'd just muddled through as best I could, hoping love would be enough to not screw Persie up.

Have I squeezed too tight? I loved her more than anything. From the moment I knew she existed, my heart had been hers. Everything I'd done, I'd done out of fear for her safety. When she'd asked me about Leviathan, I'd been as honest as I could: it was an unknown threat, but he was dangerous. The only thing I'd omitted was the depth of their bond—that he'd named her. But that was only to stop her from thinking about herself, and her name, in a different way. A bad way. At least, that's what I'd convinced myself.

Oh, and the ominous gift he intends to give her. I'd left that part out, too. It would only have cast a shadow over her life, the way it had cast a shadow over mine and Wade's. She'd have constantly looked forward, instead of living in the moment. I hadn't wanted that for her. I'd wanted to bear that weight for her. And, deep down, I still hoped I could stop it. I'd stopped evils before. If I threw enough firepower at the problem, why couldn't I save my daughter, too? Then, she'd never have to know she'd been in peril.

"We thought the dangers were over, didn't we? We thought we'd have a normal life when all those old troubles were over with." I dwelled on the distant memories we all shared, the old Rag Team. Now, we were moms and dads, complaining about wayward kids and stressing out over exams and homework and lunch prep instead of global cata-strophes. And there must've been something in the water, almost two decades ago, because kids had come left, right, and center. Finch and Ryann had a wedding and Diana soon after, followed by Kes, five years later. Astrid and Garrett had Merrick the same year that Diana and Persie came into our lives. Then Santana and Raffe had trumped us all by adopting four kids! Marius was nineteen. Azar, their only daughter, had just turned seventeen. Both of them so beautiful they literally stopped traffic. Then they'd adopted Cy, a feisty ten-year-old with a love for all bugs, which had led to a few unpleasant discoveries—scorpions running loose in the coven, beetles in his hair, that sort of thing. And Angelo, who was six going on sixty. He cracked me up, sometimes saying things that sounded like Nash.

I should give him a call. The new Muppet Babies, as Finch called them, stopped by from time to time, but it had been a while since we'd made proper plans to see each other. Too long. I supposed adult life did that.

I should call Tatyana, too. She was the one person from the old squad who wasn't around anymore. After a messy breakup with Dylan about ten years ago, she'd packed up and headed back to Russia with Saskia. I hadn't checked in with her as much as I should've. Though I guessed it worked both ways.

"Our work is never done, it seems," I told the bird, though it wasn't listening to my human problems. In addition to the Leviathan issue, magicals had been disappearing recently, and we didn't know why. We'd been tracing the incidents and trying to locate the missing people, to no avail. Another reason I had to keep close watch over Persie. Her name and her vulnerability could well make her a target, and I wouldn't have been able to live with myself if anything bad happened to her.

Suddenly, the door opened, and in walked Tobe, Persie, and Genie—the latter two looking guilty as sin. I hurried in from the balcony.

"Harley." Tobe bowed, his wings ruffling. "Apologies for the interruption. I am afraid I have rather disheartening news."

"Is that so?" I put my mom voice on, as Persie refused to meet my gaze. I knew it couldn't have anything to do with her lessons, since Tobe had brought her here. And she was a model student. My mind whirred to try and figure it out— something harmless, probably. A prank or joke that Tobe hadn't found funny. Other than the occasional slap on the wrist for that kind of thing, Persie had a clean record. A fact I couldn't have been prouder of.

"I thought I would leave your daughter with you while I take Miss Vertis to her father," Tobe continued.

Genie huffed a sigh. "And what a treat that'll be."

"I'm sure it won't be so bad," Persie reassured her, her voice tight with anxiety. I liked Genie, even if I occasionally had concerns about the Atlantean's impish influence. The two of them were like cream cheese and jelly—a pairing that shouldn't have fit, yet somehow did. She always brought Persie out of her shell, coaxing her out of her room when she otherwise would have buried herself in sketching and books.

"He'll throw the book at me. And you know how heavy those things are." She flashed Persie a resigned smile. "In fact, if you listen really closely, I'm pretty sure you can hear the vein in his temple popping from here."

My daughter laughed, but not much. The pair of them clearly knew they were in deep crap. I just didn't know what sort of crap... yet.

"What did they do?" I asked.

"I discovered your daughter and Miss Vertis attempting to approach Leviathan's enclosure," Tobe replied. "Indeed, they might have achieved it, had the gargoyles not warned me of their presence."

What?! After everything I've said? The peaceful afternoon

turned sour in a heartbeat. I gripped my mug to try and stop the world from spinning. She knew better than that! I'd told her of the danger. I'd warned her so many times. What was she thinking, trying to sneak in behind my back to see that slimy creature? This proved it. That girl needed a helicopter parent, nearly eighteen or not. I'd never let the "if you live under my roof, you live under my rules" cliché slip out of my mouth, but I felt dangerously close.

"We shall be going, now." Tobe gave Genie a stern look.

"Lead the way, Beast Maestro."

He grumbled in the back of his throat, bordering on a reluctant chuckle. "Maestro?"

"I think it suits you." She looped her arm through his, and he was too gentlemanly to pull away. Instead, he escorted her out of the room like they were heading to a swanky ball. I even caught sight of a half-amused, half-bemused grin on his face as they exited. That girl had a way of winning over just about anyone, even in a situation like this. The only person immune to her charms was her father, which was probably for the best.

Persie stayed by the door. Head down, shuffling awkwardly, she emanated remorse. The question was—did she feel sorry because of what she'd done, or because she'd been caught?

"Go easy on her." Finch's words came back into my head. I paced a little, tapping the side of my mug frenetically. I had to keep calm. If I blew a fuse at her, she'd run in the opposite direction. Yes, she needed reining in, but there were ways to go about it. I had to keep reminding myself of that.

Silence stretched between us. Then, all at once, our voices rose in a clash.

"What were you—" I jumped in.

"Before you start yelling, I just want to—"

"—thinking! I *told* you about Leviathan. I've warned you about—"

"—make it clear that I didn't have a choice. We don't know what his deal is. I don't know what his—"

"—going there, so many times. I thought you understood! Do you think I make these rules up for a laugh?" I had no idea if she was even listening.

She held my gaze, wide-eyed. "Mom, will you listen to me? I'm trying to explain!"

I fidgeted with the pendant around my neck, the same one Isadora had worn. The Merlin heirloom made me feel closer to those I'd lost along the way. I clutched it tight in my palm and tried to draw strength from it. My parents had never had the chance to deal with a teenager. I often wondered what sort of teenager I'd have been, if things had been different. I had a feeling I would've been just as headstrong. They might've wanted to kick me out of the nest, by the end of it. So perhaps I owed Persie a chance to remedy this.

I took a steadying breath. "Then explain."

"I know you didn't want me going near him, but I had to! You don't know why he's a threat to me. Isn't it better to find out, instead of wondering?" She shoved her hands into her jeans pockets. *My* jeans, but I wasn't about to bring that up now. "He won't speak to you. I thought... I thought he might speak to me."

"You shouldn't have done that," I said flatly. Without magic, she was vulnerable in most magical situations, which I supposed added to my overprotectiveness. But this was on another level. Leviathan spelled pure, unadulterated danger. And she had nothing to defend herself with, even if she'd taken Genie with her. Even an Atlantean was no match for someone like him.

"Why not? He's behind magic glass, and I had Genie with me. Plus, I knew Tobe was around if we needed help." Her eyes hardened. I hated seeing her like this, set against me. "I need answers, Mom. I can't keep pretending everything's fine, when there's this secret about me that nobody knows. Why shouldn't I know what the deal is between us? It's better than not knowing and waiting for some... *whatever* to take me by surprise!"

She had a point. A very good one. And, with her eighteenth birthday fast approaching, I didn't know how much longer we had before Leviathan finally gave up his secrets and revealed the true extent of his threat. But...

"It's my job to keep you safe." I didn't know what else to say.

She looked away. "How do you plan to do that, when you don't even know what kind of danger I'm in?"

I heaved a sigh, speechless. I didn't have an answer. Only a silence that spoke volumes and a gathering dread in the pit of my stomach.

THREE

Persie

_____

"See, you can't give me an answer!" My voice took on a pathetic note. A high-pitched, unnatural sound, as though I'd sucked in a whole balloon of helium. What was it about being in front of your mom, knowing you'd done wrong, that regressed you back to childhood? I summoned what I hoped sounded more like maturity. "No one can... aside from Leviathan."

"It doesn't matter if I don't know the specifics. I know he's dangerous, and that's all that matters." My mom tapped the side of her mug, a jarring sound that pecked at my skull with woodpecker precision. "And I know how to protect you. I've been doing it your entire life, and I was protecting people long before then, too. Do I need to remind you that—"

My eyes threatened to roll back into my sockets. "That you saved the world... twice. But this is different! I don't want to fight anyone. I don't want to save the world. I just want the truth." I bit the inside of my fleshy cheek. Anything to stop my voice from rising again. In the famous words of Michel de Montaigne, fabled philosopher of the French Renaissance: *He who establishes his argument by noise and command shows that his reason is weak.* Or, more simply, once you shouted, you lost the argument.

"We don't know the truth. We only know what we know." My mom kept tapping. An endless percussion that made me want to stick wax balls in my ears, Odysseus-style. "And I've faced Leviathan before. He's as nasty as they come, and twice as tricky. It's not a matter of walking up to his glass box and asking for answers. That's not how he works."

"Does it matter? You have no answers, but Leviathan *does* have answers. You don't want me speaking to him, but he's the only one who knows the truth. Catch-22 doesn't even cover it!" I looked at anything and everything other than my mom, from the sea glass paperweights she kept on her desk—a gift from the Atlanteans, in vivid shades of blue and green—to the pieces I'd painted that adorned her walls. Abstract splashes of color and light with flavors of Kandinsky, poured from my mind into my paintbrush and onto canvas. They'd made sense when I'd painted them. Now, not so much.

"It's for your safety, Persie." The party line, stuck on repeat.

"I'm eighteen in less than a week, Mom. I'll legally be an adult. If that's not the point when you stop babying me, then when will it be?" Desperation crept into my tone, constricting my throat. "How long are you going to stuff me in bubble-wrap?"

My mom froze. "I'm not! I'm helping you, even if you don't see it now."

I dug my thumbs hard against the denim belt loops. "But wouldn't it be better if we got ahead of anything Leviathan might have planned?" After all, knowledge provided the best form of defense. Know your enemy, and that sort of thing. Although, I didn't even know *why* Leviathan was the enemy, only that he was dangerous. More than that, I longed to be able to protect myself, instead of feeling as though my mom had to do all that for me. How could I ever be independent, living my own life, if we carried on like this? I'd be in perpetual child limbo.

"It's all taken care of. You just have to stay away. That's all I ask. That's all I've ever asked." Her eyes hardened—my eyes. The color of the sea on a summer day. My gift from her, like the dark curls from my dad.

I stood my ground. "What do you mean, it's 'taken care of?' Since when?"

"Since the moment I found out you were coming into our lives, I've been putting defenses in place. He's not going to get you. I won't let him." She peered down into her coffee. I wondered what she saw in there. Enough hope to convince herself it was true?

"He's broken through before, though, right?" I knew all about his eerie message to her by the SDC's pool, when she first found out about me.

"Yes, but almost two decades is plenty of time to shore up the defenses. Melody and I never stopped working on solutions." Her body language gave more away than she thought.

An Empath should've been better at hiding her emotions, but doubt and guilt radiated from her in waves. And she wasn't finding any answers in that mug. Ironically, it was a chipped, ancient mug with "#1 Mom" half-scratched off the ceramic. A Mother's Day gift from about a million years ago.

I gulped down a lump of tension in my throat. "Maybe I've got a solution that suits all of us."

"Oh?" She lifted her head, wary. A red strand of hair narrowly avoided a caffeine dip.

"Actually, it's something I've been thinking about for a while, same as most people my age." I gulped again, to try and shift the pesky lump. "The SDC is my home, but..."

Ah, how do I phrase this? I didn't want to come off as ungrateful or spiteful, or like I was childishly trying to win this argument with underhanded tactics. But if I didn't say this now, chances were, I never would.

"I think I'd like to move to another coven." I wiggled my tongue inside my mouth, wondering if those words had actually come out of my mouth. "It's hard enough here, with the Merlin dynasty hovering over me—Little Miss Magicless. But it's even harder under Leviathan's shadow, with you and Dad treating me like I'm made of glass."

Mom walked forward, compelled by maternal instinct to come closer. And I had a childish instinct to step back. "Persie..."

"You don't want me to go near Leviathan, and I get that you know more about him than I do. But you have to see it from my perspective. It's a huge temptation, having him nearby and knowing there's this big gap in who I am that only he can reveal. So maybe I take myself out of the equation. Maybe I put some distance between us, so I don't keep wondering all the time." I kept talking, determined not to clam up. "The SDC is your territory. It belongs to you and Dad. I see your names, and I hear all those stories about everything you did before you had me, and I'm so proud that you're my parents. But... I want something that's mine. A place to start fresh."

Mom fell silent, pausing halfway across the room as though someone had flipped her off-switch. "I... didn't know you felt that way."

I took a deep breath. "I'm nearly done being taught here. Plenty of people move on when they're my age." Her eyes burned into me, but not in a harsh or angry way. The heat of sadness, more than anything else. Confusion, maybe. "Genie and I were looking through some prospectuses for other covens. There's one in Austin that sounds like it was made for me. They've got this Mediocre development program, where Mediocres get specialized training to boost their abilities. And it's pretty there, so I can keep up with my painting, and there are programs that Genie's interested in, too."

Mom stepped closer, weirdly cautious. As if I were a fawn she didn't want to spook. "Persie..."

"I realize this is all a bit of a shock, but I know you'll come around once you've looked at the prospectuses. And it'll get me away from the SDC, and from Leviathan, and I can start building a life of my own, and—"

"It's not that," she interrupted, closing the gap between us. Her hand grazed my upper arm, her expression gentle and sympathetic. "A Mediocre development program wouldn't do you any good, Persie. You aren't a Mediocre. You don't have any magic at all. I hate to put it so bluntly, but it's the truth."

Ouch. That never got easier to swallow.

"That's why it's better if you stay here," my mom went on. "We can protect you here. You might not have magic, but you're still a Merlin, and we have one of the best non-magical relations departments in the US. This coven doesn't belong to your dad and me—it belongs to all of us. You belong here."

"What if I want something else?"

Mom relaxed her hold on me and stepped back, turning her eyes downward. "We can revisit it in a few years, once we understand the threat from Leviathan."

A few years?! Speech evaded me. Literature liked to keep its madwomen in attics—take the wife in Jane Eyre, for example—but I'd wind up as a basement dweller, hiding out until I hit forty. The magicless girl who vanished into the darkness and never emerged, driven insane by her over-bearing parents.

"Besides, the magical world might look like it's at peace, but it's not safe out there for someone like you. Your name and your... uniqueness make you vulnerable." Mom softened her voice. A sure sign that I wasn't going to like what she had to say.

"What does Dad think about this?" I shuffled away from her touch. It felt too much like a shackle around my arm.

"He... agrees with me." Her hesitation said everything.

"Does he, or are you just saying that?" I bit my tongue so I wouldn't spew out something I wouldn't be able to take back.

"He's always saying he wants me to be happy. If he knew I wasn't happy staying here, he'd let me leave."

My mom lifted her chin. A mannerism I hadn't inherited. "Your dad wants what's best for you, and he knows that means staying here. I'm not the bad guy here. I'm trying to keep you alive."

"Not everything is life and death!" I exploded a little—at least, enough to make her eyes widen in surprise. "Saving the world twice is great and everything, but it's messed with your head. You think everything is a catastrophe waiting to happen, when all I'm asking for is the same thing a million other eighteen-year-olds ask for! Freedom."

"You aren't the same as a million other eighteen-year-olds," she reminded me. As if I needed reminding.

"Aren't I?" My eyes turned steely. "I don't have magic. That makes me the same as most of the population."

Mom clenched her jaw, her cheeks sucking in. "Persie, you asked me to see things from your perspective, and I *do* understand your frustration. But see things from mine. You're my only child, and there's a monster who wants something from you. I can only fight him if you're near me."

Because I'm so useless and defenseless that I need you to stand up for me? It saddened me, looking at my mother, to wonder how much this stemmed from my lack of magic. I was constantly second-guessing my relationships with everyone around me, and it sapped so much of my energy, making it harder to think and breathe clearly.

I loved her more than anyone else in the world. But I wondered if she'd ever see me as an equal, with my own ideas and capabilities and contributions. Eighteen was a milestone for a reason—the ascent into adulthood. But she didn't seem to realize that. Instead, the older I got, the harder she appeared to cling, refusing the inevitable truth. One day, I would leave. One day, I'd be my own person.

I found some grit at the back of my mind. "And we're right back where we started. You haven't listened to a word I've said."

"I have, Persie, but I'm asking you to listen to me in return."

I straightened, pulling my hands out of my pockets. "We're never going to agree on this. So, as long as you won't let me speak to Leviathan, and I don't get answers, I'm going to start looking for other covens to call home—somewhere to put as much distance as possible between me and this secret that's followed me my whole life. If you won't help me, then I have to help myself. I won't wait for the axe to fall."

I turned, even though I knew we weren't finished. Unspoken words lingered heavy in the atmosphere, like clouds gathering, chasing me out of the room. The lightning would strike later, after simmering awhile. Holding my head high and putting one foot in front of the other, I resisted the urge to storm out of there. And I refused to let the clouds break now, with silly tears stinging my eyes. For once, I might have won an argument with my mother. At least temporarily.

Brushing away the hot tears that had fallen regardless, a quote from Voltaire popped into my head: *A long dispute means that both parties are wrong.* It seemed he'd missed an important exception in the case of Merlin women—what if we were both right, in a way? In either case, arguing with my mom left me feeling like a salted slug, all dried up and fizzing. The brief victory meant nothing, not when we'd both pay for it in future tension.

Between Genie and me, seeing eye-to-eye with our parents verged on the impossible.

FOUR

Persie

———————

The Physical Magic classroom sweltered in the late-afternoon heat. Balmy bronze sunlight sashayed through the windows and draped everything in a syrupy glow. Half the students propped their chins lazily on their hands, eyelids heavy, moments away from an elbow slip that'd jolt them right back into reality.

At least it's a good excuse to keep out of Mom's way. I tilted my notebook against the lip of the desk, positioned away from prying eyes. My pencil etched gray strokes, the soft scratch barely audible above the commanding voice of the preceptor: Alyssa Soanoke, Jacob's wife, who'd taken his birth-given surname after he'd changed it from Medina. A one-woman dynamo with a mysterious past. People said she'd been in the magical Secret Service, or that she used to be a bounty hunter. Others said she had a full-body tattoo of a phoenix, which meant she was part of an ancient cult—the rumors changed year after year. I didn't know which I believed, if I believed any at all.

"Oi!" She rapped her pointer against the board. "I get that it's late in the day, but I'd appreciate it if you didn't nap during my class! This isn't kindergarten."

Everyone sat up a little straighter, and I kept right on doodling, half pretending she had my attention. As preceptors went, she was one of the good ones. The kind who spoke to her students with respect and made her lessons interesting. Even for a magicless dunce like me. We were getting into the theory of Physical Magic, from the early twentieth century to present day. Usually, I'd be scribbling down notes and hanging on her every word, but the argument with my mother had stolen away all my concentration. And... not to sound petulant, but what was the point of learning this stuff if I could never use it? At least I had purpose in drawing.

"This is Kyu-Ho Min, one of the finest magicals from South Korea, famous for his unique hex work and manipulation of Elemental abilities. This recording was taken in 1972, during the Global Magical Expo. There is an entire library in the Seoul Coven dedicated to his Grimoires—all of which are filled with experimental spells and ingenious methodologies." She paused. "Well, perhaps not an entire library, but definitely a bookcase. And there are books written about his personal style in magical combat—some of which you'll be able to see here." She tapped her pointer against the board, which doubled as a cinema screen.

A square-jawed, dark-haired warrior spun and twirled like a dancer across the board, magic sparking out of him like fabric: silky and uniform in its spirals. It didn't even look as though he had to raise his palms, he moved so fast and fluidly. Bright colors exploded in the face of his assailant.

"Here, he uses a preemptive strike of flurried hexes to startle and disorient his attacker, and immediately follows through with a swipe of Air to further unbalance his opponent. You'll notice he jumps in with a hex to the chest, designed to immobilize." Alyssa stared at the grainy film with adoring eyes. "The reason we use him as an example is because, as you can see, there's no hesitation between each hex and the switch between his abilities. One follows the other in quick succession, so his enemy has no opportunity to adapt."

Diana raised a slender hand. My cousin's Esprit—a cuff bracelet with an opal the size of a scarab beetle—slipped down her wrist. "Is he still alive?"

"Sadly, no," Alyssa replied. "He died under mysterious circumstances in the 1980s."

"Then I guess he wasn't that good," Diana murmured. A few snickers rippled around the room.

Alyssa pushed back a curtain of thick chestnut hair flecked with fiery auburn. "What is the first rule of magical combat, Miss Merlin?"

Diana replied without pause. "Hit first, ask questions later."

Sounds about right to me. I shaded in the snout of a

monster, a creature conjured from the depths of my tense brain. I had no idea what it was. A griffin-looking thing with the head of a turtle and the body of a scaly horse. Weird to imagine, but my imagination liked to dip into the weird from time to time. It kept things spicy.

Alyssa did not look amused. "While that may serve you well in some circumstances, you know very well that's not the first rule. It's respect, Miss Merlin. I suggest you show some to a magical far greater than any of you can ever hope to be, who was taken before his time."

"Sorry, I wasn't trying to be obtuse." Diana turned more serious. "I'm genuinely curious. If he's as good as you say, how come he got knocked off?"

"Come on, Di." Marius ran a hand through his super-model locks. "Why do you like the grisly stuff so much?"

"I'm interested." Diana shrugged, batting baby blues at the preceptor, who looked annoyed by the display. Diana was the broccoli of the SDC—you either loved her or you hated her. I fell into the former category, but then, I knew her better than most. She used a lot of bluster and humor to hide a lack of self-confidence, even though she had nothing to be concerned about. Still, they say the prettiest girls are the ones with the most self-doubt.

Alyssa twisted her pointer between her palms, and I sensed a different storm brewing. "Precisely because he was that good, Miss Merlin. I'd expect you, of all people, to understand the threat that comes with great power. People want it for themselves, or they seek to remove it if they can't have it. It took him twenty-four seconds to floor his opponent in this video—another famed magical by the name of Barnaby Pierce, of the London Coven, at a time when the best magicals in the world were coming directly out of England. So you can imagine the outrage. Kyu-Ho became a champion in those twenty-four seconds, and a target."

People are scared of things they can't control. My mom's fear of Leviathan, for example. Still, I felt sorry for the guy on the screen. He'd worked hard to succeed, and someone had killed him for it. The green-eyed monster had far more sway than any physical monster, because it could infect more people in one fell swoop.

Azar looked up from her notes. "He invented the Hexent moves, didn't he?"

I mustered a half-smile. You could always rely on the Catemaco-Levis to break up an imminent argument. A skill they'd had to learn fast, with Santana's fiery temper and Raffe constantly quarreling with his inner djinn, Kadar.

"Very good, Miss Cate—Azar." Alyssa gave up on the long double-barrel. "He did. Otherwise known as the Min Spiral, it is a deadly combination of a hex and an Elemental ability used simultaneously. Few are able to master it, even now."

"Are you going to teach us?" Diana turned her cuff around on her wrist.

Alyssa made a frustrated face, pursing her lips. "I… can't do it, personally, but there are plenty of books on the art. You can find some in the library if you want to research it in your own time. It's also… uh… not strictly on the syllabus."

It's frowned upon, you mean. I drifted in and out of the conversation, focusing on the fine details of the monster I'd sketched into the margins. The delicate curve of a nostril, the spark of life in an eye that I imagined to be green, if I had colors. And the shine of light on each of those horsey scales, to urge it into three dimensions.

"Ooh, nice kapafin." Genie leaned precariously on her chair, the legs straining.

"Huh?" I replied, sharply scratching up with my pencil tip to detail some fine hairs on the beast's back.

"That thing." She pointed to the creature. "It's a kapafin. Third-turtle, third-horse, third-bird. There was a picture of one in my favorite book when I was little. Never seen one in real life, though. I don't think anyone has. Is there one in the Bestiary that old Tobe's keeping quiet?" I glanced at her. She was jittering with all the excitement of a kid on Christmas.

I shrugged. "You'd have to ask him. I don't think I've seen one in there, though."

"Didn't people say he sold his soul to a djinn?" Merrick cut into the class debate. A hulking, six-foot-six man, with his mom, Astrid's, dark skin and razor-sharp intellect. He might have looked intimidating, but he had a heart of mush. The kind of person who stopped to let a snail pass in front of him.

Alyssa grumbled under her breath. "There are some who said so, yes. But I suspect it came out of jealousy. People will do anything to denigrate the reputation of someone who's truly gifted."

"It would explain why he died mysteriously, though." Marius chewed the end of his pen. I'd never wanted to be a pen more. "Making deals with the djinn comes at a steep price, most of the time. Unless you get a more benevolent one."

"There was no djinn deal! He had discipline and a gift, and he suffered for all his hard work. That's something most of you could do with learning—hard work!" Alyssa switched the film to a newer video. She'd clearly had enough of having someone she admired brought under scrutiny. I'd have tried to offer her some support, but I rarely spoke in class unless the preceptor asked me a direct question. *Shy, but very capable. Could do with putting her ideas forward more.* The same old school report for as long as I could remember.

"Who's up next?" Diana sprawled, feline-like, across her chair.

Alyssa smiled. "Someone you might recognize."

"It's my dad, isn't it?" Diana groaned, all her bravado disappearing in a haze of embarrassment, which quickly turned to relief as the next video began. "Thank Chaos, it's Aunt Harley. I thought you were going to put on that video from the 2024 Magical Olympics. The one everyone turned into a meme."

I looked up, and my insides tensed. My mom stood at the edge of an arena, speaking to my dad. Our earlier argument rushed back, unraveling all the meditative work my sketching had done.

"I wouldn't do Finch the injustice of showing everyone *that* particular video." Alyssa smirked, but I sensed she wouldn't have minded putting it on to keep Diana quiet.

"Earth calling Persie." Genie lobbed a scrunched-up ball of paper at my face.

I recoiled from the missile. "Huh?"

"What's going on up there?" She wiggled her finger at my head. "You went all… sad."

I shaded in a few feathers to try and get my thoughts back on track. "It's nothing."

"Your mom laid into you, didn't she?" Although Genie might have been older than any of us—older than my mom, even—Atlantean minds developed differently, so she acted the same as any teenager. It might've sounded strange, but we'd all gotten used to the age disparity after the first wave of integration, twenty years ago.

"We… had a difference of opinion. Let's just say that." I really didn't want to talk about it, but I had to get it off my chest. "I ended up telling her about moving to a different coven."

Genie stared at me. "Seriously?" She hurriedly checked that Alyssa wasn't watching us. Fortunately, the preceptor had returned to a heated debate with Diana and the other students about the previous video.

"I did. And I might regret it now. Anyway, how did things go with your dad? I'm guessing it wasn't too bad, since you're in class."

"The usual lecture, and a few truths of my own." She grinned. "I swear you and I are connected by the brain. He got me so annoyed that I just blurted out my plans for the future, too. And he didn't like them one bit. He wants me to study at an Atlantean university, to get in touch with my heritage. I think part of him misses the old world, so to speak. Anyway, I told him, for the millionth time, that if he wanted me to get in touch with my heritage, he never should have taken me out of Atlantis. Cue him giving me the usual spiel about necessity. I said I was going to forge my own path out of necessity, and I wasn't going to take any of that stuffy, antiquated crap. He told me we'd talk about it another time, and I haven't seen him since. He's probably constructing a cage for me as we speak."

"Trouble in paradise?" Diana leaned into our conversation.

I laughed wryly. "Parents."

"Your mom?" Diana eyed me, her blue gaze whirring like an X-ray machine.

I gestured to Genie. "And her dad."

"Girls!" Alyssa shouted, giving us serious stink eye. Diana pretended to look forward again, waiting until the preceptor carried on with a deconstruction of my mom's arena battle, before continuing the conversation at a whisper.

"Is it the… secret thing that no one talks about?"

"When is it not?" I lamented. The whole family knew about my monster sitch. Well, my cousins weren't supposed to, but they'd overheard a thing or two.

Diana nodded in understanding. "She's worried about you, that's all. My mom's worried; my dad's worried. Every-one's worried."

"I know." I aggressively shaded a few scales, ruining one. "But I'm worried, too. Worried about what this means for my future if Mom doesn't let me out of her sight."

"Hey, it's like when you get a pimple. It's all red and angry the first day, but then it settles and eventually goes away, and everything's smooth again. Unless you pick at it, and then it gets worse." Diana offered a reassuring smile, showing her sweet side. "Have a chat with your mom and dad, keep it calm, and the pimple will resolve itself."

I laughed. "What do you know about pimples?"

"There's a lot that glamour can hide." She winked, and the tension in my tight smile eased slightly.

"I wish one could hide me," I half joked.

"It can't be that bad, can it?" Diana looked dubious. "You hardly ever argue. I'm sure it'll blow over."

I set my pencil down and stared up at the video playing out on the board. "I don't know if this one is going to. We want two different things. She wants me where she can see me; I want to get out of here and see more of the world."

"Ditto." Genie smiled sadly. The other pea in my pod.

I sank back into my chair and watched the familiar film play out. My mom, a few years after she'd had me, taking part in the North American Expo. I knew how it ended. The famous Harley Merlin flooring a giant woman in two minutes flat and the crowd erupting into applause. Squinting, it could've been me up there, aside from the hair color. We had the same face, the same eyes, and the same stubborn heart. I loved her. She loved me. And that love and similarity had somehow built a powder keg between us over the years. One spark, and it blew.

Let me go, Mom. Let me walk down my own path. Let me fight my own battles, the way you got to. I glanced at the classroom, which had fallen quiet. Everyone was transfixed by my mom's prowess. The shadow I lived under. She didn't realize that her shadow would stunt me if I stayed in its darkness. I needed freedom, I needed air, I needed something new—something that belonged entirely to me—or I'd suffocate.

FIVE

Harley

———————

She'll be in *Physical Magic by now.* I tried not to look at the huge vintage clock in Waterfront Park's latest brunch hotspot, Holland Days. I guessed they thought they were clever with the word play. In a better mood, I might've agreed. Instead, I tipped back my second mimosa and downed half of it in one go. Ryann and Santana gave me a curious look—code for, "What the heck happened that warrants two mimosas in less than fifteen minutes?"

"Long day," I grumbled in reply to their unspoken question, drinking the rest and signaling for another. I knew I'd hate myself for it later.

Astrid checked Smartie's screen. "It's three o'clock."

"I know." I exchanged a conspiratorial look with Wade. We'd organized this brunch about two weeks ago, since detailed planning was the only way to have quality time with friends these days. I'd tried to bail due to wayward offspring, but Wade had insisted we show up. He thought it might take my mind off things. If only.

"This place is nice." Raffe glanced around, oblivious to the elephant in the room. I smiled, despite myself. He hadn't changed a whole lot, and I was glad of that.

Sometimes, surrounded by my married friends, I forgot that almost two decades had passed since we were all young and childfree. We'd sat in a different place then, in a different establishment, but the view had been the same. Lovers and families, strollers and dogs, runners and cyclists—they all followed the same paths around the park that they always had. Only their faces changed; the kids becoming the adults and having kids of their own. Just like us.

I nodded and poked at my plate. "How long has it been open?"

"A few months, I think." Garrett wiped his mouth on the corner of a napkin, also oblivious to the telepathy of women.

"What's wrong?" Santana came out with it, simultaneously feeding Slinky, who was draped around her shoulders. He hadn't aged a day. Bastard. "You've got a face like thunder, and the bartender looks like he's thinking about watering down your third mimosa. Either you've gone rogue, or you've got teenage daughter problems."

I toyed with the stem of my mimosa flute. "That obvious, huh?"

"Only to us." Ryann nodded, her voice soothing.

"And the bartender," Santana muttered.

"Persie wants to change covens," Wade answered for me. I

offered him a grateful smile. He had a way of keeping things simple that I lacked.

A shocked ripple spread out across the table. Even Raffe set down his fork, though Kadar had been ranting about how hungry he was two minutes earlier. The djinn hadn't calmed down over time, but he'd become one of us in his own right. And he adored his kids more than anything—the kids all three had technically adopted. I'd never seen him quieter, or more angelic, than when he'd held a two-year-old Marius in his arms for the first time.

Astrid wiped her glasses on her shirt, frowning. "Why would she want to do that? The SDC has everything she could need, and we've got the best non-magical department in the country."

"Well, you say that, but there are other covens that are equally good. Maybe she wants to see Europe, or Brazil," Garrett chimed in. "And lots of them have programs that we don't, like—" Sharp looks from Ryann and Santana silenced him. "Uh, never mind."

"I could just about deal with that, if it weren't for..." I sucked in a nervous breath. "You know."

Raffe shifted into Kadar, his skin burning scarlet. "What has that scaly devil done now? Has he harmed Miss Persie? I am already ravenous, and, since Raffe has denied me these sandwiches, I would not mind taking a bite out of an ancient Purge beast to satisfy my hunger."

I gave a weak chuckle. "Thanks, but I don't think it'd do any good."

"Why's that?" Ryann asked, after a sip of her drink. "Melody still didn't find anything to keep Leviathan at bay?"

"Nope, nada. And if she hasn't found anything in eighteen years, I doubt she will now. Tobe has reinforced hexes on Leviathan's box, but I'm not sure I'd pit them against Leviathan's determination." I sagged, feeling miserable. "I don't know what he wants from my daughter. All I know is, he wants *something*. That's why I can't just let her wander off to some other coven. I need her here, so I can protect her no matter what."

"And she thinks you're being unreasonable?" Santana stroked Slinky's vivid feathers.

I shrugged. "I pretty much told her that I was banning her from going anywhere for the foreseeable future." I tore up the corner of a napkin, leaving a snowfall of scraps on the table-top. "And it sucks, because I hate monitoring her all the time like she's in a police state, but what else can I do when Leviathan's gunning for her?"

"Wade, what do you think?" Ryann prompted.

He looked stoic in his resolve, but a hint of remorse glinted in his eyes. "I agree with Harley. We need to keep Persie safe, but I wish she didn't feel like we were putting a stranglehold on her. That's how it seems, and neither of us knows how to make her see *why* we're doing this."

"And, with her eighteenth birthday coming up, you're worried about the gift he might bring?" Astrid folded her hands on the table, as though we were in the middle of an interview.

Wade and I looked at each other. "In a nutshell, yeah," he replied.

"My offer is still on the table." Kadar huffed and puffed, sending up wisps of angry black smoke.

"I'll keep that as a backup, but... we need to make sure we've got all hands on deck when her birthday comes around, in case things take a Leviathan-shaped turn." I hated admitting I needed help, but these were my people. They'd do everything they could for Persie.

Santana stopped mid-stroke of Slinky. "Are we talking weapons, hexes, the whole shebang?"

"All guns blazing." I swallowed the creeping guilt that edged up my throat. I was asking for an army without letting the target know she was a target. "I hoped Melody might still come through with a solution. That hasn't happened, obviously, so it'll be down to us, when the time comes."

"But her birthday is soon! Like, four days away!" Ryann looked as though I'd slapped her with a wet fish. "If Leviathan is coming for her, then we don't have long to prepare!"

I shook my head and tried to offer her my best apology face. "No, we don't. And I don't even know what we *can* do, besides being there for her and using everything we have to defend her."

Just then, a figure rushed up to the table and plopped down in the empty seat beside Ryann. Red-cheeked and breathing hard, Finch leaned over to kiss his wife. Ryann smiled and playfully batted him away. Even when he was late, he managed to bring some levity to any situation. Flashing a grin, he swiped up a glass and took a sip, only for his smile to fade rapidly as he took in the hangdog faces. "Who died?"

"Persie is in trouble." Kadar stuck out his proud chin. I guessed he was about five minutes away from snatching up his fork and going to face Leviathan himself.

Finch's expression darkened. "What do you mean? Is it Leviathan?"

"You'd know if you were here on time." Santana shot him a sarcastic smile. Twenty years later, their love-hate relationship was still going strong.

"Sorry, I didn't realize you'd added me to your Von Trapp family. Would you like me to start singing 'Do-Re-Mi' before or after I find out what's going on with my niece?" He turned his attention back to me as Santana rolled her eyes. "Seriously, Harley, what did I miss?"

He liked the news even less than the others.

"So, you don't know if Tobe's hexes and Leviathan's stasis will hold him back, for some reason, Melody's still a no-go, and you still don't know what nightmare jack-in-the-box he's got prepped for Persie's eighteenth?" He downed the drink he'd pilfered from Ryann. Merlin minds thought alike.

"A gift," I corrected.

"Oh yeah, because he's got eighteen years of My Little Ponies waiting for her." Finch shook his head. "His idea of a gift isn't going to be sunshine and rainbows, Harley."

I sighed and held on to Wade's hand.

"Go easy, Finch," he warned. "And we don't exactly know that. Echidna helped us before, and Leviathan helped us, in a roundabout way. It could be a useful gift, or it could not.

Which is why we need to prepare for all scenarios, including the worst case."

"I'm guessing you haven't told her about it?" Finch eyed me.

I puffed air through my lips. "No, but I know we can keep him away from her if we have to. I have a better idea of what to expect." My determination to give my daughter an ordinary life was one of the main reasons I'd kept the secret. Why tell her, if it didn't have to go down like that? We had power, we had strength, and we had everyone on our side. If Leviathan struck, he'd have to face all of us. And we'd faced worse... right? Heck, I'd faced Leviathan and won once before. I'd do it again. Plus, Wade was right. I'd spent so long thinking Leviathan would bring something bad, I'd never stopped to think that it might be something good. Then again, nothing came from him without provisos.

"Correction. You *hope* we can keep him away. Well, looks like I came along at the perfect time." He flexed his fingers and cast Santana a pointed look. "First, and I know this is going to sting, but cut the girl some slack. The harder you try to control her, the more reason you'll give her to distance herself from all of us. And that's the last thing anyone wants, with Captain Tentacles on the hunt. She needs to know we've got her back."

Ryann put her arm around Finch's shoulders. "If she's anything like Diana, she just needs time to think and calm down. I wouldn't be surprised if she comes to find you tonight, to have a quieter conversation about everything."

I wonder if Wade and I look like they do: a team. They spoke on the same wavelength without it sounding like they were ganging up on anyone. A seamless double act that had taken years to perfect.

"And maybe tell her everything you know, if you want to convince her that we're the sane ones." Finch tilted his head until it lay against Ryann's. "Otherwise, you look like demented, super-controlling parents who want to squeeze all the joy out of her life for no reason."

"Finch." Ryann jabbed him in the ribs.

He laughed. "Sorry. I went a little strong with the teenage mindset there."

"If she hasn't started throwing darts at a picture of my face, I'll talk to her again." But still, there was a part of me that didn't know if I could break the truth to Persie. If I told her about this unknown gift, there'd be more questions I couldn't answer, and I was terrified that would only push her farther away. Or, worse, that it might push her toward Leviathan.

"Ah, so that's why she came by to ask for my dartboard." Finch reached across the table for my hand. "This'll all work itself out, Harley, as long as you're honest now, and you give her your reasons for staying quiet about it. I know it will. The trouble with the two of you is, you're the same—an unstoppable force meeting an immovable object."

Is that true? Are we the same? I saw so much of me in her sometimes. Other times, I didn't see any of myself at all. I saw someone with walls around her that I couldn't get through, no matter how I tried. Maybe that was the immovable object Finch was talking about.

"How come Melody hasn't found anything, anyway?" He took some of the heat off me for a second. "After eighteen years, you'd think she'd have *something*. Looks like the Librarian is slacking, now that she's on the wrong side of thirty-five. I blame Luke. But then, I always blame Luke. He's an easy target."

I graciously accepted my third mimosa from the server, even if it'd taken him ages to bring it. "It just isn't in her mind palace, but she does have hexes and spells that she thinks might be useful. She's promised to get them in place before Persie's birthday."

"What, she's coming here? How did you swing that? The pair of them are harder to get hold of than a doctor's appointment." Finch stole a piece of toast from Ryann's plate. "I had to *book* to see them, a month in advance!"

"Are they still on their traveling spree?" Ryann smiled wistfully. I could almost see images of Bali and Mexico and New Zealand flashing across her eyes.

"The never-ending voyages of Luke and Melody." Finch waved his ill-gotten toast dramatically. "I'd just caught them after a six-week stint trekking around South America. Apparently, there are lots of tribes in the Amazon, and plenty of ancient Mayan and Aztec temples, with secret knowledge that she was desperate to learn. And where Melody goes, Luke goes."

Garrett finished off his waffle. "I wouldn't have the patience. You'd think that, being a Librarian, you'd have all the knowledge you'd ever need, and that'd be that. No need to uncover more."

"For some, the pursuit of absolute knowledge is a lifelong commitment." Astrid peered up at him with a knowing smile. She might not have been a Librarian, but she'd dedicated her entire life to the same cause.

"Have you heard from Nash?" The older I got, the more I thought about him. He drifted in and out of our lives like the seasons, dropping in whenever we least expected. He'd never been as close to the Rag Team as he was to the new Muppet Babies, but he had a calming presence and a sage mind that I could've used right about now.

Finch smiled sadly. "I dropped in on him a few weeks back. He's still at the cabin, happy as a clam, ready to fling knives at any intruder. I pity the postman, that's all I can say." He lowered his gaze, and I sensed bad news in the air. "Huntress has stopped biting his ass, though—the postman's, not Nash's. It's weird to think of her getting old, but she's no spring pup anymore. Honestly, I can't even picture Nash without her."

Ryann looked heartbroken. "You said she was okay!"

He wrapped an arm around her. "She *is* okay, but I think he's preparing for her sunset, so to speak. She's already had a freakishly long life as a Familiar, but even that won't last forever, and she's getting tired."

"It's going to kill him." Tears filled Ryann's eyes.

"Hey, she's not gone yet." Finch kissed her forehead softly. "Why don't we head out to the cabin soon? You can bury your face in her fur, feed her something naughty by the fire, and make sure she has a sunset that no one will ever forget."

Life and death had a funny way of making everyday problems shrink into insignificance. Nash loved Huntress, and he had to brace himself for a future without her. I loved Persie, and I wanted to protect her to my last breath, so I'd never have to face the same fate.

"I'd like that," Ryann murmured.

Wade smiled at them and gave my hand a squeeze that said, "I love you." I squeezed back. Regardless of how bad things got with Persie, I still had him by my side, through thick and thin. We'd started this journey together, and I knew he wasn't going anywhere. My partner in everything, even navigating the treacherous waters of a teenage daughter bound to an evil monster.

"Speaking of old friends, I got word from Erebus the other day." Finch sounded nervous. Barely a week went by when Erebus didn't check in about something or other, though the former Child of Darkness had adjusted to mortal life fairly smoothly, in the end. Mostly thanks to Finch playing advice columnist over the smallest human problems. Bigger ones, too. I could still remember the day Kaya went into labor and Erebus had the freak-out to end all freak-outs. He'd kept phoning Finch, insisting he come to Italy to help. Apparently, he hadn't been there for the births of his ill-fated hybrid children in antiquity. Finch had refused, but he *had* talked Erebus through the labor, which was a conversation I'd never forget. I doubted Finch ever would, either.

"And what did he have to say?" Wade's guard went up. He'd never really agreed with the decision to just let the two of them wander off into a very different kind of sunset together. I hadn't either, but we'd been overruled. And I supposed they'd kept their promise to stay out of the way.

Finch fumbled with his cutlery. "They're thinking about sending Jason to the SDC."

I almost spat my mimosa all over the table. "Pardon?"

"They might be a pair of happy hermits, but Jason's a sociable kid—they want him to be around normal magicals, so he can integrate into society. Which begs the question, why do they want to send him to the SDC? Normal, we are not." Finch forced a laugh. "Anyway, I think that's parent talk for, 'We don't want to screw up our kid.' Little do they know, it doesn't matter what you do, they all end up a little screwy."

"Finch, don't say that." Ryann gave him a disapproving look.

He put up his hands in mock surrender. "I don't make the rules." A sly grin tugged at the corners of his lips. "Man, imagine if Jason turned out to be the most normal one out of all our kids."

"Ours have good heads on their shoulders," Santana replied defiantly. "Cy might be slightly obsessed with bugs, but I'm sure it's just a phase. Or a sign that he's going to be a great entomologist one day."

"Merrick knows what he wants out of life. That boy has his sights set on a government position—envoy to covens all over the globe. He wants to help wherever he can." Garrett smiled proudly, and Astrid shared in it.

Finch chuckled. "Any coven will jump to attention if all eight feet of him turns up on their doorstep."

"I think Diana's still weighing her options, and we don't

have to worry about Kes for a while." Ryann added to the customary child exhibition, where we took turns crowing about the merits of our offspring. Usually, I had a good brag about Persie's art, but with talk turning to other covens, my mouth stayed shut.

The only one who never weighed in on the child parade was Dylan. He and Tatyana still spoke, and they'd managed to keep up a firm friendship, but we were all waiting for the day when both of them found someone special. There'd been partners here and there, but none of them stuck. Not because they still wanted to be with each other, but because... Actually, I had no idea why they could never get a relationship to stick. Both of them were catches.

Smartie beeped, cutting through the conversation before it got too competitive. Astrid swiped the screen on autopilot. Even at brunch, she never let her first love out of sight. Her eyes scanned a series of windows that popped up, taking in information at a mile a minute.

"What's happening in the cyberverse?" Finch craned his neck to get a better look.

Astrid furrowed her brow. "Another magical has gone missing. Texas, this time."

"That's the third this month, right?" My heart sank. We always got there too late.

"There's a potential fourth, but we're still waiting to hear more about the circumstances. One of them was... how shall I put it? Shady. So they might have disappeared for a different reason." Astrid started typing frantically. "I'm sending a message to the field teams to get them over there.

The longer we delay, the less chance we have of finding this latest missing magical."

"Has there been any news of any of the others?" Wade interjected.

Astrid shook her head. "Nothing. It's like they just—"

"Vanished." I finished the sentence for her.

SIX

Persie

---

reathless in a world with a violet sun and scarlet skies, I raced across a barren landscape. Huge drops of black rain crashed to the ground, inky splashes spreading underfoot. One struck my shoulder and sent an icy cold shiver down my arm. But I kept running, silky fabric billowing behind me. I'd always been a jeans and t-shirt girl, with the occasional summer dress thrown in just to surprise people, but glancing down, I saw a dark crimson gown. Grecian style, pinned at each shoulder with a gold Medusa head pin, it draped my sprinting figure. The silky fabric wrapped around my legs whenever the hot wind blew in a new direction, feeling like Medusa's snakes had slithered down to trip me up.

Just keep running. Don't look back. My golden sandals snagged in a tangle of black roots, their thorns biting my skin. I stumbled for a split second, only to regain my balance and dart forward with renewed adrenaline.

Suddenly, my feet skidded to a stop at the brink of a gaping canyon. With the terrain so flat, I'd almost missed it. Panting hard, I dared a look over the edge. Nothing but darkness, stretching down into an abyss.

Crap, crap, crap, crap! I couldn't jump it. My golden sandals might've looked Grecian, but they didn't have wings.

A blood-curdling roar split the air, and my shoulders hunched against the sound. Fear pierced my heart like a javelin. My brain didn't want to look, but my body had other ideas. Slowly, I turned.

In the distance, getting closer by the moment, a cloud of red dust churned across the harsh terrain. Something big was coming. *It can't hurt you. Not here. It's not real, remember?* I tried to convince myself this was true as the dust cloud neared.

I glanced left and right, searching for an exit, but there was nothing but jagged canyon edge and desolate landscape as far as the eye could see. And if I stepped back, I faced a long fall with a messy ending. Out of the corner of my eye, I spotted a different creature, watching from a tumble of thorny weeds. Small and round, and seemingly made entirely from white fluff, it stood out against the hellish world. Big black eyes observed me. I blinked, and it disappeared, making me wonder if it had ever been there at all. It didn't matter. I had bigger fish to fry. Much bigger.

The dust cloud stopped, and a gigantic figure loomed out of the red vapor. Walking tall on two muscular legs, the creature showed itself. Its body bulged with strength, dark gray fur displaying the hard contours of a humanoid torso, which grew more wolf-like at the extremities. Coarse, oily fur spiked up from its thick, overlong arms and legs, and its hunched shoulders made it look perpetually stooped. Its face was all wolf, with a long snout and dark lips peeled back to reveal dripping fangs. Two pointed ears flicked back and forth, while a set of glaring yellow eyes observed me hungrily.

A loup-garou. I had no idea how I knew the name, but I was certain of it. Not to be confused with your run-of-the-mill werewolf. This beast had a different pedigree—bigger, stronger, faster, hungrier.

"Stand back!" I shouted desperately, panic rising. The hot wind blew, and my dress whipped back with the current.

The loup-garou didn't listen. It stepped closer, and the ground trembled beneath me.

"Don't come any closer, or I'll—" What would I do? Shout it to death?

It took another step, and I braced myself for the impact. But instead of sinking its horrible fangs into me, it did something very strange. Slowly, it sank to one knee and bowed its head, chin touching chest. Its great claws sank into the dirt, its ridged spine rising up and down with every breath.

"W-What are you doing?" I stammered.

It growled, digging its silvered claws deeper into the dirt.

"What do you want me to do?" I swallowed, trying to take away the dryness in my throat.

It growled again and pushed its head forward.

Does it want me to... stroke it? My legs took over, against my will. I walked toward the beast, even while my mind screamed to run in the other direction. But it was almost as if the wind was changing trajectory, giving me a gentle push forward.

For a moment, the beast looked up. Its ragged face softened, its eyes unreadable as they met mine. Its lips slid back over its fangs and it bowed its head again, leaning forward. My hand stretched out like it belonged to someone else, and my fingertips grazed the loup-garou's furred snout. It whined in the back of its throat, as though it liked it. A huge beast transformed into a puppy by the touch of my hand.

What the—?

The hellish terrain vanished, and the creature and I disappeared, too.

I awoke to birdsong and the pale tinge of dawn creeping through my curtains. Mouth dry and eyes drier, I sat up, upsetting a tin of colored pencils and two sketchbooks. The former clattered to the floor, making me wince. My mom's bat ears would hear it a mile off, and I didn't want her to come running. Why undo all the intricate avoidance work I'd put in for the last four days after The Argument?

I didn't even change into PJs. I poked my face out of the dark green hoodie I'd fallen asleep in, like a mole daring to poke its head above ground. The button of my jeans had made an indent in my stomach, branding me. Most people would've been a sweaty mess after waking up from a dream like that, but I'd had so many that I guessed I'd gained immunity. It tended to be the "during" part that had me petrified. Don't get me wrong, when these dreams had first started, I'd screamed the place down. But once I realized the beasts couldn't follow me into the waking world, it got easier to deal with. Time had helped, too. I'd had these dreams my whole life, and I'd learned to either put up or shut up.

"Musclebound man-wolf. That's a new one." I picked up my sketchbook and made a note in the top right corner of a fresh page: *Loup-Garou.* Some people had dream diaries; I had a dream sketchbook. Lots of them actually, full of creatures I'd seen in dreams.

Freud would have a field day. I chuckled to rid myself of any residual fear and got up to gather my fallen belongings. Placing them on the desk in my bedroom, I paused by the mirror. Dark circles ringed my eyes, and my cheeks looked feverishly pink. I touched the back of my hand to them and felt a faint heat.

What if this heat had come from that dreamworld's searing wind? It wouldn't have been the first time, and it never got easier to consider. The landscape changed each time: jungles, icy tundra, cities, deserts, wetlands, et cetera. I'd woken shivering from snow-blanketed worlds, or soaked through from water worlds, or sweating buckets thanks to rainforest worlds. Cause and effect couldn't always be shaken off. But they were still just dreams.

Right...? I wondered if I should speak to my mom about it, then immediately stomped on the idea. Hearing about them only put her on edge, and now wasn't a good time to add to her worries. Or give her any more reason to insist on keeping me here.

I rubbed the sleep out of my eyes. These dreams were a

weirdness that still didn't make any sense to me. My family had no history of them. Doctors and psychiatrists couldn't explain them. They just... were.

My phone pinged from somewhere in the mountain peaks of my twisted bedsheets, the sleek circle lighting up. I hurried over and swiped my hand across the surface. A hologram shot up—Atlantean technology that'd been sneakily introduced into mainstream tech—and a slideshow started to play. Pictures of Genie and I, from childhood to now: the two of us wearing elf ears at Christmas; our faces smeared with cake; one of us getting thrown up into the air by Tobe; our first formal dance, and so on. I watched, grinning like an idiot.

"Happy birthday!" Genie's voice cut through at the end, and a banner exploded to life.

Eighteen years old. The hologram faded, and I picked up the phone to message her back. And ask what she was doing up at half past five in the morning. Genie was not an early bird. I paused as I saw a different message from Genie—one I'd missed last night, having fallen asleep before: *Hey! After ur bday, we should get moving on the future. Let's chat about new covens. Take a step 2ward beautiful, beautiful independence. Mwah x.* Her dad had kept her busy over the past few days as penance for the Bestiary thing, so we'd only spoken in passing. I considered asking her to come and talk about it now, but the little blue light that indicated Genie's availability had gone out. Evidently she'd programmed the hologram to send so it'd be the first thing I saw when I got up.

I couldn't love you more, Genie Vertis. I typed out a thank you and slipped the disc into my pocket. Facing the mirror again, I stared at my reflection.

"Austin. I think Austin could be good for us." Sure, a Mediocre program might not do much for me, but they had other programs. They even had a non-magical program, if memory served. It didn't have the prestige the SDC's had, but it wasn't in San Diego, or anywhere near my family or Leviathan. That put it way up there in my book.

Anyway, I can think about all of that tomorrow. Right now, I had a birthday to look forward to.

I perched awkwardly on the beautiful fountain at the front of the Grand Del Mar, waiting for Uncle Finch to arrive. I'd never been anywhere this fancy before. Palm fronds rustled in the warm breeze, and the tumbling water made me wish I'd gone to the bathroom before leaving the SDC. The hotel itself was a terracotta masterpiece of Mediterranean and Arabian fusion, which had somehow found its way to San Diego. And I was here to have a special birthday lunch with my uncle at the Addison restaurant. My mom had definitely shanghaied him into picking this place, to make it *memorable.* I'd have been happy with tacos from a truck. Naturally, I was already thinking about forks, and trying to remember if the salad fork was the longer one.

One of the busboys came out to check on me, asking, "Can I help you, miss?"

"Oh, um, no thanks. I'm just… waiting for someone," I

replied nervously, checking my phone. If the preceptors thought I liked to be quiet during their classes, they'd never seen me out in public. Another reason I needed to get out there, into the world, before I gave up and slapped "hermit" on my forehead.

Late, as always. I looked up again, but the busboy hadn't gone.

He smiled. "Would you prefer to wait in the lobby? You might get wet, sitting there."

"No, I'll be okay."

"Well, feel free to change your mind." The busboy wandered off, with a glance back at me. I'd done my best to dress up a bit. My mom had tried to get me to put on one of her fancy dresses, but I'd settled on one of my favorite summer dresses instead: a black maxi dress with red roses embroidered onto it, with capped sleeves that made me feel like I could flamenco, if I knew how. Now, I wished I'd swallowed my pride and accepted one of my mom's dresses, which would have suited the unprecedented levels of fanciness. I looked nice, but not posh nice. Not designer label nice.

It's fine. Once my uncle is here, I won't notice. I scanned the driveway for any sign of him, though I doubted he'd arrive by car. Excitement bubbled up inside me, taking over the awkward nerves. Uncle Finch sat at the very top of my list of favorite people in the whole world, just behind Genie. He also held the title of being my closest friend in the family. An ally, through and through. We hadn't had much of a chance to spend time together lately, which I guessed was why he and my mom had planned this lunch. A chance to catch up without being stuck inside the SDC.

As though summoned, he tumbled out of a hedgerow to the right of the driveway and dusted himself off. He strolled toward me casually, a couple of leaves and a twig clinging to his tufty, strawberry blond hair. Not a speck of gray, thanks to his Mimicry.

"Sorry I'm late. I got caught in traffic." He scooped me in for a hug.

"You came by chalk-door," I retorted, unable to resist laughing.

He pulled away and gestured to the empty hotel fore-court. "And you wouldn't believe how many people were all headed here. Rush hour in the chalk-door network."

"What really happened?" Already, I felt calmer.

"Kes wanted to show me a spell he'd been working on." Finch smiled fondly. "He toasted the lab. Seriously, fire everywhere. I think I've still got a lungful of smoke."

I gaped at him. "Is he okay? Do you need to go back and help him?"

"Nah, he'll be fine." Finch waved a blasé hand. "I put out the fires, no one got singed, and the alarms didn't go off. Not sure if that last one should worry me or not. Anyway, he's busy scrubbing the place clean. Character building."

"Are you sure?" I'd hate to miss lunch with Finch, but Kes was only thirteen. "We can do this another time if you need to head back."

He put an arm around my shoulders and gave me a firm look. "It's good for folks to learn how to clean up their own mess." His expression softened. "Besides, today's your birthday. A birthday lunch when it's not your birthday is just... well, lunch."

I smiled, satisfied he wasn't going anywhere. "Should we go inside? The busboy is hanging around like he's worried I'm going to rob the place."

"*Pfft*. With prices like this, they're the robbers." He flashed me a wink and linked his arm through mine. "Let's go, birthday girl."

Together, we walked across the beautiful forecourt and headed into the lobby. Another collision of cultures met us inside, somewhere between the Hamptons and Spanish villa, with marble pillars and a sleek tiled floor. Fresh-cut white roses sat on a central table, and huge potted plants added a touch of color. It even smelled expensive.

"This way, Mademoiselle. We mustn't keep the tiny food waiting." Finch led me away from the lobby, following the signs for the restaurant.

I giggled, thrilled at the prospect of spending a couple of hours with my uncle. "Thank you for bringing me here."

"My pleasure, mon petit pois." He grinned back at me. "I learned some French for the occasion."

"Bien sur."

He tilted his head like a confused dog. "Huh?"

"Never mind." I felt the weight of the last week slough away, and my lighter heart cemented its resolve to leave the SDC. Just getting out of the coven for an afternoon had improved my mood drastically. Imagine what it could do in the longer term, and with a greater distance.

"Your mom caught me before I left." Just like that, he pierced my elation with a parental pin.

"Oh?" I fumbled with the clasp of my purse.

He gave my arm a squeeze. "Relax. She hasn't sent me on a covert mission to talk some sense into you. If she had, you'd never suspect a thing." He laughed softly, putting me back at ease. "But... have you guys had another chance to talk about *the future?*"

"No," I said simply.

"Not at all?"

I tried to stay positive. "Nope. Today's the first time we've made anything other than small talk. Kind of a birthday truce."

His face scrunched up strangely, as though he were disappointed. "I thought she might've spoken to you."

"Why?" My curiosity pricked up, alerted by the concerned tone in his voice. "Is there something she needs to tell me?"

"Well, it's about time she told you the secret of aging, now you're at the ripe old age of eighteen. I'll give you a clue: snail mucus." He smiled, but it didn't quite reach his eyes. "I'm sure your mom will talk to you when the time's right. But—and I've said this to her too—you should cut each other some slack. You're family. You love each other. And you're not always going to agree, but you owe it to each other to hash it out. It's not a household with teens unless there's some door slamming, but it's up to both of you to open the door again. Does that make sense?"

I snorted. "How did she take that?"

"I wouldn't dare repeat it, or I'd need to wash my mouth

out with soap." He cackled, never wasting an opportunity to take a playful jab at his sister. "But that doesn't change the facts. You're more similar than either of you will admit. That's going to cause some major headbutting. But it'll also bring you closer together, if you let it. I'm not saying she was wrong or you were wrong. Frankly, I don't think either of you were. But if you leave the SDC in anger, you'll regret it. You'll miss her, and she'll miss you, and neither of you will know how to bridge that gap, and you'll both miss out on so much. Don't let that happen, is all I'm saying."

"I forget how wise you are sometimes," I replied quietly, turning over his words.

He chuckled. "I can be sensible when it comes to people I care about."

I dwelled on his words on the way to the restaurant. To my surprise, Finch breezed right past the maître d' and weaved us around the tables, ignoring the curious looks of waiters and waitresses. He didn't stop until he reached the kitchen. Steam erupted volcanically from cooking surfaces, and the clang of pots and pans thundered in my ears as the chefs shouted to one another.

"Uh, Finch? The restaurant's back there." I tugged his arm, but he kept on, hauling me to the back of the kitchen and out into a smaller courtyard.

"We have to make a quick stop first." He cast me an apologetic glance. "I realized I forgot your present. Ryann told me to pick it up before I left, but did I listen? Nope. Je suis un idiot. See? French."

I looked back at the kitchen door, the delicious scent still infiltrating my senses. I wanted the tiny food. Plus, I was worried one of the chefs might come out and see whatever Finch was about to do. Mind wiping was a moral gray area, but it still happened if the occasion called for it.

He sketched a chalk-door onto a nearby wall and whispered the *Aperi Si Ostium* spell.

"It's fine. I don't need a gift," I insisted, nervous about getting spotted. Plus, if the gift happened to be back at the SDC, it meant bursting my temporary bubble.

"Maybe not, but Ryann would pop a blood vessel. Harley, too—she threatened to torch one of my first editions if I forgot." He ran a stressed hand through his hair. "I can't believe I left it behind. I blame Kes's arson attempt."

I glanced once more at the kitchen door as the lines of the chalk-door fizzed and sank into the wall, creating a doorway. "It'll take five minutes, tops," Finch assured me. "The maître d' won't even have time to strike our names off the reservation list." Finch pushed open the door and shoved me through it.

I staggered forward, expecting to see the SDC. Instead, color and beauty and magic bombarded my eyes. Before us was a calm riverside beneath a starry sky—a nighttime fairy-tale hidden away inside an interdimensional bubble. Glittering firefly lights swayed in the willow fronds, strung paper lanterns glowed pastel through the dark, and floating candles in lotus holders drifted on the water. White tables stood on the riverbank, decorated with sprays of wildflowers and candles in glass jars. Gauzy ribbons had been tied to the backs of the chairs in shades of purple, pink, yellow, and pale green. There were flowers everywhere I looked, the blooms overwhelming some of the smaller trees.

I caught sight of creatures dancing in and out of the willows and skating across the surface of the river, chasing the flamboyant dragonflies that darted here and there. Faeries with gossamer wings skirted over the water, their delicate feet barely touching the surface. Fauns carried trays of sparkling drinks as a band of satyrs played panpipes beneath a big willow, accompanied by selkies who sang from the edge of the riverbank.

"Finch!" I punched his arm.

He laughed and gave me a tight side-hug. "Surprise!" he shouted, in sync with the partygoers, who'd all turned to raise their glasses to me.

My closest friends and family, all in one place. My mom and dad, Aunt Ryann, Genie and her dad, Diana, the Catemaco-Levi clan, Astrid, Garrett, Merrick, Dylan, Tobe, Jacob and Alyssa, Dr. Krieger, and the Smiths—AKA, my grandma and grandad. I even spotted Luke and Melody, along with Nash and Huntress. People I hadn't seen in such a long time!

I spotted my cousin and gave Finch another stunned look. "Kes isn't scrubbing, you fibber! You deserve an Oscar for that! I didn't suspect anything!"

He winked. "I'll add it to the trophy cabinet."

"Do you like it, Miss Persie?" Tobe emerged with a champagne flute, doll-sized in his giant paw.

"I love it!" My heart swelled with happiness.

"I am pleased." Tobe smiled, and handed me a glass of sparkling peach juice from a passing tray.

I realized there was more to that smile than met the eye. "Did you do this?"

"I played a part, under your mother's orders." His golden eyes sparkled. "She said you had a fixation upon someone by the name of Mr. Tumnus when you were an infant and thought you might enjoy the fauns. I confess, I do not know how they correlate, but I hope they are to your liking."

My cheeks burned. "She didn't tell you that!"

Finch snorted. "What's a birthday party without a couple of embarrassing skeletons coming out of the closet?"

"Ah… perhaps I was not supposed to mention that." Tobe held out his glass. "Nevertheless, I hope you enjoy your party. Happy birthday, Miss Persie. Let us toast to a long and prosperous life!"

My mom and dad came toward me, glasses raised. "Happy birthday, sweetheart."

All of this, for me? Never in my life had I seen a more beautiful sight. I took everything in, from the faint ripple of a faerie's wing skimming the river down to the last bluebell. It didn't even look real. It was as though Mom had reached inside my head and pulled out my ideal dreamscape, free of gnarly monsters with anger management problems. I smiled at my parents and clinked my glass against theirs. Maybe they did know me better than I thought.

SEVEN

Persie
_____

"How did you manage to keep this a secret?" I sat on the riverbank with Genie, the two of us kicking our feet through the cool water. "I can just about get over Finch's performance, but you'd normally have let something slip weeks ago!"

Genie sipped her peach fizz and leaned back onto the grass. "She didn't tell me until this morning. Your mother's a wily one." Genie smiled, but I sensed she was a bit bothered. "She told my dad ages ago, to make sure I got here on time. He took a risk, though. See, he made out that he was taking me to a Ganymede service this afternoon, to try and whip some tradition into me. Naturally, I spent all day trying to think of a way out of it. So imagine my surprise when I find out I'm coming to your surprise birthday party."

I copied her and laid back in the grass, staring up at the

starry sky. "For what it's worth, I know you wouldn't have said anything."

"No, they were right to keep it from me. I can't keep things from you. And the look on your face was worth it." She turned and grinned at me. "Happy eighteenth, my beauty."

I grinned back. "Why, thank you."

"How does it feel?"

I shrugged. "So far, it feels… the same."

"That's because we're still in San Diego. Once we're on the loose, it'll feel different," she promised.

I twisted onto my belly and observed the party. Thirty or so guests milled about, enjoying the music and the drinks and chatting to one another. Little groups had splintered off, with my classmates dancing under the willow to the satyrs' music, while Kes kept the younger children busy. He looked long at the older group every so often, no doubt wishing he could join them instead of being stuck on babysitting duty. Luke, Melody, Nash, and Huntress sat at a different table, with Nash feeding Huntress scraps as she lay at his feet. My aunt and uncle had branched off with my mom and dad, the four of them sitting at one of the tables with plates from the buffet, loaded up with my favorite food—a whole spread of soft tacos with any filling you could want.

"You did good, sis. Perfect party for a freshly minted adult." I heard Finch say. "What were you doing on your eighteenth birthday?"

My mom picked at a taco. "I didn't have an eighteenth birthday. I was working at the casino."

"We had dinner the weekend after, though," Ryann pointed out. "Mom cooked a roast for you, and she made apple pie with 'Happy Birthday' written on the top in pastry."

My mom smiled faintly. "I'd forgotten that."

"Too busy self-flagellating?" Finch gave her a knowing look.

"What were *you* doing on your eighteenth birthday?" she shot back. She sounded tense, though I didn't know why. My mom usually loved a party.

Finch whooped so loud he frightened a passing faun. "Wouldn't you like to know? But if I told you, I'd have to kill you. Now, have a few more of these, and wild Harley might make an appearance." He took a glass from the poor faun's tray and set it in front of my mom. "When was the last time we saw her, *hmm?*"

"It's been a few years." My dad put his arm around my mom and leaned in for a kiss just as Genie jumped up and grabbed my hand, hauling me away from the imminent smooching.

"Come on."

I brushed grass off my dress. "Where are we going?"

"We're going to dance!" She yanked me toward the big willow tree before I had the chance to protest. I had zero coordination, so this would undoubtedly end in disaster and many stepped-on toes. If anyone made it out unscathed, I'd be shocked.

"Genie! I can't!" I complained, even as she swung me around.

"Nonsense! Everyone can dance!" She giggled and swung me again, urging me under her arm. "See? It's easy."

Merrick stepped in. "You mind if I dance with the birthday girl?"

"Be my guest!" Genie pushed me into his arms and whirled off to dance with Marius, leaving me to navigate a jig with Merrick. Fortunately, he also had two left feet, so we pretty much just bobbed about in front of each other until we got over our self-consciousness. Laughter fizzed up my throat as he tried a couple of twirls and turns, spinning me out and bringing me back in, before we carried on with some manic hopping that made the satyrs roll their eyes.

I'd been to formals and balls at the SDC, but they were nothing like this. This was... otherworldly. A party I'd never forget. And though I might've been furious with my mom over the past few days, I couldn't help but let go of some of that anger. She'd done this for me. She'd crafted this memory, and that deserved a bit of the slack that Finch had spoken of.

Speaking of whom, Finch had just leapt into the center of his circle, having hauled everyone over from the parental table. He danced about, Highland-Fling style, while the others cheered him on. Ryann looked mortified, but not enough to stop a smile from edging onto her lips. She knew what she'd married, and she loved him for it. Plus, my parents' friends—these people who'd been part of my life for as long as I could remember—had no intention of letting him have all the fun. As Melody jumped in to take his place, he stepped back out into the circle, everyone whooping and hollering as though they were at a competition.

This is perfect. Utterly perfect.

The music stopped and the older contingents moved back toward the tables, panting but happy. Some color had come back into my mom's cheeks, and she looked... radiant. I turned away when my dad scooped her in for another kiss. No kid wanted to see that. Ever. Even if it meant they had a healthy, loving relationship, which I knew couldn't be said for a lot of people's parents. My gaze settled on my grandparents, who danced together a little way away from the unofficial dancefloor.

I bet they looked at each other like that when they first got together, too. They weren't my biological grandparents, but they'd been there all my life. So many Sundays spent in their fragrant kitchen, watching my grandma cook something delicious while my grandad sang to her and chopped vegetables.

"Ready for another one?" Genie took my hand as the panpipes started again, this time with a slightly slower tune.

I shook my head. "I need a breather."

"No way! You're the birthday girl. You have to dance until your legs give out."

I heaved in a breath. "I think they're about to." All of that spinning and twirling had made my stomach churn. Not to the point where I was about to throw up or anything, but I was certainly feeling a bit discombobulated.

"Are you okay?" Kes peered at me with maturity beyond his years. "Can I fetch you a drink? I think there's water, if you don't want any fizzy stuff."

I put up my hands and chuckled thinly. "I'll be fine, I just need a minute."

"Hey, just give her some space." Genie tried to shoo everyone away, but they wouldn't listen. They kept crowding. Meanwhile, a cold sweat snuck up the back of my neck. See, this was why I didn't dance. It made me dizzy, same as roller-coasters and horseback riding.

"Great party, Pers." Marius dipped to kiss me on the cheek. My knees suddenly turned wobbly, but I didn't know if it was the dizziness or Marius Catemaco-Levi dropping a casual kiss on my cheek.

Diana's hand shot out to catch my arm. "Are you all right, Persie? You don't look so good."

"You do look a bit pale." Marius put his hand on my shoulder. "Do you need to sit down?"

Genie muscled in. "She just needs a minute, give her some room to breathe!" But her eyes suddenly widened. "Persie?"

There were too many people. Too much light, too much color, too much noise. I backed away from the dancefloor, my temples throbbing. Panic and pain collided as I struggled to come to grips with the weird sensations flowing through me. I wanted to scream and I wanted to cry, but nothing would come out. My friends followed out of concern, but I put my hands up in a gesture that I hoped showed I didn't want them coming closer. I was too freaked out, and if anyone tried to touch me, I'd burst into tears or fall apart or... worse. They stopped and stared at me as I stumbled backward. Genie tried to break free of the pack, but I shook my head at her.

"Persie, what's wrong?" she asked, her face etched with concern. "Sit down for a sec and take some deep breaths."

Kes reappeared with a glass of water and put it into my hand. "Here, drink this."

I struggled to lift it to my lips and took a sip, only to spit it out a second later. It burned like acid on my tongue.

By now, everyone had their attention fixed firmly on the crazy birthday girl. My mom looked completely freaked, her mouth open and her eyes bugging out of her head. I noticed her hands shaking, terror written across her face.

"Persie?" Dad's voice cut through the deafening buzz in my ears.

Mom joined him, both of them walking quickly toward me. "Persie, we need to get you out of here. You're going to be okay, but we need to go. Now." She didn't sound sure, and I didn't trust whatever was happening to me. It hurt like someone had lit a fire in every cell, and it felt *powerful*. Like I could explode at any moment and take everyone down with me. It didn't make sense, but I didn't want anyone getting hurt.

"Stay back!" I screamed. A weird echo of the dream I'd had this morning. Only, they weren't monsters. I was the one acting like a wild creature. "Please, stay back." My throat burned white hot, my tongue feeling as though it had swollen to twice its normal size. My chest clenched in a vise of pain, like I was trying to breathe through a snorkel that someone had stuffed full of cotton wool, overworking my lungs to try and catch some air. And my vision now refused to clear, no matter how many times I blinked.

"Persie, you're not well. We need to help you." My mom took another step forward.

"Don't! Just stay back! Stay away!" My brain felt like it was moments away from blowing out of my skull. In front of my blurred eyes, an image flashed—a watery cave, with shadows darting between the rocks. It disappeared as quickly as it had appeared, but it left behind a stone of dread in the pit of my roiling stomach.

Finch pushed to the front of the crowd. "Tell us what's happening, Persie. Do you feel something? Explain it to us."

I fought to lift my head. "Something's... coming." I sensed it, clawing into my skull and body. A numbing cold, akin to being trapped in a block of ice. Only, the ice was in my veins, my organs, and my skin. It came from within. All of a sudden, my vision went black. I could feel my eyelids blinking, but it made no difference. Darkness surrounded me. Not unconsciousness, but shadow. Thick and impenetrable.

A voice whispered in the back of my mind, startling me. A voice I didn't know, and yet... recognized.

Happy Birthday, my darling...

EIGHT

Harley

P anic set in, adrenaline shooting through me. Persie looked like a ghost. All the color had drained from her face, replaced by a bluish, waxy sheen. Her lips turned a deathly purple, and faint cracks of broken capillaries spider-webbed across her cheeks. And her eyes… *Chaos help me, her eyes.* They'd turned milky white with blindness. Her hands flailed wildly, trying to touch something solid.

"Persie, we're going to help you," I said with a trembling voice, trying to get closer to my daughter. "You have to come with us." I knew who was responsible for this, and I wanted to tear his neck off his slimy shoulders. Ordinarily, I could compartmentalize and focus, to solve a problem. But this was my daughter we were talking about. And, at the moment, I wanted to hold her and take the pain away so badly that I could barely think. I reached out for her and she batted me away hard enough for the impact to reverberate.

"Don't come near me!" she shrieked, as eerie, pearly white tears trickled down her face. "It's not safe! Don't come near me!"

"What? I need to take you out of here!" I tried to reach for her again, only to get another panicked flailing. She suddenly pitched forward and hit the ground, her fingers clawing at the grass, tearing up big tufts. That was the final straw. I couldn't watch anymore. I had to help her. She could bat me away all she liked, but I was carrying her out of there. I made to lunge for her, but a tight hand grasped me by the elbow and pulled me back.

"Listen to her, Harley." Melody looked as pale as Persie. Her big eyes shone with concern.

"I can't stand here while my daughter's in pain!" I barked.

Melody swallowed anxiously. "Harley, she's Purging."

"What?" Wade shook his head in disbelief. He tried to run for Persie, but this time Luke caught him before he could, holding him back.

"She can't be. You need to be magical to Purge. It's not possible!" I snapped, pulling away. But Melody held tightly to my arm. "Let go of me, Melody! I need to get to her. This isn't a Purge; this is some trick Leviathan is pulling. And I swear to Chaos, if she... if she..." I couldn't even say it. No mother could. The thought couldn't be put into words. But I felt the stab of it in my heart nonetheless. If anything happened to her, I'd be... There wasn't an entry in the English dictionary that covered what I'd feel.

"I'm as stunned as you, but it's the truth. I can sense it building inside her. She's Purging. And it's going to be a powerful one." Melody raised her palms to release a spell, only to drop them again. "There's nothing I can do to help her. If I put a buffer on her to ease the pain, it'd only prolong the experience."

"Then what do we do? I can't just leave her like this!" I hissed as Persie began to scream. It was the sound of someone in unbearable agony, pushed through choked sobs. Her muscles stretched and strained, her entire body turning a blotchy red. The purple spiderwebs raced faster through my daughter's blood network, as if her veins were collapsing. She strained harder, her cheeks turning an angry shade of red. More spiderwebs forked down her bare arms, right down to her fingertips. I could see every ridge of her spine, as though the bones were trying to push right through her skin.

Beside me, Kadar overtook Raffe. "I can restrain her, to stop her from hurting herself."

I stared helplessly at my daughter as Melody continued to restrain me.

Kadar ran toward her, only to stagger back as Persie abruptly stood. Her milky white eyes had turned black, blinking alien-like at Kadar's shocked face. Unnerving silence echoed across the riverside. Everyone waiting. Everyone watching. No one knowing what would happen next. Kadar took a step forward.

And then all hell broke loose. Black fire erupted in a circle around Persie. Her body bent violently, her arms splayed out and her head flung back, as though she couldn't contain what was inside her. Suddenly, the ring of black flames lifted up, spinning faster and faster around her. It stopped abruptly with a deafening crack before imploding into Persie's chest.

"Persie!" I howled.

A glowing black streak painted her throat, and dark smoke began to spill out of her mouth in a powerful torrent. It pooled on the grass in front of her, only feet from Kadar. Huge limbs formed and rapidly took shape. Four scaly legs with glinting talons led to a bulky body, complete with a whipping tail that carried a spiny barb. My first thought was: dragon. But then the neck and the head started to form multiple necks and heads. Armored scales climbed from the communal belly and slotted up each neck toward gnashing fangs. They had dragon-like faces, with long snouts and fanned-out bone frills. They were dark red with black armored scales, covered in shivering spines, and weaponized with two pointed horns apiece.

"A hydra!" Genie's eyes bugged. "Atlantis used to have one protecting the bank vaults. They had to get rid of it when it… ate a few of the guards."

Tobe narrowed his feline eyes. "I do not believe one has been Purged since the days of Ancient Greece. The last was Purged by a Child of Chaos's hybrid offspring, shortly before the endeavor tore them apart." He rested a paw on my shoulder, realizing what he'd said. "Hybrids were too powerful to be contained in mortal bodies, which is why they died. Miss Persie is no hybrid."

But what is *she?* A magical with no magic, who could Purge without ever using a drop of Chaos? It didn't make sense.

And it didn't matter now. Persie was in danger, and a hydra stood between me and her.

"Rag Team, with me!" I shouted, taking command. It'd been a while since I'd used that term, but I didn't just mean the originals. Melody, Luke, Nash, and Huntress were part of us now. Even if the old dog wasn't as spry as she once was.

The youngest kids were pushed back by the older children, while the old crew formed a line, palms going up in quick succession. Nash swiped a few sharp knives off the buffet table, and Ryann took out the channeler that Krieger had made for her. A silver orb with a conductor in the center, it allowed her to use the residual Chaos that had clung on, long after Lux had left her. She only had a weak Fire ability, but we needed everything we had.

"Back me up!" I yelled to the group. Grounding my feet, I dug deep into my twin affinities and pulled a strand of each into my core. I felt it swirl in my chest, forming the ball of raw power that let me control monsters. Only, I had no idea if it would work on something as powerful as this.

A hydra head shot forward, aiming for Huntress.

"STOP!" I bellowed, my throat burning with the sheer volume.

Spotting the danger, Tobe tore off at a pounding sprint. He barreled into Huntress a moment before the hydra, grabbing the husky and rolling free of the creature's jaws. Infuriated, the seven hydra heads screeched. Two more heads shot forward, targeting Melody and Ryann.

"STOP!" I boomed, louder this time.

The hydra jolted to a standstill, the three attacking heads

twitching as though they were buffering. But I knew my hold was weak. With so many heads to deal with, this wasn't your average beast to control. It was more like trying to wrangle a herd.

One head broke free of my influence. It lunged for Kes, who had slipped away from the group of kids for a closer look.

"OBEY ME!" I screamed as loud as my lungs would allow. They seared inside my chest, the effort threatening to crack my ribs.

The head stopped, inches from Kes's head. He stood there in shock, all the color drained out of his face. Almost nose-to-nose with a hydra head, the poor boy looked like he might pass out.

Just then, Tobe began to sing. He held Huntress in his strong arms as he walked back over to where I stood, not missing a note. The song drifted across the riverbank and the hydra heads reeled back, listening to the sad tune. They swayed strangely as the ballad mesmerized them. The hairs stood up on the back of my neck. Not for the first time, I felt as though I was hearing something I shouldn't be: an ancient melody, unheard for generations. I didn't understand the language, but the hydra did. And, between my beast control and Tobe's voice, we had the creature where we wanted it.

With the hydra heads swaying like reeds, Tobe plucked a Mason jar from inside the shadow of his wings. I'd never understood how he kept so many things in there, but grati-tude overcame the mystique. Unscrewing the lid, he approached the hydra and set the jar at its feet. Not once did he stop singing. Transfixed by the melody, the heads didn't even seem to notice as they began to disintegrate. They turned to black smoke and spiraled into the confines of the Mason jar until just Persie's limp body remained on the ground. Only then did Tobe stop and screw the lid on tight.

I raced forward with Wade at my side. "Persie?" I hauled her body into my arms while Wade supported her flopping head. The spiderwebs had gone, but she still looked deathly pale. I shook her gently. "Persie? Can you hear me?"

Please, please, please, wake up! Tears welled, and my heart felt as though it were on the brink of shattering. I needed her to pull through. I needed *her*. My little girl. If I lost her because of that vile snake, there'd be no power on this Earth that could stop me from decimating the bastard. And I'd blow away anyone who stood in my path. I shook her a little more, seconds shy of pounding on her chest until my arms gave out. She had a whole life ahead of her. This couldn't be it. It just couldn't.

She stirred, blinking her blue eyes. Immediately, hysterics took over. She struggled against me, panting hard. "What's going on? What the hell just happened?"

Wade looked at me, and realization dawned. "This is the gift he was talking about," he said bitterly.

"What gift? What are you talking about?" Persie stared at us both, on the verge of tears. She sounded so small and frightened, and all because we'd withheld one not-so-tiny detail. The time for honesty was long overdue.

"Leviathan's." Tears jabbed at my eyes. I'd been right—of course Leviathan's gift wasn't going to be something nice.

And this was it. A gift unlike any other. No, not a gift... a curse. One that was as much of a surprise to us as it was to her; the revelation that Persie wasn't quite the non-magical we'd thought.

Persie peered up at me. "What do you mean? What happened?"

"You Purged," Finch said. He knelt beside her, his voice calm.

"I... *what?*" She scrambled out of my arms and gaped in disbelief. "That's not possible!"

No, it shouldn't be. But I just watched it happen. I kept my thoughts to myself. Something had clearly changed, but we didn't know what. Persie had no abilities to speak of, yet she'd just spewed a hydra, a rare and legendary beast not seen since Ancient Greece. None of this made sense. But it all pointed to one entity. The one who'd started all of this.

"It has to do with Leviathan," Wade said.

Persie hit us with a defiant glare. "You know what's happening, and I want to hear the whole truth. Now. You owe me that much."

A tear dropped onto my cheek. "Yes. Yes, we do."

NINE

Persie

—————

All that glittered was not gold, and all that had sparkled on this riverbank had lost its shine, too. The party atmosphere morphed into tense anticipation before everyone ventured back to the SDC to give my parents and me some space to talk at the long trestle table. Even the willows ceased their whispering, eager to hear the truth. The food went cold, the fizz went flat, and the mythical creatures retreated back to their Mason jars, obeying the specific lilt of Tobe's songs—one for each species.

I folded my arms across my chest. Defensive or protective, I didn't know yet. "Go on."

My mom glanced at my dad, both sheepish. She fidgeted with the edge of the tablecloth. "Leviathan and I have a history. It started when I needed his mother, Echidna, to break my Suppressor so we could fight Katherine and win. You know that. But you don't know what I gave her in return." She picked up a napkin and touched it to her lower eyelid, to catch a tear. I could count on one hand the number of times I'd seen her cry. Furious and confused and hurt as I may have been, seeing her on the edge of losing it was an added struggle for my overwhelmed mind.

My dad put his hand on her back, rubbing small circles. "It's important you understand the gravity of the situation your mom was in when she made the deal with Echidna."

"Deal?" I gulped down a phantom fishbone in my throat, but it wouldn't dislodge.

They'd never mentioned any deal before. I sensed trouble on the horizon, an ugly truth that I wouldn't like. But I'd finally reached the point of no return, and so had they.

My mom's breath hitched, and I pushed away a twinge of pity. Until I knew the full story, I couldn't settle on an emotion. "In return for breaking the Suppressor, Echidna wanted to name you. My firstborn. Before Katherine killed her, she made sure I knew that her death did not void our deal, but instead passed the mantle on to her son, Leviathan. It became his promise to fulfill."

My stomach took a nosedive. "But… you said Persephone was a family name."

"That's not entirely true." My dad rubbed his stubbled chin, where grains of gray brushed against dark brown.

"Leviathan visited me after you were born, when I was alone." My mom cleared her throat. "I was weak from the labor. He named you before I could stop him. It was a spell of some kind, which bound you to him."

My name came from him. The fact twisted in my gut like a

rusty blade. My mom had never referred to me by my full name, ever, but I'd always found it pretty. It flowed off the tongue, full of history and gravitas. Persephone Merlin-Crowley. The kind of name someone could be proud of. To hear that I'd been given it by a monster made me feel sick all over again. And the beauty that I'd once seen in that name faded away, like the glowing lanterns that hung from the trees. It changed everything. He'd molded that name, and so he'd molded me too.

I battled angry tears, but I heard them wavering in my voice. "And that's why I Purged? Because of that spell?"

"Yes and no." My mom wiped her nose on the napkin. "He told me, right after he cast the spell to name you, that he'd return on your eighteenth birthday to give you a gift. He didn't explain what the gift would be before he vanished. I tried to speak to him so many times afterwards—Tobe and Melody, too—but he wouldn't say another word. I think he enjoyed holding it over us."

Through tear-blurred eyes, I sought out Genie for encouragement. She'd wandered off to the riverbank, refusing to leave until I was done here. Normally, I was her right-hand woman. Today, she filled that role. Her eyes found mine and a small smile lifted the corners of her lips. A movement that said, loud and clear: *I'm here. I'm not going anywhere.*

"Wait. That can't be right." I returned to the conversation. "Purge beasts can't leave the Bestiary, so how did Leviathan visit you? And how... how did he get inside my head? He spoke to me. Is that because of the spell, too?"

Air hissed through my mom's teeth. "He spoke to you?"

"For a moment, back there. He... wished me Happy Birthday." The bitterest of ironies.

"That scumbag!" My mom looked about ready to tear the tablecloth to shreds. I wondered if there was some backstory to her fury, or if it was just the invasion of my skull. Either way, it was my head he'd tapped into, and I wanted answers.

In the face of her sudden burst of anger, I tried to stay calm. "Which brings us back to the question—how is he doing it? How is that even remotely possible?"

My dad toyed with the stem of an empty glass, while his mouth twisted in shared resentment with my mom. "Leviathan is a Purge beast, yes, but he's ancient. Older than Tobe, even. He may even be older than the Primus Anglicus. With that sort of heritage comes immense power. That's why Tobe keeps him on ice." He paused, his expression hardening. "However, he had to be unfrozen so your mom could learn how to fight against someone with immense power before battling Katherine, and they unfroze him a couple of other times, to collect samples of his blood and tissue for research that Remington was doing."

My mom tilted her head up to chase away fresh tears. "Tobe tried to deny the requests, but he got overruled."

"So, you're saying he might not have been totally contained?" Shivers pinpricked my spine.

"It's a logical conclusion." My dad sounded bitter. "I don't know how he sends his mind out, or whatever it is that he does, but he's found a way around the enclosure. At least on a psychological level."

My mom nodded morosely. "And Tobe suspects that

Leviathan has been experimenting with thawing and refreezing his enclosure, due to some discrepancies with the frost on the box that he's noticed in Leviathan's hall. Although he can't say for certain. He's never actually been able to catch him in the act. And that monster is crafty, to say the least."

Leviathan isn't confined to the Bestiary anymore. Physically, he remained in his box, but he'd discovered ways of getting into mischief without his body. I'd heard him in my head, for Pete's sake. And the very idea that he could thaw himself left me, ironically, cold. I had to comfort myself with the thought that the box still held him fast. If it didn't, he'd have been out here right now, enjoying the party and his stupid gift firsthand.

"Why didn't you kill him? You said you fought him, and since you're standing here now, I'm guessing you won." I directed the blunt question at my mom. "If you were so worried about him getting to me, why didn't you get rid of the problem?"

She shook her head. "It's not that simple. The deal is hereditary. Echidna asked him to make the deal happen, and he obeyed. But it wouldn't stop there. Basically, history would repeat itself. If he died, he'd pass it to another ancient monster who'd see it through. And so on. There's no escaping it. I couldn't kill him when we battled, and it wouldn't change anything if I did now."

No escape. The words buzzed in my head like furious bees. If that were true, then no amount of distance that I put between myself and the SDC would matter. I narrowed my gaze at my mother and she held it sorrowfully.

"That's why you didn't want me to go to another coven. You knew it wouldn't make a difference, didn't you?" Frustration leaked into my voice.

My mom sighed under the weight of so many heavy truths hitting her at once. "From the moment I made that deal with Echidna, our fates were sealed. Neither of us can get away from it, but I *can* keep you safe. I can help you fight Leviathan, once he reveals what he wants from you."

Which is what, exactly? He hadn't informed me of any extra details, either.

I swirled flat peach fizz around in a glass and stared at the blush liquid. "That's the part I really don't get. I understand that you probably thought you could stop this, like you stopped Katherine and Davin. You misjudged him. Fine. But I don't understand why Leviathan would give me a Purge as a gift. How does that fit into his plan?"

"I don't know." My mom hung her head. "I don't know why. I don't know if it'll happen again. And I don't know what his plan is. But this is why I don't want you to leave, Persie. This is why I want you near, so I can help you through whatever comes next."

My dad nodded enthusiastically. "We'll confront Leviathan. We'll fix everything, once and for all. We'll make sure you're safe—that's all we've ever wanted."

A switch flipped inside me. "If that's all you've ever wanted, then you should've told me the truth. Do you have any idea how it feels, to know you weren't even named by your parents? To know that you've had some monster's prints all over you from the day you were born? To know that the name you were proud of is actually a curse?" My body vibrated with rage that I couldn't control. Someone had shaken up all my fizz, and now I was about ready to explode. "I asked you so many times if you were telling me everything. You lied. And I took the hit for it."

"Persie, I'm sorry. I know you're angry, but if you'd just calm—" I cut my mom off before she could finish.

"How can I calm down when I just heard that monster's voice in my head? How can I calm down when I know he's got some plan for me? How can I calm down when I don't even know who I am anymore? You left so much out—*so* much!" My heart rattled at a sprint. "I gave you chance after chance to come clean, and you didn't take any of them. Call it lying by omission, call it bending the truth, call it what you want, but it's still a lie. One that's shaped my entire life! And I... I honestly don't know how this can be made right again. So no, you won't clear this all up for me. I'll clear it up my damn self. *I'll* talk to Leviathan. Maybe he'll fill in the blanks, since you two find honesty so freaking impossible!"

"Remember what was at stake." My dad's voice cracked. "If your mom didn't agree to Echidna's demand, we wouldn't have been able to beat Katherine."

I scraped back the chair and got up, aware of their eyes on me. Looking at Genie, I saw a supportive smile and gave her a subtle nod in return. I was done. The aftershock would get me later. People would talk about this party for months, but I figured they'd make up their own minds about what happened here. But they didn't have to take it home with them, and they weren't feeling all the feelings that collided inside me: sadness, confusion, hurt, and fury.

Genie hurried over at my signal, already one step ahead. I needed a magical to get me out of here. She strode at my side, making me feel less awkward and alone just by being there.

"Are you okay?" she whispered.

"I will be. Please, get me out of here. Not to the SDC—anywhere but there."

She nodded. "Can do."

Genie hadn't yet uttered the spell to get us away from this nightmare when something gripped my waist and wrenched me backward. For a split second, terror gripped just as hard. Had Leviathan come back to claim me for his grand, unknown plan? No. The lasso of Telekinesis dragged me to the edge of the long table, where my mom now stood, visibly shaking. Her palms were up.

I wrestled past the lump that balled up in my throat, dumbfounded. "You said you'd never use magic to control me."

My mom dropped the Telekinesis faster than you could say "major betrayal."

"I'm sorry, but you can't wander off like this. It's not—"

I cut her off. "If you say it's not safe one more time, I'm going to lose what's left of my mind! You swore you'd never use Chaos against me. I guess that's just another thing you lied about."

My mom clasped her hands together like she was praying. "Persie, forgive me. Instinct kicked in. Leviathan isn't done, and you can't face him alone." She looked desperately at me. "Please, Persie."

I had no idea what to do with my hands, except ball them into fists. "There's nothing you can say that will change my mind. There's nothing anyone can say. You got me into this mess, and I'm going to get myself out of it. So, either help me or stay out of my way. That's the only choice you've got to make here. But if you touch me with magic like that again, don't expect a choice in the matter."

My dad walked slowly to my mom's side.

Oh, here it comes. More of the same. I braced for the broken record, all the while fending off hot tears that threatened to spill. I just wanted this day to be over. *Happy eighteenth, eh?*

"She's right, Harley," my dad said quietly. "We can't put this off anymore. Leviathan already came to her, and nothing stopped him. Not this bubble, not the hexes you and Melody used. Nothing. It's time for her to go to him. You should take her."

My mom sagged in his arms, melting into a weeping puddle. "But what if he hurts her?"

She cared. I knew she cared. That's where all of this came from, when it boiled down to it. And I cared that she was so upset, but my head was so full of insanity and hydra and Leviathan and Purging that I didn't know what to do or say to make any of it better. How could I try and comfort her when I couldn't even comfort myself? And I knew that any words that came off my tongue right now would be laced with a venom I didn't mean.

"You'll be there to stop him. Hexes might not have

worked, but you're still you. You controlled him before. If he acts out, you can do it again," my dad reassured her.

She controlled him before? That was news to me, but so was a lot of what I'd heard today. She'd said that they fought, but I guessed I'd misinterpreted how the battle had played out. She evidently won with her beast control rather than brute force.

My mom steadied herself again and stood tall. Heaving in a shaky breath, she nodded. "Okay."

"What?" I had to be sure I'd understood her.

"Your dad's right." She hiccupped pitifully. "It's time."

TEN

Persie

After the fake, starry night of the riverside, seeing daylight had the same jarring effect as emerging from a movie theatre. The Bestiary basked in the late afternoon amber that shone through the dome overhead, but the sun's touch refused to warm me. Instead, a numbing cold coursed the tributaries where my blood should've been, and my forearms prickled with goosebumps.

There is no folly of the beasts of the earth which is not infinitely outdone by the madness of men. Herman Melville's words had never rung truer. Leviathan had caused this mess, but my parents had exacerbated it with their lies and omissions. They'd been so focused on protecting me they'd failed to see that, without all the details, I wouldn't be able to protect myself.

Now I'm finally getting the chance to put my money where my mouth is. Moving through the glinting glass boxes under the curious eyes of countless creatures, we headed for Leviathan's hall: my parents, Tobe, and me. Genie had asked if she could come along, but the request had been vetoed.

"Are you sure of this?" Tobe asked, his talons clicking on the marble floor, threads of silver and gold forking through the grayish-white material.

Is he talking to me? The eerie presence of the other beasts made it impossible to concentrate. They'd fallen unnervingly quiet, staring as I passed by. Not even the gargoyles neared the glass. Maybe they knew I'd had enough of a fright today to last a lifetime. Or, maybe they knew that something far scarier awaited me.

"Yes," my mom answered. "We have to deal with this now, before it gets any worse."

I Purged a hydra! Does it get worse? Who was I kidding? Of course it could get worse. We all knew it.

"You do not sound certain, Harley." Tobe paused in front of familiar doors.

I stepped forward, trying to copy my mom's chin-up trait. "Well, I am."

Aren't I? The simplest solution tended to be the best one, but speaking directly to Leviathan no longer seemed like the simplest or best solution. Nope, it seemed like the most nerve-wracking thing I'd ever done in my life. And I wished Genie could've been here, to lend me some of her courage.

"Very well, Miss Persie." Tobe dipped his head and opened the door with an elegant flourish. "Rest assured, I will not leave your side. You will not be alone in this, I swear to you."

"Thanks." I swallowed hard. My throat twisted so tight that sucking in a breath felt like a mammoth challenge.

The cold dropped to Baltic conditions the moment I put a foot inside that hall—atmospherically and internally. About the same temperature as the frost between my mom and me, which showed no sign of thawing. Although, in fairness, she did look sorry. No, sorry was way off the mark. She looked as though she were single-handedly walking me to the gallows, all shaky and grim.

"I'll be with you too." My mom walked level with me to the enclosure at the far side of the gloomy hall. A few anemic lamps tried their best to cast some muted light on the situation, but the darkness gobbled it up.

"Even if you don't like it?" My tone softened, the walk over providing an antidote to the venom that'd been on my tongue. No matter how upset I might've been about the secrecy, I was glad to have my parents here. The cavalry, in case anything went wrong.

She gave a strained smile. "Exactly."

I stopped a few yards shy of the enclosure. Fresh, frosty plumes spread out across the glass interior, as if someone were breathing against it, watching us from the shadows within. Dread turned my feet heavy.

Spots of stinging cold burned sharply at the nape of my neck and tingled out across my back, like someone trailing unwanted fingertips up my spine. No, more like someone was sneaking up behind me to whisper something deadly in my ear. Or worse. More patches of goosebumps shivered over my skin, white hot and freezing cold at the same time. An allergy to the beast in the box.

The frost melted away from the glass, revealing wall-to-wall smoke so dark and thick you wouldn't have known there was glass at all. A huge cube of light-swallowing black. I stumbled back in shock, caught by my dad's hands. Two seconds ago, I would've tried to push him away. But a lot could change in two seconds.

"You have come." A grim laugh muffled its way through the fog. And the voice echoed strangely, deep and resonant, and seemingly all around me at once.

Tobe slammed a hefty paw into the glass in a way that would definitely get a person kicked out of an Aquarium. "I knew you were thawing yourself, Leviathan! I would chastise you for it, but I know it would do little good. I have suspected for some time."

"Yet you never thought to ask?" The grim laugh turned smug. "A useful trick. If you want to chastise anyone, it ought to be those who came to take samples of my being. Samples that did not belong to them."

"I had no choice," Tobe said bitterly. "Nevertheless, you *will* behave now."

The smoke unfurled, and I saw Leviathan for the first time. He became more than the voice in my head, and more than the hushed-up mystery that had covertly chased me through the years. The name that made every adult in the SDC tight-lipped and nervous. The beast himself.

A twisted demon, swaying on the teal rope of a coiled

serpent tail. Where I had sun-starved, freckled skin, he had a patchwork of scales and armored plates, brushed with an oceanic palette that I'd used a few times in my dream sketchbooks. Cerulean, cobalt, cyan, sapphire and ultramarine—all of the striking blues, nothing powdery or pale—blending into glinting iridescent patches of skin and scale. It looked pure black, but when the light hit, tones of emerald and olive green showed through faintly. And there were several transparent sections—a pearlescent membrane of some sort—with blue lights and organs pulsing inside. His whole terrifying form had a mesmerizing quality that made it impossible to look away.

He looked primed for war. Bulky arms covered in armor plating, and hands that clacked jagged silver claws against the glass. Huge sea-urchin spines protruded the length of his back and his jutting jaw, and long, crooked teeth reminded me of an angler fish. The dangling, gray-white appendage that hung over his face only added to the image. A pulsing green orb nestled at the end, matching the rhythm of his internal lights.

Am I the prey you're trying to entice? I blinked rapidly, trying to stave off the hypnotic effect of all the glowing lights.

"Leviathan," I murmured, startling myself. I hadn't meant to. My tongue had spoken without my permission, like he had control of it and wanted to hear his name.

His eyes met mine. So human that I could almost forget the rest of him, his eyes were a shade I'd never be able to replicate properly in paint: a pale tone of blue just kissing white-flecked silver, or the faintest hint of lavender, depending on how the light caught his irises. Tobe's paw shot out and pushed me gently backward, making me realize that I'd stepped way too close to the glass, drawn in by his gaze. I shook my head, feeling unsettled by the magnetism I felt.

"Welcome." His voice cut through me. Soft and violent, both at once. "You are here. At last."

I cleared my dry throat. "You knew I'd come?"

"I hoped." His strange eyes glittered, and that lavender sheen flashed.

"Don't bat your fishy eyes at her, Leviathan." My mom stepped in, putting an arm in front of my chest. "You gave her no choice but to come here. You whispered in her freaking ear and made her Purge a giant hydra."

He didn't take his gaze off me. "A hydra? Intriguing."

"We're lucky it didn't kill anyone. You deliberately did this so she'd speak to you. Don't pretend otherwise." My mom hated this... thing. The disgust warped her face into a mask of fury. But I wanted to hear what he had to say. I'd come to hear him out, and that was exactly what I planned to do. Even if he scared the living daylights out of me.

"I called. That did not mean she would come." He chuckled, the green orb taking on a pink tinge. "Tell me more about this hydra."

I felt a nervous flutter. "Me?"

"Who else?" he said simply.

I pushed against my mom's arm, feeling the resistance. She still thought I needed protection. But his soft tone made me think otherwise, weird as it might have been. "I'm still trying to wrap my head around it, to be honest. I guess that's why I'm here—to find out more."

"In good time." He smiled, all the rows of his teeth mashing together in perfect tessellation. "First, I should introduce myself properly. I am Leviathan. By now, you likely know some stories about me."

"Yes," I replied dumbly.

"Ah, but I am not what you have heard." He scraped a silver claw toward Tobe. "He is the only one who vaguely knows me. And that is not saying much. One day, I hope you will be close to me. I hope you will know all there is to know. In a way Tobe here could never understand."

"I think I know you plenty," my mom interjected, stepping in front of me.

Leviathan scowled, his blue lights turning red: a warning. "Why do you keep doing that?"

"What?" she shot back.

"Acting as though I intend her harm?" His body relaxed, the red fading. "I do not. It is the last thing I want."

Is he telling the truth? With so many scales and such distracting colors, it proved hard to read his face. He sounded honest, but lies could tumble off tongues without anyone being the wiser. The last hour had taught me that.

I skirted around my mom and approached the glass, ignoring her hiss of protest. "What *do* you want?"

"To know you." His tail flicked faster. "For you to know me."

"Bull!" My dad exploded, causing me to jump. He walked right up the glass and practically pressed his face against it.

"What are you playing at, huh? What's your game? Your mother wouldn't have made that deal all those years ago just for you to get to know her."

Leviathan rose higher on his tail, the muscled coils lifting him easily. "I gave her a gift. Nothing more."

My mom slammed her hand against the box. "What gift did you give her that made her Purge like that? I've never seen anything like it in my life!"

"That is the gift." Leviathan smiled at me and my insides shriveled up. He had major creep factor, especially when he spoke softly.

"Purging beasts?" I choked on the horror of it.

He tilted his head forward in a nod, his spines bristling. "I prefer 'birthing monsters.' But yes. That is the power."

No. That terrible pain and suffering, again? Over and over again? I stumbled and thought I might pass out, but Tobe swooped in to keep me upright. His gentle paws held my shoulders as I leaned back against his solid chest. The only thing between me and the floor.

"You have been blessed," Leviathan continued. "Echidna's gift is now yours. My mother died at Katherine's hands, but her Chaos remained on this plane of existence after Gaia gave back what had been taken. It had nowhere to go. It belonged to Echidna and could only be given to a vessel who had her blessing: you. You were always the one who would carry it. My Persephone."

His Persephone? Over my dead body. How could he even call it anything close to a gift? No magic, no normal abilities, but the power to spew up rare, formidable beasts that tried to eat the people I cared about, and hurt so much I couldn't even think about it without flinching. I didn't want it. I'd have torn it out if I'd known how.

I sighed and sank against Tobe. "Happy freaking birthday to me."

ELEVEN

Persie

———————

"**D**o not be alarmed." Leviathan swept closer to the glass. "There is nothing to fear."

I held onto Tobe's arm and tried to muster some forti- tude. I'd asked for this. I'd *wanted* this. I had to face the truth, no matter how difficult it was to comprehend. And if I sank back and gave up, I'd be showing that I wasn't capable of handling my own problems. My mom and dad shouldn't have been the only ones standing up against the monster.

"It's not ideal." I steadied myself and approached the box from a different angle, a hint of sarcasm spiking my tone. "I'd be lying if I said I was thrilled about it. I mean, is it going to almost kill me every time? Does it get easier? Will I always recover so fast?" The recovery part still surprised me. I still ached a bit and had some lingering fuzziness in the brain, but I thought I would've been feeling a lot worse after what I'd been through.

Leviathan slithered along the ground to meet me at the far side of the vast container. "Fear not. You will answer your own questions in due course. It will take time to master, but it makes you magnificent. A wonder."

"A monster factory?" I watched his flicking tail. Anything to avoid staring into his unsettling, human eyes. Looking into them made me feel less afraid, and I knew I couldn't let them fool me.

"A Mother of Monsters," he corrected. "A queen amongst peasants."

I glanced at my mom and dad, who'd turned silent and sullen. "But Purging usually comes from magic."

"Magicals Purge when their bodies cannot contain Chaos. You are more powerful than that. You will Purge because it is your gift to bring life." Leviathan pressed his scaly hand to the pane and I resisted the urge to put my hand there, too.

"Can I give the gift back?" I had to ask.

He shook his head slowly. "No returns."

"How many times am I going to Purge?" I tried to ignore the absolute panic that barreled through my veins, since I didn't want this so-called gift one bit. The idea of Purging things left and right was far worse than having no magic at all.

Leviathan settled back onto his coiled tail and swayed rhythmically. "I cannot say for certain."

"How often did your mother?" I'd heard about the fabled Echidna a lot today, but I'd heard of her before, too. When you'd been regaled by the Merlin Tales as many times as I had, all the secondary characters popped up from time to time. Echidna didn't feature as often as, say, Davin, but I knew enough of the sacrifice she'd made at Katherine's hands. Honestly, I didn't like the Katherine stories as much as the other stories. It never felt good to know that a relative had been a power-hungry tyrant who'd almost destroyed the world.

Leviathan leaned back, a claw scratching at his chin. "My mother's emotions influenced her birth rate."

Cool, so don't get angry, don't get sad, don't be happy, don't feel anything. How hard could that be? I took another peek at my mom and dad, who'd stayed remarkably quiet, given how close I stood to Leviathan's enclosure. My dad held a stoic expression, likely for both our sakes—my mom's and mine. My mom, on the other hand, visibly struggled to control her emotions. A mixture of pain, helplessness, and hatred competed for prevalence on her face. Her eyes glinted with tears of anger and sadness. Anger at the monster in front of us, and sadness for what she hadn't been able to prevent.

"It is a unique ability." Leviathan brought my attention back, his glowing orb turning a darker shade of green. "Only Mother possessed it before you. It is hard to anticipate how it will manifest in a mortal."

"But it can be controlled, right?" *Oh Chaos, please tell me it can be controlled.*

He scraped a barnacle off a shoulder plate. "I do not know. Take deep breaths, perhaps."

"Riiiight. Deep breaths. That'll fix it." I clenched a handful of skirt in my fist.

He laughed, and the sound was frighteningly pleasant. "You never know."

"I thought you wanted to help me." My voice hardened. "No offense, but this isn't useful."

"I said I wanted to know you."

"And that's all?" I narrowed my eyes to slits. "Like my parents said—Echidna made that deal with my mom and passed it to you for a reason, and it wasn't about getting to know me. What do you get out of this?" There was a reason you never looked a gift horse in the mouth: because you might not like what you find. But I had to crack this Trojan horse wide open or I'd go mad with all the unanswered questions.

Leviathan laughed, colder than before. "My mother was persecuted for eons because she could birth monsters. And her children, in turn, were persecuted. Then she was incarcerated, simply because she created life. She died for it." He jabbed a scaly finger at my mom. "What will *you* do, Harley? The tables have turned. Will you lock your own daughter in a cage? Will you see her as a person... or a *monster*? You have been quick to make the judgment in the past."

My mom paled. "She's not a monster."

"You are correct." Leviathan smoothed his fingertips over the pane, like he was caressing my cheek. "She is special. I only hope your resolve remains in days to come."

I shot a look at my mom, but she wouldn't look at me. In the space of a minute, a different kind of ominous sensation had brimmed up through the marble floor and into my body, starting at the legs and working up. Every part of me now bubbled with this monster ability. The gift that couldn't be returned. It was *bound* to me now, the way my name had been bound to Leviathan from birth. I had changed, without realizing and without permission. Finally, I started to understand my parents' all-consuming fear. A great unknown stretched ahead of me. Anything could happen next.

All I know is, I'm no monster. But that wouldn't convince others. If I had no control over the monsters I Purged, then why not paint me with the same brush? If anything, it made me more dangerous than whatever I spewed out. A lion tamer who wasn't in control of their lions was nothing but a disaster waiting to happen. But imagine if you couldn't stop them from collecting more and more lions.

"Can't you tell me *anything* else about this curse?" I sucked annoyed air through my teeth.

Leviathan flashed that hideous grin again. "Gift. Not a curse. And you cannot expect immediate answers. That is Chaos's beauty. The wonders of discovery!"

Anger flickered in my chest. "You can't give someone a curse like this and then just push them out into the world."

"Persie, perhaps we should talk about this outside?" My mom finally broke her silence, and that defensive arm moved to steer me away.

"Her name is Persephone." An irked note slithered into Leviathan's voice.

"Her name is Persie, and she's coming with me." My mom tried to grasp me, but I slipped out of her reach. I knew I should be honest and tell her I was five seconds from a mental break, but I couldn't do it. My stubborn tongue twisted in my mouth and wouldn't ask for help. Part of me still wanted to punish her for keeping this secret for so long. It'd caught me unawares, and now I had fears and worries about my future that I'd never anticipated hurtling from every direction. All because she hadn't given me the chance to prepare myself.

Who'll ever accept a girl who can birth monsters at the drop of an emotion? There it was. The worst part of all of this. Not the actual Purging, not the lies, not the shock of it, but what it meant for me going forward. I'd been on the outskirts my entire life, and this had just pushed me to the farthest boundary possible.

"No, Mom. I want you to go." I clenched my fists. "I can't talk to you right now. My head is already a mess without you adding to it. Please, just go."

My mom's face fell, and that wounded look broke off another fragment of our splintered relationship. I expected her to rant and rave and fight to stay—but she didn't. Her hands flopped to her sides and she nodded, defeated. A feat that Katherine Shipton and Davin Doncaster had failed to accomplish, but I'd managed with just one utterance.

"Okay, Persie. I'll go." She lifted her head to shoot a last sniper glare at Leviathan. "This isn't over yet."

He smirked through his shark teeth. "Goodbye, Harley."

I saw a muscle twitch in my mom's jaw. She clearly wanted to punch the victory off Leviathan's face, but she turned and left without another word, Dad following after her. Pieces would need picking up, I felt sure of it. But at least for now, I could be alone with my questions and Leviathan.

And Tobe. He'd said he wouldn't leave me alone, and he was a Beast Master of his word.

"This is better." Leviathan caressed the pane again. "Forget Tobe is here, and it's just the two of us. My Persephone."

I jabbed a finger at him. "You cursed me, Leviathan! *Cursed,* not gifted. And just because I'm fighting with my mom doesn't mean I'm going to go running into your arms, so you can stop with that." I took a deep breath, just like he'd suggested before. "I'm not a damsel, and I'm not a fool. I've heard enough about you to know that you've got an angle in this. And I promise you, here and now, that I will figure it out. It is only a matter of time."

"Isn't everything?" He chuckled, unbothered.

Tobe peered down at me in amber-eyed confusion. "Do you wish to leave now?"

I hesitated. "Yes, but I wanted to give my mom a five-minute head start so we don't bump into each other in the coven."

"Ah." Tobe's feathers ruffled in amusement. "Then allow me to help. You must be thirsty after all you have endured today. Come with me." He took my hand and led me away from the enclosure. But Leviathan wasn't the sort of mythical beast to let anyone else have the last word.

"Farewell, Persephone." He kept up his formidable grin, each serrated tooth glinting out the Morse code of a secret I couldn't decipher.

But I will find out what it is.

TWELVE

Persie

———————

T he whirlwind of emotions that Leviathan had set swirling inside my head suddenly took a detour, pushed away by the overwhelming awe that took my breath away. We'd somehow stepped into the silent greenery of a forest, though I didn't remember coming through a wardrobe. Just an average door had led to this world of wonders.

"How have I not seen this before?" I tried to absorb everything at once, giving myself a sensory overload.

"It is my serenity." Tobe purred contentedly.

"I can see why." I could no longer hear the thrum of the atrium. In fact, I couldn't hear any sounds from the coven at all. A comforting quiet enveloped us as we walked a leaf-strewn path between enormous redwoods that seemed to lean in, their branches shaking against the breeze. Autumnal colors tinged the leafy carpet, hues of bronze and scarlet and rich brown. People didn't give brown enough credit as a color, I thought.

The forest went on as far as the eye could see, giving way to the darkness of shadows. I guessed they came to a stop somewhere, but Tobe had clearly constructed an illusion of some kind to make the greenery look like it went on forever. A few birds fluttered between trees, startled by our presence. Well, *my* presence. They adored Tobe, swooping down to perch on his broad shoulders and peck at him playfully before flapping off again. A robin with a plump red breast hopped along a branch above us then dropped down onto Tobe's head, staying there as we walked.

"I thought you'd have Purge beasts in here or something," I remarked, smiling at the cheeky robin as it nestled between Tobe's ears.

Tobe chuckled. "I prefer not to bring work into my private domain, as wonderful as every beast may be. Besides, these birds amuse me with their mischievous antics." He gestured to a rainbow-feathered bird that trilled as it flew between trees. "That is a lorikeet. I have a collection from all over the world."

"It's beautiful."

"I am pleased that you think so." He took a right off the main path and my eyes almost burst out of my head. Ahead stood a whole freaking cottage, complete with white walls and a white picket fence that enclosed a garden of wildflowers. An oversized rocking chair sat out on the veranda, and shiny gray roof slats gave the house a chocolate box feel. In the center of the garden, a fountain babbled happily. He really had created his own little paradise in the Bestiary.

It took a moment to find my voice. "Does everyone know about this place?"

"Very few. To keep it peaceful." He flashed his fangs in a smile. "I built it all myself. Every tree you see here was planted by my own hand."

"No way," I gasped. By the size of the trees, the project must've started decades ago, if not centuries.

"I have watched them grow, as I have watched so much grow in my lifetime." His voice turned sad. "Only, these do not die. They will one day, but I may be gone before that happens."

My heart suddenly ached. If I hadn't been so worried about vomiting up another Purge beast, I might've teared up. I tended to forget how long Tobe had been alive. He'd watched the world change time and time again. He'd seen civilizations rise and fall. He'd watched people he cared for come and go, including the woman who'd created him. No matter how strong he might have been, that had to be hard. So he'd turned to the one thing that wouldn't leave him— nature. A private den of redwoods as old as he was, that might even outlive him.

"Don't say that," I said softly.

"All things must die, Miss Persie. It is the one thing we may rely on in this world." He walked up to the picket fence and opened the gate. "Now, would you care for some tea?"

I followed him through the gate, marveling at the sweet scent of the wildflowers and their sprays of colors, which complemented the rich green of the grass. "I don't drink much tea, but I'll give it a go."

"Sit here. I will prepare something palatable for you." His claws scraped the back of a lawn chair, which he set up on the veranda. I obeyed and he went inside, leaving me to enjoy the scenery. The dome overhead tricked the eye into believing it was outside, with nothing to interrupt the glass, allowing the afternoon sunlight to pierce through the canopy in gauzy ribbons.

A few minutes later, Tobe reappeared with an entire tea tray that looked even daintier in his gigantic paws. He laid out a teapot, cups, saucers; the whole nine yards. He'd even rustled up a slice of cake for me, though I had no idea what Tobe himself ate.

He sat down opposite, and the lawn chair groaned. "You will forgive me if I do not eat with you. I fear this chair would give way if I did."

I laughed. "Thank you, Tobe."

"It is the least I can do, after what you have endured." He positioned his chair so it faced his garden. "I imagine you did not expect your birthday to be so eventful."

"That's putting it mildly." I let him pour me a cup of greenish liquid before raising it to my nose suspiciously. It smelled of fresh-cut grass and mint. "Can I ask you something?"

He poured a cup for himself. "Of course."

"Did you know about Leviathan giving me a gift?"

Tobe took a sip. "I did, Miss Persie. However, before you ask, I was not at liberty to disclose the information. It was not my place to go against your parents' wishes."

"Then let me ask you another question—do you understand why they kept it from me?"

Tobe set down his cup. "They were certain of their ability to prevent this from occurring, and I had no reason to think it impossible. I know Leviathan's nature, and though he can be wily and underhanded, I had more faith in your parents' determination than I had in his. Perhaps that makes me foolishly optimistic. Regardless, I underestimated him, and I did not once think that he might pass his mother's ability to you. So, to answer your question, I do understand... and at the same time, I do not."

"No one can give me a straight answer." I tried a bit of the tea and found myself pleasantly surprised. Sweet and refreshing, with a hint of spice at the back of the throat.

"That is because there isn't one," Tobe replied.

I switched angles. "Do you think they did the right thing? Do you think they should've kept it from me?"

"There is little use in dwelling on past actions, Miss Persie. When you have lived as long as I have, you come to learn that." He put a paw on my shoulder. "However, that does not make it any easier to bear when everything is still raw. Your parents are also guilty of underestimating Leviathan, but fear was their greatest motivator. And fear has a way of clouding judgment and sense. They did not want you to live under a burden and have it mar your childhood. They wanted to bear that weight for you and try to resolve it themselves so you wouldn't have to suffer under it."

"But it affected everything." I took another sip, letting it warm me. "It's shaped my whole life."

He gave my shoulder a squeeze. "Perhaps it may be easier to think of it from this perspective—your mother was forced into making the deal with Echidna as a means of putting an end to a great evil. She did not ask for it, and she has lived with guilt since the moment she learned about you. But know this: she had no choice." He took away his paw and sipped some tea. "Your mother has always been the sort of woman who wants to fix everything in her own way, and she usually succeeds. Now she feels she has failed when it mattered most. More than ending Katherine, more than ridding the world of Davin, more than any challenge she has previously faced. Imagine how that must feel."

Why'd you have to go and put it like that? I clutched my teacup in both hands and observed the birds that chattered in the trees. I noticed their nests, painstakingly put together with twigs and bits of Tobe's fluff and anything they could find to make it homey. In a way, that's what my mom had done. She'd layered the lies around me with tufts of half-truths and twigs of misjudgment to try to soften the eventual blow, but the winds of Leviathan had come and blown the nest right out of the branches. And now we just had the debris of what remained.

After a moment of letting me digest his words, Tobe went on.

"That is not to say that you have no right to your anger and confusion, or that it is insignificant. Your mother must also put herself in your shoes." He looked at me fondly with those magical golden eyes. "For you are now in a worrying predicament, and you must work together to overcome it."

"But," I said, my fingers trembling around my cup. "What if I can't control this?"

We could go back and forth forever trying to figure out who was right and who was wrong. But Tobe had hit the nail on the head—we were in a terrible spot. I had received a strange and terrible gift that I didn't want: a curse. What would happen to me if I couldn't get a handle on this ability? Would they really throw me in a box, like they did with Echidna? I didn't want to believe it, but what if I became too dangerous? So many questions, so few answers.

Tobe leaned back in his chair, the whole thing straining. "I know a thing or two about Purge beasts, and I know a thing or two about people. I may overlook things at times, but there is not a great deal that evades my knowledge. Perhaps you might take a page from the book of professional monster hunters."

"There's a book on that?" A faint flicker of hope wafted in my chest, but the merest breath could snuff it out.

He laughed softly. "Not a literal book, Miss Persie, although there may be something hidden away in the library. What I meant was, think of yourself in that capacity: as a hunter of monsters—though I abhor the term 'hunter'— instead of the person who brings these beasts into being. Learn to contain the monsters you create, and you may have an easier path to controlling the outcome of your... ability." He downed the dregs of his tea. "Or, as your mother might put it: clean up after yourself, and no one will have anything to complain about."

"You've heard that one, huh?" It usually came when I'd spent days in my room, hard at work on a painting, to the point where dishes and laundry had piled up around me. Maybe I'd been training for this my whole life, without realizing it.

Clean up my mess. Part of me liked the sound of it. My job, my duty, my way out of this, in my own hands. A way to loosen the leash around my neck and prove my independence. No, it was so much more than that. It was a way to prove that I could be just as much of a Merlin as my mom, and my uncle, and my cousins. Standing and fighting on my own two feet.

"Consider it," Tobe urged. "I know you will feel the desire to flee from this, as is natural. But moving to another coven would not serve any purpose. As conflicted as you currently are, at least you are in a place where you are understood and loved. You are home, and a home is hard to find."

I watched a sleek blackbird pluck a strand of dry grass with its orange beak and flap back to its nest above. There, the bird threaded it into the outer layer of a half-built nest. A poignant sign that, even if the nest fell apart, it could be rebuilt. And even if it was never the same as before, it would still be home.

Dammit, Tobe. The people I loved, the people I knew, the people I called family and friends were all birds of a feather, and we flocked together. This was my home, and I had it better than a lot of people out there. But didn't birds also leave the nest eventually? Just because I left, that didn't mean I couldn't come back, did it?

I watched the blackbird a while longer, then exhaled as if I were pushing the whole day out of my lungs in one go. "I'll consider it."

THIRTEEN

Harley

It had been a while since I'd sat in the Alton Waterhouse Room, but the familiar prickle of tension was still in the air. I had so many memories in this room, including many with the people who were with me now: Wade, O'Halloran, and Astrid. I'd have taken a lengthier trip down memory lane if Persie wasn't at the forefront of my mind. But while she was safe with Tobe, there were other dangers to distract my attention for a while. A double-edged silver lining, if such a thing existed.

"Two more have shown up in St. Louis." Astrid swiped Smartie's screen and holograms powered up. They displayed two figures, slowly turning 360°. A middle-aged man with extra chins and thinning hair and a young woman—more of a girl, really—with a pixie cut and a startled expression. The sight of the girl made the mom in me ache. She belonged to someone out there. I thought of my own daughter, and I ached for her too.

"Same symptoms as the others?" O'Halloran squinted over the top of his glasses to observe the turning figures. He'd gotten old. There was no gentle way to put it. *He'll have to step down soon.* I shrugged the thought off. The SDC without O'Halloran was like bread without butter. Then again, I'd thought the same thing over twenty years ago, when Alton—the great man this room was named after—had been the director.

But O'Halloran still had the vitality of someone half his age when it came to matters of magical importance. And his trusty leprechaun, Diarmuid, still perched on his shoulder. The tiny man seemed to run on a mix of rage and lewd humor, and he hadn't aged a day. Maybe that was the secret.

"Ach, what de ye think?" Diarmuid scoffed. "They're goin' te come wanderin' back te spill all them beans te folks? Nah, they've got mush fer brains now, ye mark me words."

Wade ignored the leprechaun. "You're sure? They all have the marker of mind-wiping inside their brains? It's definitely been checked?" He had become the primary expert on all things amnesiac. He'd even published several essays on it.

"For certain," Astrid confirmed.

"See, what did I tell ye?" Diarmuid gave O'Halloran a nudge to the skull. "Mush."

"Are they showing signs of having any memory at all—babbling, random muttering, that sort of thing?" I kept my tone hopeful. I needed some good news after the day I'd had.

Or maybe I just need to feel like I'm useful somewhere.

"They don't have any recollection. Or at least they don't have the capacity to voice it." Astrid typed something into Smartie and different images emerged. The same two figures, now camouflaged by bruises and cuts. The young woman's startled expression had turned haunted, while the older man could barely open one eye. He'd also lost his extra chins, now bordering on gaunt.

"Ach, would ye look at 'em? It's like the before and after ye don't want te be seein'!" Diarmuid crowed.

I sucked air through my teeth. "They were beaten?"

"Tortured," Astrid corrected.

Tortured. The word made my heart clench, like a fist had seized it. Missing magicals were one thing, but tortured magicals... As awful as it sounded, people with malicious intentions tended to kill witnesses and informants instead of leaving them alive. To keep them living and send them back out into the world, post-torture, suggested that someone was sending a warning.

"Stranger still, they showed up in St. Louis, but neither of them knows anyone there, and I don't mean because of the mind-wipe. We ran a Chaos check with the Krieger Detector after they were found wandering by the St. Louis Coven. The young woman, Zara Gilchrist, is from Portland, Oregon. And the man, Howard Hickins, is a native of Bardstown, Kentucky."

"Aye, but that don't mean a kitten's whisker." Diarmuid hopped down onto the workbench. "These folks don't want ye knowin' where they snatched the goods, so te speak."

I cocked my head. "I think you might be right. Just

because these two are from Kentucky and Oregon, it doesn't mean that's where they got taken. We should dive deeper into bank transactions and locations from before they went missing."

"Way ahead of you." Astrid flicked up an image of a blank bank statement. "It's been wiped. Phone records, too. Just like the other magicals who've reappeared. We've only got their names because you can't wipe the slate clean on Chaos signatures."

Diarmuid pulled a grim face. "Aye, not yet anyhow. Ye just wait 'til folks start turnin' up without a sniff o' Chaos in 'em. Drained dry as a kipper."

"We're trying to be optimistic," O'Halloran muttered.

Wade lay his hands flat on the table where we'd come up with a thousand schemes. "I'd like to take a look at them myself, if the UCA will allow. And I'd like to take Jacob along with me since he's helped a lot with my research. I'm not saying we'll be able to reverse what's been done to their minds, but we've been developing a new method, which might work better than past attempts."

O'Halloran gave a nod of approval.

Diarmuid did the opposite. "It ain't right, pokin' at brains."

"Well, it has to be done, if we're ever going to make some headway." Wade gave the leprechaun a sharp look, which said, *Please, for the love of Chaos, shut up.*

"I'll send a message now. See what can be arranged." Astrid tapped the screen at lightning speed. "I can't imagine why they'd disagree, since they're as stumped as we are."

"How many does that make?" I asked, trying to shove down the fear and uncertainty I felt inside. *Persie is with Tobe. She's safe for now. You still have a responsibility here.*

Astrid opened another window on her beloved device. "Over the last five years, somewhere in the region of 150. An estimate, considering not all of them have reappeared, and some might have vanished for their own reasons." She peered more intently at the screen. "If my graph is right, the first two years we had an average of two disappearances a month, and that upped to five a month in the last three years—give or take."

I considered the data. "And, whoever they are, they're still keeping the numbers relatively low so there's less chance of messing up and getting caught. That'd be my guess, anyway."

Astrid nodded. "I'd be inclined to agree."

The question remained: *why?* With every missing magical that reappeared, we asked that same question. But whoever these people were, they'd completely evaded magical authorities. Leaving no trace behind.

"And we still have no leads." With visible frustration, Astrid pushed her glasses back up onto the bridge of her nose. "Five years, and we have nothing."

"Someone ain't haulin' their weight," Diarmuid remarked unhelpfully. *Everyone* was working hard on this, but the invisible enemy provided little by way of clues. Besides, Melody had worked eighteen years to keep Leviathan away from Persie and look how that had turned out. All the preparation in the world didn't mean success.

No, don't think about that now. Focus.

"Any connection between the latest victims and those we've seen before?" I grasped for fresh hope. Astrid crushed it with a shake of her head.

"No similarities in appearance. No connections between victims. No apparent target age range, abilities, locations. *Nothing* to help us narrow the search. It still seems like random selection."

Diarmuid stopped his pacing and lifted his head sharply. "Hobbies? Jobs? Bad haircuts?"

"There are commonalities here and there, but it isn't enough to make an assumption with," Astrid replied. "Everyone who has disappeared seems very... ordinary. Unless that's the common denominator, that they're all ordinary?"

Diarmuid snorted and looked at me playfully. "Unlike that daughter o' yours, eh?"

"What did you just say?" I felt my throat constrict. It was hard enough returning to work after everything, without the little twerp casually bringing it up.

"Diarmuid!" O'Halloran's voice held a warning. "Rein it in, before I hand you back to Tobe."

"*Pfft.* I'd like te see ye try," Diarmuid muttered. "I'd smash yer hands before ye got ten steps."

Wade put his hand in mine and held my gaze, centering me. "Ignore him. You know he struggles with verbal diarrhea."

Diarmuid folded his arms huffily. "It ain't like it's a big secret no more."

"That cat may be out of the bag, Diarmuid, but that

doesn't give you the right to speak about one of our own like that. She deserves respect, not derision." O'Halloran swiped up the obnoxious creature and plonked him back on his shoulder.

"And if ye ever pick me up like that again, I'll deck ye!" Diarmuid protested, but he didn't try to get down again. He just sat there, scowling. His default setting.

O'Halloran shook his head and looked over at Wade and me. "I'm sorry about him. Personally, I think it's for the best that everything's out in the open. At least this way, Persie knows what to expect."

"Aye, she'll be a right ol' Puff the Magic Dragon, spewin' up smoke." Diarmuid chuckled to himself.

Say one more word, and I swear to Chaos. I gripped Wade's hand tighter. I'd had no time to process what had happened with Persie, and Diarmuid seemed intent on pushing all the wrong buttons.

"Of course that's not how we see her," O'Halloran continued, casting a sharp sideways glance at the leprechaun. But when he turned back to us, his face was pained. "However, I do have concerns. This monster ability isn't something we're familiar with. After that hydra... we don't know what else she might Purge."

"Sounds like you and Diarmuid are pretty much on the same wavelength." Bitterness dripped from my words and Wade squeezed my hand again, trying to keep me calm. "The coven isn't at risk, if that's what you're getting at."

O'Halloran's lined face softened. "She's one of us. We're not against her; we're here for her. I only meant to say that everyone will need to be vigilant to address the concerns that people are going to have."

Everyone's going to be scared of her, you mean. It broke my heart to think that Leviathan had made Persie a pariah. She was quiet enough without that nasty viper adding to it. I'd been so afraid of her retreating from us, her parents, that I hadn't stopped to think about her retreating from everyone.

"We've been through worse," Wade chimed in to restore my optimism. "This is nothing we can't handle."

Diarmuid threw his head back in a cackle. "Ye say that now, but ye've never had a monster-spoutin' bairn before. Ye shouldn't be so cocky. Who's te say this ain't worse than what ye've dealt with before?"

"Because I won't let it be." My palms shot up and spat a line of Telekinesis at him. I was sick to death of the munchkin and his attitude problem, talking about my daughter that way. The threads wrapped around him, and I closed my fist, making the lasso squeeze around his ridiculous little body. Anything to shut him up, just for a second or two.

O'Halloran intervened with a sharp bang to the table. "Harley! Enough!"

I released the leprechaun, albeit reluctantly. "Don't tell me he didn't deserve it."

"I'll rip yer ginger head off and toss me gold coins down yer neck, ye—" Diarmuid lunged for me, but O'Halloran got there first. He grabbed his tiny companion and held him tight, not taking his eyes off the creature.

"I think we should bring this meeting to a close, before

war breaks out." O'Halloran gripped Diarmuid tighter as the irritating cretin wriggled, trying to get free. He hurried to the door. "Astrid, keep me in the loop, okay?"

"Always, director," she promised. He exited rapidly just as Smartie pinged. "Oh. Just got the reply. They say they can send the returnees to us in the next hour for interviews, so Jacob and Wade won't need to go to St. Louis."

I exchanged a knowing glance with my husband. "In other words, they want to palm the responsibility off to someone else?"

"They're a small coven." Astrid shrugged. "At least here, we know they'll get the right care."

Wade got up. "Then we should get to the infirmary and help Krieger and Jacob prepare for the new arrivals." He took my hand and ushered me to the door, where I could still hear Diarmuid yelling up the corridor. It riled me up all over again.

Speak about my daughter like that again, and you won't be seeing the end of the rainbow, you'll be seeing the end of my fist.

FOURTEEN

Harley

"You'd think they hadn't done anything over there. As if these poor souls had not been through enough, they had to fall into the hands of Cronenberg! As lazy a physician as he was a student," Krieger complained. "Why, I believe he would rather have let them die than do any actual work." He flipped open a chart sent from St. Louis with the traumatized duo, though Krieger looked like the traumatized one right now. Two hours had passed since the duo arrived, and Krieger and Jacob had been hard at work ever since. This was the first time they'd come up for air after running test after test to gauge the extent of the damage.

"Cronenberg?" I didn't recognize the name.

Krieger pursed his lips. "The physician in St. Louis. We were at university together. He was always scraping through exams by the… how do you say it? Skin of his teeth?"

"Are all physicians German?" Wade joked.

"The best ones usually are, but Cronenberg brings our average down." Krieger set the chart on a nearby table. He picked up a pen in an arthritic claw to scrawl notes on a clean page. The ink came out shaky, like a spider scuttling across the lines. He'd gotten frail in his advancing years, his fingertips trembling as he flicked the pages. But he had Jacob, his son and heir apparent to his physician empire, to help him. I had no idea what we'd do when Krieger retired, but I knew what he'd do. He'd mentioned plans to move to the Arctic Circle to study the aurora borealis: a personal pastime, waiting in the wings for the day the doc would be free to explore it.

"You want me to do that?" Jacob smiled. The mid-thirties suited him, and he'd grown to be as handsome as he was smart. Because of his Native American and Latino ancestry, he didn't look much like his adoptive father, but the affection in his kind eyes showed that they were family in the way that mattered most.

"Would you? I don't have the right glasses on." Krieger handed off the pen and the chart.

The physician and scientific engineer famed for inventing the magic detector. Now, I doubted he'd be able to fix a screw on his own invention without Jacob's help.

Jacob began to write, speaking aloud to keep Krieger involved. "Both patients showing a fear response when introduced to stimuli on screen. Neither patient able to articulate, likely due to mind-wiping. Vitals remain stable, but there are multiple internal and external injuries." He looked up. "Did I miss anything?"

"They show signs of re-experiencing." Krieger flexed his fingers. They cracked loudly.

"Re-experiencing?" The term wasn't familiar to me.

"The state of involuntarily reliving the traumatic experience in a physical sense—spasms, defensive reactions, that sort of thing. A symptom of PTSD," Krieger explained.

Jacob poised the pen and glanced back at Wade and me. "It's a way for the mind to process what it's been through. But if they have no flashbacks due to the amnesia, it puts the brain under even more strain."

"Excellently put." Krieger patted his son on the back.

"There's no mention of night terrors in the notes, but we'll monitor them tonight." Jacob tapped the pen against paper and frowned. "Alyssa wanted to have dinner. I'll have to reschedule. Unless she wants to come have a picnic here."

It boggled my mind that Jacob had a wife. I still remembered him as a teenager. The kid the Smiths took in, and then had to forget through no fault of their own. His first love had turned out to be one of Katherine's cronies, whom she'd killed in front of him. Luckily, life had gone a little smoother for him since. And I loved Alyssa, his wife, almost as much as Jacob. Fiery and assertive, she'd spotted Jacob on her first day here seven years ago, and she'd gone for what she wanted. He'd been wary of love for obvious reasons, but he'd been bowled over by her. Literally, at times.

"She wouldn't mind helping you watch the patients, I am sure." Krieger beamed contentedly. He was as smitten with his daughter-in-law as the rest of us. "I would offer, but..." He trailed off with a sad note.

"Your sleepless nights are done, Dad. You've earned it," Jacob said softly. "Why don't you go ahead and get out of here? I've got this."

Krieger smiled gently in a way that seemed to hold deep meaning. "I know you do." With that, the old man nodded to us and turned to leave.

Jacob continued. "Anyway, where was I?"

"Night terrors," I prompted, waving to the older doctor as he exited the room.

"Right." He started writing again, the doctor in charge now. "Both are experiencing pain, tremors, nausea, and sweating. The above are to be monitored closely. Thus far, neither patient is responding to magical or non-magical treatment for the amnesia."

"You can heal their physical injuries though, can't you?" My thoughts flitted to the girl. Sixteen years old and covered head to toe in bruises, cuts, burns, and lesions. I hadn't been able to look at her for long. When I saw her, I saw Persie, and I couldn't deal with that right now.

"We're working on it," Jacob assured. "There's just so much to repair. Whoever did this to them tried pretty much everything to get *something* out of them."

That poor girl. "Have her parents been found?"

"She doesn't have any."

"A foster kid?" The cracks in my heart splintered a little more.

Jacob nodded.

"What about the guy? Does he have family?" Wade's tone

was thoughtful. I quickly understood what he was getting at: a possible connection.

Jacob checked the chart. "He has a wife and two sons, both waiting for him in Kentucky. They were going to come visit, but the UCA forbade it, considering the circumstances. We're sending them updates on his situation instead."

Wade sank down onto a nearby bed. "I thought I might've had something there."

"You thought maybe they were only taking people without anyone to care if they disappeared?" I sat beside him.

"Exactly." He ran a hand through his dark curls, flecked with a few strands of gray. His wizard hairs, as I liked to call them. "Do you think they're stable enough for me to try some magic on, Jake?"

Jacob set down the chart. "They're awake, but confused, so we might have to keep it brief and have some sedative on hand in case things take a turn."

"I'll be as quick as I can," Wade replied. Tension lines creased between his eyebrows—a sure sign of inner stress. I put my arm around his waist and hugged him close, knowing that we were bonded in our stress and fears. About everything.

I pulled back and peered up into his eyes. The eyes I'd loved for twenty years of my life. "Nobody knows mind-wiping spells like you. If there's a way of reversing this, you're the man for the job."

He brushed his thumb across my cheek. "I just hope I can help them."

"You will, one way or another," I assured him.

Jacob grinned at us. "Some things never change, huh?"

"Weren't you just talking about picnics?" I laughed.

"It was a hospital picnic, which isn't exactly romantic." Jacob beckoned us to follow him toward the ICU. He tried to keep his tone light, but the growing tension as we neared the ward was palpable. "For one, you can't have candles with so many flammable things around. If one of the oxygen tanks sprung a leak, this whole place would go up."

Our good humor died as we entered a secure room with two sets of quarantine-safe sliding doors. The girl was sitting up in the nearest bed, rocking slightly and clawing the edge of her blanket. The man, on the other hand, sat eerily still, staring unblinkingly at the opposite wall. Both looked like they'd been through a battle—on the losing side. Chunks of the girl's short blonde hair were missing, some parts singed to the scalp. And the man had so many bruises on his face that everything had puffed up to inhuman proportions. As Jacob went to the girl's bedside, Wade and I stood quietly near the doors, taking in the pitiful sight.

"Zara?" Jacob spoke slowly and gently. "Zara, these are my friends, Wade and Harley. You might remember them from before. Wade wants to talk to you. Is that okay?"

Her eyes darted left and right, like she was following some unseen creature on the bed. "Zara?"

"That's you," Jacob replied. He put his hand on her forearm, and she stiffened.

"Another trauma response?" I whispered.

Jacob took his hand away. "Apparently." His eyes widened in sudden thought. "Actually, maybe you could sit with her and keep her calm while Wade talks to her? I'd like to test a theory."

Breaking away from Wade, I walked around to the other side of the bed and sat down. Gingerly, I put out my hand and let Zara decide if she wanted to reciprocate. She flinched at the sight and her eyes flickered wildly toward me. But the moment she saw my face, her shoulders relaxed, and her hand reached out. Her fingers gripped mine tightly, as though I might be the only thing in the world she had left to cling onto. And her eyes finally focused on mine.

"You're safe now." I shuffled closer and put an arm around her shoulders. She nestled into me and buried her face in my shirt. Quiet sniffles drifted upward, and I felt dampness through the fabric. She was crying.

"That's what I thought," Jacob said, his voice heavy. "She's not afraid of you, like she's afraid of us." He gestured to Wade and himself.

"Does that mean...?" I started, covering the girl's ear as I held her.

Jacob swallowed. "Men. I can't say for certain, but I think the perpetrators were male. I'd have to see what Howard's response to you is, to gauge his reaction."

I nodded, turning back to the girl, wrapping her in my arms. "You're okay. I'm here. I've got you. I promise, you'll get through this. We won't let anything bad happen to you again."

I realized, with sudden tears of my own, that I wasn't just speaking to her.

Wade approached. We looked into each other's eyes as he reached out and placed both hands on either side of Zara's temples. She seized in my arms, gasping for air. I held her and stroked her hair gently, whispering soothing words.

"You don't have to be afraid. I know this is scary, but we're here to help."

In front of me, white sparks of Chaos threaded out of Wade's hands and into her head. Her body went limp, but I kept right on holding her, as though *my* life depended on it, too. I hadn't been able to help Persie when it mattered the most. I wasn't going to fail Zara as well. Not on the same day.

"Do you sense anything?" Jacob asked.

"Not yet." Wade closed his eyes, and the white threads brightened. A spell of his own design, written in the Grimoire that he'd vowed to complete by the time he was fifty. I'd made the same vow, but with that deadline fast approaching, I doubted I'd make it. I hadn't yet written a single word.

I glanced down and watched little bursts of light exploding through the layers of skin and bone. Wade's magic, digging deep for evidence. The glow was mesmerizing. I kept watching, transfixed, until Wade snapped me out of it with a quiet gasp.

His eyes shot open while his hands stayed in place. "There's been some heavy-duty magic in her head. Magic I've hypothesized about, but never seen. Dangerous stuff, due to the possibility of peripheral damage."

"I guess whoever did this didn't care about that." Hatred boiled up inside me, aimed at our invisible enemy.

Jacob frowned. "Do you think it's an ability or spell work?"

"Hard to say. All I can feel is the residue of what's been left behind. And it's potent." A muscle twitched in his jaw. "I'd say it was done by an expert in memory spells. Someone more adept than me."

"Is there an ability that matches that?" I looked to Jacob, the Sensate, for an answer. "I know the ability is forbidden by executive order, but is there a rarer ability we might not know about? To get around the order?"

"No," he said simply. "That order covers variations."

A bead of sweat trickled down the side of Wade's face. "If it's not an ability, we're dealing with someone hugely powerful."

We'd thought we were done with powerful people wanting to cause trouble, but we should've known better. Now we had Leviathan *and* this to deal with. Whatever it was.

The color of Wade's threads turned slightly pink as they thrummed into Zara's temples. He was trying something else. I continued my maternal stroking. Whorls of light spiraled and darted across her head, literally trying to jog her memory.

A few moments later, he pulled his hands away and severed the magical tie. "Try again."

I jostled her gently and she stirred in my arms. "Zara?"

"You're still here." Her eyes filled with fresh tears. "You didn't leave."

"You remember me?" I said.

She nodded slowly. "Harley?"

"That's right. What's your name?" I prompted, keeping every extremity crossed.

"I... I don't remember." Her face clouded over with confusion. "Do you know who I am?"

"You're Zara." I struggled to suppress the pain in my voice. "Zara Gilchrist."

She mustered a faraway smile. "That's a pretty name. Who is she?"

"She's you," I urged, like it would make a difference. "You're Zara Gilchrist. You're in the infirmary at the San Diego Coven. Do you remember why? Do you remember what happened to you?"

"San Diego?" She giggled strangely. "I've never been there."

I held her gently by the shoulders. "Do you know where you're from?"

"I'm from..." Her giggles turned to rapid breaths, her eyes darting wildly again. "I don't know where I'm from. Am I from San Diego? Is that why I'm here? Did I have an accident?" She looked down at her bandaged arms, horrified. "Is that why it hurts?"

"You're from Portland, Oregon." I fought back tears. She looked so lost and scared. It reminded me of Persie at six or seven, when I'd lost her in Waterfront Park. I took my eyes off her for a second and she wandered off. I found her half an hour later. But by then, we were both in tears. Up until today, it had been the scariest moment of my life. Screw Katherine and her Challenges, and screw Davin and his schemes—losing my little girl for those thirty minutes had trumped any fear they'd ever ignited in me. The thought of losing her forever was the only thing worse.

Zara blinked. "Portland? I've never been there, either."

"You tried, Wade, but I don't think it worked," Jacob said sadly.

"Wade? Who's Wade?" Zara kept staring at me.

I pulled her back into a hug as Jacob took up a syringe. "It doesn't matter. You just need to sleep, and you'll feel better. Just remember: you're safe and you're going to be taken care of. We'll get you through this, one way or another." My gaze drifted up to meet Wade's. Tears welled in his eyes. I knew he was thinking about another scared young girl, just like me.

Jacob injected the sedative. A few moments later, Zara's body relaxed in my arms. I rolled her back onto the bed and tucked the blanket around her. On the other side, Wade fluffed her pillow. Anything to make the poor kid more comfortable. But it was like putting a band-aid on a severed leg. She'd wake up again, and the re-experiencing would come back. And we might not be here when that happened.

"It looks like we're at another dead end." Jacob dropped the syringe into the hazardous materials bin. "I'd say these two are the lucky ones, since at least they came back, but they've still got a long road ahead."

"Are there specialists who can help?" I took two tissues from the box on the bedside table and passed one to Wade.

Jacob nodded. "Astrid is arranging for them to come and take these two to a special facility."

"Like the one in Paris?" My heart lurched. Odette had been murdered in one of those places. She'd still been granted her happy ending with Remington, in an otherworld somewhere. But she'd been a Librarian, while Zara was an ordinary magical. Who was to say that the people who did this wouldn't find Zara and finish the job? What would be her happy ending, then?

"It's higher security than Paris. They'll be safe there." Jacob turned away. His shoulders sagged wearily. He and Alyssa didn't have children yet, but I knew they'd been trying for a while. A long while, actually. Perhaps he was putting himself in a father's shoes, imagining how he'd feel if Zara were his.

Somehow, things like this felt sadder when they happened to the young. I guessed that was why Persie's situation hurt so much. She'd lived eighteen years, and now she probably thought her life was over. All because that stupid snake had "gifted" her something she didn't want. Something that would make everyone look at her differently.

But not me, and not your dad. We'd never look at her differently.

"Should I test Howard's response to me?" We might as well settle this now, so we could report that we'd made the tiniest step of progress.

Jacob turned back around. He looked tired. "Yeah, let's try it."

Leaving Zara to her artificial sleep, I crossed to Howard. He hadn't made a peep since we'd come in; he just kept staring at the opposite wall. I approached with caution, but he didn't seem to notice me.

"Howard?" I said tentatively.

He whirled around. For a second, he did nothing. Then, to my horror, he screamed so loud I thought my eardrums might burst. I staggered away from him and put my hands up in a gesture of peace. But he didn't stop. His screaming continued as he tried to shuffle away from me. With a panicked expression, Jacob approached him from the other side. But the moment he saw Jacob, he stopped and sat still and quiet, returning to his staring competition with the wall.

After a few silent, breathless seconds, Jacob sighed. "I guess that's my theory out the window." He took another syringe and injected Howard, who quickly flopped back and started to snore. Jacob's brow furrowed before he went on. "But Howard's reaction, it looked more like conditioning, or reinforcement. I'm not saying it's definitely deliberate, but he had a pretty intense response. More intense than Zara's response to me or Wade."

"Why would someone do that?" Wade approached me and held out a steadying hand. The fright had almost knocked me to the ground.

Jacob smiled faintly. "Do you remember how Finch put a dent in that love spell when he was in Atlantis? You know, he started feeling like things were off when he should've been head over heels?"

"He won't shut up about it, especially when he's in the doghouse with Ryann." My heart rate finally slowed to a normal pace.

"It could be that the people who did this are trying to

prevent a similar problem. Howard has a wife. Maybe his torturers thought he might remember something if he made it back to her, so they conditioned him not to say a word, on top of the mind-wiping." Jacob took off his latex gloves with an elastic snap. "It would explain the differing reactions. But it's only speculation. It could just as easily be the simpler explanation—Zara had a male torturer; Howard had a female."

Wade went up to the bed and put his hands on Howard's temples. "There's an easier way to find out if you're right." As before, he sent in the white threads, and then the pink. I watched him concentrate until he came out of his focused trance.

"Well?" I prompted.

"There have been serious cowboys tromping through there. More damage across his brain, as a whole. They definitely added something extra that's not in Zara." Wade lowered his hands. "Whether that fits your hypothesis or not, I don't know. But, these two have been mind-wiped in very customized ways. Another fact that points to someone very powerful performing these spells. I wonder if it's the same across the board for the returnees."

Jacob pulled out his phone and wafted a hand over the disc. "I'll update Astrid and see if she can get you in to see any more of the victims. There might be some red tape to cut. But that's your thing, isn't it?" He meant it as a joke, but it hit a nerve. One that had been bugging me a lot recently.

I want that quieter world. Being Secret Agent Harley and running through mission after mission had lost its sheen. A long time ago, to be honest. The Merlin legacy came with a crap ton of responsibility. And it was exhausting. Ten years ago, maybe even five years ago, I was still riding the wave. Now it had crested, and I felt beached. I was tired of seeing sad things and cleaning up the mess, only to take it all home with me.

"You know us," Wade replied with a grin. "We eat red tape for breakfast."

But what if I've lost the taste for it? I was tired of everyone looking to me for salvation, because, well… it *hurt* to take on their problems. They became my problems. My emotions. My stress, my strain, my energy. Yes, I'd saved the world. I'd had to. But maybe Persie was right—not everything had to be life and death.

"Harley?" Wade gave me a nudge.

I forced a smile. "Our favorite meal."

Wade gestured to the two sleeping figures. "The number of vanishing magicals is steady, but we need to get ahead of it before it gets worse."

Around me, Wade and Jacob continued to talk about important matters, but my mind wandered to the idea of that quieter life. Where my decisions and duties weren't filled with danger, other people's suffering, and wild goose chases. I wanted career fulfilment that didn't rely on the turn of a key in a prison lock as the endgame. I wanted to help people, but in a career where there weren't such high stakes—maybe working with children who needed care.

"It's going to need a special task force. I'll speak to O'Halloran about it on our way out. Hopefully, the UCA won't take their time in agreeing. Harley?"

"Huh?" I snapped out of it.

"What do you think?" Wade pressed.

I sighed. "I think it's time to dig deeper and get to the bottom of this."

I'd fight until I had no fight left in me. A quieter life would have to wait.

FIFTEEN

Persie

Technically I was eighteen, but I might as well have been eighty. Gritty sand had replaced my corneas, my lymph nodes had swollen to the size of golf balls, and my internal organs felt as though they'd done a couple of switcheroos on me. My heart had definitely found a new home in my throat, and I'd forgotten what it felt like to not have my stomach churning like I was in the middle of a continuous ferry voyage. Multiple Purges in a short space of time would do that to a girl. Not to be blasé about it, but I was already sick and tired of this curse.

I slumped on a chair in one of the Physical Magic training rooms. "How has it only been two days since my birthday?"

It felt like weeks, and Leviathan's gift had been the one that just kept on giving. A foolish part of me had hoped it would be an infrequent thing, this Purging lark—perhaps once a week, or once a month, something manageable.

Instead, I'd been hit with five Purges in two days. In an effort to lessen the collateral damage of my Purges, I'd seen very little except the inside of my bedroom after returning from Tobe's den. I didn't want to admit it, but I'd been glad to have my mom and dad around. They'd bottled up my Purge monsters as fast as I'd Purged them. Fortunately, the beasts hadn't been as violent as the hydra, but they'd made up for it in quantity. They'd been smaller beasts, though my mom hadn't given me much chance to see what I'd created, which part of me also felt glad about. But the terror of feeling the Purge coming hadn't abated. I doubted it would for a long time—another part of the so-called "mastery" that would miraculously make sense, according to Leviathan.

So much for handling it myself. So far, it was the opposite of what I wanted out of life, which was how Genie and I had ended up in here. Alyssa had agreed to let us use the room to work through some beast-catching tactics. But so far all I'd done was struggle to stay awake. Purges, as it turned out, could come at any moment. Even in the middle of the night, waking me from rare sleep.

"Time is a fickle mistress when she wants to be." Genie jogged over and hauled me up. "No snoozing on the job."

"What job?" I resisted the tug of her hands. "I just want to sleep forever."

"Not on my watch, Sleeping Beauty." She tried to pull me up again. "You said it yourself, the only way to control this is to control the monsters. Getting ahead of this is right at your fingertips—I can feel it. Which is why I'm here to help you learn."

I sighed. "Tobe said something similar."

"And Tobe is the Beast Master for a reason." She pulled me out of the chair and led me to the center of the room, with me dragging my heels the entire way.

"Is it way too bright in here, or is it just me?" I shielded my eyes against the glare of sunlight that bulldozed through the windows. The Physical Magic room reminded me of a dance studio—not that me and my terrible coordination had ever been inside a dance studio. Well, not without immediately being kicked out again for the safety of everyone else. Mirrors lined one wall, with a mahogany-beamed ceiling overhead. Scuffed parquet floor gave way to large, gray squares of springy stuff, intended to lessen the impact of any falls between competitors. It looked so cozy, primed for curling up and dozing off.

Genie kept a hand on my arm to stop me from running back to the sidelines. "I think you Purging your very own quintet might have something to do with it."

I lolled against her. "Only five? I thought it was more. I definitely blacked out during one of them." I had to make a joke out of it, or I would actually stop to think about the monsters that had come out of me. Every time I dwelled on it for more than a minute, it wigged me out completely—on top of the exhaustion factor.

"Here. I brought you a present in case you started to get tired of this, so I probably should've given it to you before we even came down here, but hey." She left me standing and sprinted for her bag. Hurrying back, she pushed a flask into my hands.

"Coffee?"

She laughed. "Something much, much better."

I unscrewed the top and took a whiff. My nose wrinkled instantly as my nostrils stung against the scent of something fishy. Nope, *rotten* and fishy, with a hint of sour milk. "What is it? Or do I not want to know?"

"It's an Atlantean brew for stamina and energy." Genie tipped it to my lips. "You get used to the taste after a while."

"Because it burns off your taste buds?" I closed my eyes and took a sip. Regret slid across my tongue and down my throat. It didn't just smell rotten, it tasted rotten, with a frogspawn consistency that added insult to injury. In all my life, I'd never tasted anything like it—sour and foul, with a potent taste of the sea, if the sea had gone bad.

"It'll make you feel better." She smiled, but we'd never been good at keeping secrets from each other. I could read her like my favorite book. And, on this particular chapter, I saw concern in her gray eyes, glittering with a touch of anxiety.

I gulped down another mouthful for her sake. "I think it's more likely to make me hurl, and then Purge again."

"What? No! Put it down!" Genie's bravado cracked like an eggshell. Ironic, since everyone except her had been tiptoeing around me since my birthday. "It was supposed to help you!" She lunged for the flask, but I lifted it out of her reach.

"I was kidding," I reassured her, though my friend's alarm didn't inspire much confidence. It looked like I wasn't the only one trying to figure all of this out.

Her face relaxed. "Oh, thank Chaos. I thought you meant it."

"Are you bothered by it?" My stomach clenched, not sure if I wanted to hear the answer.

Her expression transformed into a mask of astonishment. "No, of course not. You're still you. I just hate that it's affecting you like this, and no one would let me near you the past two days."

"Maybe this is why." I waggled the flask at her and coughed up a halfhearted chuckle, plus a glob of whatever I'd just swallowed. It was far worse on the way up than it'd been on the way down.

She sighed heavily and looked toward the mirrored wall, watching our reflection. "I should've been there, even if it was just to hold your hair back."

"My mom really sent you away?" I would've liked to have my friend there, if only to keep me sane within the four walls of my bedroom. Someone to keep me entertained instead of fretting all the time.

Genie put her arm around my shoulders. "I think she wanted it to stay in the family for a while, at least with everyone still gossiping about what happened. Don't worry, though. I've been smacking silencing spells on everyone I've overheard. Got myself an official warning from Old Halloran for my efforts."

"Genie!" I gasped. I admired her chutzpah, but taking such a huge risk wouldn't do anyone any good. If anything, it would be inclined to make folks more afraid of me if they knew my best friend had turned vigilante.

"What? I'm not too scared to defend the honor of my best friend. I think O'Halloran understood, but he had to give me some kind of punishment, or people would've thought he was playing favorites." She met my mirror image with sad eyes, determination clear in the set of her lips.

"Well, maybe ease up on the silencing spells. I don't want you getting kicked out because of me." I leaned into her, feeling a faint buzz vibrating through me. The Atlantean brew, and whatever sordid things had been blended up to concoct it, were starting to work their magic.

Genie grinned. "I'll save them for the worst offenders." She spun me around to face her. "Now, what do you say we start beast-catching?"

"About that." I took a deep breath, hoping my stomach would settle. "I'm not even sure I *can* catch them."

"Tobe wouldn't have suggested it if you couldn't," she pointed out, not taking any of my nonsense.

"But I'm not a magical."

Genie still wasn't having it. "Five Purge beasts say otherwise."

"This curse hasn't given me any additional abilities—I've tried. And if I don't have any Chaos aside from this Purging business, then I don't have the juice to catch what I create." The gray square of springy stuff looked comfier by the moment. Perhaps, if I slept long enough, I'd wake up and find that none of this had happened. "Maybe it'd be better if they locked me up in the Bestiary. I mean, it's not always going to be smaller beasts, is it? At least then I wouldn't be a risk to anyone."

She held onto me and ushered me toward the mirrored wall. "What do you see, Persie?"

"A very tired, grumpy, fed-up girl." The plump, purple bags under my eyes could've seen me through a trip around the world, and my skin seemed so thin and translucent that I could see the bluish tentacles of my veins. A map of my existence, marked on my flesh.

"Do you know what I see?" Genie's voice softened with her expression. "I see *you*. I don't see the curse, just my smart, funny, creative best friend. And do you know what else I see?"

I glanced at her. "What?"

"Strength. So much strength." She sounded proud and sad, all at once. "You demanded that your mom take you to face Leviathan. You could've run or tried to hide from this, but you didn't. You stood up at your party and you let everyone know you weren't going to let this beat you. The Purges have taken it out of you, but you can push through. I've seen you do it before. I've seen you stay up all night to finish a painting, or a book, or cram for a test. You've always finished what you started, and I've always been there to wave the pom-poms. I know you can do it again. And I'm going to be here, cheering you on the whole damn way."

I reached deep to drag myself away from the edge of a pit of despair. "Do you promise one thing?"

"Anything," she replied, not missing a beat.

"No more special brews." I adored this girl. No one did motivational speeches quite like her, and having my own personal cheerleader felt nothing short of incredible. It was the fire I needed to get over my fatigue and my fear.

She flung her arms around me and pulled me into a bear hug. "You've got yourself a deal."

A few minutes later, we stood on opposite sides of the gray fighting square. And I may or may not have felt like a prize idiot, clutching a Mason jar in one hand and a bag of entrapment stones in the other, with no idea what to do with either. Genie had dug a book out of her bag called *Art of the Hunt* by someone named Victoria Jules. A list of practice drills took up the first four chapters, and we were trying out a few of them.

"Pretend I'm that hydra, but with fewer heads." Genie stuck out her hands like naked sock puppets, making them twist and snap like raptors as she stalked up and down the far edge.

I covered my mouth and laughed into my palm. "How am I supposed to take this seriously when you do that?"

"Hey, I'm giving you my best monster moves here." Genie put her hands on her hips. "Should I pretend to be something a bit more human? A vampire, maybe?" She pulled a funny face, her lips retracting to show her perfect teeth. She gnashed them together, as frightening as a mildly irritated bunny.

I set down the jar and the stones. "I don't think this is going to work without a real monster. I won't know if I can actually do it. It's not like I can catch *you* in a jar."

"Are you feeling Purgey?" Genie arched a hesitant eyebrow. After her last reaction to me potentially Purging, she was evidently worried about the prospect. And who could blame her? I had no clue what might come out if I *did* Purge. Spinning the roulette wheel of beasts wasn't a game I wanted to play, even with Genie here as backup. If it escaped and ran rampant through the SDC, we'd be in humongous trouble.

I paused and searched for any of the usual symptoms— cold sweats, itchy eyes and skin, a burning in my chest, and the sudden influx of saliva you got when you were about to be sick. I had the itchy eyes, but that had nothing to do with Purging; only a side effect of the sleepless nights.

"I don't think so," I replied, semi-hopefully.

She tapped her chin in thought. "Well, if you want to try with a real one, maybe we could ask Tobe to borrow one? You know, for safety's sake." Her eyes widened in a lightbulb moment. "Oh, or we could take a look at some material from the Basani Institute. I read an article about it the other night, after your mom kicked me out."

"The *what* institute?" The name rang a bell.

"Basani Institute. Home of the Monster Hunters." She nodded her head excitedly. "They've developed these puzzle box things that bypass the need for entrapment stones. Very... uh, what's that film your uncle dressed up as for Halloween?"

"*Ghostbusters?*" I remembered Diana dying of embarrassment when he'd turned up in a khaki boiler suit, pretending to skid a box at her feet. Although the embarrassment might've had more to do with him licking Ryann's face and calling himself "Slimer."

"That's the one!" Genie shouted triumphantly. "And those things are way more efficient than entrapment stones, if you believe what you read on the internet."

I bought into her infectious enthusiasm. "Do you think we could get our hands on some?"

"If you name drop hard enough, I reckon we might be able to." Genie winked. "There are perks to having the Merlin name."

After two days of hurling up Purge beasts, I was ready for a dose of hope. Leviathan's shadow loomed over me, but shadows couldn't thrive in the light. If I fed the flames of optimism, maybe I could chase Leviathan so far away that I could almost pretend this wasn't his fault.

"Don't find fault, find a remedy," I thought aloud.

Genie frowned. "Huh?"

"Henry Ford."

"The old car guy?"

I nodded absently. He wasn't my usual source of wisdom, but his words cemented the determination in my heart. I needed to make a change in my life if I wanted to deal with these Purges myself. And that had to start at the very beginning—with my mom.

SIXTEEN

Persie

R eturning to an empty apartment in the Fleet Wing—
named after the former site of the SDC—I sought
refuge in my bedroom. I had every intention of waiting for
my mom to come back from wherever she was, but the
Purges had taken their toll. Ensconced in the comfy covers,
sleep tempted me like a wanton mistress.

Where is everyone? My exhausted mind struggled to focus.
But with my smoky offshoots keeping them on constant
guard, it seemed odd that my parents would suddenly disappear. Then again, I had them on speed dial and they could
chalk-door to me in about five seconds flat, so I supposed it
wasn't a massive deal. A note had been pinned to the fridge:
*Dealing with coven business. Back soon. Ring IMMEDIATELY if
you get Purge symptoms.* But no specifics, like when they'd left
or how long "soon" would be.

"Here's hoping I don't Purge before they get back," I whispered to the ancient stuffed bear on my bed. My beloved Thread Bear, a name given to him by my Uncle Finch. He didn't reply, but I sensed him listening, and that gave me comfort enough to drift off.

I stirred to the whine of a flying bug. My eyes opened slowly while my hand swatted on instinct, sending the buzzing critter on its way. Above me hung a dense canopy of humungous, dark green leaves, with cerulean sky poking through. Yellowed moss clung to moist tree trunks, and creeping vines swayed like hidden pythons. The humidity covered me in a sticky glaze, turning the air viscous. Even the boughs of the jungle trees seemed heavy and languid, buckling under the sweltering heat of the tropical atmosphere.

I sat up to better gauge my surroundings. My limbs were cooperating, my lungs were taking in the thick air, and my eyes were definitely looking at this jungle terrain, but my mind whispered, *None of this is real.* I'd gone to sleep and tumbled headfirst into a dream.

Please, not another monster dream. I've had enough of monsters for a while. I waited for the crash and crack of something charging toward me through the fecund undergrowth. But nothing came except the sounds of the jungle—the creak of tree branches, the rustle of animals hidden in the greenery, and the drip of condensation hitting lower leaves.

"I haven't been in a dream jungle for ages." I spoke aloud to ground myself in the dream, hearing my voice among the sound of the trees and the hidden critters.

I got to my feet and wiped the sweat off my brow. I expected my t-shirt and leggings to cling, since that was what I'd gone to sleep in. But glancing down, I realized I wasn't dressed for bed anymore. A floaty white dress of gauzy cotton trailed all the way down to the ground, adorned with a lion-head pin at each shoulder. I fumbled for my hair and felt loose curls and two hard barrettes on either side of my head. Unclipping one, I stared at the unfamiliar item. Shaped in gold to look like a harp, or a lyre, the entire thing glittered with sapphires and diamonds.

"Weird." I slotted it back into my hair and squinted around. The lack of monsters had me puzzled.

I'm here, so now what? A loud splash drew my attention. I whipped around, trying to locate the sound, but the jungle and its lush flora and fauna muffled everything.

I stood perfectly still, and another splash rewarded me. It came from up ahead. Gathering the flowing skirts of my dress, I tiptoed toward the sound. A moment later, I froze on the steep edge of a hole in the ground. One more step, and I would've fallen right into it. With my heart racing, I looked down into the hole and saw a deep pool beneath me. The water lay perfectly calm and impossibly clear, tinged with vivid turquoise.

A cenote. A natural underground reservoir of water. Santana and the Catemaco-Levis had spoken about them a few times after their yearly trips to Mexico, talking about how they were usually filled with kids dive-bombing and swinging into the pool. Not this one, though. And there was one other person here: a shadowed figure of a man, standing in the middle of a narrow suspension bridge that crossed over the pool. He had his back to me, a hood over his head. At least I thought it was a hood, but it might have been part of him.

My feet began to move without my permission, heading to the suspension bridge. Putting one hand on the rope banister, my heart beat with sudden urgency—but this time, the urgency came from *him*. I had to reach the shadowy man. I didn't fear him or his shadowy form; I feared he would disappear before I could get to him.

"Who are you?" I called, walking tentatively down the bridge. It swayed violently, but my eyes fixed dead ahead. I wasn't afraid. If it snapped, the pool would catch me. If I didn't reach him in time, I felt I would lose something inexplicably valuable.

The silence turned thick, like everything else in the jungle.

"Tell me who you are." I hurried faster along the rope bridge. He didn't answer, though I thought I saw his head dip to his chest.

My feet hit the solid planks of wood and I ran for him, hand outstretched. I barely slowed when I touched his shoulder. My fingertips passed straight through him. A cold sensation shivered up my hand, as though I'd stuck it into an ice bucket. Still, I didn't feel any fear, only confusion.

"Hello?" I shouted, the rock walls of the cenote throwing my voice back to me. The perfect, natural echo chamber.

"Here you are."

I spun around in surprise, but there was no one there. The reply had come from inside my head. A voice I recognized.

"Leviathan?" I whispered, not wanting the name to echo back.

"My Persephone," he said.

I scanned the platform and noticed two drying footprints where the shadow man had stood. "Why are you in my dream?"

"We parted on bad terms, and I wished to make amends. I am sorry that I alarmed you. It was not my intention." His voice susurrated all around me.

"Are you sorry for giving this curse to me?" I looked up at the edge of the cenote, trying to spot that figure again.

Leviathan chuckled. "I will say it again: it is a gift. It is yours. It has always been yours. It is your legacy."

My legacy? Hadn't I longed for one of my own? Perhaps, that age-old saying had come back to bite me: *be careful what you wish for.* Or, perhaps, this really could be the start of something. A way to put myself on the map. I beamed giddily at the thought, my entire being floating on a wave of sudden positivity, my head swimming with the warmth of the jungle. Purging monsters didn't have to be a death knell to life as I knew it. Purge beasts powered the Bestiary. Their energy was invaluable. What if I could turn it into something useful?

"I see that you are thinking." Leviathan disturbed me again. "Thinking is beneficial. The sooner you come to accept this, the better it will be for you." Silence echoed in my head briefly before he continued. "I must confess that I lied to you before."

I sucked in a syrupy breath. "What do you mean?"

"I *do* want more than to get to know you. I want to help you," Leviathan admitted. "I could not say so in front of your mother. She would never believe it. She would think there were conditions to my help. There are not. I want you to do well, and to succeed. That is all."

I shuffled to the edge of the platform, my eyes wide and excited. That warm feeling sank deeper into my chest, coating my heart in honeyed delight. "You want to help me?"

"More than anything." I could almost feel him smiling inside my head. "Come to me. I will show you the truth. I will show you the world. I will show you what it could be like."

The shadow man appeared again on the other side of the rope bridge. My heart jolted with that same fear of losing him, whoever he was. Was he Leviathan? Or someone else? I had no idea, but everything inside me wanted to follow him. I darted across the platform and up the rope bridge, Leviathan's words falling away. The shadow man disappeared again, only to reappear a short distance away, one arm leaning casually against a moss-speckled tree.

I have to know who you are! I sprinted after him. The pattern repeated, over and over. I got close and he vanished, then reappeared again, leading me on a frantic chase through the jungle. I tripped on vines and exposed roots more times than I cared to count, and sweat dripped off me by the bucketload, but I couldn't give up. I had to know.

Suddenly, I skidded to a halt at the perimeter of a clearing. An overgrown plinth rested in the middle, and on top of the plinth, a large glass box, snarled up in so many creepers that it looked like it'd been strapped down. Dark blue flowers spotted the thick vines, their leaves bright white aside from thin tiger stripes of sea green. It looked like the box had been here for a long time.

"Where are you?" I cried out, moving closer. I couldn't lose him. I had to be near him. He made me feel floaty and light, euphoric in a way that I hadn't in... forever.

The shadow man appeared behind the plate glass, dark palms pressed to the pane. "I am trapped, Persephone. Help me, so I may help you."

I touched my hand to the glass, caressing it. "You said you didn't have any terms." He might have been in a different form, but that voice couldn't have belonged to anyone but Leviathan.

"It is not a term. I can only help you from outside my cage." Leviathan's creepily human eyes showed through the swirling shadow of his face. "Without my body, I am nothing. I cannot give you the help you need. I have to be free."

I pulled my hand back. "But you're in my dream. I don't have the power to free you from here, even if I wanted to."

"You only have to let me out in this dreamworld." His voice swam with anguish, inspiring sorrow in me. I didn't want the shadow man to be sad. "Free me. So I can help you."

"Tell me the truth, first." I stepped away slowly, though my heart urged me to move closer again, and his shadowy fingers raked the glass in desperation.

"The truth... Persephone, this is your destiny." His eyes

shone brightly, mesmerizing me. "You were not born by chance. You were born because Chaos needed you. It needed your strength and integrity. Chaos wanted you to take up my mother's mantle."

I drifted back toward him, hooked by his words. They surrounded me like a woolen blanket on a cold night, making my heart swell. "Chaos needs *me?*"

"You are the generator. You are the personification of its cosmic energy. You *are* power itself." His voice lulled me into a dopey smile, and my chest swelled with the prospect of being important.

"I like the sound of that." I giggled and quickly covered my mouth. Nothing about this should've been funny, but I couldn't help it. Laughter just bubbled up of its own accord. The colors of the jungle were so bright, and his eyes looked so inviting. I had nothing to fear from him. It was only a dream.

Leviathan pushed a hand against the glass, and it turned weirdly human, though tinged with blue and green and black. "Release me into your dreamworld, Persephone. Let me aid you."

Drawn by his hypnotic voice and the magnetic pull of a light that glowed in the darkness of the enclosure, I approached the door to his prison. All the while, my eyes stayed fixed on that throbbing light. My hands came up as though they belonged to someone else, but I didn't mind. He'd made a persuasive case for his freedom, and what harm could he do within the parameters of my dreamworlds? *He promised to help. He wants me to succeed.* Chaos *wants me to succeed.* My woozy brain seemed convinced that he had good intentions, but it was too foggy to be sure. Plus, I couldn't really focus on anything other than that steady green flash. Even the verdant greenery of the jungle had faded into the background.

I hesitated moments away from opening the door, though I wasn't sure why. As I paused, a creature dropped down onto the top of the enclosure, snatching my attention away from the spellbinding glow. I had no idea where it had come from, but this beastie wasn't new to me. A fluffy cotton ball of a creature, with two wide, black eyes. They blinked at me now.

This is realer than I think. Through the marshmallow cloud that had become my brain, it proved hard to tell if the thoughts were mine or if they belonged to the strange puff-ball. It sounded like my inner monologue, but who knew? For the first time tonight, a spike of true terror javelined through my heart.

"No." I scrunched my eyes shut and sucked in a deep breath, making myself feel it in my actual lungs. It was cold and dry.

I forced my eyelids open a crack. The jungle no longer existed, replaced with the icy darkness of Leviathan's hall. Right in front of me stood the glass door to the monster's enclosure, my hands a few inches from the lock. I scrambled backward as Leviathan burst out of the black smoke inside, his dagger-like claws scraping the pane.

"Let me aid you. Free me," he implored.

I sleepwalked here! I remembered running through the jungle. Me, chasing the shadow man relentlessly to that clearing. I hadn't run through any kind of jungle—I must've run from my bedroom to the Bestiary, playing Leviathan's twisted game.

"You lied!" I snapped. "You tricked me!"

"It was the only way I could communicate with you." That strange flash drew my eye, emitting from the appendage on his forehead. The angler-fish bulb, used to entice sea creatures closer to his jaws. "But my motive is true. I want to show you what you could be. For that, I need to be out of this cage."

I shook my head, trembling at the thought of how close he'd come to escape. "Even if I had the magic to let you out of your box, I wouldn't trust you as far as I could throw you." I heaved in a steadying breath. "You lied for your own benefit. You tried to hypnotize me into letting you loose. This isn't about helping me at all, it's about helping you!"

"I did not lie about that." Leviathan stretched his mouth in a creepy grin. "This is your destiny."

I took another step back. "What are you talking about?"

"You will rule this world, in the image written in your legend. *This* is your destiny." His bioluminescence pulsed faster.

"*My* destiny? My legend? This is ridiculous! You're making stuff up." I stood my ground, ignoring that flashing orb in case it drew me in again. There was a chance he wasn't making it up, but I wasn't willing to accept that. It sounded like storybook nonsense; something his mother had told him to make him feel better about life in a box.

Leviathan laughed. "Well, not yours alone. We are bound; this, you know. But our bond is deeper than you realize. We will rule over a world of eternal Dark, filled with my brethren. An underworld crafted into the only world. And you will be my queen. It is decreed. The legend of Persephone will come to pass. You will reign over the beasts of Chaos at my side. Their mother. My wife. My *Persephone.*"

Persephone. the name the monster had bestowed upon me. I looked at my attire. It was just my t-shirt and leggings again, but in the dreamworld it had been distinctly *Grecian.* Was my name more than just a name? Was it about the myth herself?

Abducted by a smitten Hades, the young Persephone was trapped in his underworld against her will. Her mother, Demeter—the goddess of the harvest—looked high and low for her, until Helios—the all-seeing sun—finally took pity and told Demeter what had happened to her daughter. Nothing of the earth had grown while Demeter despaired, and the people pleaded with Zeus for help as their bodies grew weak. Zeus forced Hades to return Persephone to her mother.

But it was too late. Persephone had already eaten six pomegranate seeds. And, in Greek mythology, if a person ate food from their captor, they were bound to them. To save the people from starvation, an exchange had to be made. Persephone would spend part of the year in the underworld, at Hades' side, and the rest of her time would be spent on the surface, with her mother. That was why the harvest came in seasons; life grew when Demeter's daughter could visit her, but when Persephone was forced to return to her dark husband, Demeter's despair overtook her once more.

Persephone, the goddess of the underworld.

"No." I backed away, bile rising in my throat. "I don't want any part in *that*. You're not getting out, and you're not having your underworld on Earth. I'll stop you, and that starts with keeping you in that box! You can rot in it, for all I care!"

It's just a name. And those ancient legends had nothing to do with me. They'd expired when the Ancient Greek deities fell out of favor, if the original Persephone had even existed at all.

"The monsters deserve freedom. Sooner or later, you will come to understand that the magical world has been living on borrowed time. Its exploitation of monsters must end. We are not fuel." Leviathan showed no sign of concern, like he could already see the endgame in sight. "You cannot fight this."

"I *will* fight it," I seethed.

"Not when you see that they are your brethren, too." Leviathan grinned, his teeth snapping together. "My gift will show you the truth. You will see what it is like to be one of us. And you will understand, at last."

The hall door burst open and Tobe tore in on all fours, his claws clacking on the marble as he barreled toward me. In one smooth movement, he scooped me up into his furry arms and waved a paw at Leviathan's enclosure. A thrumming shield went up, blocking him from view. But not before Leviathan had the last word.

"You are a traitor to your kind, Tobe! I will have a special place in my hell for you!"

Tobe didn't dignify Leviathan with a response. Instead, he carried me right out of there, so close to his chest that I heard the rapid drumming of his heartbeat through his fur. He might not have shown it on his stoic face, but he was afraid. And that made two of us.

SEVENTEEN

Persie

———————————

B ack in Tobe's forest dwelling, I finally got to see the inside of his cottage. I sat in an armchair, enveloped in an oversized tartan beside a roaring fire, clutching a cup of coffee between shaky hands. It looked like any countryside cottage might—quaint and homey, with too much crammed inside—only everything had to be bigger to accommodate a Beast Master. Unfortunately, even the sight of Tobe-sized couch cushions couldn't warm the chill inside my heart.

A bird flapped past the window, casting a dark shadow that made me sink deeper into the armchair. It perched on the sill, with sleek black feathers and glinting black eyes. Just a raven, or was it an omen to round off this weird night? As a chill pinched my spine, Bram Stoker's Dracula sprang to mind. *"Come, we must see and act. Devils or no devils, or all the devils at once, it matters not; we fight him all the same."*

"Are you feeling unwell? I could concoct a sleeping brew

instead of coffee, if you require it." Tobe crouched on his haunches, his golden eyes a burnished bronze in the firelight.

I burrowed deeper into the plush cushions. "I'll be alright. I think it's just shock." Truth be told, I felt hideous. Worse than during the training session with Genie, worse than after my last few Purges. And the warning signs that threatened another spewing session were all in place—a cold sweat up the nape of my neck, a quickened pulse, a churning stomach.

"Your parents are on their way," Tobe assured. "They can take you back to your room whenever you feel ready."

"Tobe?" I lifted my weary head to meet his gaze. "Why didn't you see me on the security system?"

His furry brow furrowed. "It is as mysterious to me as it is to you. I happened to be on my rounds when I heard your voice. I believe Leviathan may have deciphered a path of blind spots through the Bestiary that avoids the mirrors, guiding you along it while you were sleeping." He growled uncomfortably. "I will install more mirrors as soon as you have been safely returned to your bed."

"Do you think he could have figured out something similar for the rest of the coven? I walked a long way, and nobody stopped me." If that monster had a grasp of the SDC's layout, then he already had too much information.

Tobe nodded reluctantly. "I think that is a logical specula- tion. After all, we know he visited your mother in the infir- mary, after you were born. That would have required some knowledge of that kind." He turned to stare into the fire. "I will ask Astrid to heighten security in the hallways, and to look over the recordings from this evening. You should not have been able to get so far without someone sounding the alarm."

"Thank you, Tobe." I let the warmth of the coffee cup feed my numb fingers. "Thank you for coming to get me."

"I would never allow any harm to come to you, Miss Persie. You are dear to me." A purr rumbled in the back of his throat. "However, I must ask a question. What did he say to bring you so near his enclosure?"

As I relayed the ominous news that Leviathan had given me, Tobe's ears flicked back and forth like honed radar dishes. And, when I finished, he covered my hands with his paws.

"Pay him no heed. I do not know how to prevent him from entering your dreams, and for that I am sorry, but if his physical form stays incarcerated, he is limited. None of this will come to pass. Together, we will prevent it," he insisted.

I wanted to believe him, but Leviathan had looked so complacent about my refusal. As if he was so certain that I'd come around, that he didn't even need to contemplate failure. Still, hearing Tobe's words gave me a shred of comfort.

Then again, Tobe is one of the free Purge beasts... He could go where he liked, more or less. Maybe he didn't understand how it felt to be locked up in the way that Leviathan and the other Purge beasts did. Which could mean that he didn't appreciate the enormity of their resolve.

"I wish he'd stuck his 'gift' where the sun doesn't shine," I muttered.

Tobe mustered a stiff chuckle. "I know you do, Miss Persie. We all do, but we should not think like that. The past and the present cannot be changed. Only the future can, and that will depend on your strength of character. For what it's worth, I would trust that feature of yours to the ends of the Earth."

"Good, because it might be the end of the Earth if I mess up." I gazed into the coffee cup and inhaled the soothing scent.

"If you are the Persie Merlin-Crowley that I know, there is no chance of it." He laid his head on the armrest. I resisted the urge to stroke his soft fur, though I knew he wouldn't have minded.

Just then, my mom and dad arrived. The door swung open on their pale, terrified faces, and they didn't pause for any niceties. They ran toward me and I sprang up from the armchair, falling into their welcoming arms.

"What happened, Persie?" my mom asked in a tone that was at once fearful and relieved.

My dad hugged us both to him. "Are you all right? We thought you were with Genie, or we'd never have left the apartment."

"I came back early." I clung to them as if they were a lifeboat in a treacherous storm. "And I fell asleep. That's how it started." Taking a deep breath, I repeated the story I'd just told Tobe.

"The legend of Persephone?" Mom said. "Well, for starters, I'm not a goddess and he's not Hades. And he's not tricking you into being his wife with any pomegranate seeds, so how's he planning to make this happen?" My mom had her action hat on. Otherwise known as her coping mechanism. "I might get in touch with Erebus or Lux, see if they have any information—they know Chaos better than anyone."

I nodded in agreement. "Or you could summon Remington and see what he knows about any Chaos legends regarding Persephone, since he's the Child of Darkness—see if they differ, or how it could play out without the usual characters. Either way, I have no clue how he intends to do it." My throat lurched strangely, somewhere between a hiccup and a dry heave.

Oh no. Not now...

"As I have said to Miss Persie, as long as Leviathan remains inside his enclosure, he cannot hurt anyone." Tobe raised himself back up onto two feet. "And I intend to increase our security measures once you have departed."

"You were right all along, Persie," my mom said, looking at me as if she were seeing me for the first time. "You must've sensed what was coming, deep in your subconscious."

I squinted. "What do you mean?"

"You have to get away. We have to find a way to keep you from the Bestiary altogether." She paced, leaving my dad to keep hugging me. Another one of her coping mechanisms. "Leviathan clearly has a way of slipping around obstacles and getting into your head, but maybe he couldn't if we got you far enough away."

"But what about my Purges?" The thought of being away from the SDC no longer comforted me. I hadn't got a handle on this Purging yet. But I couldn't deny the logic. Like a radio signal, the farther I got from the transmitter, the lower the strength of the transmission, at least in theory.

I can't always rely on my parents or Tobe to bail me out. If Tobe hadn't walked by Leviathan's hall, I would've had to get myself out of that situation. And, though I was afraid, I knew from my dream that I was capable. With Hell on Earth on the table, I *had* to take myself out of the equation. It was time I stepped up to my legacy, and not the legacy Leviathan had spoken about.

It was time to live up to the Merlin legacy. The thought gave me a sudden rush of confidence, which quickly gave way to...

"We'll find a way to deal with—" My dad's words got cut short by my body buckling out of his arms. I flopped to the ground on all fours, my muscles wrenching to throw up the latest smoke beast. I might not have been able to control the Purges or what came out, but I'd come to terms with the different Purge sensations. And this one felt small. No ring of black fire, no cracking bones. Manageable.

The smoke poured out of my mouth onto the floor, taking shape before I'd finished hurling it into existence: webbed feet and a leathery back, with dark wings unfurling. Its bright blue scales glinted with a sheen like a gas spill, flecked with pinks and purples and darker blues that shifted between colors with the flicker of firelight. A gaping mouth appeared, filled with sharp, dripping fangs and a slavering tongue that dribbled black goop onto the floor. Above that, two beady eyes darted around the cottage. For a moment, it fixed those eyes on me and its head dipped strangely, sort of like a bow.

"A gargoyle!" My mom whipped a Mason jar off one of Tobe's shelves and slid it under the creature. Meanwhile, my dad clattered down a bag full of entrapment stones, where green light-ropes shot out and lashed across the creature. It howled as the ropes dragged it down to the floor, trying to bite at its restraints. With its shrieks ringing in my ears, it began to disintegrate back into smoke, filtering into the waiting jar. I knew it had to be done, but that sound—it stuck with me a while. There'd been despair in its fight, like any creature struggling for its freedom.

"It looked odd, didn't it?" My dad collected the jar and screwed on the lid.

My mom nodded. "I haven't seen a blue one before."

"I shall contend with this." Tobe took the jar from my dad and cast me a remorseful look. "Take care of yourself, Miss Persie. And, remember, you have the strength to combat this. I know you do."

"We should get you home." My dad helped me to my feet and my mom joined him on my other side, the two of them propping me up as we followed Tobe from the cottage. I homed in on the jar in his paws, where black smoke swirled furiously.

And that sound, that pained sound, rang in my ears. Did any creature really want to be trapped inside a box? Would I fight like that if they came for me?

EIGHTEEN

Persie

_____

"You'll get a stomach ache." My mom eyeballed me across the table as I devoured half a loaf of toast. Crumbs and butter formed a grainy paste around my lips, which I hastily wiped away to get back to shoving food into my mouth.

"Who knew that Purging monsters burned so many calories?" I joked, attempting to look innocent before hastily finishing another piece.

She folded up her newspaper and set it down on the counter. "Are you going somewhere?" She nodded to my athleisure fashion statement: an old gray t-shirt with a worn-out slogan for some bar that didn't exist anymore, and a stolen pair of my mom's high-performance, breathable, expensive sports leggings.

"I said I'd meet Genie." I kept the rest vague.

"Do you think that's a good idea? Now that we know what

Leviathan... uh... wants, perhaps it'd be better if she came to you instead." She didn't sound forbidding, just maternally concerned. Last night had given everyone a shock, especially since that particular monster had revealed he had *romantic* intentions toward me. Ugh. I'd anticipated nightmares filled with that slimeball trying to woo me in a thousand rose-tinted dreamscapes in a thousand sleazy ways, but I'd slept surprisingly well after we got back from the Bestiary. No nightmares, no dreams whatsoever. It was the first good sleep I'd had since my birthday.

I flashed her a crumby smile. "You suspect a surprise corona-tion? He'll jump out of the shadows and slap a crown on my head? Or were you thinking something more along the lines of a dozen roses and a box of chocolates he picked up from the gas station?" I rubbed my tummy. "Actually, chocolate doesn't sound so bad." I obviously didn't mean it, but she looked so jumpy and weirded out. I just wanted to soften those hard edges a little bit.

"While I appreciate the comedy show, this is serious... and seriously disturbing." She clenched her coffee mug so tight I worried it might shatter.

"Preaching to the choir, Mom. But if I spend another minute in that bedroom, I might paint myself and become a living mural." I put on what I hoped was a casual smile. "And I don't want to risk napping, in case I end up back at Leviathan's hall, where he actually *might* try to lay on some flirtation. If I keep busy, I'm lessening the chance that he'll slither back into my head."

My mom sighed. "Okay, but don't be gone too long. And

make sure you keep your phone on so you can call if you need me. I've got some things to do, but I'll be there as soon as possible."

"Where's Dad?" I hadn't seen him all morning.

"He went out on some business, but he should be back this afternoon." She stared intently into her coffee, her forehead creased.

Some things... some business. The usual party line when it came to work stuff. The vaguer, the better. Her work took her on all kinds of missions, and I barely knew any of the details, but her frazzled expression piqued my interest.

"Is everything all right?" I wondered if it might be the same thing that had taken them away yesterday.

She looked up. "I hope it will be."

"Have you had a chance to think about what you said last night?" I munched my way through another piece of toast like the Very Hungry Caterpillar.

She pretended to look over the front cover of the newspaper. "Your dad and I are still working on a solution."

"Without me?" I bit back the note of irritation that threatened to seep in.

"No. We're just putting together some ideas, and you're welcome to add your own. We can discuss it as a family when he gets home." She scrunched the corner of the paper.

Oh, I'm welcome *to add some of my own?* Why did I have a sinking feeling that they'd only get shot down? I tore off a chunk of toast and used the mouthful to stop me from saying something I'd regret. After last night, the mood had thawed a bit, and I didn't want to ruin that by turning it into permafrost.

"How about the Children of Chaos? Any luck on that front?" I pressed, anxious for something solid—a foundation to work from.

My mom made a face that told me she was chewing the inside of her cheek. "Erebus said he'd have to think about it, Lux has dropped off the face of the Earth, and Remington is on Chaos business, so he's got a cosmic 'Do Not Disturb' sign on his otherworld. Even Dylan's ring isn't working. I sent a message to Melody, asking for an updated version of the spell or to get a fix for the ring, but she hasn't gotten back to me. At your birthday, she said that she and Luke were about to leave for a two-week expedition to Easter Island for Librarian research into powerful protective hexes. Ones that might still help you. I'm guessing they have no signal out there."

I checked the clock on the oven. "Well, let me know. I need to head out or I'm going to be late." Finishing off my eighth slice of toast, I dusted the crumbs from my face and made my way toward the door.

"Be careful, Persie," she called after me. "And call if anything happens."

I half-rolled my eyes with my back to her. "I will."

"And, Persie?"

I glanced back. "Yes, Mom?"

"You can keep the leggings. They look better on you, anyway." A chuckle followed as I ducked out of the apartment, mortified.

Back in the Physical Magic training room with Genie, I tried to concentrate on getting a Purge going. I must've looked like a complete weirdo, doubled over with burning cheeks and bulging eyes, trying to cough up a beast that didn't want to come out.

Stubborn monsters. They line up to pop out whenever I don't want them.

"I think I've got performance anxiety." I gave a subtle nod in the direction of Kes and Diana, who'd walked into the training room about five minutes after we'd gotten started. They kept to their side, but I noticed occasional glances. Kes looked on with boyish enthusiasm, apparently forgetting that he'd almost had his skull crushed by hydra jaws. Diana's gaze had more affectionate wariness, one hand ready to shoot up and dispense with a beast if it appeared.

Genie smiled. "Don't worry about them. You take all the time you need."

"The setting is wrong." I stopped pushing, terrified I might accidentally fart or something. I was among friends, but still…

She frowned. "You want to go somewhere else and try it?"

"No, that's not what I mean. I can do this anywhere, but it probably won't make a difference. I need to recreate the conditions that caused Purges before." I took deep breaths until my cheeks returned to a normal temperature. "According to Leviathan, it's got a lot to do with emotional state. Anger, sadness, et cetera."

Genie's mouth twisted. "I can't believe you can say that bastard's name without wanting to punch something. Preferably him."

"I'm choosing the high road. Besides, Tobe said that, as long as he's locked up, he can't do anything. I trust Tobe. So I'm focusing on what I *can* control... maybe."

"Then you're a bigger person than I am." Genie picked up her flask of water and took a swig. "But I'll support whatever you choose. With that in mind, which emotion should we start with?"

I thought for a second. "Anger, I guess? It's probably the easiest one, and I don't want to end up in a puddle of tears."

"Hey, Kes, Diana—can you give us a hand with something?" Genie shouted to the duo, who were practicing Physical Magic drills in the opposite corner.

"I guess we're making this a spectator sport," I mumbled.

Kes bounded over, with a more reluctant Diana bringing up the rear. She gave me a knowing look. "You're trying to Purge, aren't you?"

"Only so I can learn how to contain the beasts," I said. Her expression eased a little.

"Well... good for you, Pers." She patted me on the back. "You show these suckers who's boss."

Kes punched the air. "I can't wait to see what comes out of you!"

"You want to try phrasing that differently?" Diana arched a perfect eyebrow at her brother, whose cheeks immediately reddened, deepening the freckles on his face.

"I meant…" He shuffled awkwardly. "Uh… what did you need us for?"

"To throw some insults at our girl here." Genie looked nervous. I guessed she hadn't wanted to bear the sole responsibility of lobbing insults at me. "We have to get her angry, but also try to keep it as civil as possible."

I braced myself, though my stomach had begun to churn nervously. "Say what you like. I'm ready to get furious." I wasn't sure it would work since I already knew their intention, but I supposed it would depend on what they chose to say.

They exchanged uncomfortable glances for a moment before Diana drew in a breath, preparing to throw the first punch. "You… um… you don't get out of your bedroom enough, and it makes you look ill sometimes."

I snorted. I heard that from my mom on a regular basis. "You can go harder than that."

"I feel bad!" Diana protested. "And I can't think of anything to say. If you were an asshole, it'd be simple. Believe me, I'd have the insults locked and loaded."

"You won't ever live up to the Merlin legacy because you don't have any magic!" Kes blurted out, prompting a brief, stunned silence.

"Kes!" Diana shoved him, her eyes wide.

He rubbed his arm, pouting a bit. "What? She said to go harder."

I chuckled. "You're just stating the obvious there, Kes." Although, deep down, I felt a familiar flicker of annoyance. A flame that could be fueled into some kind of powerful emotion, with the right encouragement. Maybe more sadness than anger, but still...

Genie flipped back her long, silver-white braid. "You Purge some ugly-ass beasts, and one almost ate Huntress."

"Not exactly an insult, but this is good. Keep it coming," I urged, closing my eyes.

"Nobody understands your paintings. They don't look like anything." Kes came in with another unexpected dig. But Diana and Genie quickly undid his insult.

"That's because you have the artistic appreciation of a mole rat," Diana shot back.

"Art is in the eye of the beholder," Genie agreed. "It's about feeling and emotional response, not realism."

I opened my eyes to find Kes gawking at them. "She said we had to insult her! I like her paintings too. They're cool. But if I said that, it wouldn't make her angry."

"Oh, right..." Genie flashed me an apologetic look. "This really is hard, Persie."

"Stick with the Merlin thing. Tell me about my shortcomings. Go." I closed my eyes again, anxious but ready to feel some rage.

"Your mom and my dad saved the world, and you can't even save yourself from your own creations." Kes really had a knack for this. I heard him yelp and knew Diana had swatted him. But he'd gotten the ball rolling.

Genie's voice chimed in, hesitantly. "Your mom knows you need to leave, but she's not going to let you do it on your terms. She wants to make all your decisions for you. She screwed up before, and she's still not listening to what you want."

The flame inside me sparked. As far as triggering went, Genie had hit a definite nerve. Then again, she knew me better than anyone. My mom understood that distance was the best way of keeping Leviathan out of my head, but she'd dodged the conversation this morning. Sure, she'd *said* I could add my suggestions to the family pile, but would she actually agree to one of them? Survey said, *no chance.*

"Keep going," I urged. This was good.

"You might not be accepted into another coven because you don't have any magic besides Purging beasts." Diana added a real zinger. "That's no good to anybody. Leave it to you to develop a talent that's worse than nothing at all."

Kes jumped in. "People are afraid of you. They think you might unleash something that will eat everyone alive."

"Your mom and dad don't think you can control these Purge beasts, and I think they might be right. If you mess up, people will die," Genie interjected. Her tone sounded wounded, like she hated saying every word. But it helped. It really, really helped.

My hands automatically balled into defensive fists. Their words were working, but I knew they would never say the whole truth. So I decided to. "Before I was even born, my life wasn't my own. Leviathan had plans for me, my parents had plans for me. Everyone had their opinions and lies and secrets, without stopping to consult me on any of it. They put me at the bottom of the food chain. They think I'm some vulnerable mouse who can't stand up for herself." My eyes opened and strength rode in on a wave of building anger. "Well, they're wrong. I'm every bit a Merlin, magic or no magic, and I'm going to do everything in my power to show them how much they all underestimated me. I'm taking control of my own life. I'm in charge of my future!"

The cold sweats crept in, and my heart palpitated wildly. Familiar pressure clenched my stomach and pushed my lungs to the limits of my ribcage. But I wasn't going to flop forward and endure the indignity of Purging my next beast on all fours. If I wanted to prove I could stand on my own two feet, then I needed to start now... literally. I bent at the waist, doubling over, but I didn't fall. Gritting my teeth, I forced my body to straighten.

With a howl that shook the mirrors, I flung my head back. The torrent of black smoke I unleashed shot upward in a spiraling column then arced back down to the floor, where it took on solid form. On the rear of the beast were bronzed lion legs and a flicking tail, which gave way to a huge, furry body. Eagle feet with sharp talons switched up the forelegs, the vibrant yellow talons blending into the lion fur. A proud neck formed next, leading up to an eagle head of white plumage—a strange mix of feather and mane—with two feline ears sticking out.

It was a griffin.

I gaped at it, hands shaking. Of all the creatures I'd Purged before, this one actually took my breath away. I doubted I'd ever seen anything so beautiful, and... it had come from me. Its majestic yellow beak opened in a deafening bellow, between a screech and a roar, and a crack appeared in one of the mirrors.

Just what I need—seven years of bad luck on top of everything else. I shook off the momentary awe, trying to get back in the right mindset. Beautiful as it was, it couldn't stay here. It had a one-way ticket to the inside of a Mason jar.

Huge golden wings tipped with black shot out and flapped aggressively. Fully materialized now, the griffin saw me and ceased squawking. It bent a leg back and dipped into a bow, the same way the gargoyle had done.

I'm not your queen, and I'm not your mother. My anger took over from my astonishment as I remembered why this creature had come into being. Not its fault, sure, but not mine, either. And anger worked better than sympathy for what I needed to do next. It thrummed through my exhausted veins, giving me an extra boost of energy. Exactly what the doctor ordered.

"We have to catch it!" I yelled.

The griffin's head shot up, its noble golden eyes narrowing in confusion. I had to suppress the faint pang of pity that struck me in the chest. Maybe it was because it reminded me of Tobe, or maybe it was because it didn't have scales and a bad attitude. Either way, it had to be dealt with.

"On it! You get the jar and the stones while we keep it busy!" Genie jumped in front of the baffled creature. Her barrette glowed as green sparks erupted out of her. Beneath my feet, cracks appeared in the training room floor. A moment later, thick vines shot out and wrapped around the griffin, pulling it downward. Meanwhile, Diana grabbed Kes and dragged him to the edge of the room to keep him out of harm's way.

The griffin lashed out at Genie and the vines, its sharp beak making quick work of the restraints. Lunging through, it headbutted her full in the chest and sent her sailing backward. I sprinted to her side, but she waved me away.

"You know me. It's all good." She jumped back up, her body crackling with a strange, bronzed energy. Her eyes transformed into burning orbs of that same bronze, and when she brought her palms together, sparks jumped between them.

Diana ran back with her palms up. Another member of the full Elemental club, it would've been easy to feel inferior.... but not today. She sent out a wave of Air to knock the griffin back, but it spread out its wings to catch the gust and hovered menacingly, its eyes burning with rage.

"Incoming!" I lunged for Diana as the griffin divebombed us, knocking her out of the way of its open beak.

"I've got it covered." Genie let the energy build inside her before unleashing it in a fierce surge. It hit the griffin in the face, making it reel back with a screech. Sailing back, it crashed into the mirror. Glinting shards showered the floor, but the griffin wasn't done with us yet. It eyed me dubiously, a quieter caw coming from its mouth. The sound made the back of my neck tingle. It was oddly recognizable, as though it wanted to understand why I was doing this.

I'm not what you think I am. I ran for Genie's bag and snatched out a Mason jar. I grabbed the entrapment stones too, but they didn't matter so much. I couldn't rely on them any more than I could rely on having people around to do my dirty work for me. I had to find a way to do this on my own if I ever wanted to get out of the shadow of Leviathan... or my mom.

The griffin prepped for a charge while Diana and I got back to our feet. Genie stood ready, a matador waiting for the bull. And it took the bait, hurtling toward her on its mishmash legs. Genie opened her arms wide and let the griffin barrel into her. I winced at the impact. Nobody should've been able to survive it, but Genie wasn't just anyone.

"Genie?! Are you okay?!" I gripped the Mason jar and tried to spot her in the tangle of limbs and feathers and fur.

Silence echoed back.

"She's hurt." Diana's eyes widened in horror.

Just then, the griffin exploded into the air on a pulse of crackling bronze energy. It shot across the room faster than my eyes could follow and slammed into the far wall, shattering the rest of the mirrors. At the opposite side, Genie rose upward, totally unharmed and brimming with raw Chaos. She seemed to float toward the griffin, as it struggled to get up.

"Now!" Genie instructed.

I sprinted for the downed beast and shoved the Mason jar underneath its bowed head. Too weak to fight against the pull of the jar, its body disintegrated back into black smoke and twisted into the glass. I waited until all of it was inside before jamming on the lid and pulling it close to my chest.

When it was done, I turned my attention to a very glowy,

very frightening Genie. I'd seen levels of this during manda-tory training sessions, but I'd never seen it reach this kind of powerful peak. Most Atlanteans had the four Elemental abili-ties plus one extra, and the tattoos on Genie's face repre-sented each one. Sitting just under her right eye, the outline of an owl: her fifth ability. The Atlanteans called it "Athena's Wrath" but we called it the Verso ability—the power to absorb energy and expel it as raw, brute force or use it to bolster other abilities. The harder she got hit, the more powerful she became.

She touched down and discharged the remaining energy into the ground with a sonic boom that nearly took down a roof beam. "I'm going to hurt tomorrow."

"Do you ever Purge anything... smaller?" Diana laughed nervously, her eyes flitting toward Kes. He sat on the ground in total awe, gazing at Genie as if she were a rock star.

I tilted my head to the side. "I think it depends on the level of emotion."

"Have you thought about meditation? Because I don't want to see what comes out when you're *really* pissed off." Diana brushed some fallen ceiling dust out of her auburn hair.

I bit my lip. "Neither would I." My gaze lowered to look at the smoke swirling inside the jar. "Which is why I need to learn how to catch these things myself. I can't rely on people always being around."

And they seem to want to listen to me, at least when they're first created. So far, two of them had done that. If I could capitalize on that momentary pause to catch them, then I might really have a shot of being able to do this by myself.

"What are you thinking?" Genie panted.

I picked up her flask of water and handed it to her. "That institute you mentioned—the one with the puzzle traps?"

"The Basani Institute." Genie nodded thoughtfully. "If we can get you a bunch of those traps, you'll be set."

"Basani? The place that trains the monster hunters?" Diana frowned.

"*Trains* them? I thought they just lived there." My intrigue was piqued.

"They do and they don't," she replied. "Lots of monster hunters live there when they're not roaming around looking for beasts, but they have this famous training program for would-be hunters. Pretty brutal entry exam, if you believe the stories."

"That's it! That's what I've been looking for!" I jittered with excitement. "Puzzle traps sound good and everything, but I'm guessing they'd work better if I actually learned how to use them properly. If they train monster hunters, then that's where I need to be."

Genie joined in my enthusiasm, clapping me on the back. "And I bet they even train people how to catch monsters without magic. There are beasts that can dampen or block abilities, or even play tricks with the mind, so hunters have to be trained in non-magical techniques too."

"Imagine what I could do with that kind of specialized training." I grinned, hope rising through me. "It's perfect!"

"It's in Ireland." Kes poked his head into the conversation.

I peered at him, feeling my stomach sink. "What?"

"It's on this remote island near Galway. I've read all about it—thanks for the credit by the way, sis. You only know it exists because I wouldn't shut up about it." Kes rolled his eyes at her before turning back to me. "They've got an open entry exam the day after tomorrow, coincidentally—they hold them four times a year, so this is stellar timing." He paused, frowning. "Well, it would be if you weren't on parental lock-down and all. You might not be able to get your mom and dad to agree at such short notice."

"The young one has a point." Genie downed half her flask in one go. "Ooh, maybe you could persuade them that the Institute is the perfect distance from Leviathan."

I exchanged a dubious look with my friend. "They won't buy that. They didn't mean *that* much distance, I guarantee. And my mom will just offer to get some of the puzzle traps for me if I tell her it's about that."

I'd always felt drawn to the Emerald Isle. Ireland was in my blood, as much as my Merlin-ness, a place rich with mythology and culture and mystery. My parents used to say we'd visit, but work always got in the way. Maybe it was time for a solo trip to the land of my dad's heritage.

I fixed a firm gaze on my cousins. "You can't say a word about this to your mom and dad. If I decide to go, you have to keep it to yourself. You know I wouldn't usually ask you to keep secrets from them, but this is important."

"And don't go telling my dad either, though I don't know why you would." Genie chuckled, bringing some levity back to the situation. But when she turned to me again, her gaze was serious and genuine. "If you're off on a jaunt to Ireland, I'm coming with you. After all, two heads are better than one. And seven heads are no good for anyone."

Kes smirked. "I don't know, I thought the hydra was cool."

"It tried to eat you!" Diana protested.

"And that's why you can't say a word about it. If I don't do this, people really could get eaten," I pressed the point. Making this work hinged on them, especially as Kes seemed to have some Institute intel that we might need.

Diana gave a slow nod. "We won't say anything, but you'll have to make sure that your excuse for getting out of the SDC is watertight. If Mom and Dad come interrogating, Kes will fold like origami."

"Hey!" He folded his arms across his chest. "You'd break before I would."

"We both know that's not true." Diana grinned and looked back at me. "Seriously, it's going to have to be ironclad. If it's not a solid excuse, your mom will be the first to smell a rat."

I straightened up. "Then maybe I should just tell them the truth. That I'm leaving for everyone's sake."

"You're eighteen. No one can stop you," Diana agreed.

Kes shrugged uncomfortably. "And that's the easy part."

"What do you mean?" I frowned at him.

He looked sheepish. "Well, you need to figure out how you, a non-magical—no offense—are going to convince the head huntswoman that you'd be a good fit for the Basani Institute."

"Ah... right." When he put it like that, my mom and dad seemed like the least of my problems.

NINETEEN

Persie

———

The following day, we hatched our scheme… and it began with Kes. Considering that it happened to be a day full of lessons, we had plenty of time to establish our plan without having to worry about any meddling parents listening in. My mom and dad had tried to get me to take a few days off, but, good student that I was, I made a show of feeling bad about skipping out on my education and promised to run out if any Purgeness struck.

"Lunchtime means go-time." Genie flashed me a grin. We'd tucked ourselves into a recess around the corner from the Hexes classroom, where Kes would emerge any time now. After yesterday's encounter, it'd become obvious that my cousin was the primary expert on all things Basani, and we were on a tight deadline. But we couldn't just knock on the door of his family's apartment and ask to speak to him. As

Kes had said yesterday, any unusual behavior would put my mom on the scent. We'd hoped to corner him earlier that morning, but it turned out Kes liked to be prompt to his lessons, getting there way too early—and that was coming from me, the queen of punctuality. We hadn't been able to catch him.

A loud siren went off, ricocheting through the hallways of the Education Wing. Three blasts for the end of a lesson. The sound of my childhood. I wondered what life would be like without it dictating my every move, five days of the week. In truth, what would I do without *all* of this? The hallways, the preceptors, the friends, the people... The comfort zone of home, which I'd soon be stepping out of.

"He's coming! But not alone," Genie whispered, peering around the corner.

I hung back until he passed the recess, only to watch as two other kids deliberately shoved past him. They knocked him so hard that he stumbled forward, his face scrunching up as harsh laughter shot back in his face.

"Not the big Merlin now, are you?" one taunted.

The second one nodded like an idiot. "Your cousin is twice the magical you are, and she doesn't have any magic at all."

I had to resist the urge to leap out and pummel those kids, with my Purging taking on a life of its own. I couldn't risk accidentally unleashing a griffin or hydra on them. But where were Kes's friends, running to have his back? I knew he wasn't as popular as his sister, but I hadn't expected to see this. Watching him stand there, not saying anything as the bullies strode away, hit me with a major jolt to the heart and a dawning realization.

That's why he gets to his classes so early. For some, classrooms provided a safe haven from whatever lay out in the hallways—sometimes the only safe haven, until the last bell rang and they could hurry home. But Kes was sweet, and helpful, and nice—who would pick on him? These morons, apparently. I vowed that, when I had more control over it, I'd spew up a Purge beast on those bullies if I ever saw them hurting or upsetting my cousin again. But, for now, we just needed to snag Kes.

"Kes, we need a word." I pounced and whisked him away a few yards up the hall. I guessed taking him by surprise after dealing with those two cretins wasn't the best idea, but we didn't have a backup. His mouth opened and closed like a beached fish, but I didn't give him a chance to protest as I pushed him over the threshold into the enemy territory of every boy his age: the girls' bathroom. Genie barreled in after us, sending out blue sparks that locked the door.

He backed away from me, going into panic mode. "Are you insane? I can't be in here!"

"It won't be for long," I promised. "It's the closest bathroom to the Hexes classroom."

"You couldn't have walked me another ten yards to the boys' bathroom?" He dipped his chin to his chest, as if looking at this sacred space might burn out his retinas.

"We need to talk." Genie leaned up against a sink with the air of a rom-com bad gal.

"I said I wouldn't tell anyone! I haven't, I swear!" he squeaked.

I walked up to him and put a hand on his arm. "Relax. We know you won't say anything."

He lifted his head tentatively, his mouth curving into a smile. "Does this mean you've come to ask me for help?"

"How did you know that?" Genie shone her phone light at him, like he was under interrogation. "Who have you been talking to?"

"I know all about the Basani Institute. You've decided to go for that exam tomorrow, haven't you?" He cheered up in the space of a second. He was obviously excited to talk about the place.

I eyed him cautiously. "Maybe we have, maybe we haven't. For your sake, it's best you don't know for certain." I played along with Genie's cloak-and-dagger routine, knowing that this would probably be the highlight of Kes's day. "However, if we *were* to head out there tomorrow, we might be in need of a bit of Shapeshifting ability to charge up a couple of Ephemeras."

Genie had come up with the genius plan of nabbing the devices from one of her dad's forgotten trunks, which were all packed with stolen booty from Atlantis. Included in the loot was a handful of souped-up, Atlantean-style Ephemeras that had been passed down from Genie's infamous grand-pappy. They worked the same as a surface Ephemera, but for a longer time. Perfect for our needs. If nobody saw us leave, nobody would know we'd… well, *left*.

"You're sneaking out?" Kes's eyes bugged with excitement. "That's so cool. I always knew you were cool."

I put a finger to my lips. "We need you to keep mum about this."

He nodded silently.

"And we need your Shapeshifting ability to charge these puppies." Genie whipped out the golden orbs and rolled them around on her palms with dexterous fingers. "Persie and I can gussy up like other people and slip out without raising any alarms. We'll deal with the parental fallout later."

"I thought you were going to ask your mom?" Kes peered at me. "Did she say no?"

I hesitated a moment too long.

Kes nodded in understanding. "You didn't tell her, did you?"

"The conversation didn't even come up. We were supposed to have a family discussion, but both of them ended up working late. And if I'd had the chance to ask, she'd have been on her guard about me pulling a stunt like this," I explained. Honestly, I'd come close to telling her the truth a few times. But then my dad had come home from wherever he'd been, and the two of them had muttered through a few hours of stressed conversation. Things they clearly didn't want me overhearing. Plus, it was better to ask forgiveness than permission, right?

"Sneaky, but probably sensible," Kes replied. "Moms go crazy when they think their kids don't need them anymore. My mom picks fights with Di over the tiniest things, and I know she regrets it when it escalates. It's like this weird tug-of-war to assert authority over someone who's getting close to real autonomy. You know?"

I gaped at him. "Yeah... I do."

"Someone get this boy a leather armchair and a couch." Genie laughed. "And two hours of my time to psychoanalyze the living daylights out of my family problems."

"It's all a matter of psychology," Kes said, matter-of-factly. "The teenager wants to test the boundaries, to gain independence and a sense of adulthood, and the parent fights against it out of a residual sense of responsibility."

I patted him on the back. "I bet when you're eighteen, you'll just therapize your way out of any conflict."

"I'll have to start practicing now." He leaned back against the wall, a bit more comfortable in his surroundings. But he still couldn't look at the tampon dispenser without immediately looking away again. The poor boy couldn't have gotten any redder if he'd tried, though it was an endearing blush color, somewhere between coral and crimson, with a dusting of brown from his freckles. My hand itched for a paintbrush. With so much going on, I hadn't been able to resort to my favorite pastime.

Genie clapped her hands. "Back to business, before he Freuds us into forgetting why we came here. What do you say, Kes? Fancy giving your cousin and her best pal a helping hand?"

He cocked his head to one side—a trait he'd inherited from his dad. "If I were to help you, that would make me an accomplice. I don't know if I like that idea. Staying quiet is one thing, because it's not direct involvement. But giving you two Ephemeras' worth of Shapeshifting ability is aiding and abetting."

"You've watched one too many cop shows, my friend." Genie still looked impressed. "This isn't grand theft or some crime against magical kind. This is your cousin pursuing that independence you spoke about because her mom is winning the tug-of-war."

I nodded. "Come on, Kes. Help us out."

"And what if my mom and dad found out? It could cause a family rift, and I wouldn't want that." Kes shook his head, but a glint of mischief shone in his eyes. "I'm just not sure it's worth it."

I paused, reevaluating him with newfound respect. "What do you want in return?" It seemed that little Kes was growing up and resorting to extortion. I felt like I was watching a baby take his first steps, and I couldn't have been prouder.

He feigned innocence. "Who said I wanted anything in return?"

"Your face." I chuckled.

Kes pushed off the wall and tried to puff up his chest. "Okay, here's the deal. I'll help you—on one condition."

"You scare me, Kes." I laughed stiffly and shot a glance at Genie. We hadn't prepared for an exchange, and I wondered if we'd be able to cough up whatever it was he wanted.

He grinned at me, morphing from skilled diplomat to puppy dog and then back again. "'Let us never negotiate out of fear. But let us never fear to negotiate.'"

"John F. Kennedy," I marveled.

"I'm glad someone in this place is on my wavelength." A flicker of hurt flashed across his face for a second, but he covered it quickly. "Don't you want to know what my condition is?"

Genie shrugged. "Smartass syndrome?"

Kes cast her a sarcastic smile. "In return for helping charge the Ephemeras, I want to go with you."

"No chance." Genie immediately shook her head, but I wasn't so quick to dismiss the request. Deals weren't exactly my favorite topic lately. Still, he deserved to be heard out.

Kes was glancing between the two of us, his face still showing false bravado, but I made him look at me. "Why?"

He looked down. "I've... got a bit of an obsession with the Institute and its Head Huntswoman." His cheeks flushed again, and he fumbled with the straps of his backpack. "Her name is Victoria Jules, and she's the coolest woman you've never read about. Our parents have their stories, but she has tales unlike anything you've ever heard. I've researched so much about her, and the Institute, and everything associated with it. I'd be the perfect guide. And I just really want to see her and the Institute for myself."

"Sounds like my boy here has a crush." Genie winked. Kes, on the other hand, didn't find it funny.

"It's not like that. I admire her." He glared at Genie. "If you knew about her, you'd aspire to be like her too. She's amazing, and the Institute is amazing. I can't let this opportunity slip by, not when the two of you want to go to my dream place!"

Mom will actually lock me in a box for this... Then again, it wasn't like we were going on some madcap mission to some-where dangerous, like she'd done countless times when she wasn't much older than I was. We were going *away* from the real danger. And Kes sounded so eager, showing the kind of enthusiasm I felt about famous writers and artists. I wasn't going to be the one to burst his bubble.

"Okay," I said.

Genie's eyes almost fell out of her head. "Huh?"

"We'll need guidance to get through the entrance exam, and he's like a walking Basani encyclopedia. We've got a better chance of succeeding if we have him with us." I smiled wide. "Plus, you heard him—he really wants to go." And who was I to deny him that? He'd made a decent case, and this was his chance to fulfill a dream. Plus, Genie and I would be there to watch him and make sure nothing bad happened.

"I'll be an asset, I swear." Kes put his hands together, praying to Genie's softer side.

After a pause, she let out a chuckle. "Remind me never to get into negotiations with a Merlin. Both of you, with those adorable faces, could sell water to an Atlantean. In fact, I think you just did."

"Yes!" Kes punched the air, his overstuffed backpack swaying. "I love you, Genie!" His exuberance went out like a light. "I mean... uh... I don't... um... I love that you *agreed*."

"Don't blow an artery, or we won't have anyone to talk us through this fabled entrance exam." Genie's tone softened, with no hint of mockery. She didn't have a cruel bone in her body. "Besides, I love *you* for saying you'd help."

Kes relaxed. "I'm in total support. Having a monster

hunter for a cousin would be awesome. I mean, it's already super cool that you can Purge monsters like that insane griffin."

If everyone thought like you, life would be much simpler. I admired his ability to meet life's problems with tail-wagging enthusiasm. Purging monsters? Awesome. Catching them? Even better. Taking matters into your own hands? Magnificent. I needed a dose of that.

"If you ever need a beast for anything—you know, if you were in trouble or something, or you needed to scare someone—Genie and I could probably do just as well." I offered him a kind smile, which I hoped relayed the subtext.

His eyes snapped downward. "I don't know what you mean. I'm never in trouble."

"If Persie's mom finds out about this, that might change." Genie cut through his awkwardness. "But she's right. You've got us if you ever need help sorting out some dingbats who probably can't count past ten." Genie had a way of scooping up the misfits and the runts of the litter and doing everything in her power to protect them.

He scuffed his shoe against the worn-out linoleum. "Thanks, but I'm okay. I just like my own company, that's all."

"And why wouldn't you? You're not half bad, Merlin." Genie smiled, and when he looked at her, he smiled back genuinely. "Right, now that we've got our mastermind on board, there's one more thing I need to pick up before we head out tomorrow. I'll get it tonight, when the coven quiets down a bit."

Kes looked as though he might burst with anticipation. "Oh, this is so awesome! What time should we meet? The exam registration starts at eight-thirty, so it'll have to be early. And you know we'll have to use mirrors to get there, right?"

"What?" Another wrench in the works.

"You have to mirror into the Institute. There are powerful hexes surrounding the island, so if you tried to chalk-door there, you'd just drop into the sea." He sounded way too cheerful to be breaking that kind of news.

I drew in a stressed breath. "Guess we'll deal with that when we get to it. And let's shoot for seven. My mom and dad will be out of the apartment by then, and there won't be too many people around. We can meet in that dragon garden no one goes to, fill up the Ephemeras, then make our way to the mirrors from there."

"Perfect!" Kes looped his hands under the straps of his backpack. "I'll see you there!"

"And remember..." Genie put a finger to her lips.

He grinned. "Not a word, I promise. Now, if you'll excuse me." In the blink of an eye, he transformed from Kes Merlin into a random teenage girl. "And don't you go telling anyone about *this*, either."

"Not a word," I parroted with a smile.

Sashaying a little too much, Kes waited for Genie to unlock the bathroom door then strode into the hallway. As he left, I heard him whisper under his breath, "I can't believe it! Everything's coming up Kestrel."

"Well, you made him a happy little bunny," Genie said fondly as the door swung closed.

"I couldn't resist. He really wanted to come." I laughed, feeling some weight slough off my shoulders. "What's this thing you need to pick up? Do you need me to come with you?"

Her expression shifted to one of conspiracy. "It's probably better if you don't, but you'll thank me for it later."

Uh-oh... That didn't sit quite right. Then again, I trusted Genie implicitly. If she had an idea that would help us out... Well, she'd never let me down before. We were best friends. Practically sisters. And that required a few leaps of faith here and there. If she had a trick up her sleeve, then I had to let her weave her magic.

"You'll be careful, won't you?" I replied eventually.

She fiddled with her Esprit barrette. "Always."

"Just don't get yourself in trouble before we reach the Institute. Watch your back, okay?" I didn't want her putting herself in a tight spot for me.

She giggled, dispelling my nerves. "This ain't my first rodeo, ma'am."

"I'm always going to worry about you," I admitted.

"Once we do this, you'll never have anything to worry about again. Aside from hacking up Purge beasts, but that'll become as normal as brushing your teeth once you know how to catch the bastards." She bounded up and looped her arm through mine. "Come on, we should get something to eat."

Heading into the hallway, my heart felt lighter. I had challenges to come, for sure, but if I could get through them, I would have hope. And, besides—if I could forgive my parents' years of half-truths, surely they could forgive a little deception on my end. Eventually.

TWENTY

Harley

———————

Darkness fell and I prepared to make my excuses. I loved Wade more than anything, but sometimes a woman needed her solitude. And after the last few days, I needed time to think. I put away the dishes from dinner and gathered up a pile of folders from the countertop. The stark contrast between my two lives—mother and agent—in real time.

"It's late." Wade leaned against the counter. "It can wait until tomorrow."

I closed the gap between us and kissed him. "If I don't do it now, I'll keep putting it off."

"So do it here." He wrapped his arms around me and pulled me close. His lips sought mine, and the temptation to linger awhile fogged my brain.

I pushed back gently. "If we keep doing this, nothing will get done."

"Best of both worlds." He grinned, pulling me close and kissing me again. One child and twenty years of marriage later, and the fires still hadn't died.

I mumbled my reply against his lips. "The rest of the documents are in my office." I pulled back. "I won't be long. Why don't you kick back with a drink? You could use a chance to decompress."

His visit to the high-security facility for the mentally compromised hadn't gone as smoothly as we'd hoped. Some of the more recent returnees showed the same signs of tampering as Zara and Howard, but there wasn't enough evidence to identify any kind of pattern or process. As for those who'd been there longer, the residual Chaos left behind by the mind-tampering had decayed to the point that it wasn't reliable anymore. He'd been so hopeful, only to come up against another dead end.

"I can think of another way to decompress." He chuckled and kissed my neck.

This time, I batted him away with playful firmness. "Persie's in her bedroom." I glanced toward the hallway. "Speaking of, keep watch while I'm gone. I'll be back before you know it. Then we can pick up where we left off. I'll be gone an hour max."

"Last time you said that, I didn't see you for twenty-four hours." He laughed and held my hand as he walked me to the door. Ever the chivalrous gent.

I grimaced at the memory. "That was different. O'Halloran sent me on an urgent mission to Russia. This is only paperwork."

"Well, if any last-minute missions *do* come up, give me a call." He smiled and kissed me one last time.

"An hour. I promise." I kept hold of his hand. "I love you, Wade."

"Not as much as I love you." It had become our signature goodbye, even if I didn't agree. I loved him more than I could put into words, but it had stuck over the years.

I kept glancing back at him until I turned the corner of the hallway beyond. There, I unleashed a breath I hadn't realized I'd been holding. Keeping secrets from Wade was a bad habit I'd picked up over two decades ago, before I realized that working together yielded better results. It didn't feel good to be doing it again.

I'll tell him once I've made a decision. I set off along the corridor with my mind racing. I wanted a career change and a more ordinary existence. But was that even possible? With Leviathan's curse on Persie, ordinary seemed further away than it had ever been. For now, with everything in flux, I just needed some time to think and put things in perspective. Figure out what was possible and what was a pipedream. And that required alone time.

Some twenty minutes later, I reached my office. I was about to pass my hand over the magical lock, when a sliver of moonlight stopped me, spilling onto the floor where I stood. My heartrate skyrocketed. The door was already cracked open. And I hadn't left it that way. A lot might have slipped my mind lately, but I *always* locked my office door.

Raising my left palm to defend myself, I pushed the door. Slow and steady, to avoid disturbing whoever had snuck inside. A shadow slunk around by my desk. Smaller than I'd expected. But they were evidently searching for something. I heard the rustle and scrape of drawers opening and closing. Meanwhile, the snitching moonlight glinted on silvery hair and a unique barrette of crossed feathers, an Esprit I would've known anywhere.

"Genie?" I flipped on the lights.

The girl stood up sharply. Whipping around to face me, she looked like a deer in headlights. All big eyes and mortified expression. And frozen to the spot.

"What are you doing here?" I prompted, trying to mask my shock with authority.

She patted her pockets unconvincingly. "I was looking for my purse. I left it here earlier when I was studying magical history with Persie for some extra credits. I didn't even realize it was missing until I tried to buy this bag online. It's got my credit card in it, and this was the last place I remember having it."

"You must really want that bag." I hadn't been a secret agent for two decades for nothing. Very few lies got past me. As fibbers went, however, Genie had all the hallmarks of an expert. Her tone was strong and steady, and she'd masked her initial panic quickly. And there was just enough embarrassment and awkwardness in her tone to fox lesser lie detectors.

"The sale ends at midnight," she replied, without missing a beat.

I checked the device on my wrist. "It's ten past now."

"Is it?" She feigned disappointment. "I thought I could get back in time. Oh well, I guess I'll have to wait for another sale." She scurried toward me, with the obvious intention of skirting past me and out the door.

I held out my arm to stop her. "What were you doing in here, Genie?"

"I told you." She stood her ground. "If you find my purse, give it to Persie and she'll pass it back to me."

"We both know there's no purse in here, Genie."

She arched an eyebrow. "There's a purse, but I don't know where I left it. Maybe I didn't leave it in here after all." A faint smile tugged at her lips. In the agency business, we called it "duper's delight." "I know this looks bad. I wasn't prying or anything, just looking for my purse. My dad will kill me if he finds out I lost it."

Adding details to gain sympathy. A+ for effort. But my instincts gave her an F for the truth.

"Maybe we should give him a call and get him to help us look?" I called her bluff. But she barely flinched.

She shrugged. "He'll be asleep, but if you want to wake him up, that's your choice." Cool as a cucumber. No signs of stress whatsoever. "Before you decide, can I ask you something?"

I frowned. "I suppose so."

"How come you've got so many college brochures? I thought you didn't want Persie going away to study."

Very clever, Genie. I would've been impressed if this were a training exercise. But it wasn't. It was my life. And we were two liars caught in a web together. If either of us revealed the truth to the other, we'd both be in trouble. *Unless...*

"I'm guessing you found my junk drawer while you were

looking for your *purse*. I visit a lot of covens and colleges for work, and I get handed a lot of literature." She could lie well, but I had more experience.

She nodded thoughtfully. "What about the non-magical colleges? And all of the… continuing education programs?"

Well, so much for that. Genie knew that brochures geared toward adults or changing careers definitely wouldn't be for Persie.

My pursuit of a normal life had branched off toward neutral territory on occasion. At least in my thoughts. We would still have ties to a coven, but we'd live outside of it. That sort of thing. Another reason I'd kept it secret from Wade until now. He hadn't gotten tired of the magical life like I had, and I didn't know how it would work to have one of us in one world and the other in a totally different one. And, until I made a decision, there wasn't any reason to hash it out. I might not choose to go down that route. Pretty much the only thing I knew for certain was that I couldn't carry on like this forever. I didn't want to. The roles of Mom and Harley, so intertwined for the last eighteen years, had started to splinter again. And there would come a time when she didn't need me anymore. If I didn't make a change for myself one day soon… then when?

"It really isn't any of your business, Genie." I switched to parent mode. "You say you weren't prying, but it sounds like you've done your fair share of rifling through my things. Why I have those has nothing to do with you. But what you've done is an invasion of my privacy. Not to mention the breaking and entering."

Genie smiled. "You're right: it's none of my business. And it can stay between us." She took a test step forward. "Besides, I can't find my purse, so I don't need to be here anymore. I must've left it somewhere else. Ditzy old me."

There's nothing ditzy about you, and we both know it. She'd backed me into a corner. I had my ideas about the future, but I was nowhere near ready to tell anyone about the brochures and my potential career prospects in the field of counseling. And I definitely wasn't ready to admit that the magical world had lost its appeal. There'd be outrage and confusion. My legacy would become a rope to hang myself with. A Merlin who didn't want to be involved in magic anymore was like a Nobel prize-winning scientist quitting to become the head of a flat Earth society. I could already envision the pleas from O'Halloran and the UCA. They'd try to persuade me to stay, offer me more money, and I'd buckle and accept. Stuck in an endless cycle until I finally retired at seventy. If I lived that long.

"You're smart, Genie." I sighed quietly.

She fluttered innocent eyelashes at me. "I don't know what you mean."

"There's such a thing as being too smart for your own good." I couldn't resist one little swipe.

"I'll bear that in mind." She walked right past me and paused on the threshold, looking back over her shoulder. "For what it's worth, I think it's good to change things up. Sometimes, it's exactly what a person needs. And... I hope you find something that fulfills you, if... certain things don't anymore."

She scooted off before I had chance to respond. But I had no doubt that her parting words were genuine, a backhanded message of encouragement that included Persie in the subtext. I had all these thoughts about changing my life completely, yet I hesitated to give Persie the same freedom because she was young and inexperienced with the world. Genie had called me out in the subtlest way.

Drained and reluctantly impressed, I crossed to my desk and sat down. All the drawers lay closed, and it didn't look like anyone had been rummaging at all. But my secrets had been discovered, and for the second time in a week.

"What do I do about this?" I said to the empty room. I clearly had to have a longer, harder think about my career prospects so I could reach a concrete decision. But that fell away to the sidelines as more pressing matters infiltrated my thoughts.

It's not like I can shadow Persie for the rest of her life. She would end up hating me. Katherine had coerced and manipulated Finch into staying at her side, and look what had happened there. Obviously, I wasn't Katherine. I was nothing like her. And I wanted that to continue in every way. My overprotection of Persie came from love, not bitterness. But what sort of life would she have with this new ability? How could I balance her protection and freedom with keeping people from getting hurt—her included?

The Everest of motherhood loomed ahead of me, and I had no idea where to even begin climbing it.

TWENTY-ONE

Persie

———

W e *should remember that good fortune often happens when opportunity meets with preparation.* Without Thomas Edison, we probably wouldn't have recorded music, movies, or lightbulbs. And maybe I wouldn't have stayed up all night beside one such lightbulb, cramming the Basani Institute's syllabus and entry requirements into my overtired brain. Through the magic of digital technology, Kes had fed me all the information I might need. And I mean *all* of it. Videos, photos, messages, emails, voice messages, pinging and pinging across my phone for my bloodshot eyes to try and process. All from underneath the rudimentary tent of my bedsheets, reminding me of happy childhood evenings spent with a book and a flashlight.

At seven o'clock on the dot, I arrived at the dragon garden. My feet dragged along in a zombie shuffle, and my mom and dad had received grunts and groans when they'd said goodbye before heading to work. My mom had been a little short herself, though. Even after her morning coffee. I guessed it had something to do with whatever she and Dad had been working on, aside from me and my Purge beasts.

"Kill me now." Genie lolled against the dragon fountain which gave the garden its name. Clear water should've spouted out of its roaring mouth. Instead, a faint trickle ran down the brownish algae that sludged over its jade green scales. Not its original shade, by the looks of it. The copper or bronze underneath had oxidized over time, with no one to give it love and attention, or a routine cleaning. Honestly, I thought it suited the design. The dragons I'd seen in my monster dreams were always some shade of green... occasionally red or black, but the green ones had the nicest temperaments. *Like living mood rings.*

"I take it you were up all night, too?" I sat on a crusty old bench.

She groaned. "So many messages. I had to turn my phone off."

"You can't fault his enthusiasm."

"I can and I will." Genie tipped her head back and closed her eyes toward the sun.

I laughed and looked around the garden. Tucked away in a lesser-walked area of the coven, it didn't get as many visitors as it should've. The flowerbeds and flagstones were snarled up with weeds, but the trees still bore plump, blushing peaches and a few pink-tinged lilies grew by the wall that looked out over the national park.

"Morning!" Kes's chipper voice cut through our slug-gishness.

Genie visibly flinched. "Not so loud."

"Sorry." He kept right on grinning. "How did you both do with studying last night?"

"I don't want to talk about it," Genie replied sullenly. "I squeezed in what I could, and I'm hoping it'll be enough."

Kes dumped his backpack on the rim of the dragon foun-tain. "It's mostly a physical test, so a lot of that stuff probably won't come up, anyway." He continued to talk, oblivious to Genie's death glare. The dramatic irony amused me. "Think of it like an obstacle course. We're talking Physical Magic, Curses, Monster Biology—things you've already learned in class, with a few off-syllabus extras."

"We need him," I reminded Genie, with a chuckle. She looked about ready to dunk him in the fountain for keeping her up all night for no reason. "And it doesn't hurt to revise old ground, to keep us sharp."

Kes turned around and finally noticed Genie's wrath. "What did I say?"

"That I should've gotten a good night's sleep," she replied drily.

"Oh... right." He lowered his gaze like a wounded puppy. "I guess I got a little carried away."

Genie skimmed her hand through the fountain pool and splashed water at him. "No baking frownies on my watch, kid." She smiled. "Persie's right. I never listen in Monster Biology, so I needed a refresher course."

His eyes brightened.

I moved to more important matters. "Did you bring the charged Ephemeras?"

He delved into his bag and took out two orbs. "All juiced up and ready to go. It took me a while to figure them out, but I got the hang of it." He rolled up a sleeve to show a few puncture marks in his forearm. Poor kid had turned himself into a human pincushion for us.

I thanked him and took mine, lifting it to eye level. A small vortex of bronze energy spiraled in the central glass canister, somewhere between gas and liquid. And the Atlantean detailing took my breath away. Intricate Kelpies and sea serpents in mortal combat, twisting and chasing across the metal surface, destined to never catch each other.

"How do we use them?" I looked at Genie.

She demonstrated like a pro, holding the orb in her hands and pressing on the panels at each pole. On one end, a harp-shaped symbol. On the other, the curve of an olive wreath. Bronzed light jumped out and slithered into her palms, disappearing to join the ranks of her other abilities. Meanwhile, she kept pressing, and the orb shrank to the size of a marble.

"Travel size." She flashed me a winning smile. "Make sure your right hand covers the harp, and the left covers the olive wreath. Press down as hard as you can, and... you should be good." I noticed a hint of hesitancy in her voice, bringing back a question I'd spent most of last night avoiding.

What if the Ephemera doesn't work for someone without any magic? I didn't know if my shiny new curse let me into the magical club or not. Although, the point of an Ephemera was to briefly give an ability to someone who didn't have said ability. And I didn't have any, so maybe I qualified anyway. I just hoped we weren't missing the small print.

Taking my Ephemera, I followed her instructions. The orb budged under the pressure of my palms, sort of like a Rubik's Cube shifting rows. A second later, the same bronze light leapt out into my hands. It took everything I had not to drop it on the ground as a sharp pinch stung at the center of each palm. Reminiscent of getting too close to a flame.

I yelped.

Genie lunged forward. "Did it hurt you?"

"It just gave me a shock." I pretended to act cool. "I'm not used to it."

Kes peered at me as if I were his latest test subject. "How do you feel?"

With the orb shrinking in my hands, I tried to feel around for the new Chaos. Disappointingly, I didn't feel much different. A bit... wired, perhaps, but I put that down to the tank of coffee I'd downed before leaving the house. Although... maybe there was a hint of something. A subtle thrum that hadn't been there before.

"A bit jittery," I replied, "but not in a bad way."

Kes grinned boyishly. "Cool."

"Who are our victims, then?" Genie's demeanor relaxed. I realized she must've been a lot more worried about me than she'd let on.

He pushed his ginger curls out of his eyes. "Whoever you like. As long as we know who they are." The curls fell back, but he left them there. "You know, this would've been way simpler if I had my dad's ability. No need for Ephemeras at all. I'm keeping my fingers crossed that the Mimicry develops when I hit eighteen."

"How about the Catemaco-Levis?" I suggested. "They're away in Mexico this week for Santana's cousin's birthday."

Genie shot me a bemused look. "Again? I swear, they're in Mexico more than they're at the SDC."

I shrugged. "She's got a lot of cousins."

"Well, it sounds like our best shot," she agreed. "But won't people wonder what we're doing here if we're supposed to be in Mexico?"

"They only left about an hour ago, so we've got a window. We can just say we had to come back for something if anyone stops to question us." My mind whirred with solutions, the caffeine kicking in.

Genie beamed at me. "Perfect. Persie the Problem Solver strikes again!" Suddenly, she clapped her hands together excitedly. "*Please* can I be Marius? Might be my only chance to get in his—"

"I'm going to stop you right there." I tilted my head at Kes and stifled a giggle. "We've got young'uns present."

Kes grumbled under his breath. "That's okay, I know everyone has a thing for Marius. My sister talks about him all the time." He did a perfect imitation of her voice. "*Oh, Mom, you should see the way his hair tumbles down so perfectly. His eyes are so pretty—they're like two pools of liquid chocolate, and I want to dive right in. Did you know, he doesn't even work out? His muscles are all natural.*" He pretended to dry heave.

Genie snorted. "You could make a lot of money impersonating people."

"It wouldn't be fair. I've got an advantage." He Shifted into a frankly horrifying split-body situation: the head of Diana and the boyish figure of Kes. Enjoying our reaction way too much, he tossed his hair around like he was in a shampoo commercial. He Shifted back a moment later, looking appalled with himself. "Remind me never to do that again. It seemed like a funny idea."

Genie and I applauded regardless.

"Now that we've all been mentally scarred, let's get back to business." I laughed and hoped he didn't feel too embarrassed. "Genie, you can be Marius, as long as you promise not to make inappropriate jokes. I'll be Azar, and you can be Cy, Kes. Does that work for everyone?"

Genie's mouth turned up in a grin. "I can keep it PG-13."

"I'm good, too." Kes nodded. "Although, you two should pretend you've got colds or sore throats if anyone tries to talk to you, so you don't have to worry about your voices giving us away. As for me, I can do a heck of an impression of Cy."

"Noted. Okay then... how do we do this?" I looked to the Shifting expert. Even though I'd never used Chaos before, I had a basic idea of the process from class. I had to feel for it and let it move through me. The more relaxed I was, the easier it would be. At least in theory.

He held up his hands and Shifted into little Cy. Hazel eyes blinked adorably in a face that had lost some of its childhood chub, which matched the rest of Cy's gangly frame. A few years younger than Kes, Cy was going to be a tall one some-day. Kes ran a hand across his borrowed hair, buzzed hedge-hog-short.

"The hair is always the weirdest part," he admitted.

I tried not to let first-Chaos nerves overwhelm me. "You might have to *tell* me how to do it. Showing didn't really help."

"Feel for the vibration of the Chaos and bring it into your body," Genie stepped in as my cheerleader slash coach. "From what I know of Shapeshifting, you have to let it wash over your skin. Here, we can do it together."

She took my hand for moral support, while I did my best to find the temporary energy inside me. It took a few minutes until I felt what I hoped was the Shifting power—a shivering, building sort of electricity that prickled in my forearms, like I'd put my hands on a generator. Honestly, I didn't quite know how to feel about it. It wasn't the bells and whistles I'd been anticipating, a big power surge that was undeniably magical. This seemed subtler, with the same kind of buzz I'd felt once when I'd downed about a gallon of energy drink and stayed up all night to work on a massive canvas. Only this didn't make me feel like I could see sounds. It just... hummed along at a steady pace. A sensation that I could get used to. Now, how I pushed that feeling into the rest of my body was the next step, and totally baffling. For magicals, I imagined it came as easily as hiccupping or coughing or blinking. For me, I hovered firmly at square one.

"Do you feel it?" Genie asked.

I nodded. "I think so."

"Okay, so imagine you're bringing it into your chest. Take your time." Her patience made me calmer. I had to remain relaxed, just like the textbooks said.

Closing my eyes, I pictured the energy moving into my center. To my surprise, the Chaos responded, pooling into the middle of my chest. I could actually feel the weight of it above my lungs, as though someone was pushing their hand down against me.

"I'm doing it!" I yelped.

Genie laughed. "You're doing great. I knew you'd be a natural at this. Next, you need to imagine that energy running down into your hands."

I obeyed, and the Chaos began to ebb away from my chest, trickling down my arms and into my fingertips. Everything buzzed with a much stronger sort of static electricity, the hum intensifying, and my heart racing at the exhilaration of it all. Eighteen years without a proper ability, and I was finally getting to experience it. This was the birthday present I should've had, not Leviathan's spiteful, self-serving curse.

"It's in my fingertips!" I wanted to dance around the dragon garden.

"Perfect, Persie." Genie gripped my hand tighter. "I can feel what you're feeling. Now, all you need to do is imagine the energy washing over you."

Kes chimed in. "And imagine the person you want to look like while you're doing it." I opened my eyes to find him hopping about excitedly, his eyes shining with pride.

Feeling more confident, I pictured the energy in my fingertips coursing back the way it had come and enveloping my body in a shrink-wrapped sheen of Shifting Chaos. A second skin. I almost screamed with happiness when it responded, moving back through me like honey until it infiltrated every limb, every cell, every vein with that slow-moving bronze.

"You did it!" Kes whooped. "Persie *who?* The only person I can see is Azar Catemaco-Levi."

I dared a peek down at myself. My skin had changed from hermit white to goddess olive, with freckles on the back of my hand that weren't mine. I wore the floral, gypsy-sleeved dress that she'd worn in class last week, and had the kind of long, slim legs that didn't turn crabby when they ran.

"Here." Genie whipped out a mirror and showed me my reflection. I gasped as Azar stared back with her unusual green eyes. A dark brown freckle marked one iris: the flagship to the dusting across her cheeks and nose. Her long, chestnut hair tumbled past my shoulders in natural curls.

"I can't believe I did it," I managed, admiring my handiwork.

Genie smiled. "I can. You can do anything, Persie. Seriously, if you wanted to be an astronaut, or a beast hunter, or freaking queen of the world, no one would be able to stop you!"

My happy bubble popped, and Genie immediately realized what she'd said. Her eyes got wide and her mouth fell open, while her hand came up to smack herself in the forehead.

"Persie... I'm so sorry. I'm an idiot." For a second, she looked like she might cry. Through all of this, she'd been my strength and support. In that moment, I understood that I wasn't the only one in this garden who was terrified about what the future held for me. I'd seen the crack in her stoic armor. My best friend might've been strong for me, but she also felt what I felt, cried when I cried, hurt when I hurt. And neither of us knew how this would play out. All we could do was hope for the best, together. "Forget that last part."

"Already forgotten," I replied, giving her hand a squeeze. "And you're not an idiot."

She gave me a grateful smile. "I'm still sorry."

"Have I missed something?" Kes interjected, confused.

I shrugged. "It's nothing."

"We should hop to it, before we miss this entrance obstacle course exam test thingie." Genie brought the conversation back around and Shifted into an identical image of Marius. I waited for the lusty jokes to come, but they didn't. A sure sign that my friend still had her mind on what she'd said.

Instead, Kes puffed out a sigh. "He really does have perfect hair and chocolate-pool eyes."

Genie and I paused a moment before bursting into laughter, diffusing any residual discomfort.

"Well! He does!" Kes protested, sending us further into hysterics.

A few minutes later, our outburst subsided. But it had been precisely what the doctor ordered to get me and Genie back into a positive mindset. Shifted and ready for action, our trio headed out of the dragon garden and away to the mirror room.

I'd heard that the mirrors used to be in the Assembly Hall, but that had changed when the SDC moved locations. Nowadays, the mirrors had a room all of their own: a hall not far from the library, where people came and went at all hours of the day. I hoped there wouldn't be too many people around to mess up our plan.

"This is going to work, right?" I whispered to Kes, as we made our way through the coven. The corridors were fairly empty, with only a few weary souls meandering to the Banquet Hall for breakfast. One or two gave us a bleary nod, but the path seemed blissfully clear.

Kes looked over at me. "Which part?"

"Getting through the mirrors."

"Oh." He fidgeted, which didn't fill me with confidence. "It should. I've snuck through a couple of times without being detected. Trips to the museums in New York, that kind of thing."

I gaped at him. "On your own?!"

The idea of my cousin wandering about in the Big Apple by himself made me feel instantly protective, and a little bit sick. He was thirteen, for crying out loud! What if something happened to him out there? No one would even know, until it was too late. *Ah... I see.* That scraped a little too close to the Mom bone. Looking at Kes, I started to understand my mom's thought process in a way I hadn't before.

"I can take care of myself," he insisted.

"Promise me you won't do that again!" My relief that the mirrors would likely work mixed with sudden panic for my cousin and his little jaunts.

He shrugged mutinously. "It depends what exhibits they have."

I was about to protest further, when we reached the mirror room. The doors stood open and the space beyond looked empty. Seizing our opportunity, the three of us snuck inside. Five mirrors loomed on a raised stage, their silvery surfaces rippling faintly. The room itself didn't have much else going for it—vaulted ceilings, a few side tables with potted plants to pretty the place up, and a black marble floor that echoed unnervingly as we scuttled across it.

"Anyone coming?" Kes murmured.

I glanced back. "Nope. It's now or... well, we wait until it's empty again."

Kes put his hand up against the farthest mirror on the right and whispered a spell I didn't recognize. *"Dare ingressum,* Basani Institute."

The surface rippled wildly for a moment, until a vision appeared and the ripples stilled. A different hall lay beyond, but the image was hazy, as if it had a layer of gauze between us and it.

"This is it! The moment I've been waiting for!" Kes braced to bolt through, but Genie stopped him.

"First things first, young Mage: we need to de-Shift. If we drop the disguises in the Institute, people will get suspicious."

Kes tapped his chin. "Then we should get it done quick, before someone here sees us."

I raised a frantic hand. "Uh, guys... How do I undo the Shifting?" Kes and Genie had already shed their fake skin and were back to their usual selves.

Genie stood in front of me for encouragement. "Let it flow away, like you're shaking off nerves. Jiggle your arms and legs if you have to."

I did what she said, trying to flail discreetly to get rid of the Shifting energy. Although, a part of me felt sorry to let it go. For a moment, I'd had magic… and I liked the sensation. Not just the actual energy part, but the feeling that I was in the same Chaos-hewn boat as everyone around me. Once I gave it up, I'd be back where I started: an anomaly, neither one thing nor another.

"Or, you could give me the Ephemera," Kes whispered, seeing my comical struggle.

I shook my head. "Not yet. There's still juice left, and I'd like to… hold onto it for a while."

"I understand." He stepped up to help Genie provide instruction. "I always find it helps if you picture the Shifting like a layer of sweat after a long practice, and you've just stepped under a hot shower. Imagine it washing away."

Using his suggestion, if only to avoid more hopeless jiggling, I pictured Azar's form sloughing off my skin and down an imaginary drain. Crackling friction bristled across my chest, moving up to my neck and face, and down to my abdomen and legs. I closed my eyes, terrified I'd end up stuck this way, ruining any chance I might've had of getting into the Institute.

"There it is." Genie gave me a light nudge. "The face we know and love."

"Thank Chaos for that." I heaved a sigh of relief, and not a moment too soon. People were coming, their chatter echoing in the hallway outside the mirror room. With a squeak that might have been fear or excitement, Kes darted through without hesitation, leaving us no choice but to chase after him.

Bursting out of the other side in an undignified stumble that threatened to turn into an all-out sprawl, my eyes bulged and my jaw dropped. The big gaps in the gray stone ruins of what appeared to be a castle had been filled in with slick sheets of frosted, blue-tinted glass. Overhead, the ceiling curved up in an impressive feat of engineering, involving a web of crisscrossing metal that reminded me of a huge cage, and precision-cut stained glass in an array of greens, blues, and golds. Beneath our feet, polished concrete stretched as far as the eye could see. An architectural blend of the new and the old, somehow working seamlessly, a futuristic cathedral.

Ahead of us, in the cavernous entrance hall and along the minimalist corridors beyond, figures in sharp, black suits went about their business. A monster hunter had to be able to blend into any part of the world. And nothing blended in quite as well as a plain, black suit.

TWENTY-TWO

Persie

A few curious eyes scrutinized us from afar, with some heads turned subtly in our direction. For some of them, it was harder to tell where they were looking, seeing as they had sunglasses on. It was more in the body language: a stiffening of the shoulders, a slight turn of the cheek, a partially raised eyebrow.

Genie eyed them right back, muttering under her breath. "Unless those sunglasses have in-built scanners or something, no one should be wearing them indoors. Only primadonnas and ass-clowns wear sunglasses inside."

"My mom says that." I chuckled. "Well, different words. But the same sentiment."

Her expression flickered strangely at the mention of my mom. "That's because she's a smart woman." It disappeared as quickly as it had appeared, but I didn't dwell on it too much.

With everything that had gone down with my parents, I assumed she still harbored a slight grudge on my behalf.

"This is so cool!" Kes distracted me with his awe, taking in our surroundings. He shuffled about happily, ready to bounce off the pristine walls in excitement.

"We should find the exam hall," Genie urged, leading the way.

Taking it slow—mostly so Kes wouldn't miss anything—we continued through the main hall. The business-formal inhabitants lost interest in us and continued about their business.

"Look at that!" Kes jabbed a finger downward. A plate of glass interrupted the sleek gray floor, and below... a stone sarcophagus. The sculpted face of a man stared back up, with a golden-hilted broadsword held in place by folded hands. A ruby the size of an egg took pride of place on the hilt, and etched lettering in a language I didn't understand ran the length of the still-shiny blade.

I cast Kes an intrigued glance. "Should we know who that is?"

He looked dumbstruck. "It's Finn McCool!" He shook his head in disappointment. "Oh, come on, you guys *have* to know who he is!"

"No idea," Genie replied.

"He's only the most famous hunter Ireland ever had!" Kes turned googly-eyed over the dead guy. "He still holds the record for most dragons captured. And since there aren't any left in the wild, I guess he'll keep it. Legend has it that he built the Giant's Causeway to Scotland just so he wouldn't get his feet wet. Oh, and he tried to throw a piece of Ireland at a rival, but it missed and landed in the Irish Sea, and that's how the Isle of Mann came to be."

I stared at the stone figure a while longer. "Are you saying he was a giant? His coffin thing doesn't look that big."

"True or not, he had the guts of a giant." Kes sighed, clearly in love with the mythos. "This is super cool."

Genie laughed. "Or super *McCool.*"

"Did you just come up with that?" Kes asked sarcastically, though his eyes twinkled with amusement. "Anyway, he's a name you should know. He ran this whole ring of monster hunters called the Fianna. Depending on the story, they're still guarding Finn while he sleeps in this magical cave somewhere, until his services are needed again."

"But he's right here," I pointed out. "And wasn't that King Arthur?"

"His *tomb* is right here. That doesn't mean he's inside." Kes looked insulted that I'd suggest otherwise. "I guess mythology likes to keep a lot of their heroes asleep somewhere. It comforts people, to think these ancient warriors might come back and save us if we need them to."

I snorted. "They must've hit snooze when Katherine and Davin came along."

"Maybe they knew other people had it under control," Kes replied, still gazing adoringly at his hero.

I wonder if they'd come back if Leviathan turned the world into Hell on Earth? I pushed away the thought and kept walking. We hadn't even made it through the main entrance hall yet, but not for lack of trying. The scale of this place was immense, like one of those European cathedrals that had ceilings so high they made you feel dizzy, with a rabbit warren of secret corridors and tunnels that branched off in every direction. All around us, people strode in and out of frosted glass doors that lined the sides of the vast hallway, moving with an air of purpose.

Pressing on, we passed display cases of magical artifacts: Esprits and old journals belonging to long-dead monster hunters, odd silver bottles that I guessed were the Mason jars' predecessors, and sophisticated projections of the Institute's rarest captures. Kes wanted to stop and stare at everything, but I gently nudged him along. If we stopped we'd invite attention, and we couldn't risk being late to the exam hall. The only time I almost stopped was in passing a display case that exhibited a single golden feather, taken from one of Tobe's wings. I wondered if he knew they had an homage to him here.

"Excuse me." Genie waved down a stern looking man with a particularly snappy suit and a Claddagh brooch pinned to his lapel. An emerald heart glittered between the curved silver hands that held it.

The man paused. "Aye?"

"Could you tell us where the exam hall is?" Evidently, she'd realized the same thing I had—without directions, we'd never find it.

He laughed with surprising warmth, considering his steely eyes. "Fresh blood, eh?"

"Something like that," Genie replied with a half-smile.

"Well, ye'll be wantin' te go up this corridor a way, 'til ye reach the case with Orion's bow." The man pointed. "Take yerself left and keep walkin' toward the stained glass o' Artemis. Lass with a bow and a stag beside her, ye'll not miss her. Head right and walk te the end o' the corridor, and ye'll see two raight big doors. That's the hall yer after."

Genie nodded, though her eyes had a glazed look. "Thanks."

"Best o' luck te yez," he said, watching as we walked away.

"Do you have any idea what he just said?" Genie whispered, drawing level with me.

I chuckled. "I think so."

"Do you think they're here for the exam?" Genie gestured to a determined duo of young women, around our age, with ponytails so severe their lacquered hair looked fake. They marched along in pressed pants and combat boots, so focused that even the black-suited regulars moved out of their way.

My insides turned to mulch. We were going up against *that?*

"Why are they holding folders?" she asked, noting the thick binders in their hands.

I turned to Kes. "I thought you said this was mostly physical?"

"It is, but that doesn't mean you can't study for it." He shrugged. "Don't tell me you're worried about a couple of cadets? I've given you everything you need to know. As long as you read most of it, you'll be fine."

"*Cadets?*" I looked back at the hallway, and spotted a few more militant looking guys and gals, ranging from our age to twentysomethings.

"Didn't I mention that?" Kes shoved his hands into his pockets sheepishly.

Genie grabbed his sleeve. "Start talking, kid."

"Well, there are some covens around the world who run cadet courses for this kind of thing. Feeder covens, if you like." He wouldn't look us in the eye. "They've probably been training for this exam for a... couple of years."

"Are you kidding?" I wanted to turn around and sprint straight back to the mirrors.

Genie let go of him and looped her arm through mine, pulling me into her side. "Look. I'm right there with you, but we're going to make the best of this. We have to. And hey— some of my best grades have come after a single night of cramming."

I couldn't reply. It was like Kes had pointed out a spot on someone's face, and now I couldn't stop seeing the cadets everywhere. Many of them carried weighty binders, filled with all the tips, tricks, and intel they could possibly need to get through this first round. And they all walked around as though they'd already gotten into the Institute, their heads up, shoulders back, marching to the beat of a victory drum. The only real difference between them was the color of their uniforms, no doubt signaling the coven they'd come from.

Kes floundered. "In my defense, I didn't think it'd be helpful to tell you." He bowed his head, but I was too busy panicking to spare him any sympathy.

Closing my eyes and raiding my mental library for anyone who might help me push through this, my brain settled on the wise words of Eleanor Roosevelt: *You gain strength, courage and confidence by every experience in which you really stop to look fear in the face. You are able to say to yourself, "I have lived through this horror. I can take the next thing that comes along." You must do the thing you think you cannot do.*

I opened my eyes. "We're doing this."

I dragged Genie along before I could change my mind. My heart pumped with adrenaline—the fuel I needed to keep putting one foot in front of the other. And, with each step, the dream of walking these halls as a resident instead of a potential trainee grew bigger, until it took up every neuron in my brain. I had no room, and no time, for anything else. I *had* to do the impossible.

Hurrying past Orion's bow and the stained-glass Artemis, our trio hurtled along the last corridor until we reached the towering set of double doors that the stern man had mentioned. Benches were tucked against the wall, all of them filled with silent, intimidating wannabes. Countless eyes made rapid judgements, a few smirks lifting the corners of sour lips. We looked out of place, but I no longer worried about standing out. We *were* different from the rest. But we were going to best them anyway.

Taking our seats on the only bench left, we waited.

After the most agonizing ten minutes of my life, the double doors opened with an unnerving screech of metal on stone, and two figures emerged. The first was a frazzled assistant with her shirt untucked and glasses slipping down her nose, overloaded with heavy stacks of binders.

But behind her stood possibly the most striking woman I'd ever seen. Not beautiful in the traditional sense, but with an aura that made it impossible to look away. Her short, strawberry blonde hair was buzzed at the sides, but the top was swept back effortlessly, hitting the balance between renegade and sophisticate. Her black eyes were too big and too dark, her nose too narrow, her lips too pale, her bone structure too severe, but it all came together in a way that made sense. In fact, she looked positively otherworldly—as though she'd come from a different planet altogether, to live amongst us mere humans.

She stood in front of the open doors, her arms behind her back to make her six-foot-something height even more imposing. On her willowy frame, a black suit had never, well, *suited* anyone so well. Although, on second glance, I wasn't sure it was black at all. More of a navy blue, paired with a shirt that had just a hint of gray—a subtle twist on the Institute's uniform.

"That's her..." Kes's eyes bulged. "Victoria Jules."

Genie looked similarly gobsmacked. "Wow."

I nodded slowly. "I think I get the hype now."

The students filed into the room beyond the double doors at some silent signal that we'd clearly missed. I'd have thought the assistant would open her binders to check off names, but she didn't. Weird, considering these weren't just any binders. They were the magical sort, used by pretty much every magical educational institution worldwide. They automatically filled with real information as students presented themselves, fueled by the same technology as the Krieger detector, tapping into the magical world's network and delivering all the necessary info in real time. But the students, mostly the cadet variety, passed through without so much as a roll call. Following suit, the three of us jumped up and scurried for the entrance. Genie and I passed by with no problem, but Victoria's hand shot out to snag Kes before he could join us. She barely exerted any effort, one arm still behind her back.

"No children. Wait here." She released him before turning to stride through the doors, her entire being brimming with power and authority. Kes must've been desperate to see what lay beyond the threshold, but he didn't move a muscle. He just stared after his idol until the doors closed in his face.

Sorry, Kes. Maybe in a few years.

Another cavernous, cathedral-like hall stretched ahead, the ground making booms out of our footsteps. To my disbelief, this one was even higher and wider than the entrance hall. It might have been more beautiful too, with a downpour of oceanic light dappling every speck of the floor and stained-glass depictions of triumphant heroes gracing the walls.

In a lot of ways, it fit the magnitude of what I was up against. An ancient seat of warriors and heroes and legends, this hall trembled with the ghosts of past battles. I might not have felt like much of a warrior myself, but I was determined to be the hero of my own story. My entire future depended on it.

Throw whatever you've got at me... I drew in a deep breath. *I'm ready.*

TWENTY-THREE

Harley

I'd left the apartment earlier than usual, under the pretense of a work backlog. In a way, that wasn't a total lie. I *was* dealing with a backlog—an emotional one, to help Persie. Checking my phone, it read half past seven: the coven's slowest time of day. And the earliest I could've gotten away without alerting my husband's suspicion. Wade had made an early start too. But he'd be on the other side of the SDC by now, at the infirmary, comparing notes with Krieger and Jacob. It wasn't that I didn't want Wade with me on this, but if things went awry and I ended up getting hurt, I needed to be sure there was one fighting fit parent to look out for our daughter. And if Wade knew, there was no way he'd let me go alone.

I paused up the corridor from the Bestiary and concentrated on a spell, a concealment hex from Finch's Grimoire.

Tobe will be on his morning rounds. He'll start with the

northern halls and work backward. A creature of habit, his schedule was easy to follow. His rarest creatures were kept in those northern halls. All but one. The dirty black mark in his menagerie that he kept confined to the east wing of the Bestiary.

I placed my hands on my chest. Slivers of powerful Chaos slipped through my skin, as I recited the words from Finch's Grimoire. *"In tenebris. Conversus caecus cculus. Et per mundi labyrinthum dissipati praemisit. Ego celatur. Et in tenebris ambulamus. Et erit tamquam umbra. Quod lux caeli. Quod atmosphaera quietam. Ego celatur."*

A shiver ran over my body. I looked to the mirror on the wall beside me, and nothing looked back. The spell had worked. I smiled, but I couldn't see the reflection of it. *Finch, remind me to tell you how much I love you and your sneaky ways.*

My hypocrisy wasn't lost on me. I'd nearly lost my mind when I found out that Persie had snuck into the Bestiary. But I was the one with the power to do something about him. It was my duty to protect her. As her mom, and as the one who'd gotten her into this mess in the first place.

My body shivering from the concealment spell, I headed into the Bestiary. Stealing along the avenues of glass boxes, I sent out a faint wave of beast control to keep the critters quiet. I couldn't have them summoning Tobe back. I was breaking two of his rules: entering covertly *and* with the aim of compelling a monster without provocation.

He'd understand. I know he would. But my actions said otherwise. If I'd truly believed that, I'd have asked for permission. The trouble was, I couldn't have risked him saying no. I usually suppressed my beast control while I was in the Bestiary, ever since having a chat about fairness and free will with Tobe. Never mind the fact that all these creatures were caged in boxes. The Beast Master had every right to set boundaries, even if the foundations were a bit shaky. But things had changed. Leviathan had crossed *my* boundaries, and desperate times called for desperate measures.

As I hurried to Leviathan's private hall, the Purge beasts stayed silent. Twenty years had honed my beast control to new heights. But it took concentration and focus. In moments of high pressure and higher emotion, the finesse evaded me. I'd dropped the ball with the hydra. I'd made up for it, though, with the rest of the creatures Persie had Purged, each one diving into the Mason jars at my instruction. And I wasn't going to drop the ball with Leviathan.

Closing the door to his hall behind me, I strode up to the enclosure. I took deep breaths to steady my racing heart. Up ahead, Leviathan had been frozen inside his box. Yet his energy—a pulse that came from behind the glass—filled the entire room.

"I know you can hear me in there," I muttered. "You've done something to this box. The freezing thing isn't cutting it the way it should."

The frost thickened across the pane.

"Is that your idea of an answer?" I glared at the crystallized patterns. "It's Persie, isn't it? She's your link to the outside world."

No reply.

The question had nagged at my mind. This kind of stasis

had kept his mother locked up, and she was more powerful than he'd ever be. Yet, he continued to break out. Maybe not physically, but in other ways. He'd managed to speak to me at the pool, and then visited me at the infirmary. He'd spoken to Persie on her birthday, and then somehow taken control of her mind to trick her into coming here to free him. It had to be Persie. She was his bridge.

Realization suddenly dawned. *The deal broke the stasis...* Our deal had been written in Chaos, and that was stronger than any hex Tobe could put on this box. The moment Persie had been created, it'd loosened the restraints on Leviathan. He'd spoken to me because she'd existed within me. And he'd come to cement the deal when she'd been born, loosening those restraints a little more. Since then, he'd lain in wait, until their bond matured with her age.

"But you still can't get out, can you?" I quelled my nerves. "If you could, you wouldn't have needed to try and trick Persie into freeing you. And she's not coming anywhere near you ever again."

The frost cracked, and the atmosphere sparked with menace.

Hit a nerve, Leviathan? I glanced at the door to his enclosure, making a decision. I couldn't risk opening it and accidentally letting him out.

Damn... Controlling beasts from outside their glass boxes was always harder than controlling them while I was also inside. And Leviathan would be the biggest challenge I'd ever faced.

"I'm going to need you to stop pretending that this ice

means a damn thing." I waited but nothing happened. The frost stayed, and the energy in the room darkened. "Leviathan, you owe me an audience."

The frost receded, melting away rapidly. Black smoke coiled inside, filling the box from pane to pane.

"If you think I'm going to speak to a bunch of mist, you can think again," I said coolly. In this form, he'd be harder to influence. Black mist was tricky to get any kind of hold on. I needed him solid.

With a tangible air of reluctance, he slowly unfurled. "The Merlin girl. Not a girl anymore. You've aged." His edges solidified until he swayed in front of me on his snaky coils.

"Mortals have a nasty habit of doing that," I shot back.

"It was no insult. To age is to grow wise." He gave a harsh laugh. "I wondered if you might visit. I am honored."

"Save it." His sarcastic flattery grated on my ears.

"This is hardly fair." Leviathan came closer to the front pane. His eerily human eyes squinted out. "You ask me to reveal myself, and do not do the same?"

I made no move to drop the concealment spell. "It's necessary."

"Ah, of course. You do not want Tobe to find you here." He grinned, his rows of teeth crunching together. "Do you intend me harm, Merlin girl?" His laughter resounded through his glass enclosure.

I wasted no time. I lunged forward and pushed my palms flat to the glass. Concentrating with every fiber of my being, I pulsed strands of Chaos into his box. They rushed forward and dissolved into his scaly chest. Two hair-thin lines still glistened in the air. A physical connection between me and him.

"Obey me," I snarled. The words scraped up my throat like knives. "You'll do as I say!"

He stared down at his chest in sudden alarm. His claws raked at the hair-thin strands that connected us, but his hands just passed through them. Five years of research and controlling every beast I'd ever come across... I hadn't known this situation would arise, but the universe had prepped me for it, anyway.

"BOW TO ME!" I bellowed. A metallic taste slithered into my mouth: blood from my throat. The sound of my voice shivered along the hair-thin strands like a guitar string. And his chest provided the acoustics. I watched his body respond to the word, his arms locking and his neck cracking. He resisted my command as best he could, his face straining.

"You are... forbidden from... doing this," he rasped.

I ignored him. "BOW! Better still—unravel those coils and lie flat on the floor!" The order expanded my lungs until they burned, shooting pains up the sides of my ribcage.

His eyes widened in shock as his body obeyed. His serpent coils unraveled beneath him, and his torso tilted forward until he was all the way down. He fought it, groaning and growling with every involuntary movement. His limbs spasmed and his tail lashed, but the impulse to submit was stronger than his willpower. At last, he lay on the ground, his chest and hands flat.

He lifted his head and glowered at me, locking onto my

position despite the concealment spell. "This is... immoral. You are breaking Tobe's rules."

"If you're planning to snitch on me, I know he'll understand." I swiped away the beading sweat on my forehead. "Don't forget where his loyalty lies."

"He is... a coward!" Leviathan spat, globs of gunk hitting the glass.

I smirked. "If he needed to, you can bet your slimy ass he'd send you right back to Chaos himself."

"Is that... what you have... come to do?" For a split second, he looked genuinely afraid. But it was likely a tactic. This monster wasn't helpless or quick to cower. He had ancient power up the wazoo and a knack for subterfuge.

"I'd love nothing more, but it wouldn't fix anything. Persie is stuck with your curse, and you'd just pass it to some other creature if I ended you." I held onto the atoms of his being with every ounce of strength I had.

His tail lashed frantically, still trying to escape my clutches. "Then why... are you here? To show... your power? It makes no... difference."

It does make a difference! He'd messed with my daughter, and now he was due a taste of his own medicine. Though I had to tread carefully. This wasn't just about vengeance.

"I'm here for the truth, Leviathan." I slammed a palm against the glass and the whole thing shuddered. "I know all about your little scheme for Persie, but this isn't ancient Greece and she's not your pawn. Your mother and I made a deal for a name; nothing else. Now, the part I *don't* know is how you're planning to bring about your vision, and what you're plotting for Persie. So spill your guts, or I'll spill them for you."

He raked his claws along the glass, the piercing sound sending a shiver through me. "I will not... tell you anything."

"Have it your way." I delved into my reservoir of Darkness. Grasping hold of shadowy tendrils, I urged them down the glinting magical wires and into his body. He writhed in pain as my mouth moved, uttering a spell I promised myself I'd never use. A curse I had in the depths of my mind, dumped there by the Merlin Grimoire. It had been one of the possible ways to hurt Katherine during her earlier rituals, but by the time I got that information, it was too late to use it.

Speaking of Katherine, I'd learned enough in life to realize that evil never truly left this planet. It only got replaced with new and improved types. I'd hung onto the curse in case I ever faced evil again. And here it was. Trying to take my daughter as his monster bride.

"*Adducere tenebris. Mutare animum. Adducere monsturum. Liberum insaniam. Unleash infernum. Pluet in obumbratio. In tenebris. Tormentum. Formido. Insaniam. Apud inferos realem mundi. Ut convertat animum. Hoc erit non ferenda. Ostende nullum misericordiae. Audite verba.*" Trying to hold three different Chaos channels at once hurt like nothing else. My shirt stuck to my sweat-drenched skin and my breath came in short, sharp gasps. Something would have to give soon, but I hoped I'd have my answers by then. Determined to fight to the bitter end, I focused on Persie and let her image bring me strength.

In the box, Leviathan screamed. His claws dug deeper into

the glass and every bioluminescent glow turned a warning shade of red. Through the transparent gaps in his scales, I saw his organs shaking. He managed to lift his torso a short distance off the ground before he flopped forward again. In that brief moment, I caught sight of his heart, pounding so fast it looked like it wasn't beating at all.

"This... is... cruel!" he roared. His scales shuddered together, making the sound of a porcupine shaking their quills. "This is... a forbidden spell!"

I glared down at his spasming figure. "Don't speak to me about cruelty." He hadn't given a second thought to the pain he'd put my daughter through—the pain and fear she'd keep going through with every Purge. Not to mention the disgusting notion of him taking her as his queen. His fear paled in comparison. Pure hatred added energy to the connecting strands between us. As the Darkness hit him, a fresh scream ricocheted between the walls of his enclosure.

"Stop!" he whimpered. Cracks began to splinter across his armored plates, where they'd vibrated too hard together. His tail lay still, his head in his clawed hands.

I shook my head. "Tell me what I want to know."

"I will... not bend!"

I sent more Darkness hurtling down the Chaos wires between us. He sucked in an agonized breath and one of his transparent patches disintegrated into black ash; his teary human eyes staring at the floating wisps as they returned to Chaos. Even Purge beasts were scared of their own mortality, despite the fact that this one had been alive for centuries. Unless this was another trick to try and get me to stop. He'd hypnotized Persie with those eyes. Why wouldn't he try it with me now that I had the reins?

I dipped into both reservoirs—Light and Dark—as his human eyes lifted up and met mine. This time, there was no mistaking it. He was running scared.

"You've got five seconds," I warned.

"Stop!" he begged. "I do… not know… the answers."

I pulled the pulses of Light and Darkness back. "Say that again. I dare you."

"It is… the truth!" he snarled. "I do not know how… Hell will come… to Earth. I do not know how… Persephone will fit… into the picture. I do not… *know!*"

I resisted the urge to hit him with another bout. "Explain."

"It… is… a prophecy. My mother's prophecy." He slumped forward, breathing heavily. "It is all… I know. I have… no details. No… instruction."

"*Converterent alica. A obumbratio. Restituerunt eum in lucem.*" I whispered the curse reversal, rapid-fire.

His breathing eased slightly. "Thank you."

"Keep talking. If you don't, I've got more where that came from." I wasn't sure I did, but he didn't need to know that. In fact, I was surprised I was still on my feet. My body and mind felt like they'd been hit by a freight train.

"Before she was killed," Leviathan wheezed, "my mother left a contingency in place. She knew her gift had to be passed on. It could not die with her. She knew I could ensure it on her behalf."

"Go on…"

"The inheritance of her gift is a catalyst. It will light the fuse to bring the prophecy of Hell on Earth." His eyes glinted menacingly. "And it has been lit."

I battled to stay calm. "What did she want from it? She didn't mention any prophecy to me when I last saw her."

"Why would she?" he hissed. "You are the enemy."

"Monsters versus humans?" I snorted, but the joke was on me.

He leered upward. "It has always been. You trap us. You incarcerate us. You treat us as though we are less than you. My mother wished to end that. She wished to see all monsters free. I grieve that she did not live to see the djinn take their freedom. It would have thrilled her, as it did me. One day, we will all be as the djinn are. And it will be thanks to my mother, who entrusted me with the task. I will not disappoint her."

Terror flared through me, racing like wildfire in my blood. He sounded dogged in his determination. As if it were already written in the stars.

I'd celebrated right along with Kadar when the djinn got their freedom, yet I didn't bat an eyelid when I walked through the Bestiary, filled to the brim with caged beasts whose energy fueled our world. But they weren't ill-treated, and if we let them run wild, people would die. This was about global safety, not cruel imprisonment. Besides, Tobe took good care of them. He wouldn't have taken up the role of Beast Master if it was immoral, or unkind. That wasn't in his nature.

"You're forgetting something, Leviathan. The djinn didn't try to take *this* world. They took their creator's otherworld, as payback for almost killing them all." I stood my ground, though I suddenly felt as though I was standing on weakened foundations.

Leviathan hit me with a pointed stare. "What do you call what you do to us? You drain us for your own ends. We may not die, but you weaken us."

"That's your narrative, not ours. Purge beasts are dangerous. They pose a huge threat to every living thing on this planet, including other Purge beasts," I said, pushing aside the faint uncertainty in the back of my mind. "Anyway, your mother isn't here, and you're locked in a box. Neither of those things will change."

A grim laugh bubbled out of his cracked lips. "The prophecy has been activated. And she *is* still here. She appears in my dreams, as I appear in Persephone's. I do not know how it will come to pass. I only know that it will. From the moment I named Persephone, I set off the chain reaction. It cannot be stopped. It is written in Chaos itself. There is nothing you or anyone else can do to prevent it."

I shrugged to try and hide my nerves. "Someone said that to me before. They were wrong."

"You asked for answers. I suggest you listen." His eyes hardened. "Whether you want to believe it or not, Persephone is fated to create monsters. *She* is the catalyst. Someday, because she exists, all of Chaos's beasts will roam free. My mother will see her dream come to fruition."

This doesn't make any sense. Except that it did. Echidna had helped us a long time ago. Now, I understood why. She'd clearly seen Katherine coming a mile off and had known how that encounter would end. With time running out for her, she'd probably predicted what I'd do to get the power to defeat Katherine and made sure the naming deal was sealed. All of those steps and trials, back then, had been for *this*: her personal goals masked as aid. Ironically, the kind of patient game that Katherine would've admired, played by a skilled competitor.

Leviathan continued. "It will be paradise for us. But it will be your doomsday. And magic-kind cannot stop it. It has already begun."

Persie... The implications were terrifying. And the fact that Leviathan didn't even know what part my daughter would play terrified me more. She hadn't asked for this. She hadn't done anything to deserve this. But, somehow, she'd started a prophecy that, apparently, none of us would be able to stop. Or, rather... *I'd* started it, by agreeing to the deal in the first place. I should've known there would be more to it than just a name. Kadar had warned me that names have power.

I snapped the Chaos strings that joined me to Leviathan and staggered away from the enclosure. Overwhelmed and exhausted, I had nothing left to say. Neither did he. But as he dragged himself up off the floor, I couldn't ignore his cold laughter. It thudded into my skull like gunfire.

Turning, I headed for the exit. Only, he *did* have one more thing to say. A parting shot to tip me over the edge into all-out panic.

"It is only a matter of time before I walk free," he crowed. "Just wait and see."

And the worst part was, I believed him.

TWENTY-FOUR

Harley

Sirens shrieking in my head, I chalk-doored right out of the SDC. Another moment in there and I'd have combusted. I needed to think, and I couldn't do it so close to that monster. Even being in the same bubble as him right now was too much for my brain to deal with.

I dropped the concealment spell and a fierce heat prickled across my face. Dry and dusty and just what I needed. I drank in the scorched air as though I'd spent the last five minutes underwater. Anything to try and clear my mind enough to get a plan of action together. But how did you even begin to fight something like this? It wasn't a person; it wasn't even a clear scheme. It was an idea, a vision, a prophecy, dangling in front of my face like a rotten carrot. Taunting me.

Think! You have to think! Freaking out would get me nowhere. Sure, I had plenty to freak out about, but I had to put that on the backburner. First, I needed backup.

Whipping out my phone, I sent out the kind of group message that no one could ignore: *Big trouble is coming. Hell on Earth big. Meet me by the oasis ASAP.* I hadn't just called on the support of the Rag Team. This required every damn hand on deck, including Finch's New Muppet Babies. I needed everyone and anyone who'd faced evil with me before.

Keeping the phone in my hand for when the replies came in, I took to pacing. I'd been doing that a lot lately. My boots thudded on the parched earth, sending lizards skittering for cover. Taking a slow breath, I mopped my face with the hem of my t-shirt. Maybe picking the middle of the Mojave Desert hadn't been a smart move. But my friends knew this place, and they knew what it meant—we only came here when something serious cropped up.

I should message Persie. I clutched the phone and stared out at the barren landscape: rusty-colored rock clusters, peppered spiny cacti, sparse shrubs, and a few skeletal trees. Meanwhile, a few tumbleweeds bounced across the dried-out ground. Feeling a tight clench in my chest, I sat down on a scalding rock and shifted around until it cooled a bit. I wasn't even sure why we called it the oasis. There wasn't a drop of water anywhere.

"Should I message Persie?" I asked a nearby lizard. The reptile eyed me as if I were an idiot. "You're right. Not yet. Not without a plan. There's no point in panicking her too." The lizard scuttled on its way, and I had no idea if I'd given it the right answer or not.

A doorway opened in the oscillating air. Two figures tumbled out.

"Melody, Luke… Thank Chaos. I wasn't sure the message would get through." I sagged under the weight of everything that had just happened.

Melody rushed up to me. "Harley, what's wrong? Is everything okay? I guess not, given your message, and… no, you definitely don't feel okay. Your emotions are all over the place, and… my goodness, they're so strong." She knelt beside the rock and grasped for my hand. "What's happened? We left Easter Island as soon as we could."

"Is it Persie?" Luke's calmer voice rang out. I adored Melody, but she talked a mile a minute, and I couldn't process it right now.

Before I could answer, five more chalk-doors opened in quick succession. Nash and Huntress strode out of the first one. Wade, Dylan, and Finch bolted from the second. Ryann, Garrett, and Astrid emerged from the third, while Santana and Raffe exploded out of the fourth. Tobe stepped out gracefully, bringing up the rear. Part of me waited for another door to open and Tatyana and Saskia to step through. Instead, my phone pinged: *In an important meeting at the UMN. I'll ring you when it's over. Hope you're okay. Tx.* I guessed a meeting with the magical UN was a decent excuse, but I still missed seeing her here.

O'Halloran was missing, too, but that had been a deliberate move on my part. What Leviathan had told me could impact how the coven, and the rest of magical society, looked at my daughter. And I wouldn't have O'Halloran making any rash decisions about what to do with her. Not if I could help it.

A barrage of voices hit me at once.

"Harley, what's going on?" Wade jumped in.

"Has something happened to Persie?" Santana's voice clashed with his.

"Is it the coven?" Raffe added.

Astrid held onto Smartie. "Or the missing magicals?"

Everyone spoke at once, a melting pot of words, making the heat and the noise feel unbearable, wrecking my eardrums and my nerves.

"Stop!" I shouted. "Everyone, just stop and I'll explain. Please."

Silence rippled through the group.

I bowed my head and stared at the dusty, red soil. "I just met with Leviathan, to pry some information out of him." I didn't lift my head to look at Tobe, but I didn't need to. I could feel his shock. "And before you give me a lecture, Tobe, just hear what I have to say."

"As you like," he replied stiffly.

"I took matters into my own hands." I raised my eyes to the desert, watching a tumbleweed get snared in a spiky bush. "And I'm glad I did." I repeated everything Leviathan had told me, leaving nothing out. Then I waited for the reactions to flow in.

"You may think your ends justify the means, but this was badly done, Harley," Tobe grumbled. "Yes, this is something we needed to know, but you should have come to me first. I have a duty of care, even to vile specimens such as Leviathan."

"Would you have let me do what I had to do?" I met his disappointed gaze.

His whiskers shivered. "No."

"Then... I'm sorry, but I had no choice." I watched his furry brow crease, a mix of emotions morphing across his face. He cared for his beasts, I knew that. But there hadn't been another choice, and he'd just cemented that.

Astrid wiped dust from her glasses. "You think he's telling the truth?"

"No. You rapped on his fishbowl, pissed him off, and he knew saying something like that would get you riled. He's full of it." Finch shrugged. But his concerned expression didn't match his words.

Kadar appeared. "Even if he spoke the truth, a prophecy is not a certainty."

"He said it himself, he doesn't know the details." Ryann nodded in agreement. "Maybe Echidna thought he'd be out of his box by now. Considering he's still in there, and it doesn't look like he can get out by himself, perhaps the prophecy is moot."

"But... what if it's not?" Garrett asked tentatively. "If the prophecy is written in Chaos, doesn't that break down a couple of obstacles? So far, Leviathan has been able to speak to you and Persie, when neither should have been possible. If he had those liberties, who's to say he won't be granted others?"

Santana lowered Slinky to the ground, where he took off to chase some lizards. "What the hell is Chaos's deal, anyway?

Why does it keep letting people do this kind of thing? Doesn't it have some kind of say?"

"I don't know," I said quietly. Wade came to sit beside me on the rock, his arm slipping around my shoulders. I sensed him trying to conceal his emotions from me. After twenty years of marriage, he still hadn't figure out how to do it successfully. Right now, I felt all sorts coming off him: confusion, anger, disappointment, panic. No good vibes at all. And I sensed some of those feelings were aimed at me, and the fact that I hadn't spoken to him before I'd gone GI Jane on Leviathan.

Melody stood back up. "Chaos works in the same manner as its Children. It can't intervene if someone wants to imprint something like this into the Chaosverse, but it can occasionally offer solutions on the sly." She fidgeted awkwardly. "But we shouldn't forget that Purge beasts are creations of Chaos. In Chaos's eyes, it may believe that they have as much right to a free existence as we do. It might not want to stop this or give us a solution, and it's not as if we can ask how it feels about the situation."

"Yeah, but Chaos is in us, too." Nash ruffled Huntress's fur. Closing her eyes contentedly, Huntress lay her head on her forepaws. I knew how she felt. This was a lot to take in. "I don't pretend to know Chaos personally, but I doubt it'd be too happy about razing our world to ash for the sake of one monster's last wish."

"That's the part I don't get, either. Why does it have to be 'Hell' on Earth?" Finch frowned. "I've seen plenty of Purge beasts who like a nice forest or a pretty lake more than fire and brimstone."

Tobe ruffled his feathers nervously. "I may have the answer to that. Purge beasts are better suited to the atmosphere of otherworlds, as that was their natural habitat before magicals came into existence. Otherworlds take many different forms, but there is one similarity: none of them are inhabited by anything, or anyone, other than a Child of Chaos. There are no buildings, no infrastructure, nothing to inhibit their roaming. I imagine Echidna's vision emulates that, destroying anything that does not coincide. It would be a hell for magicals, not beasts. Essentially, you would all be treated as Echidna believes beasts have been treated."

Finch puffed out a sigh. "Well, that makes more sense."

"Okay, say that's the plan—what do we do to stop it?" Santana brought her usual brand of no-nonsense to the table. That was what I loved about her.

"And what do we do about Persie?" Wade peered down at me. Terror spiked off him in barbed waves. "If she's the catalyst of all of this, what does that mean for her?"

Nash scratched between Huntress's ears. "A glass box and a set of Atomic Cuffs, if the UCA get wind of this."

My heart jolted. "They wouldn't. I won't let them."

"You think they'd give you a choice?" he replied solemnly. "And that'd be the soft approach."

Astrid cast me an apologetic look. "The UCA has a zero-tolerance policy when it comes to global threats. They might even arrange an 'accident,' if they thought Persie posed enough risk. I've seen it happen before."

"No..." Tears jabbed at my eyes. "They'd have to go through me first."

"They'd have to go through all of us, sis," Finch said grimly. "But we do have to prepare for the possibility. It's not going to be easy to keep it off the UCA's radar if devils with pitchforks start popping up all over the place." He was trying to make light of the situation, but I could tell that he was worried.

"And we need to consider what's best for Persie," Garrett interjected. "What if she can't control her Purges? What if she can't... fend Leviathan off?"

I shot him a dark look. "What's your suggestion? Lock her up and throw away the key?"

"If it came to it, maybe." He put up his hands in defense. "It's just that... Well, you need to look at this the way you'd look at any other mission. I know it's hard, but you might have to set personal feelings aside for the sake of Persie's safety. And everyone else's."

Finch stormed toward Garrett. "And you'd better have a long, hard think about what you're saying about my niece." His eyes burned with anger. "How would you feel if someone said that about Merrick, huh? You'd tell them to shut the hell up."

"Maybe we should all take a breath." Luke came in as the mediator. "Things will always get heated when it comes to family. So let's just take a step back and calm things down before they escalate."

Finch stepped back from Garrett, but he didn't stop glaring. I was grateful for his defense of Persie. Judging by Wade's brimming fury, he shared Finch's anger. And yet, a part of me wondered if Garrett was right. If this were any other mission, I wouldn't hesitate to make the right choice. Even if it was the hardest choice. But everything got fuzzy when it came to Persie. The thought of her locked in a box was just... impossible. There had to be another solution to this. There *had* to be.

A few moments later, with tempers dulled, Nash offered a suggestion. "Aren't we forgetting some folks who could give us a hand?"

"Who?" I looked to him, desperate for a glimmer of hope.

Finch snorted. "Ah, sis, I don't think you're going to like this."

I narrowed my eyes. "Please don't tell me you want to talk to—"

"Erebus. Am I right, Nash?" An amused grin stretched across his face. Erebus might've helped out during the Atlantis debacle, but that hadn't wiped his slate clean, not in my eyes. He'd still tugged my brother along on a string, threatening him and the people he cared about at every opportunity. And the fact that he'd been allowed to walk off into the sunset with Kaya still felt like a perversion of justice. She'd done things just as bad, yet the magical world had brushed it off because she was a former queen of Atlantis. That would never sit right with me.

Nash shrugged. "I know he's the last person you want to turn to, Harley, but he's got connections."

"He isn't a Child of Chaos anymore," Dylan said, confused. "How would he be any help?"

I sighed slowly. "He knows how to get in touch with them. And since we don't have a direct line to Lux, Remington, or Gaia, we need someone who knows how to link us up."

"Can't you use Euphoria to reach Gaia?" Melody asked.

I gave a halfhearted shrug. "She's not available for business, either. Either that, or my Euphoria has gotten rusty over the years. I tried it a few times in the run-up to Persie's birthday, trying for a last-ditch intervention, but I kept coming up against a wall of some kind."

"Could it be a Chaos embargo? Maybe she got the same warning as Lux and Erebus about getting involved in mortal problems after whatever she did to Finch in Atlantis." Nash suggested grimly. "In the years between Atlantis and these recent attempts to get in touch with her, did you ever try to make contact?"

I chewed my lip. "No..."

"She transferred your power to me, that's all," Finch protested. "I broke out of that prison all by myself."

Nash snorted. "And if you believe that, I'm a snapping turtle. You shattered reinforced, Atlantean hex-protected glass, Finch."

"It *could've* been me. And you do remind me of a snapping turtle." He pouted, but I sensed he agreed with Nash. There *had* been some extra juice in the tank back then, and it wasn't the kind that just came from a Chaos transfer. Finch had implied as much to me after the Atlantis debacle came to an end.

"Whatever the case may be with that He-Man transformation, Finch, the fact right now is, *I* can't get through to Gaia on my own," I replied. "But Erebus might know of another way through, so that's what we're going to find out."

"I can already feel that Italian sunshine on my face." Finch smirked, his mood instantly improving.

I shook my head at him. "It's not a holiday. If I'm schlepping there for that backstabber, it had better be worth it."

For the chance of sparing Persie a future behind glass, I could put up with seeing Erebus again. Hell, I'd have gone to the center of the Earth to read poetry to Davin, if I thought it would help my daughter.

TWENTY-FIVE

Harley

"Give Mr. and Mrs. Darkness our love," Santana said sarcastically. She scooped Slinky up to spare the lizards and gathered with the rest of the extended Rag Team to watch Finch and me go. Wade wanted to come along, but I'd urged him to stay, for Persie's sake. Someone had to be at the SDC for her. And Jacob had just pinged him to talk urgent shop, so it made sense for him to be the one to go back and protect our daughter.

I forced a laugh. "I'll try."

"And don't worry, the secret's safe with us." Astrid gave Garrett a firm nudge.

He dipped his head. "Sorry about before. You know I want the best for Persie. And you."

"I know," I replied softly. He'd made a good point; I just didn't like hearing it. But I didn't want anyone keeping him from speaking his mind. We needed every idea people had. That's why I had summoned them in the first place.

"Update us as soon as you hear anything, okay?" Melody waved her phone at me. "We're going back to San Jose, so we'll be nearby if you need any help. We're here for you guys, and we're here for Persie."

Nash nodded. "I'll go with them, just in case."

"And we'll be waiting at the SDC for your Italian bulletin." Raffe had the reins again, the djinn having lost interest after realizing we weren't immediately going for a second round with Leviathan.

"Be careful, okay? I'm just a chalk-door away." Wade stepped forward and kissed me on the forehead. I knew I still owed him an explanation, but it would have to wait.

I looked up into his eyes. "I'll be in touch the moment we have intel from Kermit and Miss Piggy."

A ghost of a smile touched his lips. *Almost off the hook...*

"Hey, that's an insult to all you Muppet Babies." Finch glanced over his shoulder. He had etched a chalk-door onto the face of a nearby rock and whispered the *Aperi Si Ostium* spell that would get us to Italy; the exile location of choice for Erebus and Kaya. More of a permanent vacation, if you asked me.

With the doorway ready to go, Finch gave Ryann a farewell kiss. It wasn't easy to leave everyone behind. Right now, I really wanted a full cohort of people around me, to share the weight of this prophecy and its implications. But where we were going, a low profile would serve us better.

And if we all went missing at once, O'Halloran would definitely get suspicious.

"Put on your smiley face, sis." Finch nudged me in the arm.

I smirked. "Now, that's asking a heck of a lot." Together, we stepped through.

I walked out into the most beautiful landscape I'd ever seen. Rolling green hills, adorned with tall cypress trees and neatly arranged vineyards, swollen grapes growing in fat bunches. A bronzy sunset blanketed everything in a fairytale glow, making it look like a world out of one of Persie's paintings. Up ahead, a cypress-lined path led to a Tuscan villa perched on top of a hill. It didn't look real, either, with its yellow-tinged walls and an old-timey roof.

I managed to roll my tongue back into my mouth. "They gave up on Capri, then?"

Finch groaned. "Kaya saw a picture of Tuscany and the rest is history. Nice digs, though. If I got myself exiled, I'd pick a place like this."

"That's not the point of exile," I muttered. "And you always said it'd be a tropical island."

"Between Eris Island and Atlantis, they don't appeal so much anymore." He laughed and set off up the dusty track toward the villa.

I headed after him. The Darkness duo were pushing the boundaries of their exile. There were a few other farmhouses and villas dotted around the pretty hillsides, and in the distance I saw a medieval looking spire and a few rooftops that might've been a village. They weren't supposed to be near anyone at all. Not that the UCA would enforce it, so long as they continued to behave.

"What's the kid actually like?" I fell in step with Finch. I'd never met Jason personally, but I'd heard a few things. Not enough to form a decent picture.

Finch shrugged. "An oddball, but harmless. Quiet. Up until a couple of years ago, I genuinely thought he might be mute." He smiled wryly. "Let's put it this way: you wouldn't think he was Erebus and Kaya's."

"Isn't that a good thing?" I raised an eyebrow.

"Depends on how you look at it. You'll be able to make up your own mind when you meet him. It's not as if he ever goes anywhere." Finch looked sort of… sorry for the kid.

I gestured to the glorious surroundings. "He's got all of this, and he doesn't go anywhere? It's not as if he's bound by the same rules as his parents."

"Actually, that's a bit of a sore subject," Finch replied. "The UCA can't make up their minds about him. He's half-Atlantean, with a hint of former Child of Chaos—that makes folks nervous. But if they met him, they'd probably laugh. The kid's as soft as a teddy bear made out of cotton candy. From what Erebus tells me, he spends most of his time sketching birds and butterflies and making notes on the species."

We powered up the rest of the hill to a mind-blowing sight. Our would-be informant stood in a garden paradise, complete with a spouting water fountain, elegant statues of gods and goddesses, bushes overflowing with little white flowers, hanging baskets everywhere, and gravel walkways that led to different sections of the beautiful grounds. But that wasn't what grabbed my attention. He was shirtless under a novelty apron, standing in front of a ridiculously large grill and humming to himself. It took me a moment to remember who I was looking at. He had Remington's body, but twenty years older than the last time I'd seen it. His once-dark hair had grayed, and so had the stubble that shadowed his jaw, with a few more wrinkles lining his suntanned skin. Remington didn't exist inside there anymore. This was Erebus, but... domesticated.

Erebus caught sight of us, and a grin spread across his relaxed face. His tongs clattered to the barbecue. "Finch? What a wonderful surprise. And you've brought your sister, too. The prodigal Merlin, finally come to pay her old friend a visit!"

"Merlin-Crowley," I corrected. I didn't do that often, but I wanted him to know where we stood. This was a formal conversation. And he wasn't an old friend.

Erebus wiped his hands on his apron and walked toward us. "Of course, my apologies. It is hard for me to think of you as anything other than the young and foolhardy kids you once were."

"And I still think of you as a giant pain in my ass," I muttered.

He laughed. "I see you haven't lost any of your sass."

"And I see you've gained a few pounds and gray hairs." It boggled my mind to see him all normal and paternal, with the dad-bod to go with it. The apron didn't hide nearly enough.

He patted his belly. "That is the sign of a good life, Harley. Marital bliss and a happy family—it all goes to the stomach. Indeed, in many cultures, weight is a sign of wealth and prosperity. I prefer that perspective."

"Dad, Mom wants to know when the—" a young man of around Persie's age exited the villa. He stopped abruptly when he saw us. A rabbit in headlights: his strange, wolfish gray eyes widened in fright and his arms tucked into his sides like a penguin on parade. The boy had a very striking look. Silver hair streaked with interspersed strands of sun-kissed golden brown, and Mediterranean-tanned skin with patches of porcelain white all over, as if he had vitiligo. From what I'd glimpsed before he'd bent forward, he had genetically blessed looks from his mom and dad—well, Remington. Blended with his mom's refined Atlantean features, he could've brought a whole new meaning to the word 'beauty.' If it wasn't for his major lack of social skills.

"You remember Finch, Jason." Erebus clapped Finch on the back as if they were old pals.

My eyes bugged as Jason bent into a full bow, his arms still straight at his sides. It gave the impression of a ski-jumper ready to launch. "Mr. Finch."

"And this is his infamous sister, Harley." Erebus gestured to me, making the wise decision to avoid touching me.

He bent even deeper, until his head almost touched his toes. "Ms. Harley."

I didn't have the heart to correct him. Instead, I sent out some Empath feelers to try and read his emotions and got back a crashing wave of anxiety.

"Uh... the... um... grill, Dad." Jason stayed in his bow, his cheeks turning purple from being pretty much upside down.

"You can stop bowing, son." Erebus laughed awkwardly.

Jason stood up straight. "Sorry."

"It's nice to meet you, Jason. I've heard a lot about you." I held my hand out to him. He just stared at it as though I'd waved a jellyfish in his face, so I smoothly turned it into a wave. I smiled at him as if nothing out of the ordinary had happened. "We didn't mean to interrupt your dinner."

He gulped loudly. "No. It would've... um... been rude if you had. Dinnertime is for... uh... family."

"Yes, I suppose it is." It didn't sound like he meant to offend me; he was just stating the obvious. "And that's a nice way to look at it. I wish I could get my daughter to sit with us for dinner."

He looked anywhere but at me. "Then she must be very rude. Or maybe she doesn't like food. Is that why?" He tugged on the collar of his button-up shirt. "I've read about people who get no pleasure from eating, because they... um... don't like the texture. Does she have a problem with that?"

"No, it's not that. We're just quite a busy family, so we don't always get the time," I explained, aware that he had begun to sweat. I felt for the poor boy. He'd never learned to be around others, aside from the odd Finch visit. He had his hobbies, but they didn't make up for actual human contact. He'd been exiled by proxy, and that just didn't seem fair.

"It's... um... important to make time." He brushed a shaky hand through his zebra hair. "Right, Dad?"

"It is, son, but everyone's entitled to do things their own

way." Erebus offered him a gentle smile. "Now, go tell your mom dinner won't be long, and to set two more places at the table," he instructed. Jason ran off without another word, clearly desperate to get away from new company.

"That kid needs to be around more people, pronto," I whispered to Finch.

He chuckled. "If he could leave, he'd probably live in the wilderness and never speak to another person again."

That's not good for him. I kept my opinions to myself, since we needed to keep Erebus on our side. Besides, if the UCA were still hemming and hawing about what exile rules should apply to Jason, it wasn't exactly the boy's fault that he hadn't been socialized properly.

"Are you hungry?" Erebus drew my attention back.

I nodded. "We are, but I don't think we'll be staying that long."

"Oh?" He returned his focus to his huge grill. They definitely had enough to accommodate two more guests, but the idea of sitting around a table and making nice with Kaya and Erebus seemed totally implausible.

"We were actually here to ask about—" another figure stepped out into the garden, cutting Finch off. Kaya no longer had extended life, or Chaos of any kind to use, but you wouldn't have known it to look at her. She'd barely aged a day, and the way she walked still whispered power. This bygone queen definitely used her sunscreen.

"Jason said we had guests." Kaya looked at Finch and instantly looked away again. Her stance of authority fizzled to a shuffling unease. "He has decided he is no longer hungry and has headed off to the vineyards with his notebooks." She sighed, as though this was a frequent occurrence. For a moment, all of the history between us fell away and I saw a mother, worried about how her kid was growing up. A mother like me.

"We didn't mean to scare him off." I offered her a sympathetic smile. We must've done *something*, considering his insistence about the importance of family dinnertime. I guessed avoiding strangers was the only thing more important.

Erebus gave us an apologetic look. "He gets overwhelmed."

"If the magical authorities had heeded our appeal, during his infancy, we might have been able to make arrangements for him to spend time at a coven. Summers, or the colder seasons, perhaps." Kaya retrieved a straw hat from one of the garden benches and placed it delicately on her head. "They are reconsidering his integration, now that he is deemed an adult, but we have yet to receive a confirmation."

"He just needs scraping out of his shell," Finch said confidently. "You should take him to see the authorities. Five minutes in his company, and they'd integrate him in a heartbeat."

Kaya gave him a sharp look. "He is intelligent and well-mannered. Any coven would be privileged to have him. It is only his nerves that impede him, especially when meeting new individuals." She glanced at me, with a hint of hope. "Perhaps, you might offer a word to the UCA on Jason's behalf?"

I had no love for the woman, but that didn't mean her boy had to suffer. By the looks of it, cooped up with no one but his mom and dad, he'd suffered enough. I could almost imagine him with the kids of the SDC, slowly getting his anxieties ironed out. "I'll try."

Genie would take him under her wing, that's for sure. From the moment Persie came into the world, Genie had decided she'd be my daughter's best friend. Sometimes I worried about Genie's influence. But most of the time, I was glad Persie had someone she could rely on for anything and everything.

"I would be eternally grateful." Kaya dipped her head slightly. "A young man of his age should be surrounded by more than flora and fauna."

"My Persie likes her own company, too. Sometimes, it's a trial to even get her out of her room to take some fresh air. But she'd love this place." I waved a hand toward their beautiful house.

Kaya gave me a sympathetic smile. "We have one of her paintings in the villa."

"You do?" That came as a surprise.

"Finch sent it, as a Christmas present." She rubbed the back of her neck. After all the time that had passed, she still couldn't look Finch in the eye. They'd been married once, after all. "I suspect he intended it in jest, considering the subject matter. However, it continues to take pride of place in our lounge, as it did in Capri."

Finch feigned disbelief. "Me? *Jest?*"

"What was the subject matter?" She had me intrigued.

"A watery world," she replied. "It is a masterpiece, in truth. The brushstrokes are so emotive, and the colors are mesmerizing. Even Jason is fond of it, and he does not care much for the abstract sphere of art."

I couldn't help smiling. "She'd be pleased to hear you say that, even if my brother should've paid her commission."

"Is an uncle's love not commission enough?" Finch grinned mischievously.

"Look at us now, Finch." Erebus laid out his grilled assortment on a clean plate. "Would you ever have envisioned this scene? All of us content in our lives, with grown children and beautiful wives?" He crossed to Kaya and planted a lingering kiss on her lips. I glanced away, but it was sweet that they were still crazy about each other, all these years later.

Amusement flickered across Finch's face. "Well, I wasn't supposed to survive your servitude, I was briefly married to your wife, and we almost had a global takeover on our hands. So... no, I didn't think we'd ever be here, having a friendly chat in the garden of your swanky villa." He laughed to ease the tension he'd just built. "But we've already buried those hatchets."

Kaya looked like she wanted to shrink into the shadows and disappear. "I will say it until my dying breath, Finch. I am sorry for all of the former... unpleasantness."

"I know. I was just teasing." He smiled and Erebus relaxed. "Bygones are bygones, water under the bridge, et cetera."

"You'll never change." Erebus shook his head, but he hadn't lost his smile. "I imagine you cracking a joke with your dying breath."

Finch shrugged. "Isn't that why it's called gallows humor?"

Erebus closed the lid of the barbecue and picked up the plate. My mouth watered, but we weren't going to stay for dinner. I couldn't. "Now, are you going to tell us what's behind this impromptu visit, or are you going to keep us guessing? Just to forewarn you, we're good at guessing. Kaya and I love a gameshow, don't we, my love?"

Kaya laughed, her eyes twinkling. "We do, darling."

"It's about Persie." I took a deep breath. "She's in trouble. End-of-the-world trouble. And we need to find a way to contact the Children to see if they can help us out. I get that you aren't one anymore, but you must still know of a way to get in touch."

Erebus's expression hardened. "Why is it always the end of the world with you? Surely one day you could just come by for a casual visit?"

"That day isn't today," Finch replied. "That slimy blobfish of a monster, Leviathan, has gone and dumped a prophecy on us, and he's got it imprinted in Chaos. We need to fight fire with fire. Chaos with Chaos. And that calls for some of those Chaos kiddies."

Kaya put her arm around Erebus's waist. "Of course, Harley. I remember Leviathan from some of Atlantis's tomes, and they did not cast him in a particularly noble light. We will do what we can for you, and for your daughter." She covered her mouth with her hand. "You must be so worried. How could you not be, under such circumstances?"

"I am, or I wouldn't be here. No offense." I tried to keep calm.

Erebus exchanged a glance with his wife. "I will do what I can. It has been a long while since I have spoken to my brethren, but I shall try." He held her closer. "I owe you a debt of gratitude for saving Kaya from Davin. And, in truth, I've always been fond of you all. If someone is trying to hurt you or one of yours, it's personal."

"I'm flattered." Finch looked genuinely relieved.

"However, I was wrong to offer you a place at our table. You should not stay." Erebus's mouth set in a grim line. "The Italian covens have eyes on us, at the request of the UCA. I don't want them getting any ideas about us flirting with the magical world again. We've got Jason to think about. Anything that might affect his future is a risk we cannot afford to take. I'm sure you can understand our point of view."

I nodded. "We've got to protect our kids, right?"

"We do." Erebus glanced around as if he expected feds to descend at any minute. "That's why I'll still try to do this for you. I'll get in touch with Finch if I hear from my former siblings."

"Thank you." I barely got the words out. I'd been so afraid that they wouldn't be able to help. Even if it was only an attempt, it was something. And I needed that shred of hope right now.

He sighed. "But don't hold your breath. You know what Children of Chaos can be like. We're a fickle bunch."

"*Pfft.* This Tuscan air is either doing wonders for you, or it's messed with your noggin," Finch teased, though it sounded empty. And Erebus didn't look amused. In fact, he looked deadly serious, like he had a lot more to say on the subject.

No... don't burst this bubble...

"Leviathan, as you said, is a slimy creature—as slick in scales as he is in his methods. Echidna might have been worse, but she at least had the decency to die." He set down his plate. "I don't want to trouble you further, but if the prophecy is indeed embedded in Chaos, it *will* find its way to the surface. It is merely a matter of how and when, and to what degree."

"Are you saying this mission is failed from the start, then?" Finch asked.

Erebus surveyed his home with sad eyes. He took a deep breath. "I will find out more about such prophecies, to see if there is a loophole or means of prevention, but I would suggest..." he trailed off.

"What?" I hated the pregnant pause. Nothing good came after that kind of hesitation.

He looked me square in the eyes. "I suggest you prepare for the worst... I suggest we all prepare for the worst."

TWENTY-SIX

Persie

"Y ou are all here to see if you have what it takes to join our ranks," Victoria Jules declared as she strode into the spotlight. An awed silence descended over the room. She waved her hand and the polished concrete floor began to move; two halves receding into hidden recesses. The crowd peered over the newly made precipice to find a sunken arena below the hall. A gigantic obstacle course covered the arena floor—miniature mountains, a cave with a glass roof, a huge field of seven-foot corn stalks, a circle of dense forest, a deep pool... and monsters that dotted the scenes—frozen, but looking worryingly real.

A ripple of nervous excitement made its way through the thirty fellow candidates, who'd collected in cliques around a sort of holding pen. A few gasped, but quickly tried to save face by turning to their massive binders of intel. Not one of them looked like they'd expected what now lay below us.

"Are those monsters real? Why aren't they moving?" one of the cadets—a ponytailed young woman with a sharp-featured face—asked.

Victoria readjusted her authoritarian stance. "They are intricate simulations, but they will behave as if they are real." The faintest hint of a smile forced up one corner of her pale lips. "We were forced to stop using real monsters due to safety regulations. A shame, but understandable given the previous fatality rates for the exam. However, don't underestimate the simulations. You may not be at risk of death, but loss of limb is still relatively common." She smirked, but I couldn't tell whether she was joking.

My heart hammered as I scanned the fake monsters again. I counted fifteen, but there'd be more in the pool—and the forest, and the long grass, and in every corner we couldn't see from where we were. I squirmed at the edge of the arena, unable to stand still for very long. I had that pre-exam feeling of nausea, cold sweats, shaky hands, and the sense that I'd suddenly forgotten everything I'd ever learned.

"This is crazy," I whispered to Genie, who looked weirdly entranced by the arena. "It's way beyond my paygrade!"

And everyone knows we're the weak links. The burn of thirty pairs of eyes nearly gave me a rash, and the whispers were worse. Judgmental mutterings, all directed at Genie and me. Or maybe just me. With Genie's silver hair and Atlantean tattoos, they knew what she was, and that tended to command respect. Sometimes a bit of snootiness, too, thanks to old grudges. The magical world hadn't forgotten that Atlantis's former queen tried to seize global control.

Genie took my hand. "You're already here, Persie. That's the hardest part."

"Are you looking at the same thing as me?" I hissed. "I can't get through that!"

"You can. You're Persie freaking Merlin-Crowley." She grinned and pulled me closer to her. "How many Purge beasts have you faced in those dreams of yours, huh?"

I shrugged sullenly. "I lost count."

"Exactly! You've faced worse than this in your *sleep*. I doubt there's anything here that you haven't seen before." She nudged me playfully. "You didn't need Kes bombarding you with Monster Biology—you already know these creatures, all the way down to variations in scale color. You've got an advantage over these saps, believe me."

I blinked at her. "I hadn't thought of it like that."

"You have a whole Bestiary in your sketchbooks. You might as well be Tobe at this point." She smiled, and, weirdly, I felt better. "So you don't have magic at your fingertips. Who cares? You've got knowledge, and knowledge trumps magic every day of the week."

"I hope you're right." I tried to keep a positive outlook as Ms. Jules prepared to call the first candidate to the proverbial batting cage. Strangely, part of me wished the monsters *were* real. Then I'd have had a five-second break of them bowing or trying to figure out why I was important, five seconds I could use to come up with a master plan. Providing they behaved the same way as the beasts *I* Purged, that is. I hadn't tested the theory.

Victoria took a binder from her assistant. "Any volunteers?"

A bulky cadet stepped forward, egged on by his two muscular friends. "I'll go first."

"Name?" Victoria's expression didn't change, and I saw the boy's arrogance wilt into confusion. It'd take a lot to impress her, I guessed.

"Uh... Jeremiah Rollins," he replied.

"And what would be the spelling of 'Uhjeremiah'?" She offered him a cool look.

He shook his head. "It's just Jeremiah. Jeremiah... uh... Rollins."

"When you leave here, I suggest you learn how to get your name out in one go." I didn't know whether it was okay to laugh. Victoria had that air about her where she looked all business, but possibly with a funny streak buried deep down. She offered the binder to Jeremiah, who pressed his palm to the page, which was actually a thin sheet of magically charged metal. As for Jeremiah, part of me felt sorry for him. He was just nervous, like anyone would be. Perhaps this was where the actual test began, with staying cool and calm in the face of a woman like Victoria.

"Leave?" he asked, his arrogance shrinking further.

She pulled the binder back around to face her. "I have a sixth sense about these things, Mr. Rollins, but feel free to prove me wrong. I'd welcome it."

"But I'm—"

She cut him off quickly. "A Herculean, with Water and

Earth abilities. Yes, I can see that." She looked over the information that had appeared in the binder. "A captain at the Vancouver Coven's beast academy two years running. And you spent a summer working as a volunteer hunter in the Amazon. Very impressive on paper, Mr. Rollins, but paper doesn't mean a whole lot in the field."

A few snickers rumbled around the holding pen.

"I don't see what's funny about that," she said dryly. "All of you may look promising on paper. But I have seen candidates with the most pristine resumes you could imagine walk into this room. And I can count on one hand how many of *those* made it through."

The chuckles died, leaving stunned unease in their wake. But I didn't have to worry about that. I was as disappointing on paper as I'd probably be in the field. Still, I wasn't sure if Victoria actually meant what she said or if this was some sort of intimidation tactic. Surely this Rollins guy's experience counted for something; he looked and sounded, on paper, like he'd pass with flying colors.

"My assistant, Taryn, will take you down to the arena. When the siren sounds, you may begin. You will only know if you have completed or failed the test when the siren sounds again." Victoria instructed.

The assistant set her binders down on a nearby table and gestured for the first victim to follow. An elevator rose from the ground and the two disappeared inside. Shortly after, they reappeared in the cavern below, where Taryn left Jeremiah on a rocky plinth and retreated hastily. A satchel sat on the ground in front of him, likely placed there before we'd arrived, bulging in a familiar way.

Mason Jars? Or puzzle boxes? I'd soon find out.

The siren sounded seconds later, and the games began. Jeremiah leapt off the plinth and charged into the square of corn stalks. From our vantage point, I saw tails whipping and shadows darting forward to close in on their would-be capturer. Only, he'd left the satchel behind.

Strike one, I'd say...

Genie and I watched together as he thrashed through the corn stalks, oblivious to what was coming his way. Within seconds, two wolves had cornered him. Pale blue and stark white in color, their tails were disjointed, resembling thunderbolts. Gnashing their jaws, they teamed up to take Rollins down. One ran in front to distract him, while the other threw back its head and howled. But instead of a howl, the wolf let out a roar that rumbled through the arena like thunder. A moment later, lightning appeared out of thin air and forked right down at the terrified guy. He twisted out of the way just in time and threw the wolf back with his Herculean strength.

"They're raiju," I whispered to Genie. I'd met a pack of them in the ruins of a Japanese temple during a dream, a year or so ago. They'd been friendlier than these—companions to the Shinto god of lightning, if memory served.

"See, you're already a step ahead." She nudged me excitedly. "He doesn't have a clue."

Rollins ducked down and sent out a wave of Earth Chaos. The corn stalks transformed into a sea of grasping plants, snatching at the legs of the raiju. One yelped as the stalks wrapped it up, trapping it. Rollins raced toward the other creature and grasped it around the neck, holding on until the poor thing passed out. I had to remind myself that these beasts weren't real—they were only simulations. Still, it didn't seem right to treat something so noble as if it were a rabid dog. I guessed all the studying in the world couldn't give a person class. I cast a glance at Victoria. She pursed her lips, a sign of disapproval.

Leaving the raiju on the ground, Rollins cursed loudly and sprinted back to the plinth to snatch up the satchel. There must have been some sort of magical sound system rigged up to amplify everything inside the arena, because I heard those swear words loud and clear. And I'd heard the raiju yelping as if they were next to me, too.

Even with the satchel now in his grasp, Jeremiah bulldozed his way to the next stage, leaving the raiju out cold instead of putting them in jars. He skidded to a stop at the edge of a pond, his eyes scouring the water for any sign of a monster. A shadow slipped between the tree trunks at the far side of the pond—small and furtive. But Rollins hadn't seen it.

He reared back as a squat creature lurched out of the trees. Covered head to toe in a tangled mass of black hair, it reminded me of a goblin or a gnome. It was small and squat with a humanoid face and body, but utterly stomach-churning to look at: gnarled, warty features, and a bulbous, purple-tinged nose. It crept to the water's edge, swiped a smooth pebble from beneath the surface, and swallowed it whole. A moment later, it vanished in plain sight.

"Any ideas?" Genie frowned.

I nodded. "Tikoloshe. African gremlin-thing. Shamans tend to send them out when someone's wronged them. They swallow one of those pebbles, turn invisible, and sneak up on whoever they've been asked to wreak vengeance on." I remembered a fairly unpleasant encounter on an African savannah, where I'd woken up in a cold sweat after that thing had chased me for miles.

"This ought to be good." Genie tipped her head for a better view.

Rollins whipped his head this way and that. I spied a few wet footprints on the muddy bank of the pond, creeping toward Rollins, and stole another look at Victoria. Her face gave nothing away. This test was famously difficult, but not impossible. And, looking more closely, I could recognize the assists that the Institute had put in place for candidates. Tall stalks for the lightning beasts, since they could be grounded by earth. Mud beside the pond to reveal the monster's movements—if you looked carefully.

Rollins yelped and patted his hands frantically across his body, trying to feel for the creature. The tikoloshe had reached its victim, and blood was trickling down Rollins's forearm. Another bite appeared on Rollins's shoulder, prompting him to spin around in a terrified daze. His hands grasped for the beast, but the critter was too quick.

Get in the water! Splashes would be a dead giveaway. My leg vibrated with tension as I watched.

Instead, Rollins used his Water ability to surround himself with a vortex, draining the pond dry. On one side, a small shape dented the vortex. The gremlin had gotten inside, but at least Rollins had made the fighting ground smaller. I couldn't see through the wall of churning water, but I could hear the battle raging inside through the arena speaker system: shouts and expletives and howls as Rollins tried to get the better of the tikoloshe.

After an unbearable wait, the vortex fell away. Rollins panted in the center with an unconscious tikoloshe on the ground at his feet, the smooth pebble beside the gremlin. Rollins had no doubt squeezed the beast into submission, the same way he had with the raiju.

"Doesn't he realize he's supposed to be capturing these things?" Genie muttered.

I shrugged. "I keep thinking he'll remember eventually. It must be the stress."

As though he'd heard me, Rollins took out a jar and laid it next to the tikoloshe. I was a little surprised not to see the fancy puzzle boxes people had told me about. Maybe going the old-fashioned route was part of the test. With bleeding crescents turning his white t-shirt pink, Rollins waited for it to slip into the jar before plowing on to the next stage. The tikoloshe had done serious damage before Rollins had bested it, and some memory of Monster Biology told me those wounds would fester.

He walked slowly up to the mouth of a cave and froze when an almighty squawk echoed from inside. Through the glass roof, created for the spectators' benefit, a hulking creature stomped forward, emerging from the darkness. Three heads poked out first, bald and ugly with razor-sharp beaks. All three heads were attached to one enormous, feathered body, with wings so wide they dwarfed Rollins.

Rollins put up his fists. As if that would help him.

Genie's eyes bugged. "What is *that*?"

"No idea." Apparently, even my dreams had limits. I'd been on a roll with the monster stats, but this made me glad I hadn't gone first. I learned more with every stage Rollins went through. I waited eagerly to absorb what came next so I'd be more prepared when my turn came.

The monster wasted no time charging. Rollins ducked out of the way, only to get pecked by one of the heads. Mauled might've been a better description. It caught his arm in its savage beak and shook its head violently, dragging Rollins around as if he were a sack of coal. I flinched with every wrench, wanting to look away, but morbid curiosity kept me watching. Rollins managed to punch it, and the beast let him go. I gasped in nervous alarm, silently urging him to get as far away as possible before it came in for another attack. He jumped up as quickly as he could, but the vulture-headed monster was faster. It bowled into him and knocked him down, and my heart sank. A second later, the beast jumped onto Rollins's chest with its full weight and tore into him with talons the size of dagger blades. Its beaks pecked at him relentlessly until he stopped moving, and the siren blared to signal the end of the test.

"I thought you said nobody could die?" one of Rollins's meaty friends said nervously.

Victoria kept her eyes on the scene below. "I did not lie."

A gate opened in the wall of the arena and medics sprinted out with a stretcher. Meanwhile, the vulture thing retreated back to its cave to await the next contestant. The medics lifted Rollins onto the stretcher and carried him away.

"Will he be okay?" I asked. He didn't look good, but I wanted to believe the head huntswoman when she said nobody could die. Still, he'd be in a lot of pain, and that didn't make me feel good. Exams weren't supposed to leave a person unconscious and covered in bite marks.

Victoria looked surprised by my interjection. "He will recover, and once he has been stabilized in our infirmary, he will be sent home to recuperate. But an ellén trechend is not a creature to be taken lightly."

So that's what the vulture thing is. It still didn't ring any bells, but at least I had a name for it now. And names, as I'd recently learned, had immense power.

"Chances are, the nightmares will never go away." Victoria sighed and turned to address the sea of shocked faces. "Do not underestimate your foe. Monster hunting is serious business. It's not for the faint of heart. The most important factor is how you observe and act in the moment."

A bevy of nodding heads responded, including mine. I'd already learned a lot by observing, but nobody knew how they would react until they were in it. Still, it surprised me to hear her tone soften, giving a hint of humanity to her formidable façade. If anything, it made her all the more inspiring—the kind of stern yet supportive presence that I wouldn't mind learning the trade from.

"And I suggest you take that satchel when you begin, instead of having to run back for it. I would've thought that was obvious." She shook her head in disappointment. "We train hunters to capture beasts, not pummel them. What would be the use of that?"

She clearly wanted the crème de la crème for this institute, and silly mistakes wouldn't be tolerated. She had her reputation and the reputation of the Institute to protect. The Basani twins, after whom this place was named, had set a high bar for monster hunting. I'd heard about them from my uncle and mom, and the occasional online article about their heyday, and they had a heck of a record. Rollins would never have made the cut.

"May I ask a question, Ms. Jules?" I didn't know if it was allowed, but something had been bugging me since we'd arrived.

"You may, but I can't promise I'll answer," she replied.

I took my chances. "Why is the Institute here in Ireland? I thought the Basani twins were Australian."

Harsh laughter did the rounds, and disapproving eyes prickled the back of my neck.

Victoria gave another small, kind smile. "It is a valid question. One of our founders married an Irishman—the director of the Galway Coven. There was plenty of room for an institute here, and Ireland is exceptionally rich in wild monsters."

"I see." I nodded awkwardly, feeling stupid. "Makes sense."

"One needn't know every minute detail of this place to do

well in the exam." Victoria cast a frosty look over the rest of the candidates. "Although, I can't say if a lack of knowledge on the subject will help you or hinder you. I imagine I'll find out in due course. Now, who will be the next candidate?"

To my alarm, Genie stepped forward before anyone else could get a word in. "I'll go next."

TWENTY-SEVEN

Persie

―――――――――――

"And who are you?" Victoria opened the binder to a fresh sheet. I stared at my friend, my panic skyrocketing. Obviously, I'd known we'd have to step up to take our individual turns at some point, since that was why we were here. But I'd expected us to be two of the last to go, when there wouldn't be so many people watching, and after we'd gained more insight into tactics and techniques by watching more candidates.

Genie placed her hand on it, and her information appeared. "Iphigenia Vertis."

"An Atlantean." Victoria's eyebrow raised marginally as she looked over the data. "I don't like to assume based on appearance. I see enough magicals attempting to copy those tattoos, but you appear to be legitimate."

"You sound surprised." Genie smiled. She wasn't an attention seeker, but she didn't shy away from the spotlight, either.

Victoria tapped the metal sheet. "I don't mind admitting that I am. We attract candidates and hunters from all over the world, but we've never managed to entice an Atlantean to our fair shores."

"You know what we're like." Genie chuckled, and I could tell Victoria was pleased at the idea of adding someone like my friend to her roster. Atlanteans might have become part of society, but they were still a novelty, drawing in all sorts of grants and bursaries from the MUN in the name of ongoing integration.

"Yeah, a bunch of backward snobs," one of Rollins's cadet friends muttered.

Victoria whirled so fast it made *my* head spin. "If that is how you view magical variety, perhaps you shouldn't be in this room."

He took a sulky step back. "It's not like I'm going to put her in a Mason jar."

"You won't be putting anything in a Mason jar if I hear prejudice like that again." Victoria didn't raise her voice, but she didn't have to. Her steady calm held way more sway than a yell. "I accept no form of discrimination in this institute. Iphigenia deserves nothing but your respect and encourage-ment, or at least your silence. As I am sure she will respect and encourage you, despite your misguided comments."

You tell 'em, Ms. Jules. The SDC didn't accept prejudice either, but it received a lot of flack from other magicals for being the first to initiate the integration program. Even now, it had nicknames like "Atlantis 2" and "The Trash Heap." We'd been shielded from the worst of it by being amongst decent, open-minded individuals. Friction only raised its ugly head when we went on field trips and exchanges to other covens. Genie never acted like she cared, but I knew it got to her from time to time. And it was one of the reasons her dad was so keen for her to go back to Atlantis.

Victoria turned back to Genie. "It says here that you are a... Go away!" Victoria's eyes widened as a bit of her true Irishness slipped out.

A ponytailed cadet almost craned right out of her seat to get a look at the metal sheet. "What is she?"

"A full Elemental with verso abilities and a maturing Glacial ability." Victoria smiled properly for the first time, and it transformed her face into something even more remarkable.

"Good on paper, right?" Genie laughed and rolled up pretend sleeves. "Let's hope it looks as good in the test."

Victoria closed the binder. "I look forward to finding out. Taryn, please take Miss Vertis down."

"Good luck!" I reached out and gave my friend's hand a squeeze.

"Thanks." Genie squeezed back and followed the assistant to the elevator. As soon as it disappeared, the remaining candidates pushed and elbowed to get a front row seat, all of them crowding the edge of the arena wall. I took myself off to an open space closer to the door of the hall and sat down on the lip, wishing we could've gone together.

Taryn and Genie reappeared below, the assistant leaving my friend in the same spot she'd left Jeremiah Rollins. A few seconds after Taryn backed away, the siren blared. Genie didn't miss the satchel. Throwing it over her head, she took off toward the cornfield first, moving faster than I'd ever seen her move before. She was an avid runner, so I knew she was quick, but the pressure of the test seemed to have given her a boost.

Come on, Genie. I know you can do this... I clasped my hands together and swung my legs nervously as she gunned for the raiju. Standing in the middle of the corn stalks, she kept perfectly still as the wolves prowled toward her. Unlike before, they both attacked at once. She just stepped back and let them sail over her, as if she'd known what they would do. Upon landing, both of them opened their mouths and unleashed that thundering howl, bringing down two jagged forks of lightning that crackled into my friend. She didn't even try to escape it. Having seen her in the training room with the griffin, I understood why.

Her face contorted as the lightning absorbed into her, setting her aglow with power. The wolves leapt at her, and all hell broke loose. A ground-shaking explosion rocketed out of Genie and took the two wolves with it, sending them crashing into the corn stalks. I waited for them to get up and try again, but they stayed down, whimpering and smoking faintly.

Genie took two Mason jars out of the satchel and put one in front of each of the fallen raiju. They disintegrated into black smoke and slithered into the jars, which Genie promptly slotted back into the satchel.

I looked toward Victoria, who had the ghost of a smile on her face.

Silence blanketed the exam hall as Genie moved on to the tikoloshe, following the same path as Rollins. On the muddy bank of the pond, she waited. A few moments later, the hunched, hairy little man scuttled out from behind a nearby rock, ready to scoop up another pebble. Before he even touched the water, blue sparks shot out of Genie and rained down on the pond, turning it to ice.

"Yes!" I shouted, drawing stares from the other candidates. "Sorry."

The gremlin turned to her, its face a picture of rage. It hurtled toward Genie on stubby, paunchy legs. A split second before it reached her, she skated out over the icy pond to the other side. The gremlin followed her in blind fury, only to get a watery shock as Genie melted the ice with a wave of Fire. A loud splash echoed up as the wave fell, and while the gremlin floundered in the murky depths, she turned the pond back to ice, trapping the nasty creature in the center.

I could've sworn I heard Victoria snort, but when I glanced at her, she wore a blank expression.

After securing the creature in another Mason jar, Genie moved on to the next task. She avoided the vulture thing by scrambling right over the top of the cave, agile as a monkey, and headed for a circle of shadowy forest instead. After what we'd seen it do to Rollins, I guessed she wanted to come back to it later.

Someone had their oatmeal this morning. And she wasn't even breaking a sweat. As she dropped down the other side of the cave and her t-shirt rose a couple of inches, I noticed a glint of something attached to the base of her back, but a bone-shaking bellow instantly distracted me. The sound was partway between a roar and a screech—a noise I'd heard before.

A sizeable griffin—though not as big as the one I'd Purged —stomped out of the forest, and I could see Genie's shoulders rise and fall with what looked like laughter, followed by a subtle chuckle coming through the speaker system. At the ridiculousness of the encore, no doubt. As for me, I definitely wasn't chuckling. That thing dredged up a bunch of bad memories, and though my friend had faced its kind before, that didn't mean it wouldn't do some major damage. Not all griffins were made equal. This one could be way nastier than mine. I leaned forward anxiously.

It roared again, pawing the ground with its talons before pouncing, trying to snag her in its sharp beak. Genie darted out of the way and gripped its fur in her hands. Swinging her body up onto its back, she sat astride the griffin for a second, looking as majestic as a fearsome warrior queen. I didn't even see the Mason jar until the griffin started to disintegrate into it, leaving Genie to somersault to the ground in one impossibly fluid movement—the jar on the ground, one arm up in the air, and legs bent.

Hang on a second... Genie may have been a runner, but she wasn't a gymnast. The only time we'd attempted yoga, she'd been so wobbly and inflexible that the teacher had given up and just let us take time for "personal stretching." The other candidates stared at her in awe, and even Victoria looked vaguely impressed, but I smelled something fishy. Genie happened to be a freaking incredible magical, but she wasn't a kung-fu master. Still, if something *was* going on, I certainly wasn't going to point it out.

"Way to go, Genie!" I whooped. She flashed up a grin and kept going, still apparently unphased by the exertion.

Running like the wind and moving like water, she smoothly downed a five-strong group of goblins hiding under the spinning log with the swinging pendulums, all without missing a step. Then, all she had to do was collect her loot with five Mason jars while also maintaining her balance on the spinning log. A feat she managed with surprisingly little effort.

I know she's good, but this isn't right. My concerns amped up with every successful catch: three gargoyles, a golem, a kappa, and a wyvern, bringing the total to sixteen monsters. She was too fast, too fluid, too effortless.

By this point, I wasn't the only one whooping and hollering my support. She'd won over the crowd, and every last candidate applauded wildly with every catch she made. Even Victoria's hands twitched, as if she wanted to join in. Instead, she clasped them behind her back.

Whatever she's doing, I might need some of it. I gulped as she circled back to the three-headed vulture thing. Its screech turned the hall silent with anticipation. But Genie didn't wait for it to poke its three heads out. Green sparks of Earth ability flowed out of her and made the cave tremble violently, until the whole thing collapsed on top of the vultures. Another shriek pierced the air as the creature tried to get free. Seizing her opportunity, Genie hopped up onto the debris and aimed her Mason jar right at the beast. It began to evaporate, making the rocks sink down where the creature had once been.

After the vulture heads, a terrifying Kelpie became her next successful capture. It rose from a deep pool, the water a shade of darkest blue, so dark it almost looked black, and urged her onto its back with its hypnotic red eyes. She resisted, bringing it to heel before she zapped it into the jar.

Okay, I can give her that one. Atlanteans and Kelpies went hand in hand, like cowboys and horses, peanut butter and jam, salt and pepper. No displays of athleticism required. But the rest were still suspicious. And the real question was: how many more monsters did she have to catch? The siren hadn't sounded yet, and considering the length of this epic Challenge, I feared my own turn.

"Ew! What's that?" A grim-faced cadet, who clearly had more muscles than sense, pointed to the next monster.

What looked like a melting ball of flesh and fat with veiny eyes shuffled along a stretch of red-soiled desert, its floppy feet making a nauseating, squelching sound as it walked.

"This is a rarer species," Victoria replied.

The minute it saw Genie, it transformed into a good-looking man with perfect hair and a designer suit. I supposed that was what it thought Genie might like, but it didn't know my friend at all.

Genie appeared to chuckle and got ready. Bronze sparks flew out of her—the sure sign of a hex—and the glinting shards of Chaos began to quickly spin around the... whatever it was. It held the creature in a mesmerized trance, giving her the chance to slide a Mason jar under the vortex and capture it.

She brandished the sealed jar up at Victoria and yelled to us. "Tell me there aren't, like, fifty more."

"There are as many as there are," Ms. Jules replied, her eyes glittering with admiration.

"Right, so there might be fifty more." Genie stowed the jar in the satchel and headed for the only part of the arena she hadn't scouted yet. A pretty glade in the middle of a ring of vibrant trees, their leaves tinged with the reddish kiss of autumn.

From between two tree trunks, a unicorn emerged. But it wasn't like the ones that had visited my dreams. This looked like the nightmare version, with a black horn that had a pointed, gilded tip, and jet-black hair that shimmered like the night's sky as it walked. Its mane and tail carried a scarlet hue, as though it had absorbed the blood of its foes, and from what I knew of the species, its hooves were the same shade, although they were mostly concealed by undergrowth. I also knew, from past dream experience, that its eyes would be entirely white, giving the impression of blindness—but it could definitely see.

It charged at Genie with its killer horn aimed. Using the beast's momentum against it, Genie grasped the horn and yanked down hard, bringing it crashing to the dirt. There, she brought up vines of Earth to wrap around the creature until it couldn't move. Its white eyes blinked in confusion as it whinnied loudly, the sound echoing in my head long after it had disappeared into the jar.

Just then, a siren blared, making me jump so hard I almost teetered over the edge.

The end of the test... Only Victoria could say if Genie had passed or failed. But the other candidates burst into rapturous applause, having already decided that she deserved to succeed. And I clapped right along with them. Something might have been off, but my friend had put on an incredible display, and that deserved all the cheering my lungs would allow.

Victoria lifted her hand, and everyone went silent. She possessed the kind of gravitas that few people acquired in their lifetime, and even fewer truly deserved.

"Congratulations, Miss Vertis." Her voice carried without her having to project. "You have passed the entrance test and are eligible to join the Basani Institute. I commend you wholeheartedly. It's been many years since I've seen such a display. I won't forget it in a hurry."

Genie bowed. "Thank you, Ms. Jules. Does this mean I can come back up now?"

"It does." Victoria gave a whisper of a laugh as Taryn was sent to collect my friend.

Shortly afterward, we reunited at the top of the arena. Genie ran into my open arms, the two of us jumping around gleefully. I would've let myself enjoy the moment, but curiosity got the better of me.

"You were on fire out there. Did you use a spell or something?" I whispered, out of earshot of the others. A spell wasn't technically cheating, though the idea did make me feel a bit... uncomfortable.

"Nope, something much better. The thing that's going to get us both through this. Here." She slipped a hand behind her back, before embracing me again and turning us so I had my back to the wall. Before I could protest, I felt her attach something to my back. A fleeting pain jolted through me before a shiver of electricity coursed up the length of my back, making my body tingle suddenly. Fortunately, Victoria and the candidates were all distracted by the next competitor —a young woman who'd pretty much kept to herself and was now being taken down to the arena.

I pulled back and blinked at her. "What did you do?"

"Gave you what you need." She smiled secretively. "Keep your shirt tucked, and you'll be fine. It's your turn next. Use it, and you'll pass. Trust me."

I patted beneath my shirt discreetly, feeling metallic legs and a ridged back. A curled tail with a stinger on the end confirmed my suspicions. I knew this object. A scorpion amulet from ancient Egypt that my mom kept in a velvet display box in one of her office drawers.

"This is my mom's!" I whispered in shock. I knew what it did, and, while I was happy that Genie had succeeded, I wasn't okay with this. A spell came from within a person at least, but a device seemed plain dishonest. Powered by the supposed might of Ra, it granted the wearer additional strength, speed, stamina, and senses—all of the important S's.

"Okay, I might have snuck it from your mom's office last night. You remember I said I had to get something? This was it," she admitted, looking a little sheepish.

I shook my head. "This isn't right. Take it off." If there was one thing my mom and I agreed on, it was the principle of fairness and the importance of earning your success. But she'd also told me that, when the odds were stacked against you in a fight, you had to do whatever you could. I needed to get through this test. Maybe, just this once, a bit of assistance wouldn't hurt.

No! That's not how I want to win. I'd sworn to do this under my own steam, and that meant no outside help, no matter how tempting.

"It'll help you," she urged.

"You didn't even need it." I kept my voice low, in case I got us both in trouble. "You're more powerful than all of these people put together!"

She sighed, her cheeks turning pink. "I wanted to try it out so it'd be prepped and ready to go for your turn."

I reached behind my back and ripped the scorpion out of my skin. "I'm not going to cheat, Genie."

"It's no different from using a hex or an ability. This is your advantage," Genie insisted, trying to push the scorpion back into my hands.

"My mom is going to realize this is missing. And when she does, she'll come looking for me, to ask if I've seen it. When she can't reach me on my phone, she'll track me down some other way. Then, she'll find out that I'm here and..." I gulped down a breath as panic set in. And panic spelled Purge. I needed to get a handle on this before I spewed something up in front of everyone. They had enough monsters to worry about.

Another siren blared. Down below, the young woman was

being carried away on a stretcher, her hair sticking up at all ends after getting on the wrong end of a lightning strike.

"Who is next?" Victoria asked.

In a last-ditch attempt to get me to take it, Genie gave me a firm nudge with the hand concealing the scorpion. The movement drew the attention of the head huntswoman, who looked at me expectantly. If I backed out now, she'd think I was a coward, and it'd be game over before I'd even begun.

I swallowed loudly. "I'll go."

Just please don't let me Purge... please... To the Basani Institute, I imagined the only thing worse than a coward was a girl who couldn't stop Purging the very thing they hunted.

TWENTY-EIGHT

Persie

F*ear is the mind-killer.* To be honest, I'd never entirely understood what Frank Herbert had meant until this exact moment. My mind refused to cooperate, going all fuzzy and blank, reducing me to the staring moron I didn't want to be, who couldn't connect her mouth with her neurons.

"Persie." Genie gave me a sharp nudge.

The gray matter reluctantly activated. "Right, yes. Sorry."

"Place your hand here." Victoria offered up the binder and I obeyed. The shock she'd displayed at Genie's details paled in comparison to mine. "Persephone Merlin-Crowley? As in—"

"Harley Merlin's daughter." I filled in the blanks before she could. Everyone always followed my name with my mom's.

She quickly covered her surprise with an expression of

casual interest. "And I thought Miss Vertis would prove to be the greatest potential candidate today." Her eyes drifted across the details in the binder, and her forehead creased. "Oh... that must be wrong. It says here that you are classified as non-magical. Could you place your hand down again?"

I shook my head. "No need. It's the truth."

Here we go again... My stomach churned like nobody's business, and my chest had that tight, grippy feeling that suggested an imminent Purge.

"Pardon?" She tilted her head slightly.

"There's no error. I don't have any magic." My cheeks flushed with warmth as everyone stared at me. A few incredulous smirks made my blood boil. "I thought everyone knew."

Victoria closed the folder. "I wasn't aware. I knew your mother had a child, but..." she handed the binder off to her assistant. "Forgive my bluntness, but why are you here then? How do you expect to become a monster hunter without a single ability?"

My head swam, but I no longer knew if it was a fear response or a Purge response. But I wasn't going to blow this by coughing up an inopportune beast.

You don't control me. Do you hear? I shouted inwardly.

"I... uh... I have other skills that I... um... intend to apply to monster hunting." I managed to choke the words out, though my rapidly swelling throat made it difficult. "Sorry, I'm a bit nervous." I cleared my throat and tried again, digging my nails into my palms. "I've got a lot of other talents that lend themselves to the art of hunting, and I plan to show the magical world that children born without abilities aren't necessarily write-offs."

Victoria nodded slowly. "Intriguing."

"The good kind... I hope?" I forced my voice to function.

The head huntswoman said nothing for several long seconds. When she finally opened her mouth to speak, my stomach dropped in nervous anticipation. "I like your mettle, Miss Merlin-Crowley. That is one of the main traits we look for in potential candidates. And I did speak of not tolerating prejudice in this institute. What sort of figurehead would I be if I didn't stand by my own principles?" She offered a wary smile, as if she thought she were making a grave mistake. "You may proceed."

You won't regret it, Ms. Jules. I grinned at her like an idiot. All I'd wanted was a chance, and she'd given it to me. I might've been terrified after what I'd seen in the arena, but this was my dream. I had to seize it by the horns.

I glanced at Genie as Taryn beckoned to me. My friend gave me an enthusiastic thumbs-up and an ecstatic smile, though a hint of anxiety glinted in her eyes. I supposed she was wondering how I'd get on without the scorpion, and truthfully... so was I.

Heart racing like a runaway train, I followed Taryn into the elevator. It descended through the ground, obscuring the glass and pitching us into total darkness for a while. I welcomed the darkness as an opportunity to close my eyes and take some deep breaths, trying to stave off the incoming Purge symptoms. *Not now, not now, not now...* I repeated the mantra to ease my crammed brain. Anything to give the impression of normalcy. Taryn had probably seen all kinds of nerves in this elevator, but I still worried she might bring my test to a halt before it had even begun. By the time we reached the arena level, the fever had receded, and I could think a bit clearer.

Huh... maybe I am the one in control of this, after all. Finally, I'd caught a break. Except I was still walking into an obstacle course full of monsters that I had no idea how to fight.

"Good luck," Taryn whispered, as she ushered me out onto the rocky plinth. I felt the curiosity from above, but aside from Genie and Victoria, they could all take a running leap. If I focused on them, I'd only get more nervous, and nerves meant Purges.

Breathe. Just breathe. The starting siren sounded and I bit my tongue in fright. Repeating the breathing mantra, I shuffled up to the end of the plinth and picked up the satchel. I had no clue if I would get to cross the proverbial finish line. With twenty monsters to capture, I might have bitten off more than I could chew.

"Just keep calm," I told myself as I sifted through the satchel. There weren't any entrapment stones, only Mason jars. And that meant battering the monsters into submission first, to negate the need for the stones. "You can do this. Remember what's at stake. You can do this."

Putting the satchel over my head, I dropped down from the edge of the plinth and headed for the cornfield. The raiju in my dreams had been noble, beautiful creatures with sweet temperaments, but these raiju were programmed to fight.

Heading into the stalks, I listened for the sound of

rustling. But the blood pounded so loudly in my ears that I couldn't hear anything else. Cursing under my breath, I scanned the corn. Up ahead, a few of the stalks swayed unnaturally. The wolves were literally at my not-so-literal door.

Think! I racked my brain for any raiju knowledge that might be useful, but nothing came back.

Just then, the wolves pounced. The first arced gracefully through the air and landed on my chest, sending me careening backward. I hit the dirt with a thud that knocked the air from my lungs, only to look up to see the blue and white face of the beast staring down at me. Up close, it had the most astonishing eyes—a swirling galaxy of color, flecked with silver. In the near distance, I heard the familiar howl that brought lightning. And that last girl had gone out smoking.

Instinctively, my hands shot up and grasped the raiju around the neck, holding on for dear life. It flung its head left and right frantically to throw me off, but I refused to let go. I had the weight of my entire future resting on the success of this entrance exam. If I showed weakness now, I shouldn't have bothered coming.

A crack split the air, and the lightning bolt came down on the raiju and me like a ton of bricks. I buried my face in its throat as the bolt struck its mark, trying to make myself as small as possible. A yelp escaped the beast's throat, and it slumped on top of me. Scrabbling for a Mason jar, I held it up to the creature and watched in absolute incredulity as it turned to black smoke and filtered slowly into the glass.

Yes, yes, yes, yes, YES! The second raiju padded over with a mournful whine, limping along with smoking fur. Raiju were conductively connected creatures, able to pass electrical currents between each other. Evidently, the blast that struck the first beast had residually hit the second. It nudged the jar with its nose, its galactic eyes searching for its fallen friend. I reached out for the creature and scratched it between the ears, the way Huntress liked. With a defeated expression, it flopped to the ground and placed its head on its forepaws. And, though I felt a teensy bit guilty about taking advantage of the sad raiju, I slid a Mason jar between said forepaws and watched it disappear inside.

"Come on, Persie!" Genie cheered me from above. "You got this!"

I looked up at her and smiled. *Two down, eighteen to go.*

I moved forward without hurrying. The tortoise had won his damn race, and I fully intended to win mine. I planned to take Genie's way through the course and save that vulture thing until later. Maybe even last.

At the pond, I waited for the tikoloshe to appear. It slunk out of the trees and made for the water. I didn't try to stop it from swallowing the pebble. Instead, I kept my cool and watched the muddy banks for footsteps. They appeared shortly after the beast turned invisible, making their way toward me. I held my nerve until the footsteps came close enough, then hurled myself at empty air and got a mouthful of mud and a bite in the shoulder for my troubles. Undeterred, I staggered back up to my feet and waited to see footprints again.

"I'm not your afternoon snack," I muttered. Spying him a yard away, I hauled the satchel off my shoulder and swung it in a circle as fast and hard as possible. To my surprise, I felt it connect with something solid, and then I heard a loud splash. The tikoloshe coughed up the pebble and began to flounder in the water, apparently unable to swim. Driven by the thrill of my success, I waded into the pond and whacked the hairy bastard again. It ceased thrashing and sank under the surface, blending in with the fibrous algae that floated on top. Another pang of guilt clutched my heart, but I pushed it aside for the sake of the exam. Plunging my hand through the water, I lifted the beast and held a Mason jar up to its hunched body. I almost screamed with joy as it flowed into the jar.

"Go Persie!" Genie yowled, clapping so loud it nearly made up for everyone else's dubious silence.

My confidence and my adrenaline levels surged as I put my third creature into the satchel and pressed on to the griffin. It meant climbing over that vulture cave, and I had the climbing skills of an eel. I looked up and saw the cadets snickering.

You won't be laughing when I pass and you fail. I let that anger spur me on across the crumbling cave, ignoring the scrapes and cuts from the rocks as I made my way over the top. They didn't laugh so loud when I slid down the other side and strode toward the griffin forest.

The half-screech, half-roar cut right through me, making my head pound even harder. My vision blurred as the huge beast crunched out of the undergrowth, spreading its wings wide and unleashing another deafening bellow. I blinked rapidly to try and clear it, but it did no good. The fever scorched across my forehead and up the back of my neck, my throat swelling up again. My insides churned with a fresh vengeance, and the acid of inbound bile surged up my already-raw throat.

Not a Purge. Not yet! I tried to make it listen, but I'd gotten it wrong... I wasn't in control of this.

I tumbled forward onto the grass at the same moment the griffin made a charge for me. I felt it coming, but it was as though I were watching the scene unfold from somewhere else completely. The griffin rose up on its hind legs and clawed its talons through the air in warning, letting out another unholy shriek. But I couldn't get up.

"Persie!" I felt a rush of Air nearby, but I couldn't see anything except vague shapes of foggy nothingness. The griffin screeched again as it made for us. Arms encircled me and a rush of Air careened outward, hitting the griffin and forcing it back. "Persie, are you okay? Is it happening again?" Genie's voice filled my head, but she felt so far away.

The siren blared to bring the obstacle course to an end and another voice screamed through my skull.

"Miss Vertis, it is against the rules to intervene." It was Victoria, sounding as though she was at arena-level, but I couldn't see her. And she did *not* sound happy. "If your friend was going to fail, you should have let her fail. You have taken her opportunity from her."

"And let that griffin attack her, while she's clearly not well?" Genie shot back.

I writhed against her shoulder, biting the inside of my cheek against the pain. "No... she's... right. You should've... let me fail." My breath hitched. "I just need... another chance. I can—"

The Purge bombarded me before I could finish my sentence. And, to make it so much worse, I had an audience.

TWENTY-NINE

Persie

Pain ripped through my body, tearing at my skin, my muscles, my organs, until I wanted to cut it all away just to get it to stop. Every breath hurt, and I couldn't help gasping desperately. I'd have plucked out my lungs if I'd had the strength to do it. Meanwhile, my brain pulsed as if someone had set off a minefield of bombs inside, my skull struggling to contain the agony.

"Help... me," I begged, in tears. "Please." Boiled down to this—being tortured from the inside out—all I wanted was my parents. They'd know what to do, even if they couldn't take the pain away. Only... they weren't here, and they had no idea where I was.

Genie clutched me to her. "Stay with me, Persie. You've done this before, and you can do it again. I'm here. I'm not going anywhere."

A wave of agony bucked my body forward. The monster was coming, and I couldn't stop it. Panic overwhelmed my fried brain. I didn't know what might come out, but I couldn't risk anyone being near me when it did. With the last scrap of strength I possessed, I shoved my best friend as hard as I could to get her out of harm's way. She tried to run back to me, but I put up my hands.

"Don't! Stay back," I yelled, as a different person tried to step forward. The head huntswoman *had* come down to the arena. "Victoria... stay back!"

A whole freaking riptide of crippling pain exploded in my chest, and I couldn't stay upright anymore. Digging my nails into the earth, I screamed like I'd never screamed before. This was my eighteenth birthday times a hundred, and I was terrified of what was coming.

A ring of black fire ignited around my crumpled body. It spun faster and faster, with me trapped in the center. I heard it vibrating with pure, cosmic energy as the speed increased, until it finally came to a skidding halt. I only had time to snatch a shallow breath before the very core of my ribcage imploded. And up bubbled the monster I'd been making, a volatile waterfall of black smoke cascading out of my mouth and onto the ground.

Sweat dripped into my eyes as I struggled to see what I'd Purged, but it didn't seem to be taking any kind of shape. It stayed a black mass, hovering in the air for a minute. I blinked away the sweat and watched as, finally, it began to materialize, Morphing into a vaguely human-shaped mass of gauzy darkness, with two red eyes boring into my soul. Coarse black hair flowed down either side of its head. A second later, my heart almost evacuated the building as it shot forward to reveal a pale, ghostly face with a gaping mouth that opened with a blood-curdling, ear-splitting scream. No bow of respect, no brief pause, just a creature screaming right in my face, so loud it threatened to make my brain bleed.

"A banshee! Level-one threat!" Victoria's voice sounded somewhere nearby. "I repeat, level one! Everyone to arms!"

A banshee? I knew about those. I'd met one in one of my more hellish dreamscapes, and it'd nearly caved in my eardrums then, too. One thing was for certain: if Victoria was calling a level-one threat, I'd Purged a terrible danger that could wreak havoc on this hall and everyone in it.

Gates screeched open around the arena and black-suited hunters poured through. Genie dove toward me and wrapped me in a tight hug as a circle of hunters surrounded us. Consciousness seemed like a distant notion, as my head lolled on her shoulder and my eyes danced with black spots. Recovery had been faster the last few times, but Leviathan had warned that he didn't know how things would manifest in a mortal, and I guessed it changed from beast to beast. Each variety hit differently, and I'd just Purged something majorly powerful. I could sense it in my aching bones.

"Hold on, Persie." She stroked my hair gently. "They've got it covered, you just need to hold on."

"It… hurts," I rasped.

She held me closer. "We're going to get you out of here, and we're going to make sure you get all the help you need."

All around, I became aware of the monster hunters getting into formation. Armed with puzzle boxes and hard-won skill, they unleashed their collective might on the darting shadow of the banshee. Sparks of Chaos burst in the arena like fireworks, exploding in an array of vivid colors as hunters targeted the monster. It screamed louder under duress. Even so, the hunters barely missed a beat as they sent forth a barrage of Fire and Air. I watched with blurred eyes as one of them ducked low and transformed into a furry lynx, snatching up a puzzle box in his jaws. He darted forward and pushed at a series of diamond-shaped buttons with a deft paw. Faint lines ignited in a blinding glow, revealing an intricate set of patterns etched into the box itself. Soon enough, the edges of the banshee turned to wispy fronds of smoke, the puzzle box sucking the creature inside.

"Hey, get your hands off!" Genie protested, trying to keep her hold on me. Looming figures grabbed her and wrenched her away, and then they came for me. I couldn't have fought them if I'd wanted to. Harsh hands seized me roughly, and I felt myself being lifted and hauled off to some unknown destination.

"I swear to Chaos, I'll bite you if you touch me again!" I heard Genie yelling. "Let us go! She didn't mean to!"

Her voice faded as blurry figures dragged me through one of the open gates in the arena walls. I saw the stark concrete of a modern corridor on either side of me, lit with fluorescent bulbs that burned my eyeballs. The tops of my shoes squeaked as the hunters pulled me along.

"Are you... putting me... in a box?" I murmured deliriously.

One of the hunters laughed. "We don't hunt people. Even ones who Purge banshees."

"Jail, then?" I hung my head, unable to hold it up anymore.

"No, not jail," the other hunter replied.

With no energy left to expend on small talk, I stayed silent the rest of the way, drifting in and out of consciousness. I must've blacked out for much longer somewhere along the line, because when my eyes opened again, I was lying flat on my back in what felt like a soft bed, staring up at a hazy ceiling.

"Who... turned the... lights off?" I mumbled. After the savage lighting of the corridor, the subtle glow in here seemed like absolute darkness.

"I thought you would prefer a dimmer setting." I jolted at the reply.

My eyes struggled to penetrate the gloom. "Who's... there?"

A lamp turned on, and I saw Victoria at my bedside. She sat on a plastic chair that reminded me of hospitals, her fingers making a stern steeple.

"Oh..." Weakened by the Purge, sentences proved tricky. Sweat drenched my shirt and pants and plastered my hair to my forehead. I would've swept it out of my face, but I couldn't even lift a shaky hand. Everything ached, and the embarrassment and disappointment of failure only made this situation worse. Of all the people I didn't want to see me Purge, Victoria and a crowd of hunters and cadets topped the list.

"Where am I?" I croaked.

"In the infirmary."

I tried to nod, but it sent a sharp pain up the side of my neck. "Right... makes sense."

"I think you owe me an explanation, Persephone." Victoria leaned forward, highlighting her stern features. "It is not possible for a non-magical to Purge, much less such a powerful, vicious monster. How did you fool the system? Did your parents bribe someone to change the magical register?" She still didn't raise her voice, which my tender eardrums appreciated. However, her calmness had the air of an incoming storm. I imagined Victoria to be the sort of person who rarely got furious, but when she did, everyone needed to run for cover and batten down the hatches.

I shrugged wearily. "Nobody lied."

"Then *explain*," Victoria said, visibly losing patience.

"I received a... gift." I tried to find a comfy spot on the pillow. "Leviathan gave it... to me. You probably know about him. He named me, and he gave... me a gift. His mother's gift. No... a curse. My curse." I giggled feverishly. "There's a new... Mama of Monsters in town. And it's... me."

Victoria relaxed her steepled fingers. "Let me get this straight: you were given Echidna's ability to Purge monsters?"

"Bingo!" I pointed finger-guns at her and giggled some more, making me wonder if they'd put me on some meds.

She ran an anxious hand through her super-cool hair. "I imagine this isn't common knowledge?"

"Nope." I turned onto my side, curling up into a fetal position. "Sorry about the... uh... mess, by the way. I don't... get a lot of say about what I... Purge. I wouldn't have picked a banshee. My ears are still... ringing."

"And they will for a while." Victoria poured out a glass of water and popped a straw into the liquid. She tipped the top part toward me. "In fact, I imagine a few of my hunters will be partially deaf for a week or so."

I grimaced. "Sorry." I knew it was game over. After what I'd done, I was surprised they hadn't booted me out or locked me up for being a security risk. And it sucked all the more, because I had been doing well. The Purge had robbed me of my opportunity.

"You keep saying that." She brought the water closer and I managed to lean up for a few sips.

"I mean it. I didn't mean to cause havoc." I took another and another, until the whole glass was gone. "Do you think you could give me another shot? I realize I kind of messed up, but I didn't get to finish. Or, maybe you don't want someone like me around here?" I sagged back into the bed. "I didn't really know how my... uh... ability might affect my admission. But the thing is... I need this. Badly."

"And why is that?" Victoria prompted, refilling my glass.

"If I can capture the monsters I make, then no one will consider me a threat." I gulped down more water as she proffered the straw. "I don't want to be put in a glass box. I don't want people to be scared of me." I brushed away unexpected tears. "I want to have a life, Ms. Jules. On my own terms. I don't want this curse to be a jail sentence. Or worse."

I looked up at Victoria, but she wore an unreadable expression. Her big eyes gave nothing away, and she didn't say anything. Naturally, that only made me ramble more, to try to fill the confusing silence.

"I never had a say in this, but I *want* a say in my future. I need to, or I may as well give up now." More tears coursed down my cheeks, and I felt so foolish to be crying in front of someone like Victoria. It made me feel even sillier when she offered me a box of tissues, her face still blank. "And I don't want to be 'that Purge girl,' either. I have to be more than a name and a curse. I have to make something of myself, or what's the point?"

Victoria set down the box of tissues and unleashed a slow, sad sigh. "I'm sorry, Persephone, but you failed the test. Your friend intervened and, while her intentions were obviously noble, she prevented you from continuing." She gave me a faint smile of apology. "There is only one attempt. No second chance is available, no exceptions."

My breath caught. Until she'd said it out loud, a tiny part of me had still hoped. I stared at her, my mind a complete blank.

"*However,*" Victoria continued. I'd never heard a sweeter word. "I can invite you to join the Institute instead. Not everyone gains admission by way of the exam. Sometimes I handpick those I believe to be promising. Which is what I'm offering to you—a personal invitation to study here."

My hopes and dreams slotted back into place, like a smashed vase in rewind. "Are you serious?"

"Do I seem like the sort of person who makes jokes?" She smiled warmly, and the effect nearly knocked me over. It made her look like an entirely different woman. "Persie, your power doesn't need to be a curse. With hard work and training, you can turn it into an actual gift, defined and controlled by no one but you."

"You wouldn't be worried about me pouring out monsters?" I had to ask. If this was seriously going to happen, I needed to be sure we were on the same page.

Victoria flicked some dust off her lapel. "I'd be lying if I said I didn't have some concerns, but I believe this institute is the best place for you to be, given the circumstances." She smiled again. "I understand why you need to do this, and I agree with your reasoning. You should be allowed to seize control of this ability. We're going to teach you how."

I still didn't know how much was real and how much was my delirious mind playing cruel tricks. Victoria looked real, even if she was smiling. This soft bed felt comfortably real. And the residual pain of my Purge definitely packed a tangible punch.

I pinched my leg, just to be sure. Definitely real.

"So…" I grinned up at Victoria. "I'm going to be a monster hunter?"

"If that's what you want," she replied.

I laughed until my body ached all over again. "Ms. Jules, this is exactly what I want."

For the first time in my life, I'd done something on my

own. And, what was more, I'd succeeded. Maybe not via the traditional route, but maybe that didn't matter. My life's path was opening up before me, and all I had to do was take the first step.

But, in all the insanity, I'd forgotten about one slight wrench in the works. *What's my mom going to say about this?*

THIRTY

Harley

How is this day not over yet? I rested my arms on the balcony of our apartment terrace and took in the view. A few ramblers wandered along the trails, enjoying the afternoon and pausing at the lighthouse to read the plaques. I envied them, strolling around without a care in the world. What was the worst thing they had to face in their non-magical existences? Sure, everyone had their struggles, but they weren't dealing with prophecies and monsters and global threats. They didn't even know what was hidden away inside that lighthouse: the entrance to the SDC and the magical realm within.

"I thought you'd gone to take a shower?" Wade's arms slipped around my waist. He rested his chin on my shoulder, the two of us looking out at the beautiful scenery together.

I leaned my head against his. "I was about to, but then I

got this." I showed him my phone, already opened to the message Finch had sent just a few minutes prior.

The Kiddos have taken their ball home—i.e. they're not going to help. They said it's not because they don't want to, but they don't want to get in trouble with cosmic Pops. Something to do with an oath they swore to Chaos. I call BS, but what do I know? Sorry, Sis.

Wade read the message aloud, and his arms tightened around me. "Oh, Harley…"

I turned around in his arms and burrowed into his chest. "It's hopeless."

"Can Erebus do anything else to help?" Wade stroked his thumb across the side of my neck. "Child of Chaos or not, he must still have some tricks up his sleeve."

I buried my face further into Wade's comforting embrace. "It's a no-go on that too. With no power, he's not sure what else he can do. Dead-end central." His t-shirt dampened with my silent tears. "I think it's more to do with that, to be honest. Erebus is basically human now, and Finch doesn't think he'd be able to give us any actual support, so he's covering up his weakness with talk of his creator."

"I'm so sorry." He held me close, kissing my hair. "I… don't know what to say, except you did the right thing with Leviathan. If you hadn't, we wouldn't know what's coming. I just wish you would've told me."

I nuzzled harder, to hide my shame. "I know, but it was for Persie's sake. You'd have insisted on coming, because that's who you are. And that's why I couldn't tell you." I peered up at him shyly. "I didn't want to keep it from you.

While I was with him, I wished you were there. I know it doesn't make it right, but... I'm sorry for going solo."

"I get that." He tilted my chin up and kissed me softly, before giving me a harder look. "Just... don't keep that kind of thing from me again, okay? You used to scare the crap out of me when you turned all lone wolf. So, from now on, let me know what your plan is, then kick my ass if I try to be stubborn about it."

I mustered a laugh. "I promise."

"Okay, then." He kissed me again, deeper this time. A show of forgiveness that I could get on board with. If only the touch of his kiss could've made everything else disappear.

Resisting his lips for a moment, I gazed into his eyes. "But what's the good of knowing Leviathan's game if there's nothing we can do? Maybe ignorance would've been bliss." I sounded defeatist, and that suited who I was like a pair of camo cargo shorts, but exhaustion and a lack of hope did that to a girl. And with my daughter at the center of it all, I felt vulnerable and afraid.

He brushed my cheek with his thumb. "I wish I could disagree."

"I'd forgotten how it felt to be this tired." I looped my arms around his neck, feeling safe inside this bubble of two, if only for a short while.

"I know what you mean." He tilted forward until we were forehead to forehead. "I couldn't concentrate on work at all. I just kept thinking about you, and Persie, and this prophecy. I can't even sleep."

I moved closer to kiss him on the lips, savoring it for a

moment before pulling back. "I'm not closing my eyes again until I've found a way to get around this prophecy, which means I'll probably never sleep again."

"We can't give up, Harley." He kissed me back gently.

"We've never been in a situation like this before. With Katherine and Davin, we had chances to stop their schemes. There were steps for us to take, and cosmic forces backing us. Now, it feels like Chaos itself is against us, and we have no way of stopping it."

Wade cupped my face in his hands and kissed me, deeper than before. I knew why. He didn't have anything to say that would make it better. Nobody did. The Children of Chaos had backed the heck out. Lux wouldn't risk another run-in with her father so soon. Remington's lack of aid surprised me, but he'd undoubtedly undergone major changes in the last two decades, and I knew he'd gotten into a bit of trouble along the way for trying to bend the rules. He now kept mostly to himself, ensconced in his otherworld with Odette.

And he won't risk losing her to bend those rules some more. I couldn't blame him for that. Selfish as it sounded, if there'd been a way for me to spirit the people I loved away to an otherworld, I would've done it in a heartbeat. Anything to keep them safe and far away from this prophecy.

"How do we help Persie, Wade?" I turned my head away. "What's going to happen to our little girl? How do we protect her from something we can't change?" Tears trickled down my cheeks, and I saw tears glinting in his eyes as I looked back. Both of us were at a loss.

Wade held me closer. "We just have to hope there's a way.

There has to be something we've overlooked. No matter how bad things get, we can't lose hope that Persie will be okay."

I nodded slowly. "We'll keep searching, right?"

"You know we will."

"And... she'll make it through." I tried to steel my resolve. "She might be the only one who has the means to get ahead of this. If the prophecy is about her, then she might have some influence over it."

Wade smiled. "That's a better way to look at it."

"But... she's not like you and me, Wade. She never has been. It's one of the things that confuses me the most about her, and one of the things I admire most. She's quiet, she's peaceful... she doesn't know how to fight. That's how it should be, but I can't help wondering if I've made a mistake by wanting her to stay that way. Did I miss the chance to prepare her for this? Have I coddled her too much? Did I not teach her the things I should have?"

"She's tough in her own way. When pushed, she might surprise us... and Leviathan." Wade tucked a strand of hair behind my ear, and a small smile lit up his pretty green eyes. "It's always the quiet ones you've got to watch out for."

My phone beeped loudly, the blue screen flashing. I didn't recognize the caller, but now wasn't the time to start screening. It could've been Erebus or Kaya or someone from our past with more information. Startled, I fumbled for the answer button.

"Hello?"

"Am I speaking to Harley Merlin-Crowley?" an unfamiliar voice replied.

"Yes, speaking." I frowned up at Wade, who mouthed, *Who is it?*

"This is Taryn Masters, from the Basani Institute in Galway. I'm calling on behalf of Ms. Victoria Jules, the head huntswoman." She paused for effect. "I'm afraid your daughter has caused a bit of an upset, and your presence is requested immediately."

I cast a confused look at Wade. "But my daughter is here, in San Diego. There's been some mistake." Nevertheless, my heart began to hammer in my chest.

A brief silence echoed through the speaker. "Your daughter is Persephone Merlin-Crowley, yes? This was the emergency telephone number attached to her biometrics."

My heart stopped hammering and suddenly sank into the pit of my stomach. "Yes..."

"Then there's no mistake. We have your daughter here, and Ms. Jules would like to discuss the incident with you." The woman sounded impatient.

"We'll be there right away." I realized how stupid I must've sounded. My daughter wasn't in the SDC, and I hadn't even known it.

What in the name of Chaos was Persie doing at the freaking Basani Institute? And why did she decide to put herself in even *more* danger?

THIRTY-ONE

Persie

———

Broken but buoyant, I found myself being wheeled back through the Basani Institute from the infirmary by Victoria's own fair hands. I'd tried to refuse, but with jelly legs and muscles that could barely hold up my own body weight without a *lot* of lolling, I eventually gave in. The medics had been and gone, checking machines and flashing lights in my eyes, coming to the conclusion that I could leave the infirmary to go back to my friends. Now I was getting the grand tour without having to lift a finger. Well, not quite the grand tour, just a labyrinth of the same shiny corridors, cold strip lighting, frosted glass doors, and more of the black suits walking about. Nevertheless, it gave me a wider scope of the Institute. Enormous didn't cover it.

"Ah, there he is. Right where I left him." Victoria wheeled me out of an elevator and down the corridor, which led to the outside of the exam hall doors. We'd ended up where we started.

I looked ahead to find Kes perched politely on one of the hard benches. He swung his legs like a little boy, his hands tucked between clamped thighs. Relief washed over him as we approached, but it swiftly morphed into panic as he leapt from his seat.

"Persie! Why are you in a wheelchair? Do I need to call your mom, or my mom, or... this is all my fault. My parents are going to kill me!"

Victoria stopped and came to the side of the chair. "She's fine. An unfortunate Purge attack, but nothing a bit of rest and a long soak won't remedy."

Kes gaped at her. "Oh... *phew!*"

"And who might you be?" Victoria asked.

"Me? I'm... uh..." Kes sputtered, his eyes blank.

I smiled, totally understanding how a person could lose their ability to speak in front of a woman like her. "This is Kestrel Merlin. My cousin."

"Two Merlins in one day? This is going to be the strangest daily report I've made in a while." Victoria folded her arms across her chest. "Well, if you happen to take an interest in monster hunting when you're of age, feel free to come back and try the entrance test."

Kes's face brightened. "I will, Ms. Jules!"

"It appears I have a fan," Victoria whispered to me with half a smile. I chuckled as she went to the double doors and opened them, signaling to someone inside. I realized I'd probably put a hefty delay on the other candidates' trials, if I hadn't ruined the day entirely, but I was too tired and elated to think about that now.

A figure bolted out of the exam hall and made a beeline for me: my best friend, her face ashen.

"Oh, thank Chaos!" Genie launched into a python-level squeeze. "I nearly took out a bunch of those hunters when they took you away. I swear, if another one had called me 'Ma'am' and urged me to calm down, I would've made ice sculptures out of all of them. What happened?"

I squeezed her back as tightly as I could. "You'll never believe it!"

"Please refrain from threatening to ice my staff, Iphigenia, or I may have to rethink your position here." Despite her humorless tone, Victoria's eyes twinkled with the slightest hint of mischief. "I'll give you a moment." She put a hand on my shoulder and walked away up the corridor, with Kes staring longingly after her.

"Come on, spill!" Genie urged. "You'll have to talk loudly, though. That banshee blew up my eardrums."

"Join the club." I smiled, gripping the wheelchair handles as I braced to tell her the good news. "She agreed to admit me! A personal invite from the head huntswoman herself."

Genie squealed. "We're both in?!"

"We're both in!"

Kes poked his head around Genie. "Who's in what?"

"Keep up, kiddo." She nudged him away. "This is incredible! You and me, we're going to be monster hunters!" She dove on me and hugged me with just enough restraint to avoid crushing anything that'd already taken a Purge-battering. I clung on, so happy I could barely breathe. Though that might've been the hug.

Kes grabbed us both by the arms. "You both got in?! Holy crap, this is insane!" We pulled him into our celebrations, squeezing him until he squirmed away, like we were overzealous grandmas at a family gathering. "I'll leave you two to the mushy stuff." Red-cheeked, he pushed his curls out of his eyes. "But so cool, both of you. So, so cool!" He wandered off to stare at some of the trinkets in the display cases along the hall, leaving me and my best friend alone.

"I can't believe it," I whispered. "We did it, Genie. We freaking did it."

She grinned into my shoulder. "The only way for us is up, baby!" Loosening her grip slightly, she lowered her voice. "And I'm sorry about... you know, the scorpion thing. It was a stupid idea."

"No, it wasn't. You wanted to help." I pulled away so I could look at her. Nothing could ruin this celebration. "And, heck, I was tempted for a second. The thing is, I wouldn't have wanted to succeed if I hadn't earned it. Does that make any sense? The meds they gave me made my head a little foggy."

Genie crouched down and put her hands on my knees. "I get it. That's why I'm sorry. I could've gotten us both in major trouble for even bringing that thing here." She checked to see what Kes was doing, but he was too busy admiring a set of daggers in a display case. "And you didn't even need it in the end. If it hadn't been for that Purge, I bet you would've made it through anyway. You were killing it in that arena."

"You think so?" I smiled, filling up with warm and fuzzies. I'd felt so alive down there in the arena—terrified, sure, but there was nothing like danger to get the blood pumping. I was so proud that I'd done a decent job of monster hunting with zero magic whatsoever. It made getting through the stages I'd completed even more amazing.

She gave my knee a squeeze. "I don't think I breathed the whole time I was watching you. It was awesome, seeing you hammer those beasts like an action hero."

Hammer them? Thinking back, a flicker of guilt ignited in my chest. Whacking one of the creatures with a heavy satchel might not have been my gentlest moment. But now that I'd gotten a ticket into the Institute, I'd learn how to capture beasts without the need for brute force. I let that comfort me and returned to my jubilation.

"Do you forgive me for the amulet?" Genie asked sadly. She was evidently having a crisis of morality here, but I didn't blame her for what she'd done. Her intentions had been good, she'd just gone about it the wrong way.

I shrugged. "Nothing to forgive. Your heart was in the right place, though my mom might need an apology eventually."

"I'm forming one as we speak." She gave a nervous chuckle. "I just really wanted us to succeed, no matter what. I promised myself, a long time ago, that I would protect you and stay at your side through thick and thin. So I couldn't let either one of us fail."

My heart warmed. "That's the real reason you used it... You weren't just testing it out for me."

"Yeah." She looked sheepish, which hit me hard. I guessed even someone loaded with powerful abilities had doubts about their skill set occasionally. I covered her hand with mine. I loved this girl, and though she could be impulsive and misguided at times, she always meant well. She'd done it for me, and that deserved gratitude, whether I'd used it or not.

Kes ducked into the conversation. "I definitely missed something here. Are you two not okay?" He glanced between us. "Is Genie the one who put you in the wheelchair?"

I chuckled. "No, so don't you go spreading rumors. Now, come give your future-monster-hunting cousin a hug so we can carry on the celebrating."

"Future monster hunters!" Genie lunged forward instead for another cautious hug. "It's you and me, Persie! This is so cool!"

Kes grinned. "I knew you guys would do it. I never had any doubts. Well, I might've had a few, but then I was left on my own for ages to overthink, and you did turn up again in a wheelchair, Persie. Anyway, who cares—you did it!"

"And we owe a debt to our fearless guide." Genie smiled, her whole body relaxing now that she knew I wasn't bearing any grudges. I only wished we could stick with the happy atmosphere a while longer, but a black cloud still loomed, and we needed to brace for the downpour.

My laughter ebbed. "There's one other thing we need to talk about."

She pulled back. "What?"

I rubbed the achy back of my neck. "It's just... the entrance test might've been the easy part."

Understanding drifted across her face, eventually forming a grimace. "Let me guess. You're wondering how we're going to tell our parents?"

"Oooh, tough one." Kes nodded in agreement. "That'll take a PhD in hostile negotiation."

I wanted to roll my eyes, but he was right. "Getting in means we're going to be moving here for the duration of our studies."

"Good luck with that, cuz." Kes chuckled, but a sharp look from Genie shut him up. "Sorry. Not helpful."

"What if I told you that I had a bit of information to make the moving-out conversation go a little smoother?" Genie's eyes flitted toward the floor.

I frowned. "What do you mean?"

"Before I tell you, just know that the only reason I kept it secret is because it isn't my secret to tell." She peered up at me. "But we might need it, if things *do* turn sour."

"Okay, you're scaring me now." I hated secrets, especially after the whole birthday thing. Genie knew that. So if she'd kept quiet about something, there had to be a really good reason.

Genie sank back on her haunches. "I found college brochures in your mom's drawer, and they were full of programs for continuing education. Not just magical institutions, either. I think she's looking at a career change, but she wouldn't say for sure when I confronted her about it." She fidgeted uncomfortably. "She made me promise not to say a word. I intended to keep that promise, but then it felt so crappy not saying anything to you about it."

I shook my head in confusion. "But... the SDC means everything to my mom. What else would she do? What else *could* she do? And why wouldn't she have said anything?"

"You'll have to ask her when you see her." Genie took her phone out of her pocket, the screen flashing steadily. A message popped up on the screen. "Oh, crap... That might be sooner than you thought."

Kes froze. "They know, don't they?"

"Worse. They're on their way." Genie showed me the message from her dad.

Stay where you are. You are in a lot of trouble, Genie.

I didn't dare check my own phone. They knew somehow, and now we had to face the consequences. Tilting my head toward the exam hall door, I unleashed a stilted breath. "Anyone starting to wish that banshee *had* blown out our eardrums?"

THIRTY-TWO

Persie

_____

Dreaming *is happiness. Waiting is life.* But I doubted
Victor Hugo had meant waiting for his mom to come
and put a stake through his happy dream of studying at a
monster-hunting school in Ireland.

A torturous wait had ensued after Genie showed me her
father's text. She rolled me back to the Institute's entrance
hall and stopped in front of the mirrors. Victoria had
watched us go, but I was grateful she hadn't followed. If she
heard what my mom probably had in store for me, she
wouldn't think so badly about the banshee.

"Where are they?" Kes muttered, shuffling frantically on
the polished concrete.

Genie cast him a pointed look. "You want your death
sentence to come sooner?"

"I just want it over with," he replied, his face so pale that his freckles made him look like a speckled egg. "They're going to be so mad."

"I want to know who ratted us out." I wriggled about in the wheelchair to fight the numbness in my backside, wishing I felt more energized. Arguing through the residual exhaustion of a Purge wasn't my idea of a fun time.

Before anyone could reply, the mirror rippled and a five-strong group stepped out: my parents, Hector, Uncle Finch, and Aunt Ryann. Not a single one of them looked happy to see us. I suddenly understood the phrase "face like thunder," because a storm was getting ready to burst out of each of their mouths. But who would go first?

Might as well be me...

"I can see you're all angry, but before you start yelling, let me explain. I—"

My mom cut me off before I could finish. "Not here." Without another word, she walked behind the wheelchair and pushed me toward the mirror. I tried to put my feet out to stop moving, but my wobbly legs didn't provide much resistance. I didn't want to go anywhere until I'd explained myself—in case I never came back.

"If you'd just hear her out, I think you'd understand why —" Genie tried to come to my aid, but my mom gave her the same treatment.

"*Not* here." She looked to Hector. "Are we still in agreement?"

He gave a stiff-necked nod.

Agreement? How much could they have discussed since they'd found out? It had only been about thirty minutes between the message and their arrival. Their dour faces made the jelly in my legs wobble up into my stomach, while my hands gripped the armrests in alarm.

My mom carried on pushing me toward the mirror, my dad at her side.

"Why can't we talk here? What difference does it make?" I said curtly. "I've got a heck of a lot to say, so I may as well start now. Or do you have a firing squad waiting for me at the SDC?"

She leaned down close to my ear. "Not. Here."

After my mom whispered a variation on the spell Kes had used to get us in, the mirror image shifted to a darkened foyer, but it was too hazy to make out the destination. Probably the SDC, but maybe she was taking me on a direct track to some magical military school for wayward children. Regardless, I had no intention of being away from the Institute for long. The adults could discuss it without us if they liked—my mind was already made up.

But it surprised me when we arrived in a place I didn't recognize at all: a glowing grotto of a hall, filled with bioluminescent gemstones and flickering candles.

"This isn't the SDC." I found my voice. Glancing back, I waited for Genie and the others to follow us through, but the mirror rippled back to undulating silver. Evidently, they were going to be getting their tongue-lashings elsewhere. My mom had taken away my cavalry, and she never did anything without careful planning.

"Mom, Dad? Where are we?" Anxiety roiled in my stomach.

My dad put his hand on my shoulder. "Not yet, Persie."

Not yet? What the heck was that supposed to mean? They'd brought me to some unknown place, acting all cloak-and-dagger, and I didn't feel remotely good about it. They were my parents and I trusted them, but I would've felt better speaking on neutral territory. If my legs had cooperated, I'd have sprinted back to the Institute until they agreed to talk there.

My mom kept wheeling me through a network of similar cave-dwelling corridors until we reached a battered wooden door that seemed to have been forcibly wedged into the rock face. Taking out a set of rusty keys, my dad opened it and my mom pushed me into the room beyond—a study of some kind, with a broad, antique desk and empty bookshelves along one wall, though almost everything else had been covered in dust. It didn't look like anyone had been in there for a long time, and it smelled abandoned.

"Seriously, where are we? I know I went behind your back on this, and I've got an apology brewing, believe me, but you can't just wheel me off to some weird place and expect me to stay quiet about it. I have to get back to Ireland." I wanted to study at the Basani Institute and learn how to control my own Purge beasts. If she tried to prevent that in any way, she would be ruining the only chance I would ever have of living a somewhat normal life.

My parents came around to the front and faced me.

My dad spoke first, his tone firm but laced with concern. "We're somewhere safe. But now you owe your mom and me some answers."

"First, tell me why the heck you're in a wheelchair." My mom jumped in, her tone a little less lenient. "Second, I want to know why you were at the Basani Institute, and what you did there that's caused an uproar."

Straightening up as best I could, I met their stern gazes. "I'm taking matters into my own hands. Tobe inspired me, actually." I didn't mean to put him in the line of fire, but I hoped his involvement might soften the blow. "The Basani Institute can teach me how to catch the monsters I Purge. I came here to try and pass the entrance exam, but I Purged up a banshee. Ms. Jules offered me a place anyway, and I intend to take it."

I watched my parents closely, expecting an interruption throughout my entire spiel. Instead, they stayed quiet, listening to every word. If only my mom could have contained her expressions in the same way as my dad, my stomach might not have churned so much. I saw anger in the tight line of her mouth, although a momentary relief flickered across her eyes when she realized I wasn't paralyzed.

"So, you're okay, then?"

"Just tired," I admitted.

My dad ran a hand through his hair. "Thank Chaos for that. We feared the worst, with you... like this."

"My heart's still pounding," my mom added quietly.

The new softness in their voices made me feel suddenly teary. They cared about me, no matter what I'd done. I realized how worried they must've been and my guilt deepened.

My mom sank back and for a few moments, nobody

spoke. Finally, she broke the silence. "Well then, I guess I'll pack your things for you."

I blinked dumbly, certain I'd misheard her. "Wait... what?"

"I'll pack your things, to make sure you have everything you need." She looked toward the door before returning her attention to me.

Are we in some kind of alternate universe? I sat quietly, stunned. I'd anticipated ranting and raving, and hearing every reason under the sun as to why this was a terrible idea. I'd never, in a million years, expected her to get on board. Either a changeling had replaced my mom, or she was so pissed with me that she wanted me gone.

"But I... don't understand." I waved a hand around the room. "If you were going to let me stay at the Institute, then what's with all of this?"

My mom got up and took to her favorite activity—pacing. "I needed to bring you to a neutral space. You see, we weren't the only ones who heard about what happened."

"The woman who called us also called O'Halloran, and now he's panicking about the implications of your curse." My dad joined their well-honed double act. "As disapproving as we might be about your methods, the Institute was the best place for you to have Purged that banshee."

My panic took a nosedive into the realm of dread. "Crap."

"Yes, crap. And lots of it." My mom walked to the antique desk and swiped a finger across it, lifting a cotton-candy clump of gray dust. "That's why we couldn't take you back to the SDC, in case he intercepted us. This place is safe. It's the old wing of the San Francisco Coven, which your dad and I occasionally use for agent work. This used to be Remington's office. People have forgotten about it. More importantly, they've forgotten about that mirror."

"So, you're not planning to lock me in my room?" My voice trembled, and I hated that she could hear it. If O'Halloran was worried, that spelled potential disaster for me. My parents only held so much sway at the SDC. If O'Halloran wanted to restrain me in some way, he had the authority to make it happen.

She walked back and knelt in front of me. "We would never do that. We can't protect you forever, and the last thing we want is to push you away by trying to pen you in. You're a good kid—the *best* kid—with a smart head on her shoulders, and, sometimes... it's hard to remember that we don't always know what's best for you."

I tried to concentrate on my questions, but my head swam with total disorientation. "So you've decided this is best for me?"

"I wouldn't go that far," she replied, with a tight smile. "But your dad and I *have* decided to support your decision."

"I... I can't believe this." I shook my head slowly. "Seriously, I don't know what to say."

My dad checked his phone, stress deepening the lines on his forehead. "For now, just say you won't come back to the SDC until we say it's safe." His voice hitched, and my heart lurched. This must have been so hard for them both. To have it all so rushed made it so much worse.

My mom nodded, grazing her teeth against her bottom

lip. "We'll send everything you need so you don't have to return there."

"But... can't I say goodbye to everyone?" I hadn't even thought about that. Genie might have been my best friend, but there were other people at the SDC that I'd miss. I felt hollow about just vamoosing without saying anything.

My dad shook his head. "I'm sorry, Persie." He raised his phone at me. "O'Halloran is buzzing me every five minutes as it is, asking for an urgent meeting. That doesn't fill me with confidence. I'm afraid he may push for temporary... containment. We'll obviously try and persuade him against it, but we can't risk him making that decision while you're in the SDC."

"But he knows me," I murmured, tears welling in my eyes. He'd held me when I was born, I'd seen the pictures. He'd been there for every milestone of my life, and now he wanted to lock me away? It was a betrayal that stung like poisoned barbs.

My mom took my hands in hers. "I know, but right now he's blinded by panic and protocol."

"There's protocol for this?" I blurted out, incredulous.

"For threats to the coven." She sighed and rested her cheek against my palm. "The famous Victoria Jules might be able to turn a banshee into an invite, but O'Halloran can't overlook something like that. He's old school. A security magical to his core. And the coven's safety is his primary duty, especially after the troubles the SDC has been through in the past."

I blinked back persistent tears. "Can he have me extradited?"

"Not likely, with Victoria running the Institute and the place being filled with monster hunters. Even the UCA would probably agree that it's the safest place you could possibly be." She offered me an encouraging smile, but her eyes still glinted with sadness. The subtext was loud and clear —our paths would part here. Funny, how this was what I'd wanted, but seeing my mom all upset about O'Halloran and the SDC took the sheen off slightly. It changed the dynamic in a way I hadn't expected. I was getting my dream, but at the cost of not being able to go home. How could that not take a small piece out of my happiness?

A sudden, panicked thought struck me. "What about Genie?"

"Hector has agreed to support Genie's decision too." She turned her face away, her mask cracking for a split second. I couldn't fully read her expression, but it resembled... envy. After all, Genie would get to stay with me, while I didn't know when I'd next be allowed to see my mom.

"How did you manage that?" If this was true, then my mom had once again proved that she was a phenomenal negotiator.

She smiled slightly. "With great delicacy. His wife was a monster hunter, and when he heard where she'd gone, I think part of him was proud of Genie for following in her mother's footsteps. And I might have played on that, to stop him from packing her off to Atlantis."

Thank Chaos for that... If I had Genie, I'd be okay. Life without her would have been too lonely to even consider,

especially when stepping into the unknown territory of independence.

"Plus, he knows you two need each other. He may be
angry with his daughter, but he understands your relationship—he wouldn't try to separate you, not now that he
knows the stakes," my dad added with a heavy sigh.

"Then I should definitely be thanking you." I hoped I
sounded sincere. I meant it, but words were hard right now.

Just then, his phone lit up like the fourth of July. He
looked to my mom with troubled eyes. "It's Tobe. He'll have
news on O'Halloran for us." He went to the door. "I really
need to take this, but I won't be long." He ducked out without
another word, closing the door behind him.

"Thank you, Mom." I filled the ensuing silence, to prevent
the dread from creeping back in. Like a courtroom after a
trial, I didn't know if I wanted to hear O'Halloran's verdict. "I
mean it."

She glanced back at me with a flicker of renewed annoyance. "Don't thank me yet. I've still got several bones to pick
with you. Like, what the heck were you thinking, taking Kes
with you? He's thirteen!"

I stared down into my lap, knowing that whatever I could
say would sound lame. "It was part of the deal for getting us
in. I think he's kind of in love with Ms. Jules, or maybe it's the
monsters. It's hard to tell."

"He's going to be a handful when he gets older." My mom
chuckled, and her whole demeanor relaxed. "Everyone thinks
Diana is the most like her dad, but I'm not convinced. Kes is

quiet and polite, but he's got 'future rebellion' written all over him."

"The future…" I swallowed a lump in my throat. "Funny notion, isn't it?" I remembered the brochures. I wasn't the only one who'd had secret hopes on their mind of late. And, now that my dad had slipped out to take that call, I had an opportunity to ask her about hers.

My mother's eyes looked mournful, but she kept her chin up. "You'll have one, Persie. Your dad and I will speak to O'Halloran. And while we're doing that, you'll get to study at the Basani Institute with Genie."

"I meant your future, Mom." I chewed the inside of my lip, trying to tread carefully. "I'm really happy that you're supporting me, and I'm so sorry for going behind your back. I know I should've been upfront, but… What I'm trying to say is, I know you're looking at a change of career."

I braced for shock, but instead got a quiet grunt that barely amounted to the mildest of surprise. "I figured it was only a matter of time before she told you."

I fumbled around for the scorpion amulet and handed it over. "Don't be mad at her for telling me, Mom. She tried not to. But… I'm glad she did. I never knew you felt like this, and… I'm sorry you thought you couldn't say anything to me about it."

My mom turned the scorpion over in her hands. "I didn't even realize this was missing."

I eyed the scorpion with a sudden sense of foolishness. I'd allowed myself to get all riled up over a non-existent issue—to the point where I Purged a banshee. Mom didn't even look angry, just bemused. If I hadn't freaked out O'Halloran, I likely could have slipped the scorpion back into her office without her ever finding out it had gone missing, and now I'd gotten Genie in even worse trouble.

Sorry, Genie! My mom usually knew when a banana was missing from the fruit bowl. It'd never occurred to me that she wouldn't have noticed the scorpion's absence. It spoke to how much was on her mind.

"I suspected Genie had a reason for being in my office." My mom pocketed the scorpion. "But my mind's been all over the place, so I didn't have time to consider it much."

"She didn't mean any harm," I assured.

"No, I don't imagine she did." My mom glanced at her phone again, her face contorting with frustration. She turned back to me. "Genie's a good kid, and she loves you. I'm guessing she took it to try and give you an edge in the exam?"

I nodded. "But I didn't use it."

"I'm pleased to hear that." My mom smiled, wearing a hint of pride. "And, while I might not like the way she went about it, I can't fault her reasoning. She did it for you. And there's no point getting angry about it now." She patted her pocket. "I've got the amulet back, so I can just put it on my list of things to stew about later."

"Are those college brochures on that list?" I needed to understand what was going on in her head. She knew my dreams, even if she'd been against them until ten minutes ago, but I realized I had no idea what hers were. I'd been so dedicated to my future that I hadn't thought about what she'd do when I wasn't there anymore.

She tilted her head up to the ceiling, her face lost in thought. "Believe it or not, I didn't choose the path I ended up on, Persie. Chaos sucked me into this life. I look back on the adventures now and it makes me proud to have made a difference, but all of that went away a long time ago. Now, I've got a glorified desk job with the occasional mission that I don't have the heart for anymore." She sighed wearily. "It doesn't feel as important anymore, with a few exceptions. I guess it got me wondering what I would actually do with my life, if I could choose."

"I thought you loved your job," I murmured, the foundations of my world quaking again.

She shrugged. "I did, when it didn't feel like a job. Now, it's just... exhausting. I look at my agent work and I don't see the successes; I see regret. We got the bad guys, sure, but how much of your life did I miss because I was chasing them across the globe? And I'm tired of all the running and all of the expectations. In a job like that, there comes a time when getting out of bed in the morning is tough. It scoops you out and leaves you hollow, until—and I can't believe I'm saying this—you don't even care if you catch the bad guy anymore. They're a name on a list to check off and get out of the way. That's not the life I want. I *want* to give a crap again." Her gaze sought mine, and I saw the years of pressure crushing her. "Not to mention, it makes me sound like a complete hypocrite. I threw a fit when you said you wanted to leave, when, all the while, I've been wanting to get out too."

"Uncle Finch says we're more alike than either of us will admit." I kicked up the foot stands of the wheelchair and put my feet on solid ground. Her confession didn't make me think of her as a hypocrite at all. Instead, I felt closer to her.

My mom forced a laugh. "He loves that one, doesn't he?" She rolled her eyes. "In my defense, I only fought against you leaving because... well, I never got the chance to be a kid when I was your age. I wanted you to be able to enjoy your youth in safety and security, rather than spend it fighting tooth and nail to survive. I was wrong, and I'm sorry for that."

"Can you say that louder for the people in the cheap seats?" I teased, marveling at the way she was opening up to me. I knew the stories of her past, but never so personally. It was nice to hear more from her point of view.

She gave me a half-amused look, which quickly slipped into more solemn territory. "I felt like I had to make up for the deal that I made with Echidna by keeping you sheltered. One thoughtless decision, when I believed I had no other option, changed your life without you having a say in it. I felt like I'd put you in the same position that the world put me in, and I... should've tried harder to find another way. I'll always blame myself for that."

I leaned out of the wheelchair and put my hands on her shoulders. "You don't need to. I will never understand the pressure you were under back then. I only wish I could've been better prepared."

"I know..." She dipped her chin to her chest. "And I'm sorry."

With our separation rapidly approaching, I saw no reason for us to wallow in the should've, could've, would've mindset.

And I didn't want to leave without learning a little bit more about my mom—the sides of her that were usually hidden from me. The non-mom stuff. The Harley stuff. "So, what *would* you do, if you could choose anything?"

She lifted her head, her eyebrow arching slightly in bemusement. "I… always wanted to be a children's counselor. I could've used one when I was a kid." A sad smile turned up the corners of her lips. "I love working with kids. Your dad and I would've had more, if it hadn't been for Echidna's deal. I think we were worried some other force might come and snatch them or land a curse on them. And you turned out to be enough for us." Her breath hitched. "I'm happy for you, but I'm sad that you won't be home anymore. I knew this day would come, but I was struggling against it for my own selfish reasons. I know it's stupid, but… I feel like I won't be a mom anymore."

I tipped out of the chair and into her arms. "You'll always be my mom. Nothing will ever change that, and I'll only be a phone call away."

My mom laughed through tears. "I know that, but I worry. It's my job to worry."

"And that'll still be your job, but this is good. If anything, the Institute should take a load off your mind, because as long as I'm away from the SDC, Leviathan won't be able to pester me anymore." I clutched her as hard as she clutched me. "And you should probably tell Dad about the brochures. He'll want to know, and I bet you'll be surprised by his reaction. He'll understand, no matter what, because he's… Dad."

"When did you get so mature, huh?" she joked, leaning

back to smooth the hair out of my face. I noticed a glimmer of something in her eyes—hesitancy, or confusion, or disbelief. It was hard to decipher, but at least she had a smile on her face.

I grinned back. "Sometime between Victoria Jules, the raiju, and the banshee."

"The raiju?"

I cuddled back into her. "It's a long story. I'll tell you about it on the phone, once I'm settled into my new room."

She stroked the back of my head and placed a soft kiss on my hair. "I'm going to miss you, Persie, but... I'm so proud of who you've become. Prouder than I can put into words."

"I'm proud of you, too." I held her tight and let all the mayhem of my life fade away, at least for as long as we were in that room. I wanted to hug my mom and enjoy this moment, because I had no idea when we would see each other again. Together, we'd pick up the twigs and the scraps of fur and the bits of string, and we'd find a way to rebuild the nest of our relationship. True, it might never be the same again, but that didn't have to be a bad thing. And the nest would never truly be empty.

THIRTY-THREE

Harley

I'm not ready, I'm not ready, I'm not ready...

"Are you ready for this?" I held Persie in a firm side hug and planned to continue as long as I could. We'd returned to the Institute from Remington's old office, our group reconvening in the grand entrance hall: Wade, Finch, Hector, and Genie. Kes had already been taken back to the SDC by Ryann, where I imagined she'd be trying to figure out a way of grounding him that wouldn't hasten the future rebellion I sensed.

Persie peered up at me. So creative, so smart, so beautiful, and about to take her first step into the adult world. I only wished I'd had more time to prepare, which made me a hypocrite for the second time that day.

"I'm ready," she replied. "And I promise I'll stay in touch and tell you everything. Just... promise me we'll be honest with each other from now on."

I gave her a squeeze. "From now on."

And I hope I'll have some good news to tell you soon. Wade and I wouldn't be defeated by the Children refusing to help. Not yet. Not before we'd well and truly exhausted every possible solution. We had some digging to do on Echidna, and Tobe had agreed to help us. It was our last remaining avenue of hope, but it didn't need mentioning in that moment. I wouldn't dampen my daughter's excitement with talk of that prophecy. She'd wanted this so badly, and she'd done it all by herself. I had to let her have this, without tainting the memory with Leviathan. He'd crushed her enough.

"And you'll send our stuff?" Persie reached for Genie's arm, the two of them giddy as schoolgirls.

Wade scooted in to give our daughter a squeeze of his own. "I've got boxes at the ready. Although it won't be easy sending them away."

"What about O'Halloran?" Persie continued, her voice slightly pained. Wade hadn't said much when he'd come back into Remington's old office, except that we should get back to the Institute.

"He's decided to hold his 'urgent' meeting for tomorrow morning, so I'd say that's a promising sign that he's sleeping on it," Wade replied. "I'm hoping it'll make him more amenable to letting everyone carry on as they are."

And I won't get a wink of sleep until he does *come around.* Without O'Halloran's blessing, things could turn complicated. But the Basani Institute was notoriously protective of their trainees. And if Victoria Jules had taken a liking to my daughter, that could only help.

"Well then, I guess that's it." Wade pulled Persie into his chest and held her. "My little girl going off to fight monsters. Terrifying. But I'm damn proud of you, Persie. And I can't wait to hear all about it during the million calls your mom is going to make."

I chuckled as tears threatened. "I'll keep it in the hundreds, I swear."

"Be good, study hard, and... stay out of trouble." Hector wrapped his daughter in a bittersweet embrace. They'd been through a lot, and this would be tough on her dad. He'd lived for Genie for so long that I doubted he knew what to do without her around. I knew how that could be. But we had to do this, for their sakes.

Genie laughed sadly. "That's all you're going to say?"

Oh, Genie... His words sounded unfeeling, but I'd heard the nuance. He adored her with every fiber of his being.

"No, but I thought I'd lead with the practical part." Hector rested his chin on the top of her head, smiling. "I love you, Genie. I know you're going to do tremendous things, and I know your mom would be so proud of you... just as I am. I will be thinking of you. I may not call a hundred times a day, but I'll think of you that much or more."

Genie looped her arms around his neck and squeezed him in a bear hug. "I love you too, Dad."

"I promised myself I wouldn't cry." Finch pretended to sniffle and dab at his eyes, making everyone giggle. "I promised your mom I wouldn't embarrass her. Our little girl, heading off to learn how to make jam out of monsters." He sobered, a rare occurrence. "You take care of yourself, okay?

And take care of each other. You were sneaky enough to get into this together—major brownie points from me, by the way —but now you need to get through this together. And I *will* be taking all the pictures when you graduate. I want poses, cap throwing, the whole shebang, even if they don't do that here."

"I'll miss you, Uncle." Persie walked into his open arms and gave him a farewell hug. I resented letting her go even a second before I had to, but Finch deserved a proper goodbye too.

"It's okay, we don't have to say it out loud—you're going to miss me more than your mom and dad. They know. They've accepted that I'm the cool one. It's an open secret." He flashed a wink at me. "Knock 'em dead, kid."

Persie nodded. "I will."

"And here's a decent piece of advice." Finch released her, and she came right back to me. It warmed my grieving heart. "If you come across a monster that you can't fight, make sure you can run faster than the person next to you."

"Finch!" I snapped.

He grinned. "Your accomplice being the only exception. Accomplices have to stick together."

"Noted." Genie parted from her dad for her own Finch goodbye. He did give good hugs.

Finch raised a finger to offer more of his questionable wisdom. "And make sure you've got a truckload of bath salts, because you're going to hurt like nobody's business. Training is always a bitch." He flashed me a sheepish look. "I'm sorry, but there's no other way to phrase it."

Persie chuckled and laid her head against my shoulder. "I know things are going to get worse before they get better, but I'm really ready for this. I'm going to do whatever it takes to succeed, bruises and aches and all."

"I love you." I held onto her, feeling our farewell come to its end.

She smiled up at me. "I love you too."

"Stay safe, okay?"

"I will." She shuffled in for one more hug from Wade and me, the three of us gripping tight. And then, just like that, I knew we had to be the ones to step back and let her go. Kissing her forehead, I did just that. Wade followed, with Hector and Finch joining us. There we stood as Persie and Genie set off through the entrance hall to where Victoria waited at the far end beside a display case with a giant crossbow inside.

You take care of my girl, Ms. Jules, or I'll use that bow to fire an arrow into your ass. I kept watching my daughter and her best friend until they turned a corner with Victoria and disappeared from sight. They looked back a few times, but they were eager to go. Their future was calling, and they were answering.

But that didn't mean they wouldn't need us anymore. We'd always be their parents. The shoulder they'd cry on when things got tough. The people they'd call when they were in trouble. This wasn't the end of our book, but the start of a new chapter. I'd messed up by not preparing her for the future before. I wouldn't make that mistake again. She'd need all the help she could get, and, right now, the Institute was the best place for her to be.

Give them hell, Persie... I missed her already.

HARLEY MERLIN 19: Persie Merlin and the Door to Nowhere

Dear Reader,

Thank you for reading Persie Merlin and the Leviathan's Gift. I hope you enjoyed it!

Continue the journey in Harley Merlin 19: **Persie Merlin and the Door to Nowhere** — releasing **June 12th, 2020**.

Whose head will we get a peek inside next? :)

Visit **www.bellaforrest.net** for details.

- Bella x

P.S. Sign up to my VIP email list and you'll be the first to know when my books release: **www.morebellaforrest.com**

(Your email will be kept private and you can unsubscribe at any time.)

P.P.S. You can also follow me on **Twitter** @ashadeof-vampire;

Facebook BellaForrestAuthor;

or **Instagram** @ashadeofvampire

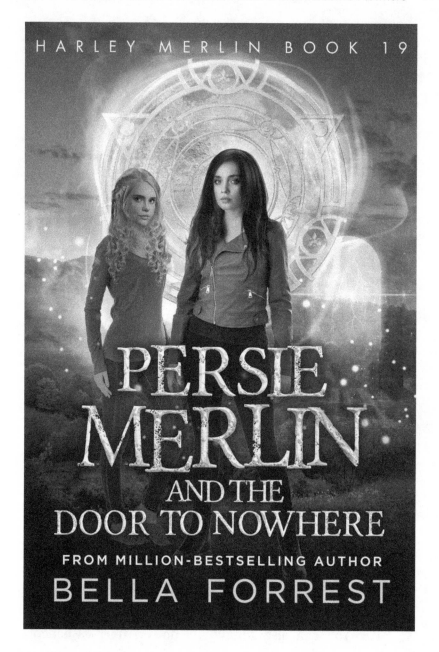

HARLEY MERLIN BOOK 19

PERSIE MERLIN

AND THE
DOOR TO NOWHERE

FROM MILLION-BESTSELLING AUTHOR
BELLA FORREST

Read more by Bella Forrest

DARKLIGHT

(NEW! Fantasy)

Darklight (Book 1)

Darkthirst (Book 2)

Darkworld (Book 3)

Darkblood (Book 4)

Darktide (Book 5)

Darkbirth (Book 6)

Darkfall (Book 7)

HARLEY MERLIN

Harley Merlin and the Secret Coven (Book 1)

Harley Merlin and the Mystery Twins (Book 2)

Harley Merlin and the Stolen Magicals (Book 3)

Harley Merlin and the First Ritual (Book 4)

Harley Merlin and the Broken Spell (Book 5)

Harley Merlin and the Cult of Eris (Book 6)

Harley Merlin and the Detector Fix (Book 7)

Harley Merlin and the Challenge of Chaos (Book 8)

Harley Merlin and the Mortal Pact (Book 9)

Finch Merlin and the Fount of Youth (Book 10)

Finch Merlin and the Lost Map (Book 11)

Finch Merlin and the Djinn's Curse (Book 12)

Finch Merlin and the Locked Gateway (Book 13)

Finch Merlin and the Forgotten Kingdom (Book 14)

Finch Merlin and the Everlasting Vow (Book 15)

Finch Merlin and the Blood Tie (Book 16)

Finch Merlin and the Legend of the Luminary (Book 17)

Persie Merlin and Leviathan's Gift (Book 18)

Persie Merlin and the Door to Nowhere (Book 19)

THE GENDER GAME

(Action-adventure/romance. Completed series.)

The Gender Game (Book 1)

The Gender Secret (Book 2)

The Gender Lie (Book 3)

The Gender War (Book 4)

The Gender Fall (Book 5)

The Gender Plan (Book 6)

The Gender End (Book 7)

THE GIRL WHO DARED TO THINK

(Action-adventure/romance. Completed series.)

The Girl Who Dared to Think (Book 1)

The Girl Who Dared to Stand (Book 2)

The Girl Who Dared to Descend (Book 3)

The Girl Who Dared to Rise (Book 4)

The Girl Who Dared to Lead (Book 5)

The Girl Who Dared to Endure (Book 6)

The Girl Who Dared to Fight (Book 7)

THE CHILD THIEF

(Action-adventure/romance. Completed series.)

The Child Thief (Book 1)

Deep Shadows (Book 2)

Thin Lines (Book 3)

Little Lies (Book 4)

Ghost Towns (Book 5)

Zero Hour (Book 6)

HOTBLOODS

(Supernatural adventure/romance. Completed series.)

Hotbloods (Book 1)

Coldbloods (Book 2)

Renegades (Book 3)

Venturers (Book 4)

Traitors (Book 5)

Allies (Book 6)

Invaders (Book 7)

Stargazers (Book 8)

A SHADE OF VAMPIRE SERIES

(Supernatural romance/adventure)

Series 1: Derek & Sofia's story

A Shade of Vampire (Book 1)

A Shade of Blood (Book 2)

A Castle of Sand (Book 3)

A Shadow of Light (Book 4)

A Blaze of Sun (Book 5)

A Gate of Night (Book 6)

A Break of Day (Book 7)

Series 2: Rose & Caleb's story

A Shade of Novak (Book 8)

A Bond of Blood (Book 9)

A Spell of Time (Book 10)

A Chase of Prey (Book 11)

A Shade of Doubt (Book 12)

A Turn of Tides (Book 13)

A Dawn of Strength (Book 14)

A Fall of Secrets (Book 15)

An End of Night (Book 16)

Series 3: The Shade continues with a new hero...

A Wind of Change (Book 17)

A Trail of Echoes (Book 18)

A Soldier of Shadows (Book 19)

A Hero of Realms (Book 20)

A Vial of Life (Book 21)

A Fork of Paths (Book 22)

A Flight of Souls (Book 23)

A Bridge of Stars (Book 24)

Series 4: A Clan of Novaks

A Clan of Novaks (Book 25)

A World of New (Book 26)

A Web of Lies (Book 27)

A Touch of Truth (Book 28)

An Hour of Need (Book 29)

A Game of Risk (Book 30)

A Twist of Fates (Book 31)

A Day of Glory (Book 32)

Series 5: A Dawn of Guardians

A Dawn of Guardians (Book 33)

A Sword of Chance (Book 34)

A Race of Trials (Book 35)

A King of Shadow (Book 36)

An Empire of Stones (Book 37)

A Power of Old (Book 38)

A Rip of Realms (Book 39)

A Throne of Fire (Book 40)

A Tide of War (Book 41)

Series 6: A Gift of Three

A Gift of Three (Book 42)

A House of Mysteries (Book 43)

A Tangle of Hearts (Book 44)

A Meet of Tribes (Book 45)

A Ride of Peril (Book 46)

A Passage of Threats (Book 47)

A Tip of Balance (Book 48)

A Shield of Glass (Book 49)

A Clash of Storms (Book 50)

Series 7: A Call of Vampires

A Call of Vampires (Book 51)

A Valley of Darkness (Book 52)

A Hunt of Fiends (Book 53)

A Den of Tricks (Book 54)

A City of Lies (Book 55)

A League of Exiles (Book 56)

A Charge of Allies (Book 57)

A Snare of Vengeance (Book 58)

A Battle of Souls (Book 59)

Series 8: A Voyage of Founders

A Voyage of Founders (Book 60)

A Land of Perfects (Book 61)

A Citadel of Captives (Book 62)

A Jungle of Rogues (Book 63)

A Camp of Savages (Book 64)

A Plague of Deceit (Book 65)

An Edge of Malice (Book 66)

A Dome of Blood (Book 67)

A Purge of Nature (Book 68)

Season 9: A Birth of Fire

A Birth of Fire (Book 69)

A Breed of Elements (Book 70)

A Sacrifice of Flames (Book 71)

A Conspiracy of Realms (Book 72)

A Search for Death (Book 73)

A Piece of Scythe (Book 74)

A Blade of Thieron (Book 75)

A Phantom of Truth (Book 76)

A Fate of Time (Book 77)

Season 10: An Origin of Vampires

An Origin of Vampires (Book 78)

A Game of Death (Book 79)

A Veil of Dark (Book 80)

A Bringer of Night (Book 81)

A Circle of Nine (Book 82)

A Bender of Spirit (Book 83)

A Memory of Time (Book 84)

A Shard of Soul (Book 85)

A Break of Seals (Book 86)

Season 11: A Shade of Mystery

A Shade of Mystery (Book 87)

An Isle of Mirrors (Book 88)

A Sanctuary of Foes (Book 89)

A SHADE OF DRAGON TRILOGY

A Shade of Dragon 1

A Shade of Dragon 2

A Shade of Dragon 3

A SHADE OF KIEV TRILOGY

A Shade of Kiev 1

A Shade of Kiev 2

A Shade of Kiev 3

A LOVE THAT ENDURES TRILOGY

(Contemporary romance)

A Love that Endures

A Love that Endures 2

A Love that Endures 3

THE SECRET OF SPELLSHADOW MANOR

(Supernatural/Magic YA. Completed series)

The Secret of Spellshadow Manor (Book 1)

The Breaker (Book 2)

The Chain (Book 3)

The Keep (Book 4)

The Test (Book 5)

The Spell (Book 6)

BEAUTIFUL MONSTER DUOLOGY

(Supernatural romance)

Beautiful Monster 1

Beautiful Monster 2

DETECTIVE ERIN BOND

(Adult thriller/mystery)

Lights, Camera, GONE

Write, Edit, KILL

For an updated list of Bella's books, please visit her website: www.bellaforrest.net

Join Bella's VIP email list and you'll be the first to know when new books release. Visit to sign up: www.morebellaforrest.com

CPSIA information can be obtained
at www.ICGtesting.com
Printed in the USA
LVHW091717160421
684704LV00001B/8

9 789925 762187